BRENT EVANS'

LAND & SEA

TIDES OF

REDEMPTION

BLAINE LEE
PARDOE

BOOK
06

WG
NOVA

Acknowledgments

This book brings to a close the first season (year one) of novels for Land&Sea. It has been quite a ride and I assure you, it is far from over. This book introduces new characters and brings back some of the established ones. The series was never about eight or nine characters. It is about a vast ensemble of people that can tell the story of this war.

Land&Sea is all about the readers of the series. We take care of our own. Thank you to the following fans of the series that graciously donated their names for inclusion in this book:

Matthew Beale
Steve Davis
Bailey Fleming
Chris Frye
David Highbridge
John Hughes
Alan Hunton
Leon Jackson
Georgia Johnstone
Duncan Kendall
Marc Lahoz
Lawrence Lee
John Jacob Lessman
Dave McComb
Ian McCranie
Andrew McKenna
Jason McLaughlin
Joseph Newman
Peter Pearson
Martin Rosales
John Bear Ross
Amanda Schrivener
Dan Shoemaker

Bill Smith
Heather Dawn Taylor
Jana Dae Thun
Bryan Wade
Thomas Wertan
Phil Walling
Geoff Watters
Justin Verret

This book includes the British Royal Marines. The British use different nomenclature for the aliens and their armor. The following is a breakdown to assist you in understanding the British terms.

British Term – American Equivalent

Sovereign – ASHUR
Blinder Ray – Flasher
Mount – Rig
Bollocks – Fish
Golem – Boss
Lobster – Crab
Skenk – Fox
Stegosaur – Turtle
Toad – Frog

Dedication:

To my grandson Trenton Davis Hester. War isn't a clean undertaking. It is violent, vicious, and deadly. Like all endeavors, it is filled with people who are forced to rise to face the challenges. The best ones have historically had flaws, either in their past decisions or their personalities. As you grow older, you will learn that our flaws often define us. They determine who we ultimately are. Through the flaming cauldron of war, we find the best and worst of each other. It creates new flaws and fixes others. War defines the fate of nations, ideologies, and in its ashes comes out the best of humanity.

That is what this book series is about.

What Has Come Before...

For at least a half a decade, an alien invasion was taking place on Earth, but humanity didn't know it at the time. The invaders landed in the oceans of the world. On July 28, 2039, they attacked. It was a bloody and costly probe, a test of mankind's capabilities around the globe that wrecked bases, sunk navies, and left hundreds of thousands of citizens dead.

The full assault began weeks later. The conflict turned coastal cities around the planet into battle zones. The military forces were equipped for fighting other humans, not genetically engineered alien species which used biotech weapons. ASHURs, Augmented Soft/Hard Unconventional Combat Rigs, proved to be the best weapons platform to deal with the aliens.

The extraterrestrials, dubbed "the Fish" in the United States, remain an elusive collection of species. Their technology is biological. Their means of communicating is unknown, as are their motives.

Every military force has run low on munitions for artillery or air support. ASHURs, and their equivalent in other nations, provide the necessary close infantry support to attempt to quell the aliens' advance. Most nations were ill-prepared for large-scale incursions from their entire coastline. Cities burned and billions became refugees, fleeing for safety as the war became a brutal urban slugfest.

By the winter of 2040, many of America's coastal cities lay in ruins or under enemy occupation. The aliens seem to be able to adapt to new technologies quickly, genetically engineering new and variant warriors for the struggle. As of yet, no one knows the alien's objectives or motivations. Despite the creation of underwater ASHURs (code-named Tridents), the Fish remain mysterious.

One officer in the DIA saw the threat before anyone else, Colonel Ashton Slade, who now heads up the Extraterrestrial Task Force (ETF) in the United States. Marine Staff Sergeant Natalia Falto was captured by the aliens in the fighting on Guam. She was a prisoner of war for months. There, the aliens experimented on her, resulting in the loss of her legs and one arm before she was rescued from her underwater prison. Both had seen the war from different perspectives, both are facing their own unique struggles.

There doesn't seem to be an end in sight for this conflict. Old treaties have been shattered and new alliances form around the world while countries fight to survive the onslaught. Everyone is looking for an edge that might help them get the upper hand on the invaders, and their human country-peers.

CYCLE I

Captain Max MacFarlane saw the alert first, a flash of crimson on his holodisplay threat board. The room where he was stationed was dark, making the red pulse of light look even brighter, somehow more menacing. US Space Force had been re-tasked with looking for incoming alien craft since the start of the invasion. Many in the public claimed that they had failed in their mission. Not catching the initial landings five years earlier was a blemish that was hard to shake. MacFarlane didn't feel Space Force had failed. They had been tasked to focus on watching human-made objects in orbit. No one had thought that a danger would come from another world.

The combat operations room was arranged with theater seating for the individual combat controllers like MacFarlane. Three large threat boards dominated the room. They were holographic displays, with the center one being the largest. The air conditioning was far too cold for his liking, but fortunately, the base commander allowed them to wear sweaters or jackets while at their post. The immediate excitement of seeing the threat light had him already sweating in his duty jacket.

Most days were filled with mind-numbing staring at displays. No one knew if the Fish were even still sending ships to Earth. So far, no one had seen an alien vessel. The navy had tangled with something off the west coast, but no one even knew what it was they were looking for—only that it might exist. It was important but dull work—not at all how he had pictured life in Space Force when he had enlisted.

Everything changed in an instant. A flash came across his board, along with a warning banner. His fingers danced over the keyboard to verify.

Whatever it is, it's fast, he thought.

"Duty Commander, I have an unidentified inbound signal on track—designating it as Alpha. Sending trajectory to you."

The image transferred to the large display that dominated the large war room. A warning buzzer sounded.

"We have an unidentified non-terrestrial target inbound," a controller confirmed.

The bright red dot dimmed for a moment, then came back.

Why is it doing that? It's like we are almost losing the signal.

"I want a plot on that bogie," came the stern voice of the female duty commander from her perch above and behind him.

His fingers moved with a speed that came from extensive training. An emerald green dotted line was thrown up on the display, showing the projected course of the inbound object. Captain MacFarlane adjusted his headset microphone. "Plot is up, sir. UAP is on an orbital insertion course. Given angle and current speed at over Mach 8, estimated impact is in the Greenland Sea, approximately eighty miles northwest of Svalbard. We are looking at impact in approximately twenty-two minutes after three orbits."

"Alert all North Atlantic commands. Send our feed to NORAD and ask them to verify our tracking," came the duty commander's voice. "Get me the base commander of the 821st Space Base Group in Thule."

The communications officer acknowledged the order as MacFarlane looked at the trajectory. Thule, Greenland, was the only base that had any chance of intercepting the incoming craft—and that was a stretch.

Given the speed that thing is moving, it's going to be like firing a gun at supersonic speeds, hoping to hit another bullet that's flying past you.

While he wasn't a fighter pilot, he knew that making that shot would take two parts skill, and one part miracle.

There were a number of muted voices on the call behind him as he continued to track the incoming ship.

"We are having a problem keeping a lock on it."

"There's metal up there, but most of it is biological."

As he tracked the speed, he noticed it was slowing.

Maybe this will give us the time we need. They're still going to need a hell of a pilot to pull off shooting this down.

Over the Arctic Circle

Lieutenant Georgia Johnstone angled the X-62 into a steeper climb as she slowly brought it in a wide arc. The G-forces already felt as if she had a dead rhinoceros sitting on her lap and the turn only made things worse. Normally she would have had some time on the treadmill before the flight, and some additional oxygen infusion. There hadn't been time before this flight. Instead the doctors had given her three injections as she had pulled on her flight suit.

I need to pour it on to hit the intercept.

"Engaging booster scramjets," she announced.

The X-62 made a series of sounds as the jets shut down and the powerful supersonic scramjets kicked in. The dead rhinoceros suddenly felt as if he had brought his entire family with him. Breathing was a struggle and with the kick of the scramjets firing up, she felt a little hot, lightheaded, and a tinge of nausea swept through her body. Her G-suit did what it could, but escaping the forces hitting her body was inescapable.

"This is Piper, climbing for intercept."

There was a momentary rumble in the interceptor as it passed through some invisible turbulence. The craft shook, but her concentration and control did not. Slowly the flight became glass-smooth.

The air controller at Thule, Greenland, signaled back. "Piper, we are transmitting live feed from NORAD. Your UAP is slowing but is still moving like a bat out of hell."

She checked her long-range radar plot. The systems aboard her X-65 had been designed for exceptional long-range sweeps—necessary when targeting enemy satellites during the war. There was nothing there, but with a few presses of the right buttons, she overlaid the data streaming from NORAD and Space Force, showing up as crimson in her HUD.

Gotcha!

"Copy that. Tallyho! I have an intermittent signal; maneuvering to intercept and engage," she managed to say as she angled the X-62 in a wider arc to align herself with the object's path. The targeting system had been designed during the Russo-Bratva War so that the X-62 could intersect with enemy satellites. It showed that she needed to decrease her rate of climb, which helped a little with the forces attempting to crush her body—but not nearly enough.

Johnstone's brain and her targeting systems were both calculating the angle and speed of the intercept as she checked her speed. *Mach 8...no one has splashed a target at this speed before.* She caught herself breathing too fast and made a mental note to slow it down.

Her interceptor rose enough that the blue sky melted away to the blackness of the extreme upper atmosphere. *The last time I was up this high, it was against Kosmos 2400.* It had been her last Russian satellite kill of the war, her fourth, and the memory came with pride. *The damn Russies cost me my seat on the International Space Station, then they ended the war before I could get my fifth kill.* Being a female Space Force pilot was a rarity, and she wanted that fifth kill and the title ace that came with it. Normally she would savor the view at the edge of space, but there wasn't time.

Her targeting system flashed *15 seconds to Intercept*, which was almost exactly what her brain had calculated.

"Master arm on, switching to ASL array. Pre-charging laser," she transmitted as she leveled out her flight path.

She shunted power to the Raytheon ASL-2 that was slung under the sleek underbelly of the X-62. The large streamlined laser was nasty and brutally efficient. It was a proven satellite killer. Against Russian satellites and Chinese balloons, it roasted electronics, usually turning most of the satellites into worthless space junk. The Russians used attack satellites with huge shotgun-like recoilless launchers that turned a space object into hundreds of bits of dangerous shrapnel. Like all things Russian, it lacked eloquence. No one knew how the ASL would affect one of the Fish ships—or even if it would. She made sure the weapon was set for its widest and longest beam.

Looking to her left, she saw a shimmer off in space. It was moving fast, swinging as if to cut her flight path. She would have preferred to come in behind it, possibly get off two shots. The problem was she had taken off with seconds to spare. As it was, she was lucky to have it cross her flight path at all. Staying with it would take a miracle, but Georgia was feeling lucky.

For a moment, she savored the sight of the target. It was nearly impossible see—not just because of the speed, but by the way it moved. As it approached the upper atmosphere, she had expected to see some wake. The air around the ship rippled, but the ship seemed to have some sort of bubble around it that was immune to the atmosphere. This craft moved differently. It was a slow-motion lightning ripple, shimmering a strange brownish hue. Her sensors painted the target, but her eyes told her just how big it was.

That thing is at least a kilometer wide and half that in length.

For a moment, she was worried that her shot was going to be nothing more than a pinprick on something that large.

The countdown clock on the targeting display ticked off the seconds, and she made her last second adjustment to her flight path.

"Coming up on target now," she said through gritted teeth.

The blur in the air crossed before her. There was the tone of target acquisition on the display and her fingers squeezed the joystick firing stud. Below her was the familiar high-pitched whine of the anti-satellite laser firing. She saw a flash as the laser hit particles in the thin upper atmosphere, lashing out at the target.

She wanted an explosion—something spectacular to signify that she had hit the massive target. What she got was almost as rewarding as she braced to fly through the wake of the fast-moving craft. The ripple that had obscured a view of the alien ship evaporated. Georgia glimpsed it. The craft resembling a brownish shellfish-like thing suddenly began interacting with the upper atmosphere with violence. It made an arc downward, then slowly turned away, giving off a yellowish heat shimmer from atmospheric turbulence as it continued to lose altitude.

That rat-bastard is shifting his trajectory to where I might be able to squeeze off another shot.

She slowed and flew into the wake of the massive ship, expecting her X-62 to be buffeted violently. There was nothing—no backwash, no clear air turbulence.

That's strange, but damn, it's welcome.

"This is Piper, target is hit. It is altering flight path and descending rapidly."

"Roger that, Piper," came back the air controller's voice from the base. "We are interpreting the data here. Congratulations."

As she slowed and descended, she tried to alter the arc of her flight path to get a better view. Her own aircraft sensors were recording heat buildup on the extended surfaces. It wasn't bad enough to be concerning…yet, but she kept her eyes darting to the data to make sure it didn't get worse.

The deceleration hit her body in a very different way. Her eyes felt like they were bulging out of their sockets as her face flushed and her skin tingled. The weight of her body pushed against the restraining harness, biting it into her chest and shoulders.

I gotta watch the Gs. The last thing I want to do is pass out.

Looking out the right side of her sleek canopy, she saw the vessel undulate, suddenly generating what seemed to be contrails as if it were trying to put some distance between them. It was slowing as well, dramatically, and an instant later disappeared under the cloud cover—streaking for Greenland. Gone was the remarkable speed. Georgia cut her own speed, angling the craft to let the atmosphere help her brake.

If I go into a dive and tighten the turn, I might be able to line up another shot.

This was going to come with a toll on her body, but she was confident she could handle it.

"Control, this is Piper," she said, banking tighter. "Switching back to jets and beginning to dive. I think I can get another shot at this bastard."

"Understood, Piper. Watch your speed on descent. Your UAP is slowing below Mach four and appears to be trying to level off."

"Noted." Georgia felt the X-62 fight her as she tightened the turn. "I can do this—one more shot to be sure…"

She had been lucky once today, so why not twice? The large laser hummed beneath her as she fought the laws of physics, attempting another pass on the massive craft that was now closing with her…

CHAPTER 1

Extra Terrestrial Task Force (ETF) HQ,
DIA Intelligence Annex, the Penetrator
Los Alamos, New Mexico, the United States

Staff Sergeant Natalia Falto stood in front of her mirror in the small bathroom and dried off. She hated the mirror a little less each day. She was putting on weight, finally, thanks to the horrible diet that the doctors had prescribed her. Her bionic legs and arm were appropriately muscled but made the rest of her body look lacking. In a weird way, they inspired her to continue to work out, if nothing else, to regain some of her body symmetry. The margin between her natural and bionic limbs was narrowing as she regained her organic body strength.

I'm probably the only person who can even spot the difference, she knew.

The replacement ear was the easiest thing to get used to. It picked up sounds better than her organic ear. The synthetic ear prosthetic was the only genuine issue she had. The skin tone on it was darker than her actual skin. According to the Marine Corps, it was a perfect match, only confirming for her the quality of military medicine.

They're fine with it because they don't have to live with it.

There had been an endless stream of medical tests inflicted on her. *They all act like the Fish have planted something inside me that is going to come bursting out of my gut.* The tests revealed a few things. The scales that she still had patches of were a "corruption" of

8

her DNA by the aliens. They didn't appear life-threatening, but remained. For Falto, the deformed areas were akin to scars, ugly reminders of what she had overcome. Daily she wrapped them with bandages. She liked to tell herself that it was so others who might see them wouldn't react. Deep down, she knew it was because she didn't want to see them. They were a hideous reminder of the worst time of her life.

The last few months had been exhausting, both mentally and physically. She was constantly giving debriefs on her ordeal, which meant reliving it over and over. *Time Magazine* had done an in-depth interview with her and her family, which she had hated. While the Marine Corps Public Affairs Office had pushed for it, she disliked making her pain and anguish known to the entire world.

Still, seeing her family had been a relief. While in captivity, she had almost forgotten what a superb cook her mother was.

Her mother had been worried about her sleeping on the floor. More than half of her time at home, she felt uncomfortable in a bed. The floor always gave her comfort. Her shrink had told her it was a leftover feeling from her captivity.

"You have unresolved conflicts you will need to resolve," the doc had said.

She assured her psychiatrist that she had no idea the depths of her unresolved issues.

When Falto had first been briefed on the war, a part of her had been worried that her mother and siblings had been killed during the alien onslaught. Her brother, Julio, had enlisted in the Army and had managed to get a seventy-two-hour pass to visit with Falto and her mother. Seeing him in uniform was a sign that he was turning his life around. Private Julio Falto had managed to put the back alleys and rough streets of Los Angeles behind him. Julio went on about how proud he was of her, something she wished he wouldn't do.

I didn't do anything to be proud of other than survive.

The Corps had seen fit to promote her and keep her on the active duty roles, despite the loss of three limbs. Based on what she had gathered of the war effort, every Marine, regardless of condition, was needed. For now, she had been seconded to the Penetrator, in the middle of nowhere, New Mexico. While the facilities were impressive, there wasn't anything to do socially. Then again, there wasn't much that Falto wanted to do out in the real world. The war had changed everything and she constantly felt like she was struggling to catch up with world events.

Learning to use her bionics required specific workouts and extended practice. At first it had been a disaster. Like learning to walk all over again. The weight differences and her lack of control over the limbs had resulted in more time on the floor than standing or walking. Natalia had pushed herself, hard, and in a matter of weeks was able to walk and even run.

Her arm and hand took more time to master. The sensations she felt from the bionic had were so dramatically different from that of her normal hand, and she often overcompensated, crushing glasses or anything else she had a grip on. It had taken six weeks for her to finally master the hand, and even then, there were times she messed up.

After toweling off and running a brush through her hair, she put on her class B uniform. As she finished, she heard a knock at the door of her tiny apartment. In four quick strides, she reached the door and opened it. Standing before her was Colonel Slade, standing in the hot New Mexico midmorning sun.

"Colonel."

"May I come in, Sergeant?"

"Of course." She opened the door further and gestured inside.

She had worked closely with Colonel Slade over the last few months. He'd pried from her every detail she knew about the aliens, even getting her to reveal things that she had almost forgotten. Slade didn't seem like any colonel she had experience with.

He's not a bad guy, for being Army.

In the dozens of hours that they had spent together, Slade had never come to visit her at her residence.

Something's up.

"I'm sorry for disturbing you in your quarters," Slade

commented, his eyes sweeping the room. "A situation has come up, one that I need your help with."

"Of course."

Slade crossed his arms and locked his eyes on to hers. "Two hours ago, a Space Force interceptor out of Thule, Greenland, pulled off some sort of miracle. She managed to shoot down an alien ship that was approaching Earth." Slade paused, letting the words hang in the air between them.

"That's great," Falto responded, surprise clearly etched across her face. Slade didn't speak for a few moments, so she continued, "That is great, isn't it?"

Colonel Slade nodded. "I've been calling it remarkable. It crashed on the eastern side of Greenland just a kilometer from the shore. This thing should be a treasure trove of alien technology. We've never had an opportunity to make a move on one before. Hell, we haven't even seen one of these things before. All we've had up to this point is radar and sonar readings."

"I take it you're going there?"

Slade shook his head. "I'm not. My boss pointed out that I'm viewed as 'invaluable to the war effort.' We are sending a team to secure the site and recover whatever we can from the ship."

"I hope they are well armed."

That brought a thin smile to Slade's face, a true rarity based on her experience with him. "You could say that. I've got elements from the Third Battalion of the Rangers prepping right now. Omega is going as well."

The mention of Omega Force made Falto cock her head. Everyone had heard of the Delta Force of the US Special Forces; Omega eclipsed their reputation over time. Omega had been formed near the end of the Russo-Bratva war. Where most Special Forces units augmented their infantry with ASHURs, Omega Force did not. It consisted almost entirely of ASHUR rigs. Where most Special Forces could be described as a precision instrument, Omega was all about brute force and speed.

"Omega's going?" she said. "You must be anticipating some

serious resistance."

"We're dealing with unknowns. We've never been able to get access to one of their ships. Chances are they aren't exactly going to roll out the red carpet for us when we show up."

Hence the need for Omega. They didn't even use the moniker of Special Forces. Omega conducted "Special Operations," which were more brutal and effective. On paper they were defined as a Special Missions Unit (SMU), something the rank and file referred to as existing "on the other wide of the green fence."

It was hard to argue with the logic.

"That's probably a safe bet."

"The real challenge is, very few people have seen the insides of the alien habitats. Our people don't know the ins and outs of working with the alien technology inside their domain. That lack of knowledge drastically limits our options."

"It would—" she started, then she realized where Slade was going. "You're here to get me to go, aren't you, sir?"

Slade dipped his head, giving her a less-than-coy expression. "Pretty much."

No! I can't believe this.

"I have done my part of the war, and then some," she replied, flinging up her hands in the space between them. "My time with the aliens cost me three limbs and months of my life. I am still struggling with the memories that I carry from being down there."

"I know," Slade replied slowly. "I spoke with your shrink. Classic mental trauma—PTSD-B. She seemed to think this op wouldn't further traumatize you."

"You talked to my doctor?"

"Of course I did. I needed to know if you were up to this kind of mission."

"Well, I'm not." They were the only words she could form to express her disdain.

How dare he think I'm ready for this kind of thing?

"Sergeant," he began after drawing a deep breath. "You are one of a handful of individuals with experience inside the alien structures. I can't replicate your experience. If I could, I wouldn't be here."

"That was a habitat. You are talking about a ship."

"We don't know that you weren't aboard one of their ships. Just because it wasn't moving doesn't mean that you were not on one of their vessels."

That concept gave her pause. It was a thought that she had not considered. At the same time, for Natalia, it didn't matter.

"I'm not sure I would be of much help to the troops going in. I'm still learning to master my bionics. I'm not in peak combat shape."

Not yet.

"I'm not asking you to fight," he said. "You would be strictly an advisor, there to consult with the military and scientists going in."

"We both know you can't guarantee that."

Slade gave her a nod. "True. This thing was brought down on land—not in the ocean. There are no signs of survivors in the recon images we have obtained. For all we know the crew was killed on impact."

"Then you aren't likely to need me," she countered.

Slade wasn't going to go down without a fight. "Maybe, maybe not. The reality is there are so many unknowns here. I need you there for the things we haven't thought of…that we can't anticipate. You lived with the Fish. You understand their thinking better than anyone else."

Pausing, her eyes went around the small apartment, and it felt as if it were getting smaller—closing in on her. Her breath was getting shallower and faster. Her skin tingled with perspiration and she realized that the temperature of the room felt like it was soaring. Natalia knew all of the signs she was experiencing; it was anxiety. The events came over her when stressed. Closing her eyes, she reined in her breathing, slowing it down, making longer breaths and holding them.

She respected Slade—everyone did. From what she had been told, he was the only person that saw the alien threat before the war started. Since then, he had been the point man for the alien intelligence and physiology. In his dealings with her, she found him to be thoughtful. Perhaps that was why his request was hitting her so hard—it felt as if it were out of character.

"I know you mean well, sir, but you have to understand something. The aliens…they almost broke me. They dissected me while I was alive. They killed good people, good friends," her voice trailed off as memories of David Chen came back to her. His death was a mental open wound with her. "What they left behind was an empty shell. I'm not the Marine I was before I went deep."

"Sergeant—Natalia. With all due respect, you are wrong. You see yourself as broken. The rest of the world sees you as having risen above all of that. What you endured would have shattered even the most battle-hardened Marine. You didn't break. Yes, they may have bent you, they certainly damaged you, but you came through it all. That makes you more badass than almost anyone else I know."

His words helped her reel in her anxiety, mostly because they were from the heart. "I don't think I can do this."

Colonel Slade sighed. "I could stand here and tell you that it is your patriotic duty. I could slop on phrases like, 'Doing this will save countless lives,' or, 'This is vital to the war effort.' I think you know I wouldn't ask you to go if those things weren't possible or true. My top brass gave me the authority to order you to go, if you refused."

"Is that what you are doing—ordering me to go?"

He shook his head. "We have spent too much time with each other for me to pull a dick move like that. If you say no, I'll honor that. I'll tell my bosses that we can do without you. Hell, they aren't letting me go. I can always say what they told me, 'You're too important for the war effort to risk.' I respect you too much to use the hammer and make you do something you're not ready for.

"But in reality, I think you *are* ready, Natalia. The Fish did hurt you. You also know that us getting possession of this ship will hurt them, badly. Sometimes the best cure for what is in your head is some good old-fashioned payback. That's what this offer really is, a chance at retribution. You don't have to fire a shot to do it, either.

We just need you there for all the things we can't prepare for or think of—that's all."

She nodded, unable to form words. It was true, the concept of some payback did have appeal.

Slade continued. "Our forces are not heading out to Thule for eighteen hours. I don't need a decision from you until then. You're smarter than the average Marine. Take this time to think it over."

"I will," she replied. "Thank you, sir."

"In training, they always tell you to apply what you experienced to get better. That's all I'm asking you to do, Sergeant."

With that, he turned for the door and let himself out. The burst of brilliant sunshine from the balcony of her little apartment made her eyes ache for a moment. Falto stood there, staring at the door after he closed it, savoring the shade.

For a few moments, she felt as if her mind were made up—that she would remain behind and not go on the mission. It only lasted for a few seconds, though, before she started questioning that path. The part that bothered her was that Colonel Slade hadn't forced her to go.

He could have just told me those were my orders. He's actually thinking about what is best for me, letting me arrive at a decision on my own.

That was what she had been missing since her recovery, the right of making decisions for herself.

When I was trapped in their little laboratory, the aliens had all of the control. Since I was rescued, I have been told where to go and what to do. I didn't question it, I didn't react to it. I thought I was being a good Marine.

Slade had upended that kind of thinking.

She moved to the small loveseat and lowered herself onto it. *I need a different perspective, someone that knows me and can help me sort this out.*

For Falto, that list was very short.

* * *

The nightmare she had was so vivid it jerked her to consciousness violently. Falto sat up from where she was lying on the floor, her hair wet with sweat, the single sheet over her body cool and damp with her perspiration.

I don't even remember crawling down from the bed to the floor.

The moment she awakened, the nightmare faded from her memory. She knew it was about the Alpha though, that much stayed with her—the alien that had been her adversary starting on Guam and during her internment.

This wasn't the first time he had invaded her sleep. It was a rarity that she got through the night completely devoid of his appearance. *The bastard's dead and he still is coming at me.* She hated the nightmares and while the doctor gave her PTSD medication, she did not take it. There was something she disliked about taking drugs. Besides, she didn't feel that they made the nightmares go away. They simply got her a few decent hours of sleep.

She knew what was the impetus for this nightmare—Colonel Slade's request. It had been all she had been thinking about since his visit.

I need to talk to someone about this—someone that can understand.

Asking her mother would not help. By default, she would tell Falto not to go.

Reaching over to her tiny nightstand, she grabbed her iPhone 24. *It's late. I don't even know where he is, but it is going to be late.* Her hesitancy was confirmed when she saw the time was 0221 hours. *He's the only one that will tell me straight if I'm doing the right thing by not going.* She spoke his name and hit the button to call.

By the third ring, she was prepared to terminate the call, but then she saw his face, shadowed in the darkness.

"Falto?" Reid Porter asked, his eyes clearly attempting to adjust to the image of her face on his phone. "Natalia, what's up?"

"I'm sorry about the time," she began. "Something has come up. I need your help."

"Don't worry about it," he said, sitting up in bed. As his sheet fell off of his body, she saw a tattoo on his arm. It was still red around the image, an indication of how fresh it was. ASHUR wings.

Damn—Porter's a pilot!

"You made the cut! You're an ASHUR pilot. Congratulations!"

He glanced at the tattoo. "Yeah—two days ago. I pilot one of the new rigs, a Warthog."

"I never heard of that one."

"You know the Corps. We always have to have our own gear. This one has a new car smell to it."

"That doesn't sound like the Corps I enlisted in. We have always been the red-headed stepchildren when it comes to equipment."

"Times change. War has a way of doing that. The Warthog is a hell of a rig, design quirks and all."

"That's great. You deserve the honor." She felt even guiltier for waking him up.

"I had a great inspiration," he replied, grinning. Falto was embarrassed, but held it in check as best she could. "So, what's up?"

Drawing a deep breath, she summarized what Colonel Slade had asked of it, keeping it to three sentences. Natalia did not go into why she was struggling with the decision. She did not convey what she was feeling. That was the best part of Reid Porter, he understood without her having to form the words. Stopping, she waited for his response.

"You don't want to go."

Falto nodded.

Porter wiped the sleep from his eyes, then continued. "You know, Natalia, you don't have to do this. You also know that if you don't, and those folks run into trouble that you could've solved, you're going to hear about it, and it'll just add to the guilt that you already feel."

"You're not helping," she said, trying to make light of his words with a chuckle.

"You and I talk every week. We fought together, lost friends together." His words conjured up memories of Sergeant Rickenburg's Lion falling in battle. "We are friends. So what I say comes from that position."

She admired Porter more than ever. *The old Reid was a weak kid. He's matured, a lot. I was gone for months in hell, and he moved on in life. That's been part of my problem, everything is the same but a little different.*

"Fire at will," she said, sensing that he had more to say.

"Alright. Take it for what it's worth…I never thought I'd see Natalia Falto afraid."

Anger geysered and flashed across her face, burning fiery crimson. "Those are fighting words, Porter."

"It's the truth, and deep down you know it. The aliens, they fucked with you. Not just physically, but in your head. You aren't at the front, but you are still fighting a war against the Fish. I have seen it with a lot of people."

Hot tears formed in the corners of her eyes, but she ignored them. "If I go back, I have to take my demons with me."

"Then stuff them in your ruck and suck it up," Porter said in a firm tone. "We all struggle with sleeping at night. I have seen some shit that I can never unsee. The damn Fish have screwed with all of us. Yes, you got it worse than others. That doesn't exempt you from duty."

Duty. The word was a bullet to her chest.

"I've given so much…"

"You have. More than me. More than almost everyone. But you are one tough bitch. This isn't about what you lost, and you know it. This is about getting on top of your emotions. You are certainly strong enough to face the Fish again, this time on your terms. The enemy within? Well, I think you're tough enough to beat that one too."

"So you think I should go."

Porter nodded. "Yes. You will never be able to live with yourself if you don't. I've seen it with others struggling with PTSD. It can dominate your life. That's not you, Natalia. You've always been a fighter. Go, but go on your own terms. You deserve that much. I think the Corps owes you that much."

She used the bedsheet to dab at the tears in the corners of her eyes, rather than letting Porter see them streaking down her cheeks. "That isn't what I wanted to hear."

"It's what you needed to hear. Suck it up, buttercup."

"You can be a real asshole at times."

"I learned from the best," he quipped. "Look, if you want two more reasons to go, I can give them to you."

She sighed. "Go on."

"First, if they are sending Omega and Rangers on this op, it's an Army show. If you go, they have a chance of succeeding because you are a hard-ass Marine, and Marines eat crayons and shit victories. The whole damn Corps will be pissed if you pass on this. Don't you dare let the Army claim all of the glory with this crashed ship. God knows they need Marine guidance or they will fuck this up."

His wording made her chuckle. "Okay, that's one."

"I got through a lot of serious shit asking myself, 'What would Falto do?' So let me share this with you. Think about this: What would Hannibal tell *you* to do?"

Evoking Sergeant Rickenburg for the second time in the conversation was a gut punch. Rickenburg would tell her to undertake the mission—without a bit of hesitation. "You know, I might have liked you better when you were a bumbling kid that couldn't keep up with the rest of the platoon."

"That kid is gone," Porter replied. "Guam changed me. *You* changed me. Now we're both hard-charging Marines, Falto. You've been away from the front too long. I don't think your story ends where you are at. Your story is far from finished."

"So, what you're saying is, stack up or shut the fuck up."

"Semper Fi."

"Hoorah," she replied. Just saying that felt releasing.

Porter is right. I've been away from duty for so long I've almost lost my connection to the Corps. If I start to falter, I will improvise, adapt, and overcome.

"Thank you, Reid," she said.

"I didn't do anything. You knew the right answer, you just didn't want to face it."

"Take care."

"You too. And do me a favor. Kick some Fish ass."

Her iPhone screen went dark. Falto ran her fingers through her slick hair, then searched for another phone number. In one ring, she heard the voice of Colonel Slade, gravely, but alert. "This is Slade."

"This is Falto," she replied firmly. "I'm in."

"Fantastic," he replied with a much crisper tone.

"I have a condition."

"Go on."

"I'm there as an independent operator. I don't want some Ranger or Omega telling me what to do. I'm not ready to be a part of a team again, not yet."

"I believe that can be arranged. I can have you there as a consultant, an advisor. We have a briefing at 0700 in auditorium one. Bring your gear—you'll be dusting off after that session."

"Yes, sir."

Setting her alarm, Falto lay on her back, and after another hour, sleep returned, sans the nightmare of her former adversary.

CHAPTER 2

Camp Viking
Øverbygd, Norway

That the Royal Marine Commandos' commanding officer was arriving in person, unannounced, was all that Major Andrew McKenna needed to know in terms of urgency. His unit, 45 Commando, had already sent X-Ray and Zulu companies back to England when the invasion started. His remaining two companies had been slugging it out with the alien-bollocks along the coast of Norway for some time.

If Lieutenant-Colonel Frye made the trip here, we are about to get redeployed.

When Frye entered his tiny office, McKenna snapped to a salute which the shorter Frye returned. "Good to see you, Andy. I trust you are well," he said, taking a seat in front of the major's desk.

McKenna returned to his chair too. His eyes darted to his desktop and was pleased that there wasn't much on the surface. He knew Frye was fond of organization and tidiness.

His office was relatively new and, in keeping with the Royal Marine standards, pitifully small and Spartan. The furnishings, while new, were cheap. The service was tight with money, preferring to spend it on the gear needed to fight the war. No one complained. Being a Marine meant that you were used to living off the land. He was thankful that he was a Sovereign pilot. At least he could sleep comfortably in his rig's cockpit.

"Very well, sir. We just wrapped up a strike at Sorreisa. Those ebony monstrosities that the bollocks use are nasty buggers—but we took out more than a few of them."

"Yes, the Norwegians have expressed their thanks already to the prime minister. They all say well done, as usual. My favorite kind of mission—minimum casualties, maximum damage. Of course, I'm not here for that."

"I didn't think so."

Frye slid his tablet on the table and activated the portable holodisplay. It flickered on, showing some sort of sea creature. At least that was what McKenna thought when he saw it. "Six hours ago, the Yanks shot down one of the alien ships that was in-bound on Earth. Our Regent 3 satellite picked it up as it came into lunar orbit."

"Is that it?" McKenna pointed to the small holoimage.

It looks like a fossil I've seen before—damned if I can remember what it is called.

"Yes. It came down in northeast Greenland. Horrible bit of terrain there, rocks and ice and snow. Inhospitable—especially with winter already upon us."

"Much like here in Norway."

"Quite," Frye said calmly. "The Chief of the General Staff and MI6 would like us to make a grab for this crashed ship. That's where 45 Commando comes in."

McKenna didn't flinch. He had assumed the moment he heard that Frye had arrived it wasn't for an inspection or social visit. "How large is that thing?"

"Three-quarters of kilometer wide, half a kilometer long. From our imagery, we believe it to be almost five stories tall."

"There's no way we can move something that big, now with the bollocks controlling the oceans." Even then, it would be an engineering feat far beyond what the Royal Navy had ever undertaken.

With half of our ships already lost, and even more crippled, this cannot be a recovery operation.

"Of course not," Frye replied. "Our lads in intelligence are assembling a scientific team to extract whatever alien technology we can recover from that ship. Your mission will be to secure the area, suppress whatever aliens may have survived the crash, and ensure the security of the team that is recovering the technology."

For a few moments, McKenna said nothing. He simply looked at the image. *Trilobite—that's it, that's what that beast looks like.* A flicker of memory from middle school came to him. As he studied the image, he realized its true scale to the ground. *This ship is massive.*

"I take it I will be allowed to bring Yankee and Whisky Companies," he said.

"Yes. For now, that's all we can spare, I'm afraid. As you know, London is half under enemy control. Many parts of the city look like they did during the Blitz. Portsmouth is in utter ruins, and we have lost more of Scotland than has made the press. You and your people are all that we can spare at this time."

Things are worse than I thought.

"Has transport been arranged?" McKenna said.

"It is a bit dicey on that front. We're going to get you into Svalbard by plane. The UN has a security base there—all very hush-hush, mind you. It's in a bit of shambles, I'm afraid, with the Americans cutting funding, but it still is operational. That will be your staging point. The Royal Navy is moving eight of our LCAC-Hs into position as we speak. You'll use those to secure your beachhead in and around the crashed ship."

The LCAC-Hs (Landing Craft Air Cushion—Heavy) were recent additions to the Royal Navy.

Eight of them—that is all that we have in the fleet! This must be of utmost importance.

"Sir, if I may, those craft have a range of 350 miles. I assume that's enough to get us there, but it will be a one-way trip."

Lieutenant-Colonel Frye nodded. "Yes. We are working out how we will get you out. It's looking like airdrops of fuel, but we are still looking at the logistics. The science team is being outfitted by MI6 and they are arranging their own transport once you give the word that the site is secure. Getting you out—well—we are working through the logistics of getting you refueled for the journey home."

Fry's words came as a caution. McKenna mulled it over aloud. "So, we are going above the Arctic Circle, in winter, devoid of practical logistical support, to recover whatever we can from a crashed alien spacecraft?"

Frye cracked a thin smile. "A typical 45 Commando operation, wouldn't you say?"

"Indeed, sir. We can freeze our arses off here, or we can do it in Greenland. I much prefer the change of scenery at this time of year." McKenna returned the wry smile.

"I thought you might. Several commands were trying to get their fingers in on this one. We've never had a shot at one of their ships before. I personally recommended your people for this."

"Most appreciated, sir."

"Well, before you extend your thanks fully, there's more you should know."

"There always is."

"The Americans shot this thing down—that much our own intelligence sources confirmed. If our spies can be trusted, they have told us that the Yanks are planning to mount their own mission to secure this ship."

McKenna rolled his eyes. *The bloody Yanks.* On paper and per treaty, the Americans were still technically allies of Great Britain. The reality was far muddier. When the United States had violated Russian sovereignty to secure the hackers responsible for the worst cyberattack in world history, they started a conflict that they clearly had not anticipated. The Russians countered in spectacular form, invading Alaska, which caught the world off guard. The US called upon NATO to support them against the Russians.

There came the rub. The Americans had started this fight. The NATO allies opted to bow out of the conflict. The Yanks had never forgiven NATO for what they saw as a betrayal. While they were eventually victorious over the Russians, the Americans cut their NATO dollars to a mere trickle. They withdrew their military bases in Europe and the UK, which crippled many local municipalities and served to infuriate their allies even more. The British press called it the "Great Recoil." They had exchanged nasty words between all parties involved. The level of animosity did not fade with the passage of time.

McKenna felt America had overreached, *as usual*. Their sending military and civilians units into Russia to apprehend the supposed Bratva hackers raised an international uproar. The incursion resulted in a nasty little battle that cost both sides some lives and set Russia's inevitable response in motion.

The Yanks love playing the role of western sheriff, riding around the world and inflicting their laws and morals. They bit the Russian bear, and the bear fought back.

"So, the Americans are likely to be there or will show up?" he asked with a hint of anger in his voice that was hard to conceal.

Frye nodded. "I trust MI6 on this. They have had assets in place for several years in the US military. The word we have is that their Omega Force has scrambled. That was why you were chosen to go. Your Yankee and Whisky Companies are both heavy with Sovereigns. If the situation becomes untenable, you possess the firepower necessary to go toe-to-toe with Omega. Of course," he added after a pause, "we would prefer that such a conflict not take place."

The Americans called their armored combat suits ASHURs, Augmented Soft/Hard Unconventional Combat Rigs. NATO had adopted that designation for a short time, but with the US's Great Recoil, each country went to their own naming convention for the power armored equipment. The UK designation was Sovereign, as in "sovereign knight." McKenna had given up on pronouncing Germany's name for their suits.

The British military doctrine had a fairly thin dispersion of their Sovereign suits in the Army. The Royal Marines were a different matter entirely. Their model was to have platoon of Sovereigns and a platoon of grenadiers, most of which were heavily armored and augmented with drones. For McKenna, the choice of his two companies was clear. *If we have to fight the Americans, we have the firepower to do so.* It was a sobering thought, one he wished he didn't have.

"Sir, what are my orders, should I encounter the Americans?" he asked after a few moments of considering the new information.

Frye leaned back in his seat. "There was a great deal of discussion about that. Much give and take. In the end, I was able to convince the Admiralty that the best orders were to empower you to make that call."

"Sir?"

"Your orders are to secure whatever technology is recoverable from that ship. When it comes to the Americans, you are to use your best judgment."

My best judgment? How should that be interpreted?

"Begging your pardon, sir, but what does that mean?"

"You're a smart officer, McKenna. You graduated Britannia at the top of your class. Your actions in Africa and in support of Ukraine during that whole bloody mess are well known. When I say your best judgment, I mean just that. We need to understand this enemy, and getting access to one of their ships is a coup for us. If the bloody Americans decide to interfere, do what you must for us to get the access we need. I can't say that the war depends on it, but we need to learn as much about these bastards' technology as possible. You are going to be far from home, cut off from meddling. Do what you think is best. I will back you, regardless of your decisions."

It was a deep vote of confidence, that much McKenna understood.

"I appreciate that, sir. I wonder if it might not be prudent to reach out to the Americans in advance of us landing in Greenland, try and warn them off. We know from experience that they don't respond well to, shall I say, surprises."

Frye chuckled. "That is understatement. We did give that due consideration. We decided they were better off being in the dark. The Foreign Affairs Minister and his people believe that the Americans are likely to be possessive of the ship, having shot it down."

"It's not their territory. Greenland is part of the Kingdom of Denmark. Have they weighed in on this?"

"Yes. Their official stance is best phrased as, 'We don't want to get involved.'"

"Cowards," McKenna growled.

"Or smart. They probably don't want to get involved in a battle where they have no interests. Where this thing went down is, for the most part, unsettled. No one in their right mind would want to live up there. They don't have the means to recover the wreckage themselves. So they are opting to bow out and let us slug it out with our former friends."

"Have the Yanks reached out to them?"

That brought a single chuckle from the lieutenant-colonel. "Yes. Typical American diplomatic effort. They issued demands of the Greenland government, claiming they had the ship down so it was legal salvage. The Greenies were less than impressed."

"If they do show, I intend to hold tough with them."

Frye's eyes narrowed. "You know, every time the Americans come up, you bristle. Is there some history there I'm not aware of?"

It was an understatement. It frustrated McKenna that he could not hide his disdain for the United States. "My family and the Americans have a history."

"So I've gathered from your service record."

McKenna tensed slightly with the memories. "I lost an uncle in Iraq. We were there to support the Americans, who had promised us all that there were WMDs there. They led us into Iraq and I lost a member of my family, someone I cared for. This is typical for them. The US loves starting wars and pulling in everyone to fight with them. They are lousy when it comes to owning up to their mistakes. They are an arrogant people, pompous, narcissistic to a fault."

"It is hard to argue that."

"In the last scrape, for the first time in my life, I was secretly cheering on the Russians in the fighting. It was one of those instances where the Americans got what they deserved. They have

27

consumed far too many movies about cowboys and sheriffs. They tromp all over the globe, stomping on other people's cultures, and cannot fathom why no one loves it when they show up."

The commander studied him. "I've known you for a long time. I trust that this won't be an issue."

McKenna felt the heat coming from his face. "No sir. My personal beliefs will not affect my mission."

"Good. Put on your best diplomatic face if and when they show."

"Yes, sir. Anyone else I should worry about showing up?"

"Iceland has been silent, much like Hawaii in the Pacific. There's an entire list of concerns with Iceland that you don't want to know about, I assure you. There's no sign of the French mobilizing anything. That doesn't mean anything; they are, after all, French. But, to address your direct query, no—just you and the bloody Yanks get to spend some time up north."

You would have thought that with an alien invasion hitting every coastal nation, the world would have come together. But no. We are still working towards our own national interests.

His mind processed the next likely threat, and that was one that made him cringe.

"Sir, do our intelligence people believe the bollocks are going to try to prevent us from securing their ship?"

That question made the older officer's face tense up. "Excellent question. It is one I don't have an answer to. Frankly, we have never had this opportunity before. We have no idea if that ship signaled his swimming buddies that it was crashing, or where. What I *can* tell you is that so far, we have seen no sign of our alien friends. That doesn't mean you should assume they will not show up."

"We would," McKenna replied. "If the tables were flipped, we would come—if only to make sure that the other side could not recover anything of use."

"Correct. While we have no idea as to how these fishies think, they have demonstrated that they are not entirely wild animals. There is a logic in how they approach battle, deploy forces, and engage with us. They adapt, in some respects, faster than we do."

It was true. The alien scouts, what the Americans referred to as Foxes but the British called Skenks, were often employed along the fringe of a battlespace, clearly feeding intel to their ground troops. The bollocks were proving themselves adept at changing out their weapons systems, being very specific for the types of missions they were on.

It would be a mistake for anyone to underestimate the aliens.

"What if they decide to make a larger fight of things?"

"We have a contingency for that." The lieutenant-colonel tapped the holodisplay controls. An image appeared of a large bomb— easily identified by its fins and markings.

"That doesn't look like a nuclear weapon."

"It isn't. After that nasty spat the Russians had in Murmansk, we didn't want you triggering the same sort of reaction. No, this is a vacuum bomb, thermobaric. It's the largest one we've ever created. All of the fun of a nuclear weapon sans the radiation. This one has been set for a ground burst. We don't want the Fish to recover that ship. So, if it looks like they are going to, you will have the codes necessary to set this off."

"Whew!" he breathed. He had worked with a lot of weapons systems in his career, but had never been assigned anything with this level of destructive capability. "Let's hope it doesn't come to us using it. As it is, you mustn't let that ship fall into enemy hands."

"Agreed. Still, we prefer to have an edge whenever possible. This bomb is one of the biggest edges we came up with."

"I would contest your words, but I tend to agree." McKenna sighed heavily. "So. I know where the party is to be held and who is on the guest list. All I need to understand is when the affair takes place."

"You have six hours to prep. The Commando Helicopter Force at Bardufoss is already readying their helis to bring you back home. From there, you will transfer to cargo aircraft and will be taken to where the operation is being staged. I have already taken the liberty of downloading the recommended loadouts and equipment lists that HQ has prepped for you. It should be on your server in a directory marked Durendal, the code name for this operation."

Six hours—this is definitely being done on the fly!

"Sir, that's not a lot of time. I have a lot to get in motion," he said, rising to his feet. "Is there anything else?"

Please, let there not be anything else…

Lieutenant-Colonel Frye rose to his feet and extended his hand, which McKenna shook firmly. "Only this. Pack your winter gear, Andy. It's bound to be a bit nippy in Greenland." He smirked just long enough for McKenna to see it, then turned to leave the small office.

CHAPTER 3

Auditorium One, Extra Terrestrial Task Force (ETF) HQ,
DIA Intelligence Annex, the Penetrator
Los Alamos, New Mexico, the United States

Captain Bryan Wade was not at all pleased about the mission his
Omega Force had been handed. Armchair generals and much of the
Army saw his unit as a hammer of war, designed to flatten and
destroy the enemy. The warhammer iconography even appeared in
Omega's unit patch. Wade knew that the work Omega did was
precise and brutal. They were a controlled fury, a monster that, when
unleashed, destroyed every appropriate target that dared get in its
path.

The problem was that most people just saw the results of their
actions. During the last war, their raid on Vladivostok had lit up the
media with images of burning fuel farms, sinking ships, devastated
Russian power armor. The Army had decided to capitalize on that
strike from a public affairs perspective, using it to recruit new
candidates for Special Forces. The PAs played up the image of
Omega as somehow being the flip side of Delta Force. It was a
sentiment that spread to the rest of the Army, and it pissed off
Captain Wade.

*I know what Omega really is, and it's not about brute force, but
precise force applied at the right time.*

There was a part of him that felt that this was a waste of his and
his people's time. *We are not some security detail. We are Omega.
We have been on multiple ops since the invasion—each one aimed at*

destroying aliens. That is our game. This isn't about that at all. They would have been wiser to tag another SF unit to this, or just let the Rangers go in.

He had been a young man in ROTC at the time of the Vladivostok raid, and it had inspired him to enlist and eventually join the Special Forces. The imagery of gallant ASHURs ripping into the Russians had propelled his military career. Wade regretted he had been in school during the war and had missed out on most of the fighting.

Wade came from a long line of patriots. His father, grandfather, and great-grandfather had all been in the service. It was not an obligation to him; being in the Army was an honor. Some of his fondest childhood memories were the Fourth of July and his father setting off fireworks. Patriotism and service had been hammered into his soul since childhood and now was the foundation of who he was as a warrior.

He had a long line of tabs and insignia to show what he was capable of. A Ranger tab; a Special Forces tab; a Special Missions Unit tab; his ASHUR wings; and the insignia of the two rigs he had qualified for, a Honey Badger and his current ride, a Python. Just a look at his sleeve set his credentials with most people. If that didn't, the salad bar of ribbons he wore on his chest usually completed the story of his life. They didn't represent medals to him; they defined who he was.

Part of his grittiness was the urgency that he and his people had been pulled off the front lines in Seattle and rushed to the Penetrator. Omega had been in the middle of planning a spoiling attack against the Fish in Lake Union. Seattle was a quagmire of fighting and Omega's presence there had been instrumental in stabilizing what little control of the city the Army had. Wade knew that his people's departure was going to be costly. It would be a price to be paid in both ground lost and the lives of other soldiers that were left to fight there. That irked him.

We fought and bled for that ground; now it will be lost and we will have to fight for it all over again.

Most operations of this type required several days of planning, if not longer. The success of US Special Forces and Operations was not just their prowess in battle, but in their meticulous planning. This mission lacked detailed planning, and that was something that chewed on Wade's nerves. He thrived on adhering to a plan—a plan with a backup plan, which had its own backup plan. Plans had been given to him out of Fort Liberty/Bragg, and it was clear that they had been rushed and lacked the level of detail that he was accustomed to. While they had thrown bodies at preparing for this mission, it was still, at best, impromptu. To him, that meant the mission was putting his people at risk.

We don't even know for sure that we are going to find anything there that is of value. Whoever cooked up this steaming pile of excrement is going to have a lot to answer for if my people get slaughtered.

Moving to the podium at the front of the auditorium, he could feel the eyes locking on him. He could feel their thoughts. *They have heard about Omega, but have never seen any of us. They are wondering if we are as big a bunch of badasses as people say. They may be disappointed. We are not presentation people. To get impressed with Omega, you need to see us in the battlespace.*

He toggled the control to the holodisplay behind him, then slid on the hand controller. "Good day," he said, which smothered the room in silence. "I am Captain Bryan Wade, call sign Crockett, commanding officer of Omega Force and acting commander of this mission. We are going to be discussing Operation 10406—code name Sulaco."

The name originally offered was Nostromo, but Colonel Slade pointed out that the reference could easily be interpreted as negative.

If I remember that movie right, the crew didn't fare well.

Wade took a sip of water, then projected the mission objectives up behind him.

"Three days ago, Space Force in Thule, Greenland, downed an incoming UAP. The alien spacecraft crash-landed on the eastern coast of Greenland."

The coordinates of the crash appeared behind him, as well as a topographical map showing the site. He worked the hand controller almost with the same precision as his ASHUR's weapons.

"As you can see, this is inhospitable terrain—rocky, uneven ice, deep snow; roughly just short of the shoreline. We do not know if there were any survivors of the crash or to what extent the craft was damaged."

Images flickering behind him showed the satellite coverage of the vessel. It was wider than it was long, with what appeared to be armored plating that overlapped on the hull. From above, it appeared very much like a giant trilobite.

There was a debris-filled trough behind the craft with what looked like bits and pieces of torn flesh, pinkish-crimson, frozen like boulders. It wasn't the size or fleshy debris that stood out, it was a faint oval shape that seemed to surround the vessel. It only extended a few meters out, but it seemed to prevent the snow from covering the ship. In many places, snowdrifts seemed to stop at the edge of the barrier.

With a click of his thumb on the controller, the image changed to a map. "Our mission is simple, at least, on paper. We will secure the craft, recover whatever is of use, and ensure that the vessel does not fall back into their hands. In doing so, we will defend the site from anyone attempting to interfere with our operations, be they survivors aboard the ship, or any other alien encounter."

Wade paused, letting the objectives sink in with the gathered group. "Omega and our Ranger support will deploy to the south, where the ground appears to be smoother. The scientists that will come in with us will need protection, and we will provide that. We will form a defensive perimeter around the vessel. Omega and the Rangers will form infiltration teams that will penetrate the target, eliminating any defenses that may remain. After we have cleared the ship, the science teams will be permitted access so that they can perform their work."

He shifted on his feet, giving him a momentary pause giving him time to make sure all eyes were on him. "There are many challenges to this mission, aside from potential alien resistance or intervention. This is an extreme environment in terms of cold. All supplies must be flown in, which is subject to the vicious weather there. The atmospherics are hard on equipment and personnel. While we are prepared for this, leveraging our experience in Alaska in the last war, it is still going to be a challenge.

"Our insertion to the target area will be by air. Our forces will transport by air to Thule. From Thule, we will be making a low altitude drop of our ASHUR and infantry forces. Thule will act as our primary logistics hub necessary."

Saying the words was one thing, but he knew the risks involved with such an operation. *Given the winds, the rocky terrain, and the snow, this is going to be a tricky operation for us to pull off.* Normally he would have a slide talking about the risks, but this mission was not just limited to the military personnel going in with him. There were several civilian scientists and engineers that would be part of the mission. *Military personnel are hard-wired to comprehend such risks—it is part of their jobs. Civilians—they tend to piss themselves.* From the looks of some of the military personnel, the flaring of their eyes, the crossed arms, and scowls—they were already understanding the complexities of what he was conveying. *I will have to brief the Army personnel on the way in, out of earshot of the civvies.*

Wade set the hand control unit down and looked out over the personnel in attendance. "Questions?"

A hand from his counterpart in the Rangers, Captain Wertan, rose in the air. Wade called on him first. "Do we have any intel on alien forces in the region? I doubt they are going to sit back and let us plunder one of their ships."

Plunder? Leave it to Tommy to use pirate wording.

Wade looked over the stage at the colonel who had kicked off the entire operation. The officer stepped forward to the podium.

"This is best addressed by Colonel Slade." He gave the colonel a respectful glance—*God knows this man has earned it.*

Slade slid behind the podium and adjusted the microphone.

"That's a good question. The reality is, we don't know. Our warfighting has been concentrated to our own coastline and bases. As such, we are unsure what may or may not be an alien presence in Greenland. We have never had a chance to get at one of their ships before, which adds some unique complexities to this mission."

Murmurs rippled through the audience at the colonel's candor. Slade was known in the Army. He had been the person that had first detected the alien threat. His work had been instrumental in giving the military the precious few victories they had secured since the start of the war.

His word carries a lot of weight with these people.

The shorter Slade seemed to sense the tension. Resting his hands on the podium, he leaned forward, as if engaging with everyone in the room. "I know what you're thinking. Are we being sent on a one-way mission? The answer to that is no, hell no! This ship is a prize. It may be a game changer for the war. Even if it nothing more than biological scrap, we will learn a lot about the Fish from studying it.

"So, in order to ensure that you are getting the best intel that we have here, we are sending along a person that has spent more time with the Fish than anyone. She lived with them for months, up close and personal. She battled them on Guam, and you all know about that battle. Staff Sergeant Natalia Falto." Slade gestured to the front row of seats with a simple nod.

An embarrassed Marine rose from her seat, turning to face the audience.

"Sergeant Falto has forgotten more about the Fish than we have learned. She had volunteered to be a part of this operation as a consultant. We're also sending a top marine biologist, Dr. Amanda Schrivener, on this mission. She was the nation's best marine biologist and since the invasion, has been studying alien physiology. Having folks like this on the ground is going to give us an edge." As he finished, Wade noticed more than a few in the audience giving nods of approval.

Having that jarhead with us should help. It was hard to deny the inter-service rivalry between the Army and the Marine Corps. Most of it was forged in tradition, and, from what Wade thought, a bit of jealousy on the part of the Marines. He had seen the footage of the fighting on Guam, and had faced the Fish on his own since the alien incursions. Based on that, his respect for the Corps had risen.

Looking at Falto, his mind raced to remember the *Time* interview with her. The Fish had cut her apart. They had used her as a biological test bed. *She lost her legs and an arm to them. By any account, she should be dead. The fact that she's willing to go says a great deal.* Still, there was a brief hesitation when it came to Falto. They had her in their possession for a long time. *Did they compromise her? Is she possibly some sort of Manchurian Candidate, waiting for some trigger to turn on us?* He didn't want to go there, but it was impossible to ignore.

One of his own, Lieutenant John Hughes, call sign Saint, asked the next question.

"What's with the thing surrounding the ship? Is that some sort of force field barrier or something we have to blast our way through?"

Slade fielded that one. "We don't know. Initially we assumed it was just heat radiating from the ship. It is warmer than the surrounding terrain, at least that is what IR images show us. Right now we don't know what it is."

That response generated more murmuring. Wade appreciated that Slade hadn't tried to sugarcoat the question or disregard it.

Hughes didn't hesitate with another question. "Are any of the other countries out there planning to make a grab for this thing?"

This was Wade's question to respond to, given the briefing his own G2, the CIA, and the State Department had given him. "Right now, as far as we know, only Greenland is aware that this thing is down, and that is because we informed them. Europe has their own Fish issues that they are dealing with. The belief is that none of them are in a position to respond quickly to this, even if they are aware of it." He opted to gloss over the fact that that Greenland hadn't given the Americans permission to investigate or recover material from the crash site. Offers were made for compensation, but Greenland had remained mute.

In this case, it is better to act and ask for forgiveness later.

There was more to that point, but not for public consumption. He had specific orders from his command that if any other country tried to interfere with his mission, Wade was to have full discretion as to how to respond, and that his senior command would back him. He had stated it directly to them that he needed that authority, and, after some debate, they agreed. *I doubt I will have to use it. No one is able to get there other than us. It's too far from their bases.* His response seemed to satisfy Hughes and the others in the room.

As the questions shifted back to the military context, Wade had retaken his position behind the podium. The questions that came were what he expected from military professionals. They wanted to know how accurate and recent the satellite imagery was. They wanted to know how much ammunition would come in with them, not to mention technicians and repair parts. It reemphasized the adage, "Amateurs talk tactics; professionals talk logistics." While he was more than able to respond to the questions, they were still reassuring. They told him that the people that would go were focused on the mission.

As the session finished and the personnel departed, Colonel Slade came up to him. "Do you have everything you need?"

"Not entirely, sir."

"What can I arrange?"

"Sir, what I need is information. I'm not sure why Omega is assigned to this op."

Slade seemed puzzled by the question. "Perhaps you can unpack that question."

"I was told by my CO that you specifically requested Omega for this assignment. I'm not sure why. This seems like something that requires delicate troops. Omega isn't that. We are brute force."

Slade crossed his arms. "You think I am wasting precious military material? Is that it?"

"Sir, Omega is designed to destroy what we are targeted against. That is what we train for; it is what we excel at. You need an enemy target obliterated, you bring us in as the big hammer. This operation doesn't need our firepower or unique set of skills."

His words clearly didn't shake the colonel. If anything, Slade smiled more. "I understand. For the record, I appreciate your bluntness. The reason Omega is going is simple—the unknowns."

"Sir?"

"Look, the Fish are highly adaptive. They are not a mindless enemy. We don't know exactly how they will respond to us making a move on one of their ships. What we *do* know is that they will not react passively. They may very well come at us and come hard. Also, there's the unknowns of the ship itself. There's no way for us to know if any of the Fish aboard that thing are alive or dead. If they are alive, they are not going to surrender simply because we board their vessel.

"I need Omega there because if I send in some other Special Forces unit or the Rangers, and they encounter problems, it'll take too long for us to get them additional support or firepower. Omega thrives on self-reliance. Every other unit is deployed, so responding would be nearly impossible. Having Omega there ensures that if the Fish strike, they will get their assess handed to them up-front and personal."

Slade's logic was inescapable. "So you believe this is going to be a shooting match."

The colonel's eyebrows rose. "I don't know. I wish I could tell you I knew for certain what you'd be facing. One thing I have learned is that this isn't that kind of war. When we fought the Russians, we understood their tactics, their logic, their approach to warfare. With the Fish, we are learning as we go. Every mistake we make costs lives and yields ground. I think that a battle is a distinct possibility—that's the best I can do for you. If that happens, I need your big-ass hammer ready to crack some crab shells."

Wade studied the colonel's face for a moment, framed with wisps of white hair on his temples. There were wrinkles on his brow and under his eyes. He looked tired, if not exhausted. This was an officer who spent his time working hard.

"I heard a rumor that during the Battle for Washington, you went out into the fighting, right on the front line," Wade said.

Slade nodded. "You heard correct."

"Good. That means you at least understand the risks you're asking my people to undertake."

"I do. I wish I was going with you, but the war effort needs me here."

Wade sighed, almost deliberately. "This is not going to be a cakewalk, that much is for sure. Don't worry. If the Fish decide to make a show of it, we will bring the music and make them dance."

"Captain, that's exactly what I'm counting on."

CHAPTER 4

Operation Sulaco
Over Baffin Bay

Falto had not put on her full combat gear since she had been captured. Parts of it had been worn before. She had donned her new standard tactical gear (STG) when working out on the treadmill, just to get used to the extra weight. With the bionics replacement, breaking a sweat had taken longer. This was the first time she had fully suited up for combat. She was wearing the same amount of equipment that she had worn on Guam, though her STG was the winter variant, as opposed to jungle. Her arctic gear was in her ruck tucked in under her seat. The plane was getting cold, despite the heaters blasting out warm air—a testimony as to the temperatures outside.

Sitting aboard the C-5 aircraft was familiar, yet somehow different. It wasn't that she was not in the presence of her fellow Marines. With her bionics, the sensations of the aircraft didn't feel the same. She understood the differences. A big part of her life was learning to live with the new sensations. As much as that was her existence, the plane just didn't feel right to her.

It's like my bionics are challenging every memory I have of how something felt.

The aircraft was filled mostly with the scientific gear and equipment needed for entry into the alien spacecraft. The bulk of the military force would await them when they landed in Thule. She had been assigned to fly with the handful of officers that had been present at the briefing at the Penetrator. So far, they hadn't talked to her much, but she didn't mind their indifference. Conversations aboard a C-5 were always a matter of yelling.

As she adjusted the chest armor, memories of Guam flickered to the forefront of her mind. She thought about Porter at first, then Rickenburg. She shared the same rank that Hannibal had when he died. It felt surreal that they could have been peers. *He was far more a Marine than I am.* She remembered when his ASHUR had been taken down by the aliens. *I wonder what he would think of me now. No doubt he would have some colorful language about this.*

Captain Wertan and the other two Ranger officers slept. *That's one thing the military teaches you, how to sleep in any situation, regardless of how loud it is.* Even with the occasional buffeting of the aircraft, the Rangers simply slept on. She was experiencing too much anxiety to employ her old skills at sleeping.

This mission might mean facing the aliens again, and that thought swirled in her head as she sat in the dull roar of the plane. She didn't fear the Fish. Her primary concern was how she would react when she came face-to-face with them. The aliens' little war with her had been more than merely taking body parts from her. They had waged a test of wills, something she understood now.

I didn't break when I was with them before—but a lot has come to pass since then. I've regained my humanity.

Even though Omega and the Rangers would be there providing security, she was worried that she might freeze or panic. *They took a lot from me.* For a moment, she mentally pictured the Alpha that had tormented her. *I was a guinea pig for their experiments. They killed good people, taking them a bit at a time.* She was fearful that when she saw them again, her anxiety might get the best of her. *I can't let that happen. I need to show these troops that I am on top of my angst. I need them to see that I am every bit the Marine I should be.*

Captain Wade had slept after they had taken off for an hour or two, then had broken out his digipad, working furiously on it. To a casual person, it might look as if he were playing a game—his intense gray eyes staring at the pad, his fingers stabbing at the data he viewed. Falto knew better. This was an officer working.

No doubt he's making last-minute changes to their loadouts and gear.

Wade moved the rubber protected digipad into a big pouch on his belt, and made light eye contact with her. After several minutes of nothing more than the rumble-roar of the C-5, he got up and made his way over to her, taking a seat next to her. "I hope you don't mind."

"Of course not," she called back.

"Hell of a mission."

She nodded. "Yes." *In more ways than you might think.* She didn't want to talk about the mission, so her mind shifted to more of a military mode. Glancing at him, her eyes focused on his assault rifle. "You SMU guys are using the XM7?" she said, nodding at the weapon.

"Yeah, you can't beat a Sig in the field. And I'm not just Special Forces. Omega is a Special Missions Unit."

"Apologies—I didn't know the distinction. Regardless, I'm pretty fond of the Remington ACR."

"I know that the Sigs are old-school," Wade replied. "I like the punch this thing has."

Falto nodded. "Those .277 Fury rounds are pretty devastating, or so I've heard."

"You heard right," he replied proudly.

"So, you SF boys get to use some non-standard stuff. Fun toys."

"You're a Marine," Wade countered. "The Corps has a long and illustrious history of having their own tanks, fighting vehicles, and weapons. It's almost as if you don't want to work with the Army."

He was right, there was no denying it. "We like the Army just fine. We just tend to be particular."

For a moment there was silence between them.

"Sergeant, do you mind if I ask you some questions?"

"No, sir," Falto replied. It was a lie. Everyone, it seemed, had questions about her captivity, what it was like. She usually didn't mind the questions, but when they came from someone in the military, there was always a mental hesitation that she struggled with. So far, no one had gotten too personal with their inquiries, but with her military colleagues, that was always a risk.

"I was told you joined this mission as an independent consultant. You're the only person I have on this op who isn't tied to my chain of command. Why is that?"

Natalia bristled a little at that, if only for a moment. "I don't want someone else calling the shots when it comes to my life. The Fish had me under their flippers for months. I guess I'm not quite ready to return to a life of people telling me what to do and when to do it."

"You're still a Marine—still in a chain of command."

"Yes, but the Corps understands and has given me leeway. That's why I was at the Penetrator."

He still wasn't convinced, she could see that in his face. "My concern is having a random element operating in my zone of control. I like a clean battlespace."

"Everyone does," she replied. "Hopefully this won't become a combat situation. If that happens, I want to assure you, I am still a Marine. If I am pressed into action, I will take it." She said the words, but she wasn't entirely convinced of them herself.

I have been through a lot since this invasion started. I haven't fired a weapon in anger since Guam. Will I be able to do it again?

Her answer seemed to satisfy him. "Fair enough. I read your reports and saw some of your interviews. No one ever seemed to ask how you ended up being captured."

There it is—a question she dreaded. She had always shifted discussion away from that question. Coming from someone in the military, there was a hint of, "How could you have allowed yourself to be captured?" While Wade hadn't asked that question, it was part of what Falto heard in her mind. There was some embarrassment that came with how she became a prisoner of war.

"I didn't surrender, if that's what you think," she blurted out. "I went down fighting."

Wade's eyes flickered, clearly surprised by her response. "I didn't say you surrendered."

"I was wounded—some of their poison needles. I blacked out. When I awoke, I was in one of their undersea complexes." The words flowed fast from her lips and she could feel some anger rising in her voice.

"I was just curious," Captain Wade stated flatly. "We saw action in Seattle. I never heard of anyone captured by the enemy, though. Sure, we have a lot of MIAs, but most of them were just buried in the rubble during a battle. I just wanted to know if they did something special to capture you—so I can prepare my people for that kind of attack."

It embarrassed Falto that she had taken offense so quickly. "My apologies. It's a bit of a sensitive subject with me."

"An apology isn't necessary. With all I have on my plate with this op, I probably should have thought about my wording better."

She shifted a little in her seat, mostly to take some strain off of her back. Lower back pain was part of her bionic replacements. Her body was having to adjust to the different weights of the bionic limbs and a change in her center of gravity. It only really bothered her when she sat for long periods of time. When she had flown before on C-5s, the uncomfortable seat had made her butt ache after a few hours.

I guess there's one good thing about having bionic legs and ass, I don't have to deal with that discomfort any longer. I've traded butt pain for back pain.

"After all of the shit they put me through, I tend to overreact sometimes."

"That's understandable. That *Time* piece about you was good. It was also damned sobering for someone like me, who has to face this enemy. I'm not sure how anyone would be after being held prisoner that deep underwater, with no idea of where you are. Psychologically that would eat up many people from the inside out."

Natalia struggled to find words, then finally said, "They cut me up. They did things to my body that I'm still struggling with. I didn't have much of a choice. If I didn't die quickly, my choice was a slow death. Even if we had tried to escape, the water is their domain. If we wanted to drown, they could have recaptured us. It all came down to the will to endure. I had family and friends on the surface, so I refused to die."

"I've faced these monstrosities more than a few times," Wade confided in a lowered tone of voice that she could barely hear over the roar of the aircraft. "Despite all of that, I still haven't figured them out. They are not ignorant. They have tactics which evolve. They have specific roles for their species. There's clearly some communication they possess. I don't know if they are following orders or operating on instinct. I can't help but wonder if there isn't someone that is behind all of them, calling their shots."

Falto understood why he came over to her. *He wants a deeper level of understanding. I'm not sure if I'm the one to give that to him or not.*

"They are not that different from us," she finally replied. "One Alpha—a Boss—he and I fought on Guam. He stayed with me, watching me suffer. It was as if he wanted revenge, or that he simply enjoyed my pain. There was some intelligence there. It wasn't animal-level, it was more. At the same time, it was different, so different that it's hard to describe. It is somewhere between cunning and ruthless. They have no empathy; they don't care about the damage or pain they cause. It's borderline arrogant, as if they believe themselves superior." She paused, realizing that she was rambling. The words just came out of her as they rarely did when she talked about the aliens.

It must be because I'm going to face them again—it's triggered something.

As if he'd read her mind, Wade coldly stated, "You're worried about facing them again."

"Any sane person would be. I've seen what they are capable of."

"So why did you come?"

Falto studied his face—the lean cheeks, his chiseled chin—all the while searching for the words to her answer. "I struggle with

46

sleep. I have nightmares about them. It's been months, but I can't seem to shake them. It's like they are living in my head. Some if it is memories, some of it is—well—fear. There is a feeling at times that I never left that place, deep down. Part of me, I think, is still down at the bottom of the Pacific, still fighting my own little test of wills with that Alpha. I hate saying it, but that's what it is." She remembered her conversation with Porter and how he seemed to understand. She could only hope that Captain Wade had the same character.

"PTSD is tough, but they have drugs for it."

"Drugs have side effects; they make you dependent. That's not who I am. I don't have to rely on anyone or anything to get by. I tried to take them for a while but stopped. They don't make you better, they simply hide the symptoms."

"Sergeant, I'm not sure that going on this operation is going to help you get better. We don't know what we are up against here. For all we know, the moment we land, they will come right at us. The variables on this are off the charts."

Natalia nodded. "I know that. I'm not looking for a miracle."

"So what is it you hope to achieve?"

She pursed her lips and felt her face get red and warm. "Everyone thinks that my time as a POW defines me. Even you, when you came over here, that's what you wanted to talk about first…me being a prisoner. Every talk that Colonel Slade has me give, every interview I do, every message I write—they are all about me as a captive. The truth is, that isn't who I am. I was a tough-ass Marine before the Fish showed up. Now everyone looks at me differently. I'm coming to hopefully put all of that behind me. I'm still a Marine. I am not defined by what happened to me for a few months of my life. I have a lot of things I need to put behind me. I want to step forward but it's hard to do with the baggage I'm carrying."

I am not a victim. I didn't do anything wrong. It was just something that happened that I couldn't fully control. She worried for a moment that the last thoughts she had may have been spoken out loud.

Wade's gaze became more intense. "Do you really care what people think?"

While she had admired his direct language before, suddenly she found herself hating it. "Everyone says that they don't care. We all have the little lies that we cling to. I guess I really do care. I don't want people to think of me as a coward, or a bad Marine."

"I learned a long time ago to not care about other people's feelings. It comes with the territory when you are a trained killing mechanism. My unit is required to do some pretty horrible stuff as part of our mission. When I first got into Special Operations, I saw what the media put out about us. I cringed when I saw SF or SO forces portrayed in movies. Hollywood either makes us out to be superheroes or baby-killers, depending on the politics of the day. I found that consumed a lot of time and got me nowhere and nothing but more frustration. There was no way to influence what other people thought. It might be worth your time to shelve your concerns about what others are thinking. In the end, all that matters is what you *know* about yourself."

His words hit home with Natalia. *He's probably right. People can either accept me for who I am or not.*

"Thank you," she said.

"Given you can find a way to suppress your concern about others —what is it that you want to be, then? What does your step forward look like?" There was a sincerity in his voice that she appreciated.

"I don't know. I'm just tired of being stuck where I am now. I guess we'll both find out when we get to Greenland." Falto leaned back in the seat, shifting slightly to adjust the low throb in her back.

"Don't worry, Sergeant," Captain Wade replied. "Omega has you covered. If you're going to be stuck on a desolate frozen landscape poking around an alien spacecraft, we're about the best fire support you can hope to have."

Natalia smiled, leaning back. *I hope to hell he's right.*

CHAPTER 5

Operation Durendal, Svalbard

The blast of cold air that hit Major McKenna as he deplaned was harsh and biting, but not uncommon. Months of being in Norway had toughened him to the arctic air of Svalbard. His eyes squinted and his nostrils tingled as he briskly made his way to the small base offices that adjoined the airfield. As he entered, he stomped his feet to shake off any snow he had carried in on his boots, and slung his kit bag onto the pile with the rest of 45 Commandos' personal gear. Someone handed him a hot cup of coffee and he could feel the warmth bring some sensation back to his fingers. It tasted a little bitter, but he didn't care.

Lieutenant Duncan Kendall, his intelligence officer, moved up in front of him. Duncan was the epitome of a good intel man. He didn't insert himself into conversations where he didn't have something to add. He didn't bog down McKenna's life with idle conversation. The fact that he approached him meant that he had something to share. "I just got the latest squirt from HQ."

McKenna looked around and spotted an office door, then walked over to it with Kendall in tow. They stepped into the dark office and found the light switch before Kendall closed the door behind them. "Good news?"

Kendall shrugged, then pulled out his digipad. "MI6 received word that several Special Forces units have been pulled off the front —their missions have been scrubbed. Humint says that they have evidence of a flight of long-range aircraft departing for Thule."

49

"Which Special Forces units?"

Do I really want to know?

"Third battalion of Rangers has a company that is being deployed to support Omega Force."

It was so hard to not roll his eyes at the words "Omega Force," that he refused to try.

That's all we bloody need! American cowboys in power armor.

"How solid is this intel?" he asked.

"Confidence is high."

"Damnation," he muttered. "I guess it could be worse."

Kendall's eyes narrowed. "How is that?"

"I have no idea," he responded with a flash of his smile. "I was just trying to be as positive as possible."

"Well, there is some good news in the latest squirt. Our sources indicate the Americans are unaware of our intentions."

"That *is* good news."

"We are moving fast enough that they haven't seemed to notice us. On top of that, our counterintelligence folks are good at giving their CIA other things to chase down. You know the Yanks—easily distracted by shiny objects."

The CIA was no longer the organization it had been during the Cold War. Starting with the lie of weapons of mass destruction in Iraq, it had become an organization that was populated with political appointees. Their failures during the Russo-Bratva War had shown incredible flaws in their methods and approaches—things they had proven unable to fix.

When we were close allies, their bumbling was something to be concerned with. Now it is something that plays to our advantage.

"Let's hope they remain in the dark until it is too late," he said.

"Indeed. There is more." Kendall pulled out an A-size printed image. It was a satellite view of the alien ship. McKenna studied it for a few moments as his intelligence officer said, "This is the latest image we have of the ship."

"I take it I'm missing something," he replied, rubbing his eyes. Weariness was as much an enemy as the aliens.

"Quite. If you look at the ship, it should have a few centimeters of snow on it. It doesn't. In fact, there seems to be some sort of barrier or field around the ship that is preventing the snow from accumulating."

Looking at the picture again, he saw that there was no sign of coverage on the ship. "That can't be good news. It could mean that the vessel is still operational, despite the crash."

"Unknown, sir. Our resident experts believe that if the ship was operational, it would move into the ocean. This field, for lack of better words, may be automated in some manner, triggered by the crash. If it is a defensive measure, that may point to how badly damaged the ship is."

McKenna disliked the response. "In other words, we have no bloody idea what that thing is or why it is somehow active."

Kendall nodded, his cheeks turned instantly red. "That is correct, sir."

I don't like it. I would have preferred that all the aliens had possessed the courtesy to simply die in the crash. This field, or whatever it is, indicates that someone aboard that ship is alive— alive enough to activate it.

He didn't mind killing Fish, but if one survived, then it was possible the whole ship was filled with survivors.

"Very well then, Kendall. Any other cheery bits of news for me?"

"They are loading the hovercraft now. Pursuant to London's instructions, we have equipped the trigger for the device in your Sovereign cockpit."

The device—the massive fuel air explosive. They had assured him during the flight in that there was no way that someone could accidentally trigger it. They had made such a point of it that he began to question whether they were lying or not. Experience had long taught McKenna that the more people took a passionate stand on an issue, the weaker their reasoning usually was. "Very well. Tell the lads we are not mounting up until we are a few minutes from shore. No point in burning off power before then."

"Will do, sir." McKenna started for the door, but Kendall interrupted him. "Where are you off to, sir?"

"I need to check my mount," he replied, zipping up his coat to brace for the bitter outside air.

He moved through the huddled mass of the members of 45 Commando and then to the exterior door. The air hit his face, stinging, as he headed for the large assault LCAC-Hs. The big hovercraft were flat on the tarmac, surrounded by sentries. The darkness of the early hours was penetrated by white lights which had to contend with the blowing snow, dimming their illumination. He went to the lead craft and climbed up the gantry.

The Sovereign aboard them were covered with pinned down thermal tarps. Technicians moved about, sliding under the tarps to dutifully check the mounts. He bumped into one tech in a parka who told him where his Sovereign was and he made his way to it, sliding under the tarp and out of the wind. He was greeted with the insignia for 45 Commando on the left torso of the mount, and under that, the logo for the Spitfire—showing a WWII aircraft flying above an outline of his class of Sovereign. Just seeing the logos gave him a strange sense of calm and familiarity.

The Americans claimed they had created the first power armor. That first generation gear had almost no armor, it was simply an augmented frame that gave the user better endurance and the ability to carry heavier weapons and gear. That generation evolved quickly to provide better protection for the wearer and even hard points for mounting weapons. Still, they were troops wearing suits. The British rushed to create their own versions, and the Royal Marines and some Army units fielded them.

It was the Russians that caused the emergence of the next generation. They started fielding bigger armored mechanized suits, some even had both a driver and a gunner. NATO countries responded with their own crash program, which led to both the ASHURs and Sovereigns. The pilot still controlled the mount with their body, but gone were the days of exposed body parts and exoskeleton suits. Armor and heavier weapons became the mainstay.

Better power efficiency allowed pilots to hang in battle longer and the weapons the frames carried were devastatingly effective.

The British Sovereign program used the same ammunition as the rest of NATO, but, in McKenna's mind, they had improved on the designs of what the Yanks called rigs. As he looked under the tarp at his Spitfire, he mentally compared it to the American's ASHURs. Where the Americans mounted weapons externally, the British went for streamlining. His six NLAWS-2 rockets were internally racked on his left torso, with small armored doors that popped open when they fired. His left arm was equipped with a RSAF Enfield, Royal Ordnance, Heckler and Koch six-barreled Gatling laser, almost entirely hidden in its forearm. Where the Americans loved their brutish lasers, the Gatling fired a stream of laser bursts that were far more effective and power efficient, at least in his opinion. The right torso of his Spitfire mounted a small chain gun on a ball joint giving it a broad field of fire.

Even the looks of the Spitfire were graceful in his eyes. The front of the body sloped forward to a narrow ridge down the front which was wider at the top where the pilot's head was positioned. There were no straight lines on the Sovereigns; everything was sleek curves and smooth contours. His own was painted white with long streaks of gray that barely masked the light hexagonal pattern of the outer layer of the armor.

The British had adopted their own naming convention for Sovereigns that was different from that of the Americans. They had opted to use the names of World War II aircraft. He piloted a Spitfire, for example, and in 45 Commando there were Hurricanes, some Hornet scouts, two Tempests, some Gladiators, a Lancaster, one Tornado, and some Meteors. The mix of mounts had been crucial to the success of his unit thus far. Concentrating many Sovereigns in a single unit had been crucial to the victories they'd enjoyed.

Climbing up on the bent knee of the mount, he activated the hatch control and it hissed as it swung open sideways, pushing hard against the inner tarp that covered it. McKenna squeezed in, closing the front hatch. He sat in a squatted position, not wanting to try and push his heavy winter boots in the mount's leg sleeves, then looked around the darkened cockpit. This was where he felt the most comfortable, in his mount. It was here that he felt the most control over his own life.

Reaching right, he activated the internal lights. Doing so made it so that he could see his frigid breath as he looked for where the thermobaric weapon trigger had been mounted. It only took a moment to see the small box that had been put in near the communications controls. It was a simple mechanism, a key, which was in the slot had to be turned first, then a small plastic cover would be flipped up and a red button pushed. Taped to the transparent button cover was a note.

Not until we land. JN.

Seeing it made him chuckle. Sergeant Joseph Newman was his technician. His leaving of little notes for McKenna was a subtle bit of humor that he often looked forward to. In this case, it was half-joke, half-warning.

There were a number of moving parts with this operation, more than he was used to. The Royal Marines were known for their mission preparation and planning. Much of this op was thrown together, a hodgepodge of personnel and hardware, with little in the form of details.

The devil's in the details, as Grandmum used to say. The little things are the ones that can mess one up the most, and most of ours are unknowns.

There were a few things he could count on. One, the Americans would be there, if not when the Brits came ashore, then sometime later. After seeing the latest intel image of the alien ship, he had to assume that the aliens would be present as well. For McKenna, it was a default assumption—one that kept him and his men alive. He also knew he could count on something unforeseen happening. There wasn't a military operation that he had ever taken part in where something hadn't gone sideways.

Glancing around the cockpit of his Spitfire, he found himself smiling. His Sovereign had served him well in battle before. His first encounter with a Lobster, what the Americans called a Crab, had nearly cost him his mount and his life. The hulking creature had moved faster than he had assumed possible. It had closed the distance with his Spitfire in a few heartbeats, seeming to shake off his shots. The Lobster had wrapped one of its huge forward claws around his Spitfire and had started to squeeze. The sound of the metal protesting, moaning loudly, was a memory impossible to shake.

The alien had actually lifted him slightly off the ground as its claw crumpled his Spitfire's armor. If not for the fast action of Colour-Sergeant Ross, unleashing his Tempest's rail gun arm into the skull of the Lobster, he might have died then. As it was, it took two weeks for the techs to rebuild his mount.

Four weeks later he had gone toe-to-toe with one of the big alien Golems—what the Americans childishly referred to as Bosses. *They all apparently think this is some sort of game. It is not.* Its deadly cutter had slashed away big chunks of his armor, and had even kneecapped him. Standing on one wobbly leg, McKenna had unleashed his four remaining NLAWS-2 rockets at once as the Golem had closed with him. The anti-tank rockets had done their job well. The cracks and holes in its chest released a torrent of high-pressure liquid that immediately turned to snow in Norway's frigid air. The satisfaction of watching the Golem drop to its knees as it bled out almost made up for the long downtime for repairs to his Spitfire.

This mount has gotten me through a lot.

He reached out and patted the targeting system. His moment was shattered as the hatch opened to the Spitfire and his tech, Sergeant Newman, stuck his head in through the hatch. "I trust it meets with your approval."

McKenna nodded. "Saw your note. I assure you I have no intention of blowing us up until we make the shore."

"Sir, I would prefer that you not blow us up at all," Newman smirked.

"I will see what I can do." McKenna then shifted subjects. "Are all the Sovereigns tucked in for the ride?"

"Yes sir. I'd have like to have brought a full B-kit for replacement parts. We had to cut weight for these LCAC-Hs."

"We all have to make sacrifices in the service."

"The Andrews I spoke to keep telling me all about weight balances and distributions, as if I care. All that I worry about is having the necessary parts to do my job."

"Now, now, Sergeant. Play nice with His Majesty's navy. We do need them to transport us to Greenland in one piece."

"They are little more than black cabs that complain about where you sit and how much you weigh."

"We should be shoving off soon," McKenna replied, shutting off the interior light and sliding through the hatch. "I suppose I should get the lads together so we can get this mission off on the right foot."

Newman helped him down, not that he needed it. McKenna double-checked to make sure the hatch was secure, then made his way to the gangway. There was much to do before they got underway, and he had already indulged himself enough in making sure that his Sovereign was ready for battle.

Five hours later...

McKenna sat in his Spitfire's cockpit and saw the spray pelt his canopy. The heater was doing all that it could to keep the Spitfire warm, but it was a stalemate against the outside weather. While it was possible to wear winter gear in the cockpit, it wasn't practical. He had tried it several times in training and found the balance between the heater and his gear was impossible to achieve. He had his thermal knickers and undershirt on—which he appreciated.

The Royal Navy captain of the LCAC-H signaled him. "We are coming up on target—estimate two minutes."

"Roger that," he replied. He then switched to the Commandos' tactical channel. "Good morning, lads. We are two minutes from debarking. I want a perimeter formed around the LCACs initially.

Then I want Whisky Company to move north, towards the alien craft and to assume a defensive posture should they react to our landing. This needs to be precise. We have no way back to Svalbard, these hovercraft only had enough fuel to get us here. As such, if you encounter the bollocks, send them to hell, don't wait for orders."

Lieutenants McCranie and Walling, commanding the companies, responded with "Yes, sir."

There was a lurch as the LCAC-H rose on the ice surrounding the shoreline. Even though he had been expecting the bump, his nerves were on edge and he found himself gripping his glove controls a little tighter. "Stand by," he transmitted, steadying himself.

The hovercraft lurched and as it did, he leaned against the turn. Years of training and practice came into play. He knew that none of his people would topple over from a lurch or change of position.

The front end of the LCAC-H rose, then the craft slowed to a stop. As it cut thrust to the skirt, it lowered. The side ramp flopped down with a deep metallic thud.

"45—deploy!" he barked into his throat microphone. Moving his legs with purpose, his Spitfire rushed toward rank and to the shores of Greenland.

It took a moment to fully process their position. The LCAC-Hs were spread out on the beachhead like a human hand with its fingers fully extended. The "beach" was really just an ice and snow bank that extended out into the ocean for almost as far as he could see. The ground rose from where they landed to a height of almost ten meters. Jagged dark rocks jutted out defiantly from the blowing snow that was coming down lightly, melting as it hit his mount's canopy.

Sovereigns were deploying, along with the support troops. McKenna briskly walked his Spitfire away from the assault hovercraft and moved north. It was there that he saw the alien spacecraft for the first time. It was brown, almost orange in color, with what looked like overlapping armored carapace plates that ran from the front to the rear. The size was daunting; it stood at least thirty meters at the front—at least what he assumed was the front. To McKenna, it appeared more like a building than a vessel. The body of the ship nearest the ground had nasty gouges and cuts in it, with pinkish flesh-like material ripped off and exposed; no doubt from the rocks it had slid across. The barrier that was so visible from satellite imagery was invisible from the surface.

"Bugger...look at the size of that beast!" came Lieutenant Walling's voice. McKenna wanted to chide him for the comment, but he couldn't because it was what he was thinking as well.

"Alright, lads, we have work to do," McKenna replied. "This isn't Piccadilly, there'll be plenty of time for sightseeing later. Right now, let's get our position established." Even as he spoke, he couldn't pull his own eyes away from the ship.

Let's hope she's not filled with aliens...because if it is, we are going to be elbows deep in them...

CHAPTER 6

Operation Sulaco
West of the Crash Site, East Coast of Greenland

Captain Wade adjusted his Python's stance in the rear of the C-130 as it hit a pocket of air and shook around him. He adjusted his center of balance to compensate, as he had done dozens of times before. He had preferred to jump out of the Stalker, the Army's latest VTOL aircraft—but none were available.

So the illustrious Air Force broke out the antiques for us.

They were a few minutes from the drop, and he was mentally preparing for what was to come. Parachuting ASHURs had been long proven but it was far from easy. With three chutes, control of the descent was tricky, made worse by the winds cutting across Greenland.

His rigger was standing at the back of the aircraft, ready for the door to open as Wade made sure the lines were clear. Without warning, his comms system came alive.

"This is Starman," the flight commander signaled. "Our advance plane reports a problem with the DZ."

"This is Crockett," he replied. "What kind of problem?"

"There are ASHURs and hovercraft in our primary DZ."

His first instinct was that it had to be a mistake. *They may have read the sensor feed wrong. Maybe it's the Fish.* Then a sinking feeling hit him. Some other country was making a move on his objective! Humans were something that he could reason with, meaning they might be better than the Fish. Then again, maybe not.

His immediate decision was necessary regardless of who was down there.

"How does our backup DZ look?" he asked.

It was a flat patch to the west of the crash site. From the last time he saw it, there were plenty of rocks near the alien ship and bits of wreckage from the ship's landing—but otherwise it had looked relatively clear.

"Backup DZ is still open for business," Starman replied.

"Then that is where we are going." Wade switched to broadcast to both his Omega Force and the rest of the expedition. "This is Crockett to Sulaco Team. Someone has apparently beaten us to the prize. There are ASHURs and hovercraft in our primary DZ. We are diverting to the secondary DZ. I want no firing unless you are given my expressed authorization." He didn't wait for replies. Instead he switched his channel back to the flight deck.

"Starman, any comms contact from the unknowns on the ground?"

"Negative, Crockett. Our advance plane did a pass and should have been visible. We tried signaling on a number of frequencies, but didn't get as much as a ping back." As he replied, the plane started a shallow dive downward.

"Show me."

The vid images went up on his screen. He zoomed in on one of the figures.

A Tornado. It is the British! How in hell did they beat us here?

It's no surprise they are ignoring us. They are an arrogant people. When we went to war with Russia, they betrayed our alliance. It was a stab in the back when we needed them most.

"Very well." There was nothing else he could say. Whatever was going to happen would have to be sorted out on the ground once his force landed.

But I'm no diplomat, especially when it comes to the Limeys.

The door to the C-130 opened and a rush of air hit his Python. Outside he saw white, then, slowly, he could make out rocks poking through the snow below. His rigger moved out on the pad. Above the door a crimson light kept his focus.

"Ten seconds," came Starman's voice in his helmet's earbuds.

Wade shifted in his saddle-seat, bracing for it. Glancing at his side, he saw Sergeant Bill Smith, call sign Brimstone, in the cockpit of his Croc. Smith gave him a thumbs-up, which Wade returned.

The light above the door went green, and a klaxon blared. His rigger pushed his chute bundle out and quickly moved aside. The trio of parachutes caught the air, jerking him out the door.

Years of training and experience kicked in. First he checked to make sure all chutes had properly opened. Once he had done that, he looked down, through the lower cockpit canopy viewport.

As he turned in the wind, he caught a view of the alien vessel, and marveled at its size. The big orange-brown hull reminded him a little of the body of Crabs, how the massive plates overlapped. His force was coming down in the long trench that the craft had cut when it crashed. It had churned up rocks and there were reddish, almost pink bits of debris that littered its wake. Mentally, he calculated the area beneath him where he thought he would be landing and was thankful it seemed to lack rocks.

God only knows how deep that snow is and what's under it, though.

The ground was closing with him fast and he prepared for his landing. When paratroopers hit the ground, they did a PLF, parachute landing fall, to disburse the shock. Doing so with an ASHUR was possible, but risky. Pilots were trained to absorb the shock with the legs of the rig on impact. During his career, he had done a half-dozen combat drops, he had never done it in snow.

The other factor he was coping with was the wind. While the pilots adjusted their approach and airspeed to compensate for the wind gusts, the weather patterns of Northern Greenland were largely unknown. While the pilot's acumen was good on getting him to the drop zone, the buffeting of the wind made his rig sway heavily, and there was nothing he could do about it except brace for the inevitable.

Wade felt the automatic flaring system kick in as he came down the last few meters. The Python hit the snow with only the crunching of snow and the protesting of the hydraulics in the legs. He bent his knees at landing and felt the oppressive weight of the rig trying to crush into the ground. The snow was deep; he sank down to his ASHUR's knees on impact. For a few pounding beats of his heart, he thought that he might fall. Shifting his own center of gravity translated to that of his rig, and after a few moments, he rose to a standing position.

As he looked over, he saw that Smith's Croc had toppled over on its side, sinking in the snow. The sergeant rolled, managing to get one leg and bent knee under him enough to push off. He awkwardly rose to his feet. The right hand of the Croc made a thumbs-up at Wade.

In the distance he saw four more ASHURs land and others who had already dropped were on the move, trudging through the snow. His tactical display showed that everyone had landed and was transmitting as operational, though Lieutenant McLaughlin's Wild Weasel showed damage to his left leg.

The curse of snow and ice is it conceals a multitude of obstacles.

Further off to the west, the dull green parachutes of the Rangers and science teams were drifting down. They had been dropped separately and some distance away to avoid injury. A Ranger might survive another Ranger landing on him. He wouldn't survive an ASHUR crunching down on him, though.

Wade went to the tactical channel for the military personnel. "Alright, people, we need to deploy to the south so that our heavy gear can be dropped. I need us to establish local battlespace control ASAP." The C-130s loaded with the equipment were circling high above. *The Brits must have seen us drop.* His tactical display, however, did not show them closing.

The ASHURs of Omega Force moved as fast as they could through the snow, moving to form a defensive position. Wade closed with the rear of the alien vessel. The ship was wider than it was long. The tail, if that was what it could be called, was a half a kilometer in length. The closer he got to it, the more it looked less like a ship than some sort of creature. The gashes that had been ripped into it didn't look like torn metal, but more like flesh of some sort, violently torn off by the rocks during the crash. He got within eighty meters of it and stopped his advance, marveling again at the staggering size of the ship.

How did they ever get something this big to fly? How do they control it? The answers were right in front of him, but were elusive. *There will be time to figure all that out later—now I need to secure our position.*

He trudged the Python through the snow, coming near one of the pieces of debris from the crash. Glancing at it as he moved past it, he saw that it wasn't at all what he expected. This was not some pinkish metal, it looked more like flesh, like some sort of meat. It was frozen, with ice clinging to it, but it was definitely not the kind of debris he had expected to see.

Are their ships organic? That's got to be impossible.

"Crockett, this is Saint," came the voice of Lieutenant Hughes. "We've linked up with the Rangers. We should be clear for the cargo drops."

"Copy," he replied, then he switched to Starman's channel. "Starman, this is Crockett, the DZ is clear for your cargo runs."

"Roger that, Crockett," he replied. "We are swinging around to align our approach."

Looking over at the C-130s, they dropped low, almost looking as if they were going to be landing on the snowpack. Out the back of the aircraft, the parachutes were tossed out, pulling pallets of gear out. They were heavy enough that the rear ramp hit the snow as the planes slowed. He saw the repair pods for the ASHURs, metallic cocoon-like shells, dig into the snow on impact. Crates with other gear deployed out of the rear of other aircraft in a near perfect pattern on the snowpack.

A quick survey of his tactical display showed that the British were moving. They were poised along the south end of the crash site, between the alien vessel and the ice-covered shore. From what he could see, they were starting to throw up a line of ASHURs facing in the direction of his force. *Is this an attempt to intimidate us? Perhaps they are simply being precautious?* Looking at the tiny dots of light on the display, he knew he would not find his answers in the display.

"Pudknocker, Saint—you two see to the Rangers, scientists, and our gear. First priority is to establish local battlespace. Deploy the perimeter sensors and have Sonic get his GRDs out there to give us some data. Next is to establish our base. Get our base set up at grid coordinate," he paused to double-check them, "Foxtrot, five. Concentrate on getting our shelters in place; we are working with limited daylight hours here."

Both men confirmed the orders as he turned his Python twenty-degrees right so he could visually see the British rigs in the distance. They looked like black statues moving slowly against the backdrop of the stark white snow. The hulking forms of their hovercraft were poised in a semicircle, providing protection from the ocean.

They weren't supposed to be here. Once more the folks, in intelligence let us down.

It was becoming a pattern to Wade. He'd seen it several times in Seattle. He understood some of it, when it came to the aliens. Predicting how another species would behave was difficult, if not impossible at this stage of the war. The British were humans, though.

You would think that the CIA or the DIA could predict what our former allies were up to.

It is best to face them now. I need to convince them that this ship is ours. If that doesn't work, we need to arrive at some sort of rapport.

He made his way down to the British line. It was a slow go; his ASHUR sank into the snow unpredictably in some spots, once almost toppling him face forward. The deep snow meant he had to lift the legs of the rig higher than usual, which made him sweat as he moved. It didn't bother him at all. Discomfort was one of the things that the military had purged from him. He had experienced every kind of uncomfortable situation the Army could conjure, from sleep deprivation to environmental extremes.

As he came down off the small plateau where his people had landed, his rig slid into a deep drift that came up to his cockpit canopy. Wade leaned into it, pushing on and through. The light powdery snow parted in his path, but only after considerable effort. Emerging from the other side of the drift, he saw a British ASHUR approaching him.

No, that's right, they don't call them what we do. What was their designation? Sovereign? Yes, that's it.

The one he saw coming at him was Spitfire. It was in arctic camouflage, white with slashes of light gray streaking diagonal across it. To Wade's eyes, it looked unarmed, but he knew better.

The Brits don't like externally mounted weapons. They are all about style, where we are all about firepower and efficiency.

The Spitfire walked towards him slowly, almost as if the pilot were sizing him up as well. When they reached a point some thirty meters apart, both men stopped, as if adhering to some unspoken order. Several seconds passed as the two war machines faced each other, each seeming to dare the other to break the silence. Wade had great patience and was prepared to stand there silent for hours if need be, but he didn't have to. His discreet comms channel came on with a cracking sound and a perfectly calm British voice.

"I am Major Andrew McKenna, His Majesty's Royal Marines, 45th Commando."

"Captain Bryan Wade, US Army SMU, Omega Force." He let his opening line hang between them, followed by a few moments of deliberate silence. *I've heard of the Commando units, mostly ASHUR-equipped, much like us.* Satisfied with the minor victory that he had not been the first to speak, Wade continued. "I am surprised to see His Majesty's forces here."

"Yes. I imagine you are. We are conducting salvage operations on this alien craft."

The polite brazenness of Major McKenna was respected. "There seems to be a bit of confusion on that point. You see, our Space Force shot down the vessel. As such, it is ours to do with as we see fit."

"That is an intriguing point. I trust you have the permission of the good people of Greenland to conduct such an operation?"

From his briefing, he knew that the State Department did not. "That is irrelevant. We shot this ship down. That makes it ours."

"I don't believe so, old boy. That isn't how these sorts of things work, not at all." There was a calmness and formality to McKenna's voice that grated Wade's nerves.

It's the cockiness…

"Regardless of what you think or believe, I am claiming this ship in the name of the United States."

"You are a bit late on that front, since we have been on the ground already and have made a similar claim for His Majesty."

Wade felt his jaw tense and he drew a long, controlled breath to temper his anger. "Look, I have no desire to argue with you on this point. The reality of the situation is that we shot this thing down, which makes it our prize, not yours."

"I am sure that from your perspective, that is the case. From where I stand, we got here first, established a military presence, and laid claim to this before your arrival. I realize that you must be very upset, coming in late as you did, but the issue was resolved before you arrived."

"I don't believe that to be the case at all."

"Well, it is a reality that you are going to have to accept."

"I don't believe you are in a position to tell me what I must accept or not. Need I remind you that I am the commanding officer of Omega Force. Perhaps you have heard of us? I am fully prepared to back up my claims for this spacecraft, if forced to do so."

"Indeed, I have heard of your Omega Force. I, on the other hand, command two companies of 45 Commando. While you and your lads are relative newcomers to Special Forces, we trace our heritage back to the Great War. You may remember that one, it's the one where you showed up rather late to the show, after all the real fighting was done."

If he wants history, I will give him history.

"I do remember that it was our country that saved your asses during the next world war."

"Ah yes, you Yanks love to play that tune, regardless if it is off-key. We could both dazzle each other with our understanding and perspectives of world history all day. Regardless, your Omega lads are a bit wet behind the ears in such matters. Perhaps you should trust people that are more experienced in such global matters. The Royal Navy and Marines have experience dating back centuries when it comes to prizes of war. It might serve you well to consider that."

"I have no intention of yielding my position to you. That ship is the property of the United States of America."

"Captain Wade, we are both far from home. Before either of us does anything rash, I suggest that we give careful consideration to our next moves."

Wade heard the words and saw them for what they were, a chance to deescalate their conversation. "We were once allies. I have no desire to enlarge the gap between our two nations."

"Nor do I. You have just arrived here. I recommend you see to your people. The nights here can be brutal. Perhaps you can use this time to confer with your government. We can reconvene in the morning, when we are both more settled."

Wade wanted to argue with McKenna, but it was a reasonable suggestion. He cringed at the thought of getting Washington involved. *The politicians are not here. They don't have to live with the consequences of their bad decisions.* Wade wanted to face this officer down, make him buckle, give up his position. *It would be only fair, given how they left us to fight the Russians on our own last time out.* He knew that vengeance was wrong, his parents had ingrained it into him but the Army had done a good job of overriding the morals they had given him. *McKenna probably wasn't even around at the time of the last war.*

Wade didn't want to have to fight the British if that could be avoided. *Realistically, I have bigger Fish to fry.* While it was amusing to fantasize about going up against 45 Commando, he knew it wasn't the best course of action. *I'd rather save my firepower for the Fish, if they decide to show.* "Your suggestion is reasonable. Until this matter is resolved, I would suggest that neither of us makes a move to explore that vessel."

"Very well. In the interest of, shall I say, cooperation, we will stop our inspection of the craft until our talk tomorrow."

Wade turned his Python around and began the trudge back up to where his command was busy wrangling their equipment and supplies.

This day is not going as I planned—not at all.

CYCLE II

ETF Headquarters,
DIA Intelligence Annex, the Penetrator
Los Alamos, New Mexico, The United States

To say that Colonel Slade was pissed would have not done justice to the word, pissed. He had been monitoring activities tied to Operation Sulaco and was stunned when he heard that the British were there. Not just any UK unit either. This was one of the elite Royal Marine units, 45 Commando. As he sat at his desk and saw the replay of Captain Wade's discussion, it became even harder to control his rage.

I was assured by the CIA that no one was fielding a counter-op against the alien ship.

Slade's relations with the CIA had been precarious from the start. According to the Chairman of the Joint Chiefs, General Frank Trevor, Slade had stepped on more than a few Washington, DC, toes with the expansion of the DIA's role in managing the alien crisis. As Trevor put it to him, "You did three things wrong, at least in the eyes of the Washington establishment. First, you were right about the aliens. You identified the threat before anyone else and escalated it. Intelligence agencies hate it when they get mud in their eye. Second, your efforts to coordinate resources against the threat that the Fish posed meant you were drawing on people from long-time agencies. In DC, people equates to power. Third, you have the ear of the president. People in power like to control who gets to the person at the top of the food chain. Being apolitical, you bypass a lot of their gates and gatekeepers. It makes it very hard for them to spin things, though God knows they try."

The CIA director had always been frigid to him. When Slade asked for resources, there were more excuses and delays than actual cooperation. The CIA resented the DIA having the lead role in dealing with the aliens. He had tried to smooth things over, even going to lunch with the director.

The old fart treated me as if I was some lowly private. Now I'm paying the price for his empire-building.

There was a knock at his door and he called out, "Enter."

In stepped his CIA liaison, Heather Dawn Taylor. "I understand you wanted to see me."

He motioned her in and she closed the door behind her. Slade gestured to a seat across from his desk and she slid into it. "You're my CIA liaison. So, I'd like to know why the Agency did not give me any warning that the British were sending in the Royal Marines to Greenland." His voice was loud, crisp, and demanding.

Anyone else would have blushed or become flustered, but not Taylor. She remained calm and collected. Normally, he admired her composure, but not so much today. "Sir, I was not made privy to any intelligence that the British were going to be engaged in a salvage operation."

"You weren't told? Does that mean that the Agency knew about it and kept it from you as well?" His anger was unabated.

"I called over to the British desk as soon as you let me know. They said that they had only inklings of 45 Commando redeploying. They informed me that they were unaware of where they were heading."

"Your wording is specific. You said they informed you. Is that the whole truth, or the Agency covering something up?"

"I'm not sure how to respond to that," Taylor replied. "I'm only conveying to you what I was told, nothing more or less."

Slade should have stopped there, he knew it. The problem was he couldn't. The stress of trying to hold together the intelligence apparatus and keep it focused on the aliens was sometimes overwhelming.

I shouldn't have to fight my own government for support. We are in the middle of a damned war.

"Ms. Taylor, I think there are two possible scenarios here. One, the CIA was incompetent and didn't know that the British were redeploying their Marines to Greenland. Two, they knew and withheld that information from me, hoping it would create some sort of incident."

Her cheeks flushed with those words, the first time that he had seen that response from her ever. "Colonel, as I said before, I am telling you what I was told."

"This mission is under the ETF command. If I had known that the British were going to be there, I would have pressed for diplomacy before sending in hard-hitting units like Omega and the Rangers. Now I have units on the ground that aren't equipped for the subtleties of international negotiations. It is bad enough that I am fighting the Fish. I don't need to be fighting with an intelligence agency that is supposed to be on the same side as me."

"I would apologize," she replied coolly, "if I had done anything wrong or had deliberately misled you."

Listening to her words, he wondered if she had been played by the CIA as well. *People that live in a universe of lies and deception would stab each other in the back just as much as their enemies.*

Slade leaned over his desk. "I understand. Your handlers are probably doing what they have been told to do as well. That's all fine and dandy. I'm trying to fight a war here, and someone in the intel community of the CIA is either incompetent or deliberately messing with me. I strongly suspect the latter. You can go back to them with a message from me."

"Yes, Colonel."

"Remind them that I report directly to the president on matters regarding the aliens and that President Bobrow has ordered the CIA to fully cooperate with my team. This isn't the time for us to be playing political games or brinksmanship. People's lives are at risk. None of this helps resolve what is happening with the Fish. If the director wants my job, he should talk to the president. Until that time, I expect nothing less from him than that he does what he's paid to do—support me and our work here."

Taylor nodded and looked as if she wanted to leave. Rising out of the chair, she made sure her green eyes locked with his. "Is there anything else?"

Ashe Slade rose to his feet as she completed her stand. "Yes. Remind him that we are humans. We're supposed to be on the same fucking side of this fight."

White House Press Briefing Room
Washington, DC, the United States

"Ms. Diamond," the White House Press Secretary said, giving a nod from her podium to Veronica Diamond. She had been in the press pool long enough to know the press secretary's expressions, even if the other reporters didn't. Her network had been critical of President Bobrow's handling of the war so far. She could see in her eyes that she dreaded calling on her. *It would be lying to say I didn't enjoy her angina*. The fact that he did call her showed more bravado than she thought the press secretary was capable of mustering.

After the incident with Dana Blaze, she had been shipped off to reporting no-man's-land. Veronica had been able to leverage the role of a victim of Blaze's raging ego for a while, but Dana had gone off and died, becoming a bit of a newscasting legend in the process. It had taken spending favors and outright clawing to get back into the White House Press Corps.

Veronica had been forced to rebuild herself. She started by being a combat correspondent for a few months. The random death of being at the front toughened her, taught her what was really important in life. In those months, she gained new perspective. Diamond was still tough and clawing to get to the top of her profession, but she did so with a certain flair, a bit of humility that she had rarely shown in the past. In doing so, she managed to get the job of White House Correspondent for Fox News. In that role, she was still fighting a war, but against her so-called peers and those in her own network who were trying to topple her.

Veronica had reassessed herself and her career path. Gone were her cutthroat ways. Dana had taught her that was only going to end one way during a planet-wide war. It had taken work and more professionalism than most reporters were willing to try, but she had reclaimed her position as a top correspondent once more— something she was proud of. Personal redemption was something she took great pride in.

I'm not the same person I was when Dana made me look like a fool. I'm back—with a vengeance.

Rising to her feet, she began her question, "Fox News has learned that the Space Force engaged with one of the alien ships a few days ago. Further, we have a source saying that we shot down the ship in question. Would you care to elaborate?" She heard the murmurs of her so-called colleagues, which was confirmation that she had skunked them.

The press secretary gestured to the officer next to her. "General Watters, I will differ to you on that." Diamond could see the momentary relief on her face as Watters took her place at the podium.

Watters was the press liaison from the Pentagon. He was an old-school warrior, having spilled blood during the Russo-Bratva War. His chiseled face and almost blocky chin made him look as if he were a character out of central casting for the role of a badass no-nonsense infantry officer. He looked down at Veronica from the podium as if she were an annoying insect he would enjoy squashing. "Ms. Diamond, I'd love to know who your sources are, given the sensitivity of this information. I was hoping to present some details on this in the coming days, but since you spilled the coffee, let me try and mop it up."

His words caused a stirring in the press pool as they all realized she had hit pay dirt.

He shifted behind the podium, resting his hands on both sides of it, less to steady himself, but more to make sure the footage of him would make him look commanding. "I can confirm that several days ago, one of our brave Space Force pilots did indeed engage with an approaching UFP. The vessel was damaged and forced down."

Another member of the press pool stole the follow-up question. "Where did this ship go down, sir?"

"That information is not for release at this time."

Veronica jumped back into the fray. "General, is there a mission underway to recover this ship?" Diamond's source had told her that there were rumors of the Special Forces making a play to retrieve it.

General Watter's eyes narrowed as he bristled at the question. "I am not prepared to confirm or deny any such operation. I can tell you this. If the United States has downed such a craft, we would endeavor to retrieve it and its contents, regardless of where it went down. At this time, this is all we are prepared to say regarding this engagement and incident." He then took a sidestep to return the podium to the press secretary.

Veronica scribbled the quote down. She used a portable holorecorder like her colleagues, but she had gone back to her roots and opted for an old-school approach—jotting down notes for the piece she would have to produce from. Glancing up at Watters, she saw that the older man had not broken his stare back.

I struck a nerve with the old bag of dirt today. With that realization, she didn't even try to suppress a grin of satisfaction. *Watters's non-answer was all the confirmation I need. Now I need to pry out of my contacts where this ship went down, and then I need to get out there before the rest of these schmucks.*

She'd need a top-notch camera person, someone with combat experience. She knew who she wanted for the job, but it wasn't going to be easy. *He's been underground since Dana's death, fearing Jay Drake's wrath.* She had kept tabs on him. *Maybe I can get him to come out of hiding. Besides, he owes me for that stunt that knocked me down a few rungs on my career ladder.*

That ship is the hottest commodity on the planet right now. No one has downed one yet. I have to be there and see it first.

CHAPTER 7

Operation Sulaco
West of the Crash Site, East Coast of Greenland

Falto had never jumped in arctic weather nor had she done so wearing winter gear. Natalia was with a platoon of Rangers who insisted they go first, before her and the rest of the scientists and engineers. When she exited the aircraft, the blast of icy wind tore at her, finding every tiny little gap in her gear to reach her flesh. She ignored the cold, staring down at the stark white ground below. Her mind was calculating where the wind was taking her and what the ground looked like.

Prior to the scientists jumping, word had come from Captain Wade that the British were at the crash site. At first, she was happy that the British were present. *We're all humans. If the Fish raise a stink over our presence, having some additional firepower is more than welcome.* From the tone of Wade's voice when he made the announcement, she gathered he was anything but happy. The realization hit her slowly as she had prepared to jump. *The Brits are not here to assist us, they are competition. We were told that no one else would be making a stab at getting the ship. This is going to complicate things, it's bound to.*

In the distance, she saw the alien ship. It was huge, almost ominous, with its wide prow short of the ice-clogged shoreline. It didn't look like any sort of spacecraft she had ever imagined, but that wasn't new to her. The Fish were an enemy unlike any human adversary. The brown and dull ochre of the ship stirred memories of her time as a POW. Those memories came with anger comingled with a desire for vengeance.

I hope when that thing landed, it killed every single one of the passengers.

Spinning slightly on a gust of wind, to the south, she saw personnel dragging gear off the DZ, and the shapes of what she assumed were British ASHURs. She swayed in the wind and struggled to control her descent path on the way down. As she saw the British force, she wondered what they were thinking, seeing the Americans parachuting down.

I doubt they'll be happy with us as their new neighbors.

The landing was softer than she expected, thanks to the snow. Her roll was far from textbook, but it had been made easier with bionic legs. She felt them, the feedback system was working as planned, but she didn't feel the pressures she used to endure with flesh legs. Rising quickly, she unhooked the harness to her chute as it was trying to pull her along with the stiff wind. Gathering her chute, her attention focused around her.

The Rangers, wearing their white winter gear, moved with speed and purpose to assemble and start gathering their equipment. Omega Force's ASHURs had already formed a perimeter, both facing the ship and the British. It took a moment for her to get her bearings, and when she did, she set off for where they were supposed to rally.

Once the personnel cleared the LZ, the C-130s came in low and slow, dropping off massive cargo containers. Many were ASHUR pods, no doubt filled with supplies and munitions. Others were full of a wide range of scientific gear, clothing, shelters, etc. The Rangers were like army ants, swarming over the cargo, moving the gear off to the pre-designated areas. Two ASHURs helped with the towing of the cargo pallets.

Falto walked over to where the shelter gear had been dragged. Joining in with the others, she silently went about her work, undoing the straps and opening the containers. Shelter was going to be critical with the sunset closing in. As the Rangers and scientists opened the containers, she went about giving directions to spread out the gear.

The portable shelters were plastic shells, embedded with solar generators. The dull white-gray shell panels could be assembled into individual domes for sleeping, or combined with other panels to connect domes or form larger quarters. The entire system had been developed at the end of the last war, when the fighting in Alaska had demanded better shelter than tents. In typical Pentagon fashion, the system wasn't delivered until two years after the war had ended.

One Ranger, a staff sergeant named Jackson, produced the plans for the three clusters of shelters they were to assemble, and started handing out orders. Falto found it assuring, once more following orders. It was strangely calming. Despite that, every few minutes, she made a point to turn and look in the direction of the crashed ship.

The shelter she was working on consisted of three sleeping domes connected by tunnels to a central hub of three larger chambers. One was designed for food prep and as a small commons space, the other two were for use by the scientists. An entire decontamination container unit was dropped, requiring ASHURs to tow it in. She took on the role of hooking up the ventilation system, a small flexible conduit that linked to small heaters in each of the large rooms. Since the shelter system had been designed for any climate or terrain, her training on it came back as muscle memory.

Staff Sergeant Jackson was dark-skinned and his tone of voice reminded her of Sergeant Rickenburg, her former NCO who had died during the fighting on Guam. As she worked, he came by and inspected her progress. "You've done this before."

"Never in an active combat zone," she replied, not looking at him out of fear that it might conjure more memories of Rickenburg. As she finished completing one hook up, she felt the air start to flow through the vent tubing.

"They say you're the one that got captured. The one that got away," Sergeant Jackson said.

"I get that a lot," she replied, turning her focus on hooking up the next section of tube. Even with the gloves on, her fingertips felt prickly, like little needles were being inserted there.

"I'm glad you're here," Jackson returned.

She turned to him, making firm contact with his gaze. "Why?"

"My people have been killing Fish since we got deployed. We still don't seem to understand them. They don't think the way we do. Most of us, when we take losses of thirty percent or more, we have the brains to disengage—live to fight another day. Not the Fish. They will come regardless of losses, no matter how badly shot up they are. They are crafty too. We had to rescue a squad that had stumbled into a warren of their spider-mines. The Fish used them as bait to lure us in. Damn nasty fight."

Natalia understood all too well. They were not mindless automatons. *The Alpha I was with, he hated me. He seemed to enjoy what they were doing to me.* "There's more to them than most people think. At times I felt like they thought we were some lower life-form."

"Maybe we are to them. Regardless, you were there, living with them. Hell, you got the Medal of Honor for surviving what they threw at you. If anyone's going to have some insights, it's going to be you."

The mention of the Medal of Honor was almost an embarrassment to her. *I didn't earn it being a POW. I got it for surviving.* To her, it never made sense, but with the alien invasion, sense was a thing that was turned on its edge. "I appreciate your vote of confidence. I will do what I can. Everyone likes to think I have all the answers. I was with them for months and a lot of what they do and how they think and why they act is still a mystery to me. I only got glimpses into their psyche."

Jackson flashed a brilliant grin. "I'm a Ranger. I'll take every edge I can get."

Falto continued to hook up the duct work. When she finished with that, she joined the scientists and offered assistance in breaking out their gear. After a few hours, she noticed that she could no longer see her breath, but she still felt frigid.

This place is the opposite of Guam. Leave it to the Corps to only send me to the extremes of the planet.

As she finished emptying a container, she felt a hand on her shoulder. Turning, she saw a tall woman with straight, black hair and a civilian parka on. "Hi, I'm Dr. Schrivener. I was hoping that I would run into you, Sergeant." She extended her cold hand which Falto shook. "I'm the head of the science team. Thank you for helping us unpack."

Falto had heard her name and had seen her at a distance, but had never spoken with her. "It's no big deal. I need to keep myself busy."

"I am a big fan," she said, then her face twitched. "Sorry, poor choice of words. What I meant to say is I have read your debriefings and reports on the alien habitat that you were held in. It was fascinating stuff."

"That isn't how I would describe the experience."

Schrivener blushed. "I seem to be tripping over my own tongue. It's just that your experience is unique. I'd love to sit with you and pick your brain sometime."

"Everyone does," Falto replied. "If you've read my reports, you know pretty much everything I do."

"The reports tell a story, but some of what I want to know, they can't tell me."

"Such as?"

"The rooms you were in, they were long separated at intervals with flesh-like flap doors. I am curious, did they serve any purpose in the movement of air in your chamber?"

Falto thought it over. At the time of her imprisonment, she hadn't paid attention to such things. Her focus was solely on survival. Her eyes narrowed as she searched her memories. "Now that you mention it, yes. Now and then the door flaps would open on their own, we'd get a light blast of air."

Dr. Schrivener nodded with her response. "I surmised as much."

"Is it important?"

"Perhaps. I have been working on a theory, one that this crashed ship might validate. Your answer fits my hypothesis."

"What is your theory?"

Schrivener flinched. "Well, from what we know about the aliens, they are masters of biological engineering. The current thinking of most of my team is that their ships are like what they've seen in movies. I contend they are like what you encountered, living organisms. Huge, but essentially living creatures."

Her comments didn't catch Falto off guard. She had felt that the organic nature of where she was held pointed to it being alive, just like the aliens inside it. "How does the air flow fit that?"

"Think of it this way: you were not being held in a chamber. In reality, you were in what is something like a gigantic blood vessel. Those flap doors you described, they were like the valves of a heart. They were opening and closing every so often to move the air, just like the circulatory system moves blood."

"Does that help us at all?"

"Maybe. If these things are living organisms, the Navy engineers are going to be disappointed. They are hoping to find the same things that they would find on a ship—you know, a propulsion system, a bridge, that kind of stuff. If my theory is right, it isn't like the ships we sail. It will be…different."

Falto took in her words. *She's making sense. Everything the Fish do seems to be all about biology. Even the experiments they did on me, they were testing my reactions.* "I guess we will find out when we get into the ship and see firsthand."

As she finished, she saw Captain Wade enter the room from the far tunnel. His face was red, either from the cold, or something else. He walked over to Dr. Schrivener, giving both her and Natalia a quick glance. "How are you and your people progressing, Doctor?"

"Fine. We should be ready to go out and inspect the ship in a few hours."

Her words brought a flat frown from Wade. "We won't be going out that soon."

"Is there are problem?"

Wade seemed to struggle to find the right words. "First, it will be dark soon. Starting our survey of the ship in the dark would compromise the security of the people. We need to at least start our efforts during the daylight hours."

Falto knew there was more to it than that. "I saw the British as I came down. Have we had contact with them?"

"I have spoken to their CO," Wade said. "We're going to talk again in the morning." It didn't sound like a conversation he was looking forward to.

"They aren't going to oppose us, are they?" asked Schrivener.

He glanced at the doctor. "There's a lot that we need to work through before we start poking around at that wreck."

"So we're not cooperating with the British?" Falto asked.

"Why would we cooperate with them? This ship is ours, we took it down. They're the ones that are encroaching on our legitimate claim." The snap of his tone told Natalia just how angry he was about the British being there.

Dr. Schrivener cut in. "Captain, this is a scientific expedition. That ship is quite big. Perhaps we should find a way to work with the British."

"Doctor, this is an *American* expedition. We don't need or desire the interference of the British or anyone else. We were the ones that took the risk to shoot at this ship. It wouldn't be here if it wasn't for us. This is a matter of national honor."

Falto heard his words and they resonated with her, as did the suggestion that Schrivener had made. During her time as POW, she wondered how the nations of the planet might react—especially when she learned how widespread the alien attacks had been. *I assumed that we would have come together in some way to coordinate our fight.* Now she saw that nothing had changed. *We are consistent as a people. We are still tripping over our petty differences.*

"I hear what you are saying, Captain," Schrivener replied, "but there's got to be some middle ground where we can work together. This ship is too important for us to squabble over."

"It's not that easy," he said through gritted teeth. "I've reached out to Washington and now I've got them breathing down my neck about this. The State Department is going to reach out to the UK to protest. The Pentagon is telling me that this is our site, our ship, our expedition. They would prefer me to 'coerce' the Limeys into leaving. This is beyond being just a mission, this is a matter of national pride. We finally gave the enemy a devastating blow and that ship is proof of it. Now the British are trying to steal that from us. I'm not going to sit back and let them trample on our victory. America earned and deserves this win." Frustration and anger rang with each sentence he spoke, but Falto didn't feel sorry for him. After all she had been through, his challenges seemed easy—almost boringly administrative.

Officers—they get paid to deal with these kinds of challenges, Falto thought.

"Captain, I'm just a marine biologist, but this is less about a military problem as it is a scientific one. Perhaps if I could speak with my British counterpart, we could arrive at a solution to this. The longer we wait, the greater the chance that whatever is in that ship is decaying. The sooner we begin our work, the better."

Wade looked at the woman like he was some bull about to charge at a hapless matador. "Doctor, this is a military operation and I am in charge of it. I'm fairly certain the same could be said of our British counterparts. This is something that will be resolved by the officers in charge."

Before she could rebut him, Wade pivoted and departed.

"Well, he's in a huff," Schrivener said to Falto once the captain was out of earshot.

"He's getting conflicting messages. He's all wrapped up in this being about America. This is about national honor to him. I don't see it that way. The whole time I was a prisoner, I didn't think of America. I just thought about getting out of there and returning to the surface. He's listening to people that are a long ways from here, who are filling his ears with things that only pump up his patriotism. There's a time and place for that. I don't think this is it."

"You are a Marine. Is this going to be shooting match?"

Falto shrugged. "If it is, the Fish will win."

CHAPTER 8

Operation Durendal
South of the Crash Site, East Coast of Greenland

Major McKenna marched his Spitfire out from his camp to where he had met up with Captain Wade the day before. He had toyed with inviting the American to his camp, but did not want him to get a good view of his Commandos' defenses or his Sovereigns. He had no trust of his counterpart, and he doubted that would change with this coming talk.

The sky was a dull gray obscuring what little sunlight reached the ground. Even at peak daylight it felt dull, almost shaded. Night was an entirely different matter. Temperatures plummeted and the darkness was stunningly black, almost as if the sky absorbed what little star and moonlight penetrated.

I hate being above the Arctic Circle, but I go where I am needed. Someday, maybe we will get sent someplace warm. I hear Crete needs liberating.

MI6 and the Foreign Desk had been giving him remote guidance. He was thankful that it was consistent. As far as the British government was concerned, the crashed ship had been claimed by their government and thus was their property. One advisor rattled off international maritime salvage laws he could quote, but McKenna had ignored that line of thinking. *This wreck isn't in the water, so that is not likely to apply.* Besides, the Americans would not be intimidated by quoting treaties or law. *It's not in their nature. They equate feelings with facts, and that blurs their logic.*

They had given him a great deal of discretion as to what he could negotiate, for which he was thankful. While it was a blessing, he also knew it came with a curse. Whatever happened, it would be his neck in a noose if it were a bad decision. Andrew was used to that when it came to military operations. He made countless decisions in battle and lived with the consequences, both good and bad. This was different, though; this was diplomacy. He had been trained in the field extensively at the Britannia Royal Naval College when he had been a student there.

There's a big difference between classes and actually negotiating with the enemy.

His science team had been chaffing to get to work on the ship, but McKenna held them at bay. If they encountered problems before the Yanks withdrew, he might be hard-pressed to support them. Besides, as he pointed out, the ship wasn't going anywhere. It merely loomed in the distance, almost beckoning someone to explore it.

Yanks before the bullocks.

Ought he to negotiate with the Americans, perhaps come up with an equitable split of the ship? He was amenable to such a proposal, but didn't want to lead with that. The Americans were aggressive in such matters, and would demand more.

It's in their nature. They believe they are superior and that they are the ones that know best...that their position is beyond reproach. It was a truly American weakness, a flaw in their national character.

It is best to not reveal how far I'm willing to go up front. Let them propose it; that's the smart move.

There was more to it than that. He wanted to argue with the American officer. His dislike for the Americans practically demanded that he hold firm, just to savor verbally sparring with Captain Wade.

These people have caused my family anguish, and I'm not about to let them off easily. Memories of his father weeping over his uncle's grave made his stomach tighten. He rarely saw his father cry, so the memory was etched deep in his brain.

Stopping almost exactly where he had the day before, he saw the approaching Python of Captain Wade. Their ASHUR was intimidating, to say the least. It was larger than his Spitfire, especially wider. The Python had a bulbous curved cockpit canopy, with only a single support strut, jutting out from the torso. It was long enough to show almost all of the pilot, and like all third generation rigs, the pilot sat in a seat. The pilot's head was just slightly above the top of the ASHUR, giving it a distinctly different look and providing the pilot with the ability to see over the top of the rig. It mounted two small missile racks near its narrow torso, one on each side, each holding three of their deadly LAWs rockets. The right forearm of the ASHUR was consumed with a large directed energy microwave weapon that was built into it. Unlike most ASHURs, it did not have a hand on the right, only the extended barrel of the directed energy weapon that the Yanks had developed. The left arm was more traditional in form, though its shoulder was heavier, equipped with two smoke dispensers—no doubt to offset the weight on the right side. The left arm was equipped with a pair of medium-size chain guns, each flanking the forearm. MI6 reported that the Americans might have developed a smoke that reduced the effectiveness of the gases that the aliens used, and McKenna wondered if this mounting was proof of that.

McKenna drank in the American's white and light gray camouflage pattern, with small oddly shaped black blocks that broke up the image. As it marched towards him, he wondered which of their suits would win in a battle against each other. *No doubt, I would have the speed over him, but if he tagged me with a weapon, the fight might be over fast.*

The Python stopped ten meters in front of him.

"Captain Wade," he transmitted.

"Major McKenna."

"I have had an opportunity to discuss this, shall I say, evolving situation, with my superiors."

"As have I."

"I'm afraid they are rather insistent that we have the lawful claim to this crash site."

"That's funny," Wade responded. "My people believe the same thing."

"We were clearly here first," McKenna said.

"This was never a race."

"Spoken like a man that has lost one," he parried.

"I have no desire to stand here and argue with you. We both know that our Space Force was responsible for the downing of this craft. I'm sure you know that. You did nothing other than show up. Our pilot who took this down risked her life to engage with it. It was a million-to-one shot to hit it once, let alone twice."

"While your pilot certainly pulled off a minor miracle, that does not improve your position in the least," McKenna countered. "My people and I were here first and established a camp and position before you were in the air."

"This is getting us nowhere." The tone of Wade's voice was that of a man whose patience was wearing thin, which made McKenna happy. "I am going to order our science team to begin to explore this ship."

"I don't think so," Andrew replied. "If you disregard us and attempt to do so, I will be forced to take actions to protect our claim."

Captain Wade chuckled. "You would be going up against Omega Force and a company of Rangers. I take it you know what we are capable of doing, if we are forced to protect our people."

"I know Omega. The Russians still have open war crimes charges against you from that little spat you had with them."

"No one gives a shit what the Russians think."

That much is true, McKenna inwardly agreed.

"Captain, you are facing 45 Commando. Much like your Omega Force, we are mostly Sovereigns, with some of the best pilots in the Royal Marines. Our track record against the aliens is outstanding. Don't believe me? Ask the Norwegians. We have accounted ourselves well in this conflict thus far, and have done so without inflicting the havoc and carnage that your Omega lads do."

"We don't inflict havoc. We are a precision military unit that obliterates our target objectives."

McKenna grinned. Clearly he had irritated Wade.

"The Royal Marines tend to be more surgical in nature."

"Who cares?" Wade snapped.

"I'm merely attempting to educate you as to who and what *you* are dealing with."

"None of that matters. I'm simply telling you that if you think you are going to send your science team into that ship, it's not going to happen."

"You'd be willing to engage in a shooting fight with us?"

"Damn right I would."

"Clearly you've learned nothing from your experience with the Russians."

"We learned plenty, Major. We learned that we need to be very selective about the countries we call allies."

"I'm sure you see it that way. We learned that your country's ego exceeded your expectations of your friends on the global stage."

"You betrayed us," Wade growled.

"You started a fight and expected us to back you up. It wasn't betrayal, Captain. It was arrogance on your part and common sense on ours."

Before Wade could respond, Andrew's comms system crackled with a pulse tone, a warning alert. "Stand by, Captain," he said to Wade as he changed channels.

"This is Range Rover," came the voice of his intelligence officer, Lieutenant Kendall. "We have contacts out at the edge of the ice floe to the east."

"Identify and clarify." Gone was the playful tone of voice he had been using to irritate Captain Wade.

"We have had eyes on two, repeat two, Skenks. Both came out of the water at the edge of the ice floe and seemed to be surveying our position and that of the ship."

"Is there a problem?" came Captain Wade's voice.

"Quite," he replied coolly. "We have alien contacts out over the water. Our little chat is going to have to be set aside for now."

Wade didn't have to be told twice; he executed an about-face and started back towards his encampment, leaving McKenna to deal with the threat. The major switched to his tactical channel. "Alright, lads, the bollocks have shown themselves. Full alert. All pilots, mount up. Let's get those hovercraft in tighter to the camp area and turned about to provide support fire as needed." He began the long trudge back to his camp, watching the tactical display as his people executed his orders.

As he swung his Spitfire along the perimeter of the camp that faced the ocean, the LCAC-Hs roared past him, swinging around and kicking up surface snow as they moved. As they settled into place and cut their fans, he saw the image of Range Rover's Tornado moving towards him. "The Skenks poked up for a few minutes, then went down, sir."

"I doubt they are here for sightseeing," he replied. "What coordinates?"

"Grid H3."

McKenna adjusted his tactical display. Where they had surfaced was not opposite of the shore where the British were poised but in front of the crashed ship. *If we saw them, they had to have seen us. What are they doing? Are they planning some sort of rescue mission of their own?* His eyes drifted down to the control panel for the thermobaric explosive. Right after his arrival, he had the device buried in the snow near the ship.

If they make a play to deny us that ship, I will blow it up.

"They have to know we are close to their ship."

"Quite. Alright. We aren't prepared to go after them in the water. Let's make sure—"

His words were cut off when there was a blast of ice right at the encrusted shoreline. Big chunks of greenish white ice spun madly skyward, then arced inland. From the hole that had been blown, an obsidian-skinned form emerged—*a bloody damn Golem!* The creature's body was covered with a tattoo pattern, almost like lightning bolts. It was more visible because the pattern shimmered a bright electric blue.

The Golem paused as it stood in front of the crashed ship, surveying the area.

"Have at 'em, lads," McKenna called out as he brought his targeting reticle in tight on the Golem. He popped the safety hatches on his NLAWS-2 rockets and the moment he got the tone of target lock, let one fly. Someone else blazed away at the hulking creature with their Gatling laser, and tiny dots of burned outer skin on the Golem spewed wisps of white smoke.

The missile's arc tightened midflight as it locked onto the creature, slamming into its left shoulder and exploding. The blast made the Golem list to the right as the black and gray smoke enveloped it.

It turned toward his line of ASHURs and extended the arm that had just been hit, still functional. It fired a blur in the air of gray pressurized water. The blast tore into Colour-Sergeant Ross's Tempest, cutting an ugly scar along his left shin and thigh. Ross, call sign Galahad, brought his big rail gun into play in response. The shot was a blur as it rode out its plume of superheated air, wounding the Golem's beefy right thigh. Liquid under high pressure shot out from the cut the rail gun round made, but only for a moment.

The ice floe off the shore exploded in two other spots north of the Golem. McKenna shifted his position, keeping his weapons on target lock on the Golem as he moved. From the holes emerged two of the massive Stegosaurs. They were large turtle/dinosaur-looking creatures. These were differently colored than those he had seen in Norway. There they had been a grayish color. These had dark shells, glossy black plates that were outlined in fine lines of light gray.

This is getting worse.

One Sovereign unleashed a recoilless round into an emerging Stegosaur, leaving a black crater on one of the large armored plates. The gigantic creature glanced at the British forces, then turned to the ship. A deafening throbbing sound, more massive than any other sonic weapon McKenna had ever heard from the aliens, filled the air from the creature towards the ship. Ripples tore through the space, cracking the ice around the base of the vessel then onto the ship itself. He could see the big brown-orange plates on the ship start to buckle under the deep pulsating waves of sound.

Lieutenant Walling, call sign Jumpin' Jack Flash, commanding Whisky Company, darted his Meteor forward and opened up with the plasma blaster that was mounted inside the right arm of his ride. The big barrel of the weapon glowed yellow as it unleashed as bolt of superheated crimson plasma at the firing Stegosaur. The searing hot plasma hit its neck, splattering on the creature's armored body, burning deep. It broke off its sonic burst, turned toward the Meteor, and fired again.

The sonic waves came so fast, there was no time for Walling to react. His Meteor was knocked back and down, as was a Gladiator from Whisky Company that moved up beside him.

Sergeant Hunton from the same company maneuvered between Walling's downed Meteor and the alien. His rocket hatches flew open and he sent a trio of NLAWS-2 rockets at the creature. The sonic ripples seemed to have offset one of the incoming warheads, sending it flying skyward. The remaining two found their mark, one hitting the tail of the beast, the other exploding near the Stegosaur's jawline. The explosion to the head tore off the lower jaw, sending it flying. The giant creature whipped around violently, a sickly blackish ooze pouring from where part of its mouth had been blown off. It let loose a loud wailing sound, deep and roaring with a gurgle to its tone—unlike any noise that McKenna had ever heard. It then flopped down hard on the ice, almost as if it had body-slammed itself down.

One of the Skenks emerged from behind a mound of ice, spraying a stream of spike-shot at the Sovereigns. Return fire in the form of chain gun bursts tore at the mound of sea-green ice, forcing the Fox to submerge again.

Those damned bogarts are going to continue to be a problem.

"Galahad, you and Jenkins reposition and see if you can get a line of fire on those Skenks if they pop up again," he said.

Before he could get a response, McKenna's own Spitfire was hit by the Golem's cutting beam. The force of the impact blew off a small piece of armor protection right next to his canopy, hitting the transparent aluminum hard enough to mar the surface as he rocked back. He had been hit by the alien cutters before, but this felt different—more kinetic. It had to be the frigid air interacting with the high-pressure water beam. The Spitfire staggered back, turning to deflect the attack. McKenna did not stand and wait for another attack, he broke into a fast run to the west.

Out of the holes that the Stegosaurs had blasted emerged several Lobster creatures. These were a bluish color, fading to pink in their claws. Two fired at the Sovereigns, with the others concentrated on attacking the alien craft.

The major switched to Yankee Company's comms channel. "Bluecap, this is Vindictive. Take your company to the northwest and lay down fire on those bollocks that are firing at us."

"Yes sir," came back Lieutenant McCranie's high-pitched voice. "Alright, lads, you heard the major. Let's move with purpose!"

McKenna's eyes caught the shift of Yankee Company's position.

As he slowed his gait, he steadied his aim at the Golem, who was once more firing away at the ship. As his reticle slid smoothly over the target, he heard the tone of weapons lock and let loose with another NLAWS-2 rocket. It tore through the air and hit the Golem in the waist. The explosion toppled the massive creature over. A part of him wanted to cheer as Lieutenant Walling's voice resounded in his earpiece. "Nice shooting, sir!"

As McKenna started to turn to the Stegosaur that remained, he felt his heart sink as the Golem he had blasted staggered back to its feet. It was unsteady, and a bit of its flesh was torn, flapping as it moved from just below where it should have had ribs, but it was still very much alive and a threat. From where it had been hit, he saw another inner layer of protection over the vital organs.

Bloody hell. All I did was tear away at his outer flesh. This bugger is hard to kill.

Before he could lock on again, one lobster sprayed him with its spiker weapon. The thin needle-like projectiles were launched at almost hypersonic speeds. These ones were large enough to see, though they were a blur of white-silver in the air. One shot whizzed past him, close enough that he could feel the wake of it through the air. The other slammed hard into his right torso with a sickening *crunch*, the impact twisting his Sovereign in place. The moaning of his Spitfire's damaged armor came in all around him, and glancing at his display, McKenna saw yellow alerts screaming at him.

Aligning his Gatling laser, he targeted the Lobster that fired at him. The left forearm armor parted and shifted aside and the Gatling laser slid out on a small rail as if it were strapped onto his Sovereign's arm. He held his breath, then released it slowly as he squeezed the trigger in his left hand control sleeve. Two power shells fired, one after the other, and the weapon began to spin, almost purring in the arm of his Spitfire as he kept it aligned with his target. It fired, he could hear the capacitor unleash the energy and saw a flicker of light as the pulses of deadly laser energy stabbed at the alien monstrosity.

As the weapon ran low on energy, the auto-fire system discharged another power round. Small black marks appeared on the hide-armor of the Lobster as his laser did its work. The shots drifted as he fired and the creature moved, no doubt reacting to the spread of fire he was dousing it with. One large claw on the front of the beast caught the last few bursts, several black holes burning almost all the way through. The lower part of the claw dropped hanging limp—proof of the damage he had inflicted.

God bless Heckler and Koch!

The remaining Stegosaur opened up with its own massive sonic blaster dominating its huge back where its spine-fin usually was located. Once more it was aiming at the crashed ship. The ice crumbled to powdery snow all around it as it raked the wide prow of the alien spacecraft. Through the rippling of the air, it was impossible for him to see with any clarity how much damage it was inflicting, but it had to be considerable.

Why are they firing at the ship? Is to stop us from getting it?

Fire from the Golem lashed out at his line, taking down Sergeant

Major Shoemaker's Hurricane. From his damage display, he could tell that the Sovereign was not completely out of the fight, but the cutter had taken off his right leg at the knee actuator, topping the Hurricane face forward in the snow. McKenna trotted to a new position as he called out to Shoemaker. "Cobbler, are you still with us?"

"Tis just a scratch," Shoemaker replied. "I've had worse."

"Fire from where you are at. We'll cover you," he replied, bringing his targeting reticle on the Lobster he had already blasted.

Let's see if you like another burst of laser fire...

CHAPTER 9

Operation Sulaco
West of the Crash Site, East Coast of Greenland

Captain Wade was already halfway to his shelters when the first shots went off behind him. The British engaged with a far too familiar staccato of fire. His own battlespace display gave him some idea of what they were against. *A Boss and a few Foxes—no big deal. The Commandos are more than a match against such a minor probing action.* A part of him was more than willing to let 45 Commando deal with an attack on their own. *Why should I have Americans shed blood for the Brits? It's almost like the Fish are giving us an early Christmas present.*

Despite the smirk that rose to his face, he knew that if the situation changed, he would have to employ his force. "Attention all, American forces, the Fish have showed up. They are engaging the British as we speak. Full alert. Captain Wertan, keep one platoon of your Rangers with the base camp, otherwise start advancing on the ship with the intent of preventing a breakthrough. Omega, form up on me. We will work our way around the northern side of the ship and lay down fire to catch them in the cross fire, if need be."

Glancing towards the British position, he saw a flurry of new activity. He heard a pair of explosions, not manmade, but something else. A few moments later, the air along the top of the ship started to ripple, fast-moving waves that buffeted his ASHUR hard. When they hit, the noise came with them. It was a deep, penetrating sound that made his arms and fingertips tingle, even through the Python's

94

armor. Ice around the alien craft flaked away, pulverized to powder and blown toward him and the Rangers that were now rushing at the battle. He saw half of them fall as the waves of sound hit them.

Wade had been hit with sonic weapons before in the fighting for Seattle. This was different. First it was the range. The Fish's ultrasonic weapons shouldn't have been able to reach him. And the force at the range he was at, it was knocking down Rangers and even staggered his ASHUR.

This is something new, something very powerful.

"Sonic," he called out Omega's GRD operator. "Are they firing at us or the British?"

"Stand by, Captain," came the younger man's voice. "Sir, they are firing at the ship."

"Are you sure?" he snapped as explosions went off out of his line of sight on the coastline.

"Yes, sir."

Lieutenant McLaughlin, Pudknocker, maneuvered his Wild Weasel beside him. It was a short, gangly ASHUR, built for maneuvering in buildings and fighting in close quarters. "We've got a pathway to the north side of the wreck," he reported.

As he finished, another wave of ripples came from the shoreline, over the top of the ship, then right at Omega and the Rangers. Wade leaned into the onslaught of sound that made his Python throb around him. His temple ached as the waves washed over them. "Let's get a move on. Our British cousins might just need some help." The thought of saving the British was something he looked forward to savoring.

Trotting the Python behind Pudknocker, he watched as the Rangers started to climb up the rear of the vessel.

They'll have the high ground on whatever is coming up from the beach.

When he reached the far end of the crash site to the north, he saw a chasm that opened up, snaking to the east. It was likely caused when the ship crashed. The ASHURs of Omega Force filed into the crevasse one at a time, some scraping the sides as they moved in.

Wade followed them in.

The crack in the ice ran some fifty meters, dropping at a steep angle. Several times his Python started to lose its footing on the icy bottom of the chasm. When they emerged at the end, Wade found himself in front of a mound of ice plowed up when the ship crashed. The big ship loomed over his force. In a strange way, the ship reminded him of a picture that he had seen in his grandmother's Bible, one of Noah's ark when it made landfall. As he moved out, he found it hard to shake that image.

The prow of the massive ship had a deflated look to it. The forward chambers, or decks, or however the vessel was organized, looked as if they were folding inward on themselves. A glossy coating of grayish ice streaked down from what looked like gashes or holes cut in the dark brown to orange hide-like material. *Is this its natural state, or is it a sign of damage from the crash?* Not knowing that answer only fed the concern that was chewing on the recesses of his brain.

The ice on the shoreline extended far out before giving way to the frigid ocean beyond. The ice floe itself was a jumble of boulder-sized chunks making it difficult if not impossible to traverse. Between the hulk of the ship and the shore was a narrow patch, some twenty-five meters wide, that was navigable. Further down the beach, gunfire still raged. As he maneuvered his Python forward, he saw an alien Turtle, a hulking creature, blasting away with a sonic weapon toward the British.

Instinct told him to act—to engage. Anger at the British told Wade to not help them. While only a second passed, it was one of the longest in his life as he weighed his options. His inner warrior overcame his personal desire for spite. "Omega, double-V formation. Gold Rush, you and Harvester move out on the ice floe and provide overwatch. Weapons hot, fire as soon as you see the baddies." With those words, Wade moved to the front of his team and started towards the British.

Gunfire from the Rangers above and to his right was assuring, but he also knew it would attract the attention of the Fish. Three

Crabs started straight at him. Initially they were focused on the Rangers, two of them firing their deadly gas weapons upward at the Rangers. The third Crab spotted Omega Force and opened up with its cutter.

The "beam" of highly pressurized liquid stabbed out and into Lieutenant Davis's Honey Badger, sending one of his shoulder plates spinning in the air and backwards, narrowly missing Captain Wade's rig. He moved his targeting reticle with precision on the center mass of the Crab and fired off a power shell, shunting the power into his directed energy weapon. The capacitors made a high-pitched humming sound as he zeroed in his sights even tighter on target, then slowly squeezed the trigger.

The DEW had no recoil, no confirmation other than the audible humming sound of it discharging. There was no beam of energy when he fired it, just a fast ripple in the air as it superheated from the microwave discharge, lancing into the large left arm forearm claw of the alien. Half of the skinny portion of that claw arm was vaporized in an instant, with some armor popping off. The remains of the claw dropped downward, limp and useless.

The other two Crabs reacted to the new threat. One climbed up the front hull of the ship, heading for the Rangers. The other unleashed a blast of gas at the approaching ASHURs of Omega. The oily graying cloud of gas swept past him, into Chan's specially modified SF Mamba. "Fuck me!" he called out, wheeling to get his rig out of the gas spray. Wade didn't check to see what kind of gas it was, but based on Chan's reaction, he assumed that it was the caustic variety, the kind that could eat armor, hydraulic hoses, and the flesh of a pilot.

Instead he focused on the Crab he had already wounded, along with two of his team. A rail gun round hit the middle of the tail of the creature, ripping off the appendage at the point of impact, sending it flailing into another Crab. Wade's own LAW rocket streaked in, blowing up one of the creature's legs on impact. Another microwave burst from another Omega rig, invisible but deadly, hit the creature's head, dropping it once and for all.

Wade brought his twin chain guns in the left arm into play on the Crab, firing a splattering spray that caught the alien's smaller rear legs. The purring of the chain guns had effect as he sawed off two of the legs, splattering the alien's gray-black blood in the process. As he shifted position and stopped firing, the Crab's ugly head snapped in his direction, its black eyes seemed to focus on his ASHUR... *no...on me.*

If the wounds hurt, there was little indication of it. The Crab on the ground was undeterred, scampering sans its missing legs, getting closer and firing its gas sprayer again, this time off to his left. Wade glanced at his tactical display and saw Chan's Mamba had superficial damage but was still operational. As he targeted the gas-spraying Crab, he saw a Fox emerge from behind a chunk of ice to his left. It leaped up and over his rig, landing on the ship, and started to scramble up the side. The Crab that was scaling the hull had reached the top, and from the spray of tracer fire that reflected on his canopy, he could tell that the Rangers were dealing with it. As much as he wanted to shoot it, the Fox climbed to the top of the hull and disappeared. His focus went to the remaining Crab.

It moved quickly, side to side, as if to shake off weapons fire. A rocket fired by Omega missed it, blowing up bits of ice in the process. Wade slowed his forward gait, concentrating on locking onto the Crab. The moment he got weapons tone, he sent another rocket downrange. This one hit the lower torso of the Crab, exploding in a brilliant ball of orange and amber flames. A bright crimson plasma burst, no doubt from Warrant Officer Pearson's Rattlesnake, splattered the head and a claw of the Crab as well. The superheated plasma melted through the thick hide-like carapace, furrowing deep and sending a plume of steam shooting out from the holes it created.

Crabs rarely showed signs of pain, but this one seemed to thrash about as it closed. Wade stopped his advance as it got closer, wary of the tail. Master Sergeant Beale's Croc unleashed three grenades from its launcher, the explosions savaging the underside of the Crab. As Wade began to step backwards for some distance to the target, the

Crab's tail came into play, whipping at an incredible speed at Beale's Croc. The lethal scorpion-like stinger stabbed into the side of the Croc, punching through the armor and knocking Beale's rig off of its feet—slamming it onto the icy ground with a sickening crunch.

Wade didn't see the shot that killed the Crab, only the aftereffects. The black eye of the Crab vaporized, replaced with a smoking hole that went deep. In an instant, the Crab's legs collapsed, and its body thudded to the ground.

Whipping around to Beale's Croc, Wade called out to the Master Sergeant. "Talk to me, Wrangler—how bad is it?"

The Croc rocked from one side to another, building momentum enough to finally get to its knees. A breathy voice came back in his comm system. "Punched through the cockpit and nicked my leg, Captain. It's getting numb. I'll be fine," he said as his ASHUR barely made it to a standing position.

"We aren't taking chances," he replied. The toxin that the Crabs unleashed in their stingers was potent.

Even if it was a nick, it could take him down. Damn it!

"You know the drill—haul ass back to the base camp and get to the medics," Wade told him.

"Sir, I'll be fine," Beale said, trying to mask his pain.

"You've got your orders, get moving."

As he wheeled towards the British position, the ice off to his left exploded right next to his formation. A block of ice the size of a cement block slammed into his rig, hard, crunching some of the armor on impact. Three of his ASHURs went down instantly and from what he could tell, at least one of them was buried under the ice.

The source of the blast was a Turtle, which emerged from under the ice and roared loudly. It was close, closer than he had been to a living Turtle before. Wade whipped his Python around in a tight loop to give him some distance as the creature's big tail snapped, hitting Dribble's Rattlesnake and sending the heavy rig skidding toward the crashed ship.

Wade took a snapshot without aiming—he didn't have to at this range—sending a pair of LAW rockets into the armored front of the Turtle. The blasts were so close, he could hear bits of shrapnel from the rockets and chips off the creature's armored plate pepper his cockpit canopy. "Get some distance," he ordered Omega as he tried to follow his own command.

Chan's Mamba had been one of the rigs knocked down by the emergence of the Turtle. From a prone position, he held both arms out and let loose hell. The microwave heater made the air ripple right into the foreleg of the beast, while his heavy duty assault rifle went to full automatic, hitting the leg, then the neck of the Turtle. The skin was thick, hide-like, and rippled under the bullets impact. Some punched through, and squirts of grayish blood-like fluid sprayed out from the holes.

He wasn't the only one firing. From the rear of the formation, a recoilless round slammed into the creature's side, exploding and fracturing one of the big shell-like armored plates. Another burst of gunfire tore into the Turtle as well.

The Turtle either didn't feel the pain or somehow ignored it. Its focus was the ship. On its back, a large vein-like projection was visible, leading to what looked like a stubby gun barrel, easily as a large as a 120mm cannon. It was something that he had never seen before, not on this scale. Out of the barrel some projectile lashed out, not at Omega, but at the looming ship. The round hit and punched through the outer hull, going deep into the vessel.

Wade brought his big directed energy weapon into play, firing off the power rounds as he aimed the targeting reticle. He was only ten meters from the creature but was no longer firing wildly—he was looking for a soft spot. Aiming for the base of the neck of the alien, he fired. The whine filled his ears and the temperature in his cockpit went up a few degrees, adding to the sweat he realized he was already drenched in.

The shot hit both the creature's neck and lower armor plates. The hide was blackened instantly and smoke rolled off it, especially from the gaps around the armored plating. The Turtle ignored it, sending another big round into the ship above him.

It made no sense to him. *We are right in front of it, but it keeps firing at its own vessel. What in hell is with that?*

The tail whipped again, this time hitting Chan's already prone Mamba, sending it rolling and then skidding into a motionless heap. Pudknocker's Wild Weasel rained in grenades and followed them up with his plasma rifle. The blistering fiery crimson plasma splattered all over the side and top of the Turtle, smoking where it burned the big creature. Still, the Turtle ignored it, firing another round into the ship.

Brimstone's Croc unleashed its M300 chain gun, filling the air with bullets and tracers as the weapon hit both of the tree-like legs of the Turtle. As Wade popped off two more power shells, power for his laser, Brimstone's missiles found the Turtle, wreathing the creature's side in flames, black smoke, and hot shrapnel.

Wade aimed for the neck again, and squeezed the trigger on his laser. The weapon discharged—his ears told him that. The flap of hide under the Turtle's chin and neck disappeared, leaving only a pristinely cut blackened hole, like a paper punch on white paper. Ugly fluids flowed out of the new hole, more than he expected. The turtle lumbered forward a step, firing another round upward at the ship. The captain could tell by the way it moved, it was in agony, and he relished that thought.

The Turtle was not dead yet. It spun in place, bringing its tail into play like a scythe cutting through dried wheat. The thick mass crashed into his Python, hitting his left leg hard, crunching armor, and sweeping both legs from out under him. The ASHUR crashed down on the ice, and as he hit, his helmet collided with the padding in the seat. His damage indicators flickered amber, and on the left leg, red. He saw a warning about hydraulic pressure, never a good sign.

As he rocked forward, a trio of explosions went off on the Turtle that now cast its shadow over him. Worry—not panic—set in that it might bring one of its feet onto him, crushing his rig, or that the tail might come down again to finish him off. Another LAW rocket impacted the alien's already damaged front leg, blowing its knee apart. He could see what looked like bone in the hole which was grimly satisfying.

With the loss of the leg, the enormous creature pounded onto the ground as it collapsed. The Turtle's mouth opened and it screeched, letting out a wail of agony that made his battered rig seem to shudder. Mid-scream, another shot, no doubt a recoilless round, devoured the head of the alien. It collapsed limp, smoke hanging in the air around it and enveloping him as well.

Out of the side panel of his canopy, he glimpsed another Fox in the distance. The Fox wasn't closing with Omega—it was simply watching the battle. It didn't rush forward, but disappeared from his view.

It probably has another hole in the ice.

His tactical display did not show any more aliens on his level, confirming the Fox had fled. The fight was still on though. The battlespace feed showed there was still fighting topside. Somehow another Crab had gotten up there, and a Fox too, perhaps from the British end of the battle. The bangs and pops from the top of the ship echoed down, but from where he lay, it was strangely quiet.

Standing took a great deal of effort. As his Python rose, he tried to survey Omega's status.

"It looks as if they are done," Saint called from his Honey Badger.

"For now, maybe," Wade said. "We should pull back to the crevasse, see if we can get on top of the ship and help the Rangers."

An explosion off to the south bounced off of the ship and the ice, echoing around him—proof that the British were still in the fight.

We probably won't get as much as a thank-you for saving them.

Wade angled his Python off to the north. There was still a fight going on atop the ship, and the Rangers were as much his responsibility as Omega was. Pausing for a moment, he glanced back at the dead Turtle.

That thing was intent on firing on the ship. If it had turned that gun loose on us, it would have taken out an ASHUR with each shot if it hit. Instead it was concentrated on firing on the ship. Why?

CHAPTER 10

Operation Sulaco

West of the Crash Site, East Coast of Greenland

Hesitating, Falto watched as the Rangers rushed out towards the ship in the dull twilight. She was torn in those few seconds, pulled between being in Greenland as an advisor and being there as a Marine. When the alert was sounded, she had instinctively grabbed her ACR and scrambled to put on her standard tactical gear, more out of instinct and training than anything else.

Her first layer of clothing was a pulse-suit, a cold weather body suit that was thin, lightweight, and used a small power unit to recirculate the body's natural heat. Everyone on the team wore pulse-suits because they dramatically reduced the need for heavier gear. The military claimed you could wear just a pulse-suit in a blizzard and not worry about frostbite. Falto didn't trust that assurance.

The procurement people at the Pentagon never actually had to count on their claims to live.

As everyone else rushed forward, she had stopped at joining the troops rushing out to face the aliens. Putting on her helmet and snugging it was a deeply familiar feeling. She lowered the visor and activated the HUD display. It was snug, she had tried on all of her tactical gear several times to make sure she wouldn't be fumbling around with straps and hooks. Still, being in the tiny universe of the enhanced combat helmet felt strange to her.

It's the smell. This is new gear. I'm used to my old ECH Mark

III.

She wanted to go, to rush forward, but hesitated. *I owe these bastards for what they did to me. They tortured me, took away parts of my body, put things in me.* There was a bloodlust that surged in her, the deep inner-Marine that demanded she take action.

It was held in check with the knowledge that she didn't have to go into battle. *They didn't bring me here to fight; I'm here as a subject matter specialist. These are Rangers and Omega Force. They don't need my help. They've got enough firepower to deal with just about anything that the Fish can throw at them.*

As she stood in the shelter, she heard a deep rumble, almost a bass pulsation that hit her and the structure at the same time. It made every bit of her tingle. *That is no military weapon; that's the aliens.* She had studied their weapons during her recovery and knew it was one of their sonic weapons. This one sounded deeper, longer, and louder than the vids she had reviewed. *This sounds like something bigger.* The quaking of her body only added to her anxiety.

Natalia closed her eyes, clutching her ACR tight to her STG-A. She pictured her former Staff Sergeant, Rickenburg, a true Marine's Marine. He was the kind of NCO that had all of the right answers, and she needed that.

Talk to me, Hannibal. Tell me what I should do.

She remembered their first meeting in Guam. He had told her what he expected of her, that he was not going to give her a break or go easy on her. Falto had replied, "You're tough and smart: I recognize that and respect it. I'm tough and smart too. I'm not as good as you... yet. But one day, I will be. I'm not going to go ask for no damn transfer. I'm going to prove to you and everyone else in the Corps that I'm as good as I think I am."

Her answer didn't come from Hannibal's mouth, it had come from her own. "Time to do some Marine shit," she muttered to herself, then threw open the door to the outdoors.

The air was frosty but the throbbing noise had stopped. Even in "daylight," it was hard to see everything; a dull washed twilight was all anyone could see, and most of the time darkness enveloped the site. She ran for the ship, almost unconsciously. In some respects, it was an out-of-body experience for her, almost like a dream. She had no thoughts in her mind, she was only possessed of action. Running was easier than before the war; her bionics didn't fatigue nor did they exhaust her as she ran. She pushed herself, going faster than she had ever run before.

She whizzed past pinkish and orange bits of what looked like torn flesh, debris from the ship's crash landing. At one point she almost fell, tripping over a small chunk of ice, but somehow managed to catch herself and avoid a face-plant in the snow. She saw the deeper footprints in the snow where two Ranger ASHURs had run a few minutes earlier.

Just before she reached the hull, she felt something, almost like an invisible resistance. *It's got to be that mysterious barrier that we were briefed on.* Passing through it took almost no effort, but she could feel it, if only for a moment. Turning back around, she reached out with her left hand and could touch it, a slight resistance. She was going to probe it more, but another deep sonic blast washed over the area. The ripples hit her again, this time not as hard given her position close to the rear of the ship.

As the waves ended, she looked skyward and was amazed at its size. It loomed above her, like a dull brown and ochre monolith. Once at the base, she could see that the plates that made up the hull provided many hand and footholds. Slinging the ACR over her shoulder, she got her grip on two plate edges and started the climb up.

It wasn't easy. Despite her return to a workout regime, she hadn't done climbing in at least a year. Her breath was strained as she strained to keep up the pace. She misstepped at one point and almost fell to the ground below. *It's the damn bionic feet!* Natalia's sensations were different with her new toes, and she corrected her approach, double-checking each foothold that she made. It slowed her ascent, but avoided what could be a fatal fall. *How did those ASHURs make that climb?* Her respect for ASHUR pilots cranked up a notch in the back of her mind.

Dragging herself on the top of the ship, she crawled to her knees, then to her feet. Looking down, she was amazed at how high she was above the ground. It was like standing atop a seven-story building. For an instant, she felt a swell of pride at having scaled the structure.

Standing on the ship she felt slightly off balance. It wasn't lying level on the shoreline. There were strange ripples on the top of the craft as well, almost as if it were a massive thick-skinned balloon that was deflated. It meant that she had to watch her footing.

Turning, she saw the top of the spacecraft. From the images she had seen prior to the mission, the top looked flat. It was anything but. The carapace-like plates were laid out in rows, and there were several rises to the bow of the ship, some several meters tall. There was no sign of entry points, no hatches or windows—the kind of things she half-expected.

Along the far edge were the Rangers, firing downward. She activated her battlespace feed in her helmet's visor and could see that there were several Crabs and Turtles, not to mention Foxes. She had never encountered the Turtles before, but based on the footage that she had reviewed during her convalescence, she was glad she had not. They were like tanks and often the aliens rode on them, like dinosaur-mutant armored personnel carriers.

Falto made her way forward towards the cracks and bangs of gunfire from the Rangers shooting down the tall and wide prow of the ship. There were ripples on the surface of the vessel, as if the chambers under them had been full but now were empty. The footing, despite the angle of list, felt secure, but the ripples were noticeable. She was winded as she moved close to the edge, lowering herself to a prone position, and bringing her ACR around.

Falto craned over the edge looking down, and vertigo grabbed her brain, turning it and her stomach violently. During her jump training, she had experienced the same sensation at heights this far up. A wave of warmth washed over her as she drew long controlled breaths to get the dizziness under control.

If it wasn't for the fighting and the fact that she was lying on a crashed spacecraft, she might have actually enjoyed the view. The eastern horizon was mostly clear, the bright yellow of the sun stabbed through the few clouds downward. She could see the white caps on the sea.

Below her, near the base of the ship, she saw the battle. To the south, the British were fighting their own private war against a Turtle and several Crabs that were going at the Royal Marines with everything they had.

Directly below her, she saw a Turtle burst through the ice, knocking over several ASHURs as if they were little more than a child's action figures. It was every bit as menacing as she had expected, if not more. The sheer size of the creature amazed her, despite all of her preparation and study. Looking to her right, she saw a Crab climbing up the sheer face of the hull of the ship, with the Rangers pouring fire onto it. To her left, a Fox, the reconnaissance alien breed, scaled the hull at a remarkable speed.

Adrenaline surged in her veins as she brought her ACR to bear on the Crab. It moved faster than she could have imagined, and she adjusted her aim several times, then switched off the safety. The sights aligned in her ECH and she could see the target. She had the shot, but hesitated, again. Her brain was screaming "Kill it!" but her fingers simply would not respond. Memories surged in her head of a different colored Crab at Guam. She hadn't hesitated then. She did what she had been trained to do. *Why can't I fire?* At the moment, she felt her body tremble. *Am I afraid? How can that be? It's just a Crab. Shoot it, damn it—fire the weapon!*

In her hesitation, she could mentally picture David Chen as he died. Other memories roared forward, all seeming to block the message to fire from reaching her trigger finger. *Pull the trigger! Just squeeze it. You've done it thousands of times before. You can do it again. Just fire!* Sweat beaded on her forehead inside of her ECH; her breathing neared the point of hyperventilation.

A sonic blast roared up from the ground. The air rippled from the waves and washed over her, throwing bits of snow and ice into her visor. There was no shelter from it, no protection. Her ears ached, igniting a raging headache that made her close her eyes for a moment. The Rangers on both sides of her recoiled, pulling back from the edge, but she did not. She wasn't sure if it was because she couldn't move, or refused to, but in the end it didn't matter.

The attack seemed to jar the clog of memories that were blocking her. As Natalia focused, she aimed at the Crab and squeezed the trigger. The ACR bucked into her shoulder like an old familiar sensation, one she warmly welcomed. Her shot hit the Crab, thwacking hard into its long body, making a tiny ripple on its armored carapace. A second, third, and fourth squeeze came easy as the Crab continued the climb.

As it cleared the top of the ship, one of its front claws struck a Ranger, sending him flying out over the edge, plummeting downward. Falto tried to ignore that image, pouring her fire into the Crab as the Rangers fell back, trying to keep distance between them and the alien. She rose to a kneeling position to fire, then to her feet. Her HUD display told her she was out of ammo, and in a smooth reflex action, she dropped the empty magazine and replaced it with a fresh one.

One Ranger threw a stacked grenade at the Crab, who surged forward, sensing the threat. It caught the tail in the blast, blowing it off. One wet piece of Crab flesh slapped into Falto's right leg, then slid down to her feet. Thanks to her bionics, she barely felt it, but the smell did rise quickly—a stench that brought back the memories of her time as a prisoner, an almost moldy rotting aroma that quickly overpowered the filters on her helmet. Falto continued to fire individual controlled shots, precise and deadly.

The tailless alien aimed one of its forward claws out and unleashed a spray of gas at a trio of Rangers. To their credit, they ran, each breaking in a different direction. One was caught in the fast-moving cloud, whipping by the high breeze at the top of the ship. Falto saw him dive towards the rear of the ship that she had just come up over, stripping off his melting armor in the process.

She concentrated her fire at the joints of the legs, and saw some results in the form of ugly black oozing goo she assumed to be blood. One of the smaller legs was no longer moving, and she attributed that to her shooting. A Ranger moved in beside her and was firing away as well, the crack of his ACR merged with her own.

The Crab reeled again, its mangled stump of a tail knocking down two Rangers in a defiant swoop. Extending out its claw, it was clear that it was about to fire its gas weapon again, when one of the Rangers' ASHURs, the Wolverine, unleashed both of its rail guns. One shot bored into the offending claw. She saw the plasma plumes of superheated air and saw the claw shattered and blown off, thrown backwards. The other shot hit the raised torso of the Crab dead on, punching deep and out the other side.

The Crab dropped hard and dead. Natalia felt like cheering, but a commotion behind her got her attention. Whipping around, she saw the Fox had finished its climb of the ship and had sprung over the line of Rangers at the edge, landing behind them. She and the Ranger next to her both turned and fired in unison, shot for shot, at the creature.

Foxes were all arms and upper body. Their short legs were strong but their massive arms were devastating. Moving almost ape-like, using its arms for propulsion, the Fox moved on the Cobra-class ASHUR as it started to unleash chain gun fire into it. The Fox swiped it with its short stubby clawed arm, ripping off two pieces of the ASHUR's armor and nearly knocking the rig over. Falto managed to land several shots, but the Fox was fast, springing towards the fallen Crab to go for the Wolverine.

She reloaded after the last round of her magazine missed. Missing pissed her off and she centered her concentration and got in control. With icy precision, she aimed at the squat head of the creature. She or the Ranger next to her must have gotten its attention because it turned to face them, leaping straight at them.

Natalia was not afraid. Panic was in her past now, shuffled deep with a myriad of other memories. *It's time to earn that Medal of Honor!* She held her ground and cool, firing as the creature landed right in front of her. Her Ranger counterpart sidestepped as he fired his ACR, trying to get a different angle.

The Fox leaned in towards her, spreading its arms wide, and

opening its massive low-slung jaw. It hissed at her, spraying spittle onto her visor. It was pure intimidation and on Falto it was wasted. She had grown up on the tough streets of Los Angeles. Natalia had struggled in life and had become a combat Marine. She had fought the aliens in their first actual battle and had survived being a prisoner of war. It was impossible to intimidate her, not with an ACR in her hands.

She aimed at the large open mouth and throat and sent three bullets right into the gaping hole.

The Fox's face seemed to lose its angry expression. The best way to describe it was a look of confusion as its eyes narrowed and it closed its mouth. For a moment it appeared to be lunging at her, enough for Falto to step backwards. Then it hit her, *it is falling.* The Fox collapsed right in front of her, a gray oozing blood-like goo spilling from the open maw onto the top of the spacecraft.

The Ranger next to her stopped firing too. "Hey, you're not one of us," he said, his voice muffled by his helmet.

"I'm a Marine," she replied with more than a hint of pride.

"Our advisor?"

She nodded.

"Pleasure to have you up here. That was some damn fine shooting," he said, turning back to the front prow of the alien ship where gunfire was picking up in rhythm and intensity. "Glad to have you here with us, ma'am," he said as he stepped towards the gunfire. The ma'am part was a minor irritant she let pass.

Pleased, Falto followed him. She had half-expected some comment about eating crayons or some other inner service rivalry poke from the Ranger, but got none. That was the best compliment she could have received.

As they got within ten meters of the where the gunfire was the most intense, the Rangers started to fall back in pairs. Another Crab scampered over the edge, this one a deep blue in color that faded to a lighter shimmer in the claws—with an almost pinkish tone to the bottom of the big appendages. It had been hit many times already. She could see the oily stains of its blood creeping out between the armored plates. Once it was over the edge, it stabbed one of its claws straight down onto the ship's hull, and unleashed its cutter. A spray of liquid pushed back until the beam of intense high-pressure water penetrated, furrowing deep into the ship.

Why is it not firing at us?

She knelt to get a steadier aim, firing away with a steady burst of shots. The other Rangers did the same; none of them broke. No doubt they too were surprised.

The Crab responded by pivoting in place on the down-aimed claw and whipping its tail at the closest pair of Rangers. The tail hit hard, crunching into their STG armor, sending both men flying toward the rear of the ship. A message crackled on her tactical channel, "Rangers—drop now!" For a moment, Falto hesitated, but the Ranger next to her put his hand on her shoulder and pushed her down flat as he dropped next to her.

There was a pair of hypersonic mini-booms from the Wolverine's twin M3 rail guns as they fired over the prone Rangers into the Crab. Both projectiles savaged the head of the creature, turning it into pulp and sending much of the head spraying out over the edge of the ship to rain down on Omega Force below. The alien creature went limp and flopped down. From the hole it had been cutting, there was a gurgle and a momentary geyser of fluid that shot back up. Two of the Crab's short legs spasmed as she checked her ammo status and rose to her feet once more.

Suddenly it was quiet. Her temples were throbbing with a headache that she had barely noticed until now. The Rangers seemed to check the edge and return. Apparently there were no more aliens to kill. She confirmed that with her own view of her battlespace display. As she stood there, her body felt numb. It wasn't just the artificial feelings from her bionics, it was the adrenaline already starting to fade. There was no resistance to the feeling, she let it wash over her.

"Good work, ma'am," the Ranger said, extending his beefy hand. "Warrant Officer Rosales." She detected a faint Latino accent in his voice, which was strangely calming.

"Sergeant Falto," she said, shaking his hand. "No call sign yet."

"That was some pretty crisp shooting with that Fox."

"Thanks."

"According to my display, we kicked some ass and took some names," Rosales said. "Decent work for a jarhead."

She flinched at the slang. "Let's not make this ugly. You don't call me jarhead or bring up eating crayons, and I won't kick your ass."

Rosales chuckled. "Deal. Well, it looks like we drove them off."

Falto surveyed the leading edge of the massive spacecraft. "For now. This isn't over."

Rosales nodded over at the hole that the Crab and cut. "You're the alien expert. Why didn't that Crab use that cutter on us? It could have taken out two or three of us in one swipe. Instead it just shot downwards."

"I have no idea," she replied, as her body shook from the last of the adrenaline was leaving her system.

"Damned peculiar."

She agreed.

Why attack the ship? We were right here, easy targets. It should have gone for us, but instead was blasting away at the ship. There has to be a reason.

As she pondered the alien's action, Falto slung her weapon over her shoulder. She looked down at where the Crab flesh had hit her leg, making sure it wasn't doing damage that she hadn't detected yet.

Just when we think we know the Fish, they do something we can't explain...

CHAPTER 11

Operation Durendal

South of the Crash Site, East Coast of Greenland

Andrew McKenna had fought the bollocks before, but this engagement felt different. Part of that was the presence of the Americans off to the north and atop the ship. He didn't feel he needed their help, but was quietly thankful they were there. If nothing else, they drew attention away from his people.

Distractions are always helpful. If the Americans want to play cowboys and Indians with the aliens, I'm all in favor of that. Every damned Lobster they kill is one we don't have to.

While the aliens fought as viciously as he had come to expect, there were several factors that he noted that were different. First, the aliens were probing more than assaulting. Two of the Lobsters had rushed towards his base camp. They fought, but did something he had never seen Lobsters do before: they retreated in good form. One of the few endearing aspects the aliens had was that they usually fought to the death, regardless of the odds. This time they struck at his base camp, then disengaged.

Why?

The second aspect of the attack that was puzzling was that the bollocks had attacked their own ship. Their Stegosaurs were equipped with larger sonic weapons than he had ever encountered. Rather than turn them on the humans, they unleashed them on their own ship. *Why?* If they didn't want the humans to recover the ship, why not wipe out his and Captain Wade's force? *Why expend firepower and energy to attack the ship?* It was annoying and confusing. *The bollocks don't do anything that isn't deliberate. Their actions were on purpose. What is that purpose, though? There's a part of this I don't understand yet.*

The fighting had cost him eight wounded, three killed, and two Sovereigns down. His technicians assured him they could repair them, which was encouraging, but the pilots had suffered broken limbs and other injuries that would impair their ability to fight. *Even having partially functional Sovereigns is better than not having them at all.*

As he stood at the British camp, he wearily looked out over the long ice floes, then back at the ship. *They'll be back. Next time they will come with more force. If we are hoping to learn anything from that ship, we need to get into it now, before they show up.* McKenna concluded that the best and fastest way to do that was to work out some arrangement with the Americans.

It was the last thing he wanted to do. *I can't look like we need their help—I can't let them think they have the upper hand.* He didn't want to cooperate with them, but it was the right choice. That acknowledgement didn't make it any easier.

His father would have disapproved. He'd died two years before and went to his grave still bitter over the death of his brother, Andrew's uncle. While the doctors told him it was the smoking and lung cancer that had taken his father, deep down, the surviving McKenna knew he had died of a bitter heart. *His Scottish stubbornness was what kept him alive even that long.* He was bitter right through to his last breath, that it was the Americans that had lured his brother off to a foreign land to die. He cursed them up until the end. The only good thing that came from his father's demise was the hope he would be reunited in the afterlife with his brother.

Maybe both of them finally have peace.

McKenna begrudgingly admitted to himself that the Americans had helped him in the last engagement. Their additional firepower had been welcome. Andrew didn't delude himself in the least about their help being altruistic. *They are just protecting the ship so they can plunder it themselves. The fact that their assistance helped us was coincidence, not deliberate. It wasn't intentional aid. Like most things they do, it was action with unintended consequences.*

He tried to put himself in the head of Captain Wade. *Would he be the one to make the first move, or is he waiting for me?* Wade struck him as a typical American military officer. There was the cockiness that came with some officers in Special Forces; that was something McKenna understood. But there was more that he had gotten from Wade. *He's got a chip on his shoulder, left over from their war with Russia. That is obvious.* This was another limitation of American thinking. *They struggle with the concept that they might be in the wrong, that they have made some sort of mistake.*

He turned his eyes to the camp itself, catching a gust of cold wind in the face in the process. Not many of his people were out in the weather, but for the major, it was the only place he had privacy…where he could work through his thinking. *This is a godforsaken place to fight and die in. At least Norway is settled; there is a hint of civilization. Out here, there is only what you bring with you, the unrelenting weather, and the bloody bollocks.*

Turning with his back to the wind, he refocused on the Americans. He organized his own thinking, making a mental checklist of what he might want for any sort of working arrangement. *Coordinating our forces militarily will be too problematic to tackle. It would come down to who is to be in overall command, and that was destined to be a battle all on its own. We need to be able to explore that ship, which is exactly why the American are here. If we can come up with the means of dividing up that task, it would save precious time.*

Sharing whatever was found was off the table as well. He doubted that the Yanks would offer up what they would discover. From what Wade had said, the view of the United States was that this was some sort of treasure, like undersea salvage, that they had the rights to.

They will be less than willing to share that treasure with us, and my own government does not want us to share what we find with them.

From his limited interaction with Captain Wade, he doubted they would make an overture with any degree of cooperation. That placed the burden for action on McKenna.

I need to go there and try to find some common ground. Otherwise we are going to be squabbling with each other when the bollocks come back. If that is the case, neither of us will win.

He raised his wrist communicator up to his face and spoke through his mask. "Lieutenants McCranie and Walling, I am going to attempt to parlay with our American cousins. McCranie, you are the senior, so you are in charge while I am gone. Keep our patrols up and see to the repairs and our wounded."

"Yes sir," they both responded.

"And good luck, sir," Walling added.

Normally he would have mounted up in his Sovereign for the journey, but that was far too impersonal. It would be a bitter cold walk, but would give him time to mentally prepare. He adjusted his camouflage sniper cloak, pulling the hood over his thermal bobble. As he walked, he caught a hint on the wind of the dead Lobsters. It only made him long to eat fish. Prior to the alien invasion, the British people consumed fish at least once a week, more for the many coastal communities. The commercial fishing community had become a hazardous occupation overnight, with many fishing fleets refusing to put out to sea for fear of the aliens. The fear was real; the aliens didn't discriminate between civilian and military ships—they attacked both with the same vigor.

Britain was attempting to start up large-scale fish farms to make up for the deficit, but it was going to take months if not years before they were productive enough to meet the demand. Rationing was being rolled out, though few outside of the UK were aware of it. The government preferred to keep the impact of the war secret from other countries. Andrew was sure that many other countries were likewise suffering, but they all strove to not let the depth of their problems be known.

As he climbed up the embankment where he had met with Wade

before, he saw the picket patrol of American ASHURs. Their camp, other than the fact that his people used tents and the Americans used collapsible domes, appeared similar to his own. As he got closer, one of their rigs, a double-barreled rail gun–mounted Wolverine, walked straight at him. McKenna wasn't worried; his own patrols would have done the same thing. In a strange way, it was comforting.

McKenna knew he would need to keep his aggressive nature in check during this meeting with the Americans. His father had always said it was his Scottish blood that got him in trouble. McKenna doubted it had anything to do with Scotland. The family has been living in England since the mid-twentieth century. *Whatever Scottish blood I've got has been diluted over the generations, that much is for sure.* Still, he knew that being headstrong was not going to help with Wade. *I'll have to keep my blood from boiling. Something that is far easier to say than do.*

The Wolverine stopped in front of him, its arms angled down so the rail guns were not trained on him. *I'm not a threat. I've got my sidearm, but that is it.* He surveyed the big ASHUR, noting its camouflage pattern. The American Special Mission Unit's ASHURs tended to use a unique color scheme. Rather than the digital pattern of grays and black on a field of white, they mixed in splotches of light and dark blue, and even a few streaks of purple. *I wonder if they know something about the alien's ability to see colours that we don't.*

"What can I help you with?" came the pilot's voice over the external speaker.

"I'm Major McKenna. I'd like to meet with Captain Wade."

There was a pause. No doubt the pilot was calling back to his base for instructions. "Follow me, sir," he said, pivoting the Wolverine in place and leading him to the camp.

Andrew could feel the eyes of the Americans boring in on him as the pilot gestured to a portable shelter. *They see me as an enemy, a threat. All of this because we beat them here.* Entering the shelter, he pulled off his cloak and took off his heavy white winter coat. A sergeant ushered him down a small corridor and into a larger domed circular chamber.

When he first saw Captain Wade, he was drawn to his gray eyes. Even as they narrowed on him, they possessed an intensity that was as penetrating as any sabot round. Wade stood at a portable table, flanked by an Army Ranger and a female Marine, judging by her uniform regalia.

What an interesting gathering.

McKenna stood erect, not as much in respect, as to put on a positive image of a good Royal Marine. "Captain Wade, I presume," McKenna said, extending his hand.

Wade looked at it for a moment, then shook it, abnormally hard, as if to make a point. "Major McKenna. I hadn't expected you to grace us with your presence."

"It was no trouble at all," he replied, turning to the Ranger. "And you are?"

The sandy hair officer extended his hand. "Captain Wertan, Third battalion, Army Rangers." Wertan shook his hand normally.

McKenna extended his hand to the Latina Marine. Wade answered for her. "This is Staff Sergeant Falto. She's a technical advisor."

Falto...that name is familiar. McKenna shook her hand. "A pleasure," he said and she gave him a single nod in response.

"So," Captain Wade said, crossing his arms. "What would cause you to come over here?" His tone was almost accusatory and was hard for McKenna to shake off.

"Captain, our countries are not on the best of terms, we both know that. We also are out here alone, with limited support. We both have the same objective, namely that alien ship. Squabbling between us is not going to help matters. It's only a matter of time before the bollocks are back for that ship."

"You aren't proposing some sort of alliance, are you?" Wade asked.

"No, I wouldn't be so bold. I do believe we should work out some arrangement in regards to that crashed spacecraft, however. I'm sure you noticed that the aliens attacked it as well as us. If they destroy it, all of this effort has been a waste. Both of us have teams to recover whatever technology is in that craft. I propose that we allow both of our teams into the ship."

Wade reacted fast. "Why would I do that? We have already been on top and in front of that ship. Any claim you have to it is moot. Possession is nine-tenths the law."

There it was, the cheekiness Wade had shown before.

"The sheer size of that ship precludes either of us having the ability to explore it quickly," McKenna smoothly responded. "Surely you see that."

"What I see is you coming here trying to barter with us to get your forces in the ship. You didn't even thank us for committing our forces to save you when the Fish showed up. That's what I see."

"Are you daft? Thank you? We had matters well in hand. While we are appreciative of your assistance, it was far from necessary."

"Why should we allow you access to the ship?" Wade countered quickly.

"Why do you believe that you have some sort of exclusive control of the vessel? My perimeter is extended out to the southern edge of the craft right now. I don't need your permission. I am simply attempting to be courteous and make sure we don't accidentally shoot each other when we explore the craft."

"You're assuming that we will allow you to in the first place."

"I don't require your permission, Captain," he stated emphatically.

Wade glanced over at Captain Wertan who said nothing aloud, but seemed to tilt his head, as if Wade should consider the offer.

It was the Marine, the one called Falto, that spoke up. "This request seems more than reasonable. It would take days for us to explore the entire ship, and that assumes it's even possible. Why not let the British explore the ship at the same time? There's no good reason for us to not cooperate, at least on a scientific level."

"Sergeant," Wade said, his teeth gritting as he spoke, emphasizing her rank. "You are not a part of this discussion. Dismissed."

Falto shifted in her stance but didn't leave. "I don't report to you, Captain. I'm here independent of your chain of command. I'm an advisor. I'm here because I have more experience with the aliens than anyone in this room. My professional advice is that we cooperate with the Brits when it comes to exploring the ship. The last thing we need or want is one side or the other shooting at each other inside that thing because we were too stubborn to work out the means to coordinate ourselves.

"Also, the Fish are going to be coming back. We all know that. If we don't cooperate, they may destroy the ship while we stand around arguing about who has what rights to what. We either work together or we all lose." There was an anger in her voice, one that went far beyond the present meeting or circumstances.

I like her.

Wade's face went crimson with Falto's words, which made it hard for McKenna to suppress his smile.

He's not used to people telling him no.

"You and I are going to talk after this, Staff Sergeant," Wade muttered to Falto. If it bothered her, it certainly didn't show in her expression. Wade turned his icy glare back to Andrew. "What, exactly, do you propose?"

"Let's draw a line down the ship. You explore your portion, we explore ours. We come up with some common communications frequencies if we need to coordinate our efforts, be that militarily or whatever else."

"No sharing of what we find."

"I was not proposing that at all, Captain. Not at this time at least. Nothing more than avoiding any friendly fire, if possible."

Wade was angry but didn't speak, which meant he was considering the proposal. "What you're asking for deviates from what I have been told to allow."

That was something that McKenna understood. In that moment, he understood a little more about Wade.

He's trying to follow orders from hundreds of miles away.

"That is something I can understand. If it will make you feel any better, my being here isn't necessarily what my chain of command wants either. My thinking is simple; I'm a Royal Marine. Part of what I'm trained to do is operate, shall I say, independent of orders from on-high. The bottom line is simple, really. We are here, not the people that are telling you to not cooperate with me. They are relatively safe, far from the action. We are both Special Forces, in our own way. That means we need to think and act on our own. Both of us have been attacked by the same alien force once already, and we bloodied their noses in the process. They will come again, you know that. I say we at least coordinate our exploration efforts, if only to muck them up."

Captain Wade still eyed him suspiciously. "Doing this, working with you, is against every instinct I have. I don't want the people I am responsible for set up for failure. Your country bailed on us in the last war, and that is something I can't shake."

McKenna wanted to argue with him about the role of the UK in the Russo-Bratva War, but he also knew that was a waste of time. "If you think the walk here from my camp to yours was an easy trek, I assure you it wasn't. A lot of my people think you Yanks start fights and expect us to roll our sleeves up and finish them for you, myself included. I have had to move past that—for the sake of the mission. Surely if I can nibble on some humble pie, you can as well."

Wade nodded. "Alright, Major. The last thing I want to do is be here squabbling with you and have the Fish blow the ship up without us getting something out of the conflict. Let's hammer out some basic protocols."

Andrew wanted to let out a sigh of relief, but didn't. For the next two hours, they went over the basics of where both sides would explore the craft, as well as all of the comms and rules of engagement should the bollocks show up. Sergeant Falto seemed at ease offering her suggestions, but he did notice her right hand fingers nervously tapping the table. He allowed himself a glance at her left hand and noticed no movement there. On closer inspection, he could see that it was a bionic replacement.

Clearly she has been through quite a bit.

Falto's presence as a consultant intrigued McKenna. *She's here for a reason, and it would serve me well to know what purpose that is.*

When they were done, Wade even shook McKenna's hand.

As he was escorted back to his lines he had thought he'd feel more triumphant, but that wasn't the case. His time with the Americans had only reinforced the feeling that he had been trying to smother—that they needed to act fast because the aliens would be returning. Other thoughts rushed to his mind as well as he thought about the meeting. As he passed his own sentries, he opened a secured channel to his own HQ.

"Walkins—send to MI6 on the scrambler bravo channel. I want whatever they have on a Staff Sergeant Falto—female, US Marine Corps."

CHAPTER 12

Operation Sulaco

West of the Crash Site, East Coast of Greenland

After he was sure that Major McKenna was clear of the base, Captain Wade spun on Falto. "What the hell was that about?"

His words didn't seem to shake her in the least, which only added to his rage. "What are you talking about, sir?" Her voice emphasized the word, "sir."

"You know exactly what I'm talking about. First, I ordered you to leave and you refused. Then you sided with that damned Limey."

"I didn't 'side' with anyone. I offered my opinion. In case you were unaware, that is what I'm here to do."

"Damn it, Sergeant, I thought we had an understanding." Memories of their conversation aboard the transport aircraft came back. He had trusted Falto and felt that the trust had been betrayed.

That did seem to shake her usually stoic expression. "We talked on the way here, yes. You asked why I came here, and I told you."

"You're a goddamn Marine. What happened to God, country, and Corps?"

"Are you questioning my loyalty because I didn't side with you? Sir, I don't care if you are superior officer—you don't get to go there. For all of your fighting, I assure you, only the dead have given up as much as I have in this war. I lost months of my life, three limbs, my hearing, and a part of my soul. I held good friends and fellow comrades in my arms as they died…slowly, painfully. All because of this enemy."

For Wade, that wasn't enough. "What about your country? I had orders that I was trying to follow. You undermined that."

Falto's anger was up, Wade could see that. Her jaw set and her eyes narrowed almost to slits as she spoke. "I didn't come here for my country. I came here because I was needed here. Need I remind you, I'm not under your command?"

"You've made that abundantly clear," Wade said through his gradually clenching teeth. "You put me in a position where I looked like a complete asshole if I didn't work with the British."

"With all due respect, Captain, you put yourself in that situation."

"Did it ever occur to you that I was following orders—orders cut by people who are looking at the big picture?"

I've got the State Department and the CIA to deal with; she has no idea the pressures being put on me.

"From where I stand, there is no big picture. The only picture that matters is the one we are in right here, right now. We're out here, isolated, forced to fend for ourselves. You're following orders from people who are worried about politics. There's no politics out here, not unless you brought them with you. We are way past the front lines. Taking orders from people too scared to be here themselves is crazy."

"You are insubordinate."

"According to my shrink, you might not be far off."

"I won't stand for you interfering going forward."

"If there's nothing else," she replied, turning to leave, "I'm going to my quarters."

Wade drew a fast deep breath, then started again. "Falto, your speaking out against me may have put this mission at risk. Did you ever consider that? There are a lot of people at high paygrades than both of us that have defined the mission parameters. Turning against me like you did, you made it so I had to go along with this. There are people in Washington that are not going to be happy with this little arrangement. You put my ass in a pretty big sling."

"I don't give a shit about paygrades or politics. As you like to point out, I'm just a staff sergeant and you're a captain. I didn't force you to do anything other than what you knew, deep down, was right to begin with. As for upsetting people in Washington, I'm very comfortable with that. It's easy for bureaucrats to sit behind desks and make calls for people like you and me to implement. What matters in the end is the people on the ground and the decisions we make—the good decisions, the right ones. In terms of your ass being in a sling, chances are pretty good mine is there right next to yours. The difference is I don't care. You need to acknowledge that you came around to a right decision and be done with it."

Before Wade could counter her points, she walked out of the room, leaving him with a view of her back as she marched out.

Damn her, she needs to be on the same page as me. She's too much of a rogue element. In the end it could cost us both.

He turned slowly to Captain Wertan. "You understand what I'm saying, don't you, Tommy?"

"I do," he replied. "I also understand what she is saying."

"So she's right and I'm wrong?"

"This isn't about right and wrong. We are isolated out here. She understands working isolated better than we do, I think. She's not some mindless Marine who will blindly follow orders because of those bars on your collar."

"You had one of your Rangers shadow her, correct?"

Wertan nodded. "Two of my people reported on her. Her shadow, and someone she ended up being alongside."

"And?"

"When the shooting started, she hesitated. No big surprise there. Even with all of the training she's had, wading back into a battle against the aliens shook her a little. She overcame that, though, and was every bit the Marine out there in the crossfire."

For Wade, that wasn't enough. "She should have just left the room when I told her to."

"Permission to speak freely?"

Wade nodded, already dreading what followed. There had not been a single time as an officer when someone asked that question that he didn't find himself disliking what came after.

Wertan shifted, resting his fists on his hips. "I think you're not going to get anywhere pushing her or trying order her around."

"Too defiant?"

"No. It's not about defiance with her. I've been watching her as have my folks. Falto is complicated. I figured her out a little in this discussion."

"What did you learn?"

"Think on this. You were ordered here, as was I. The science team was ordered here. The only person that wasn't ordered here was Natalia Falto. She volunteered. From what I have gathered, she wasn't pushed into it, she came on her own accord. She didn't have to. She's a Medal of Honor winner. She could have just told them, 'pass.' Instead, she came here. That says a lot."

Wade wasn't sure how to interpret what Wertan was saying. "What does it say?"

Since he had met Falto, Wade had considerable time to think about her and what she went through. *She didn't get that medal for fighting; she got it for surrendering and having the gall to survive. If they had taken me prisoner, I would have killed myself rather than let them experiment on me. Everyone treats her special because she didn't have the guts to kill herself.*

"She's not here as a follower. She's trying to reclaim herself. That means facing what tried to kill her. I went through something similar during one of our covert ops down in South Africa a few years ago. I nearly drowned in a river fighting with a bad guy. I never had that fear as a kid, but after that incident, sucking water into my lungs like that, I was shaken. I wasn't able to get my head on right until I overcame that fear again. It took a while, but I did it. Once I did, well, I love swimming and scuba diving."

Wade sighed. "Thank you for that. When I see her, I just see the uniform. She's as stubborn and pigheaded as every Marine I have ever met. It's not easy to let that go."

"Her time is coming," Wertan said. "When we get inside of that ship, the pressure is going to be on her. Chances are, she knows that.

She's not backing down or running from it. It might be best to let her be exactly who she is, let her act the way she is going to. My two guys following her saw it in the firefight. She could have stayed at the base, but she headed right at the danger. For a former POW, that took a shitload of guts."

It was hard to argue with Wertan's assessment, though he certainly wanted to. "We need to hang together or we will hang separately," was all he could muster.

"I understand that thinking. Anyone that has undertaken the kinds of missions we get understands the need for unity. Consider this. The mission we are on, it's not like any operation that either of us has been on before. Maybe we need to reevaluate our thinking."

"You and I are career military," Wade countered. "We have orders to not work with the British. I've broken those orders at her insistence."

"The people that are telling you what to do aren't here. I'm all about orders and the chain of command, but we are in a fluid situation. We're paid to think and act. Today, you thought first. Following orders from people whose asses are not on the line usually isn't the right thing to do."

"You're sounding a lot like Falto." It was a statement not intended to be a compliment.

Wertan grinned.

"It never hurts to reevaluate the situation and adapt to the circumstances."

Wade sighed. *Even the warrior poets are telling me I'm wrong.* "Since we got here, everything has felt wrong. We got bad intel and found out the Limeys were here. Then the Fish hit us and started shooting at their own ship. We've held our own so far, but this was just round one."

"The Fish don't know what they are up against," Wertan assured him. It was a confidence that he understood.

Tommy is probably right. We've spilled blood in the same places, fighting the same aliens.

"From your mouth to God's ears."

CYCLE III

CIA Headquarters, Langley, Virginia, the United States

Artemis (Art) Wilson, the director of the CIA, looked at Heather Dawn Taylor with a mix of dominance crossed with lecherous old white guy. She was good at masking her emotions, even from someone with the expertise and experience that the director had. "So our Colonel Slade is upset over the British arrival in Greenland. How sad for him."

She had been summoned to the throne—at least that was how her supervisor, the Deputy Director of Intelligence, had phrased it. It was never a good sign to be called to the principal's office, but she had been ordered to report in.

She knew why. Heather's last report had been scathing, again the word used by her supervisor.

We either dropped the ball when it came to telling the team in Greenland about the UK forces, or we were deliberate. Either way, we created a tense situation that had strained relations with the Extraterrestrial Task Force headed by Colonel Slade.

"Sir, you had me convey to him that we had no intelligence showing a foreign power moving on Greenland. My own check of our HUMINT reports shows that we did have some indications that the British were going to move."

"We get countless indications and hints every hour here, Ms. Taylor."

She shifted in her seat. "I double-checked, sir. You got that information but omitted it in the briefing materials I was given to pass on to Colonel Slade."

I did my homework. Everything indicates that he was the one who suppressed that data.

"Be very careful of what you are insinuating." Coming from his lips, it was not a warning, it was a threat.

"Sir—we sent those men and women to Greenland with faulty data. That information was pertinent to their operation."

"I am well aware of what was done. Based on your reports, I haven't seen where this has cost us a single American life."

"Director," Taylor said, pausing long enough to organize her thinking. "I'm confused. We are in a war. There's no logical reason that we should have held back that information."

Wilson leaned forward over his ornate wooden desk, leaning on his elbows. "This may be hard for you to understand, given that the decision was made many paygrades above yours, but it was done for good reasons. I think you should take that answer and adopt it."

Taylor internally cringed at his words. She didn't mind him talking down to her; that was something that she had expected given his reputation in the agency. She didn't mind that the CIA kept some things to themselves on certain topics. Compartmentalization was part of how the agency operated. There was something else that ate at her. This was about service personnel in harm's way. Heather was angered by that.

I have a brother and a cousin who are fighting in this war. The idea that someone, anyone, would withhold information that might put their lives at risk is wrong. There's no level of justification for it that is acceptable.

"I understand the need to sometimes withhold intel if it would compromise sources or gathering techniques. This did none of that. Worse, we now have a Special Missions Unit having to deal with the fallout of us keeping them in the dark."

It was clear from the rigid expression on the older man's face that her words were not changing his stance. "Why don't you let me worry about this kind of thing? You have a job to do, liaise with the colonel's little war effort. Until now, you've done a remarkable job of that. Continue with your assignment and let those of us that work here in Langley decide what his people need to see and what they don't."

"Sir, this isn't just about Colonel Slade. You withheld this intel from the DoD, specifically from the DIA and the whole of the ETF. We are in the middle of a war and the DoD is out there fighting it. We can't continue to operate the way we did back before the Fish showed up."

"Your *loyalty* is admirable, Ms. Taylor, if not somewhat misplaced. Did it ever occur to you that the president's placement of the DIA as the lead on the alien matter was a slap in the face to everyone in this building? The CIA has the depth and personnel to work the alien issue best. Instead, we are forced to channel resources willy-nilly every time the good colonel and his people demand them. It has put a huge strain on our agency, crippling our ability to protect this country. It was a mistake from day one—a mistake that has yet to be corrected. When you put a bunch of rank low-level amateurs in charge, these kinds of things are bound to happen. The fact that they didn't get data on the Brits is unfortunate. I chalk it up against the damage they have already wrecked on our agency—*your* agency."

It was in that moment that Heather realized who she was, not just as a CIA officer, but as a person. Resolve washed through her mind.

For my family, I need to do the right thing, not the CIA political thing.

"This just has the feel of inter-agency feuding."

We are in a war. We're better than this.

Wilson's gaze on her narrowed. "It may feel that way, but there are other ways to view this. If we keep on the way things are going, our agency becomes a shell of itself. There are plenty of countries out there that are still planning our demise, despite this war with the Fish. You have no idea the scope and breadth of the threats that are on our boards right now. As such, this is the time to make a stand. What you need to wrap your head around is that you are part of the team. If you go around making a stink about the colonel getting his panties in a wad, that muddies the waters here. This is the time for you to consider where your real loyalties lie. You were part of the agency long before you got this assignment. You keep doing what you are doing. Leave the big-thinking to myself and my staff."

He's telling me to shut up, look the other way.

Taylor understood that she was being wedged between a rock and a hard place. If she stood up for Colonel Slade, she was betraying her own agency. If she helped Slade beyond what her leaders wanted, it would help the war effort but could place her career in jeopardy.

"You've given me a lot to think over, sir," was all she dared reply.

"No one is above our reach here. I have eyes on you, Ms. Taylor. I won't tolerate agents that can't follow simple orders. Consider that as you mull over what I've told you."

There it was, the implied threat. It never occurred to her that he might be monitoring her activity. Up until now, there had not been any reason for her to think they might be watching what she did.

This was a mistake, pushing this issue and insisting on a meeting with the director. I've overplayed my hand.

"I understand, sir."

Wilson flashed her a wicked grin. "Good. You're a smart young lady. I'd hate to have to pull you from this assignment, especially over an issue such as loyalty and your patriotic duty." He then rose and gestured to the door.

My patriotism has never been questioned, until now. It's only being challenged by him, to cover up his withholding of information. No matter what I do, I need to tread carefully going forward.

O'Neil, Nebraska, the United States

Veronica pulled out the small remote control from her purse and adjusted the inflation level of her breasts. She had already used her pheromone lipstick, though she doubted it would have much influence over the man she was seeking out. As her driver cruised through O'Neil, she found herself admiring it. It was a slice of Americana from the twentieth century. Tiny little storefronts and shops, a downright quaint look to it. The small park at one end of the town had families in it, children playing. The old high school had been converted into a refugee center; a common sight in small towns in the middle of the country. Millions were fleeing the invasion, heading far inland. States like Nebraska had their populations double in a matter of months. As they had come into town, she saw the tent city filled with even more people fleeing the aliens.

It was the last place she expected to find Theodore "Fizz" Hart.

The last time anyone saw Fizz in public had been during the Senate hearings into Jay Drake. Those had resulted in a stack of federal warrants for Drake's arrest and the seizure of his US assets. Veronica had assumed Fizz had gone into some witness protection program. It took remarkably little digging to find him living in O'Neil, Nebraska. He wasn't using a new identity. Instead, from what her research team learned, he was living in a house that his grandmother had willed to him upon her death.

The driver stopped in front of the two-story Victorian home. The gingerbread trim and the large wraparound porch, perfectly shaded, seemed almost idyllic.

"Wait for me," she half-stated, half-demanded, opening the door and starting up the steps.

I know Fizz. None of this seems like the kind of place he'd be living. It's weird. This whole town feels like it's in some sort of bubble, like the war doesn't exist.

She pressed the video doorbell with a perfectly manicured and painted fingernail and waited. From within the house, she could hear the sound of footfalls on wood and some shuffling. There was a bark from a dog. Then, through the curtained glass, she saw a figure loom in front of the door.

As the door swung open, she saw Fizz. He had lost weight, easily twenty pounds worth, since his Senate testimony. He still had a little paunch, but nowhere near what he used to carry. His beard had streaks of gray in it. He looked more polished than she had remembered.

It's been a while since he has been in the field.

"Veronica…" he said, his eyes widening at seeing her.

She smiled. "Fizz."

"Look, if this is about what happened at Santa Monica—"

She cut him off. "Fizz, relax. I'm not here to exact revenge."

He said nothing for a moment, eyeing her suspiciously. "Okay—then come in."

Fizz led her to a forward parlor. A dog came in, a copper-colored Labrador, which nuzzled her knee as she took a seat on a couch that had clearly been purchased by an elderly person.

"I never expected to see you here," Fizz said, flopping down in a chair across from her.

"Look, we have history. I understand why you and Dana did what you did. At the time, if I had the chance, I probably would have done the same thing."

"Dana was a force of nature," he replied, petting the dog's head as it moved to his side and sat down.

"I have to admit, I'm surprised to find you here. I figured that you'd be in hiding."

"What's the point?" Fizz asked. "Jay Drake is the richest man on the planet. If he wanted me dead, there's not much that even the FedGov could do to prevent it. They wanted me to change my name and live somewhere safe, as if there is a place that's safe now. I came here because this is about the only place I can think of as home." He looked around the parlor almost sadly, with a forlorn expression washing over his face.

Veronica was impressed with his logic. "You and Dana got a national Emmy for her last piece. You're on the short list for a Pulitzer."

"As if they were going to have the competition, with the war and all. I didn't do what I did to win any prize. I did it because it was right and it was the only way to honor her last minutes alive." There was a longing in his voice.

Clearly he misses her.

"Fizz, I didn't come here to reminisce. I came about a job."

"What job?"

"The Space Force shot down an enemy spacecraft. It crashed on the east coast of Greenland. There's a team there now, scientists and soldiers, but so far no one from the press. I got the scoop from a source in the ETF and scooped everyone. Being the first ones there and broadcasting would be a major coup. I came to see if you would go with me, be my film and production partner."

Fizz leaned back in his chair. "It's been a while. Greenland at this time of the year, it's got to be colder than a well-digger's ass in the Klondike."

She nodded. "I've got us the right gear and have arranged for the flights. The challenge is that the clock is running."

He hesitated. "I'm not sure. It's been a while since I went up against the Fish. It doesn't exactly bring back fond memories."

"I know," Veronica said. "As much as you were a competitor, you were the *best* competition I ever had. For something like this, I need the absolute best in the business—and that's you."

For a long few moments, Fizz seemed lost in his thoughts. "I have to admit, sitting here, on the sidelines of the war, it's dull. I needed dull for a while, having been in the middle of everything at the start. There are parts of it I do miss."

"Come with me," she said in as soothing a tone as possible. "We can make some magic together…give the people a story that will excite and encourage them. A downed alien spaceship. Talk about an exclusive—and you can be the one to help me deliver it."

"I'm not sure."

"If Dana were alive, what would she tell you to do?"

Drawing a long breath, Fizz rose to his feet. "She'd probably tell me to find a way to screw you over so she could get the video for herself." Saying that out loud, he chuckled. "The truth is, I *do* miss the excitement. When my name comes up, it's always tied to hers and Drake's. A lot of people don't see me as anything but a supporting cast member. But I am good at what I do."

"So you'll do it?" Veronica said as she rose to her feet.

Fizz nodded. "What the hell. I need to find someone to watch Blaze," he said, looking down at the Labrador.

Veronica extended her hand and Fizz shook it. "Partners."

"Why not?"

CHAPTER 13

Operation Sulaco
West of the Crash Site, East Coast of Greenland

Falto moved in the domed shelter where the scientists were preparing for their penetration of the spaceship. They all pushed Steed-powered carts laden with a dazzling display of equipment. The powered devices were like augmented wheelbarrows. The Corps used them to transport ammo if GRDs were not available. They seemed to navigate the rocks and ice easily, but getting them up on the enormous alien vessel took some work.

The back of her head throbbed, a dull headache, but one she had been enduring since the firefight the day before. It was a strange place for her to get a headache, and eerily familiar. *I felt like this for weeks when I was being held prisoner.* Maneuvering through the tight space, she reached Dr. Schrivener. "Got any Tylenol?"

Schrivener gave her a sideways look. "Let me guess, headache, back of your head down near your neck?"

"How did you know?"

"The Rangers that were on top of the ship, almost to a person, have showed up complaining of a headache," she said, handing her two white pills.

Falto didn't need water to wash them down, she simply swallowed them. "What about the others—Omega Force?"

"None of them. None of the Rangers that stayed behind to protect us, either."

"So, it's something else, something connected with the ship."

Her mind raced. *Do I dare tell her I felt this before?* The last thing she wanted to do was generate fear when it might not be warranted. *Besides, it couldn't be the same thing, could it?*

"That's the current thinking. I don't have the gear here for a CAT scan, obviously, but I'd love to try and determine what caused it."

"I felt this before. Exactly like this headache—same place, same dull intensity," she said, keeping her voice low so that only Dr. Schrivener could hear her words.

"Really, when?"

"When I was being held by the Fish. I wrote it off as just part of the malnutrition. We all had it. It wasn't debilitating or anything, but we all had it."

Schrivener nodded in silence that lasted for a few moments. "It must have to do with proximity to the ship, obviously. Whatever it was that triggered it for you where you were held is probably what caused it for the people that went up on top of the ship during the battle."

Falto's mind raced with thoughts as to the implications of what the doctor said, but she didn't land on any conclusions. "So, what causes it?"

"Unknown. It could be our bodies reacting to their power source, or something else. We don't know enough about their technology to really understand it. I've been around captured aliens many times and I didn't get any headaches, so it has to be something connected with something big, like this ship or the habitat that you were held in."

"It's not dangerous, is it?"

Schrivener smiled. "You lived with it for months, you tell me. Clearly there were no long-term impacts of it on you. It just means we are all going to need some Tylenol for this part of the mission."

What she said made sense, but Falto didn't like the new bit of knowledge. It was a reminder to her that humanity was messing with technology they didn't even remotely understand.

As a prisoner, I coped with the environment down there. I didn't necessarily understand it. We were so focused on survival, we simply didn't have the strength or desire to master their tech.

"I have to assume we'll be just fine then," she said.

"Sounds like the best bet to me." Dr. Schrivener grabbed a large white MOLLE pack and slung it over her parka, then pulled on an oversized pair of white military gloves. "Alright, people, we need to move out. The Rangers are going to go with us. The weather has gotten a little ugly out there and it is already pretty dark. We stick together and work together. No one touch anything without checking with me first."

"How are we getting in?" one scientist asked.

"The Rangers think they have found a way. If that doesn't work, we have a field laser and can cut our way in, but I would prefer to avoid that approach. We don't know how the ship or any surviving occupants are going to react."

The thinking thus far was that there were no survivors in the hull of the ship. If they were there, they surely would have shown themselves by now. That was the party line of the scientists, but Falto didn't subscribe to that thinking.

There's so much about the Fish we don't know, I'm not going to trust any assumptions that I didn't come up with myself.

***

Natalia was sweating with the extra layer of clothing she wore. The science team insisted that anyone going into the ship have on protective gear, an encapsulated HAZMAT-grade environmental suit. It made sense; no one had been aboard one of the aliens' spacecraft before.

I have on my warm weather undergarments, my fatigues, the suit, my tactical vest, and a parka. It's a miracle I can move.

She kept the large hood in a ruck, along with spare ammunition. She wore her ECH, and it was rigged with a wide-angle camera to capture everything she saw. While the Rangers would be going in with the scientists for protection, she carried her own ACR and two grenades.

I trust the Rangers, but at the end of the day, it's my life that's on the line if something goes wrong.

Outside wasn't dark but it wasn't light either. The sun was setting, though from what Falto saw, it had never really risen much to begin with. Dark purple clouds blocked whatever sunlight was trying to fight its way to Greenland, turning what was left of the day into night. The Rangers had set up a guide rope from the habitat shelters to the wreck site. Every so often there were portable LED lanterns set, a string of dots leading out in the dull grayness of frozen Greenland. She helped by carrying a heavy ruck of gear, following Dr. Schrivener and a fire team of Rangers, trudging through the snow.

The wreck loomed as they closed on it. When she had gone there before, it had been at a full run. Slowly walking to the site made it seem farther away. She glanced to her right and saw some flicker of lights from the British camp. *They are setting out too.*

The agreement had been to divide the ship in half, with the Americans taking the northern half of the wreck and the British the southern. Both forces posted sentries on the upper hull of the vessel, keeping a keen watch for any sign that the Fish would be returning. Neither McKenna nor Wade could get as far as coordinating military operations, so it was a minor victory that the science teams would be able to synchronize their explorations.

The only cost of getting that agreement is that Captain Wade wants to kill me or at least ship me back to the States.

"We found two ways in," said one of the Rangers who had started to move on the other side of the rope beside her. "Looks like they are blast holes from the Space Force laser that brought this thing down."

Falto nodded but didn't reply. This was the same Ranger she had been with on top of the ship during the firefight. She cast a sideways glance at him and saw the grin under his visor. *He's probably a nice guy. He might even be flirting with me. I'm not ready for that.* As a

POW, she had connected deeply with the people being held as she had been. She had watched them die, cut apart by the aliens and their bizarre experimentations. As much as she enjoyed companionship, Falto wanted to keep most people at arm's length. *I can't deal with having people too close to me. I have lost so many along the way—I don't want to experience that again.* She knew that made her appear aloof, but didn't care. *I'm saving both of us future headaches if things go south.*

The walk was slow and ponderous, but they eventually reached the end of the rope. In what would be the narrow tail portion of the ship was a hole, roughly a half-meter in diameter. It was blackened around the edges and was slightly oval. It didn't remind Falto of any laser shot she had ever seen. *This is much larger.*

Captain Wertan pointed to it. "There's another one farther up near the top."

"Is that one any larger?" Dr. Schrivener asked.

"'Fraid not. It actually is a little smaller."

"Any idea of what is beyond the opening?"

"It's some sort of chamber, fairly big. Beyond that, it's hard to tell."

"I'd hoped to avoid any evasive work to enter. There's no way we can crawl through and get our gear in without widening that hole."

"Yes, ma'am," Wertan replied.

It was hard to read Schrivener's face with her mask on, but Falto saw a bit of nervous dejection. "Alright, Trudy, break out the laser cutter. Let's get this hole big enough for us to crawl through."

An engineer stepped forward with a laser cutter. She wore orange safety goggles and moved to the opening, bending over to inspect it carefully. Dr. Schrivener asked everyone to turn around as the engineer went to work. Natalia could hear the hum of the laser behind her as she waited.

"Alright," Schrivener called out and Falto turned. The engineer had done a good job with the laser, cutting a wider hole, easily a meter and a half in diameter. The edges where she had cut were blackened and almost brittle-charred. The inside of the chamber was dark, though Captain Wertan leaned in with a Maglite and checked it. "My team will take point," he told Dr. Schrivener. "When we have cleared it, you can come in."

Falto stared at the opening. *I'm not a science fiction fan, but everything I ever saw about exploring an alien spaceship ended with a lot of dead people.*

Four Rangers followed the captain in, weapons at the ready, visors down and prepared to engage any threats. Falto could see the beams of their lights moving around in the inside of the craft. Then a hand came out, motioning for the rest of them to step inside. Bending low, she entered the vessel.

The chamber, or whatever it was, looked like the inside of a person's ribcage, sans the organs. Large strut-like projections curved down from a bone-like center support that ran the length of the room. It was wide, nearly eight meters, and almost twenty meters in length. Near the far end, she could see that it sloped downward. The floor was spongy, flexing with each step, just like it had been where she had been held prisoner. The temperature was not as bitterly cold as it was outside, though it was far from warm. There was what she assumed to be water on the floor, several inches of it. When the lights hit it, the water was mostly clear, but there were little flecks of green that reflected the light like some sort of thin layer of emerald glitter.

Then came the aroma. It was a hint of fish in the air and an almost oily taste on the back of her tongue. That shook her more than the sight of the room. For a moment, she was not aboard an alien ship, but was back trapped at the bottom of the ocean. The assault on her senses triggered memories she wished she didn't have. Her body went rigid and she felt hot and uncomfortable.

"Alright, get your hoods on and activate your breathing units," Dr. Schrivener said. Everyone began to move except for Falto. She knew what she was supposed to do, but her body refused to comply. Instead, she began to breathe a little faster, nearing hyperventilation. It didn't feel like she was in control of her body. Even the marvelous bionic limbs didn't respond to her desire to move. Her eyes were all she seemed to be able to command, and they darted back to the opening, back into the twilight darkness of a Greenland winter night.

Falto knew what panic was, and this wasn't quite that. It was as if a nightmare was coming to life. Part of her had always compartmentalized the things that had happened during her captivity. Now those things were crashing into her reality all around her. The dangers she had faced, the pain she suffered, the losses she had been forced to endure, were no longer just memories—they were confronting her.

Closing her eyes slowly, she mustered herself against the memories, against the sights and sounds that pummeled her in that moment. She felt her right hand tremble at her side then she made herself ignore it.

I shouldn't have come. What good am I to these people if I'm paralyzed with...with...with these feelings?

Then a voice came to her, almost like an echo in her consciousness. The voice was that of Reid Porter.

"What would Hannibal tell you to do?"

Those words had started her on the road to Greenland; now she clung to them like a baby to a binky. They were comforting, safe, and brought back powerful memories and even more formidable images in her mind.

Hannibal Rickenburg had been the most God-damnedest Marine she had ever met. Part Chesty Puller, part god, all Marine. Memories of him fighting the obsidian Boss in his ASHUR were the memories she clung to in that moment. It was good and pure, it was honor, it was glorious battle. Those recollections were strong—the sights, the smells, the voices, the explosions—they crushed her POW memories, thrashing the POW memories that had momentarily overwhelmed her.

Rickenburg had no fear, or if he did, I never saw it. He was never crippled with fear. He fought, right to the end.

She was proud she had been there to see that. It defined what being a Marine was to her.

Drawing a cool breath, she opened her eyes with a new resolve, a new center of her thinking. She saw Dr. Schrivener and the Ranger who had come in with her standing in front of her, filling her field of vision. "Sergeant—are you okay?"

She nodded quickly. It wasn't much, but it was control. "Sorry, just remembering things," she muttered. Glancing down, she saw that her right hand was no longer trembling.

"You need to put on your hood."

Her hands moved on their own accord as she pulled on the oversized hood, fitting it carefully on her ECH, then sealing it. The small breathing unit kicked in after a few breaths and she felt the entire suit pressurize around her. She was still warm, still sweating, but starting to feel the coldness of her perspiration, proof that she was calming down.

"The temperature here is around forty degrees Fahrenheit," one of the other scientists said. "We can probably shed our parkas." The science team pulled their coats off and put them back through the entry hole to avoid them getting soaked. Natalia followed suit and appreciated the improved range of movement.

The Ranger who had come with her, Rosales, leaned in so that his voice wouldn't carry. "Are you doing okay? You had me worried there for a minute."

"Bad memories, that's all," Falto flatly said.

She moved forward slowly, the water at her feet sloshing slightly. Each step she took was deeper into the ship and she looked around, keeping her head on swivel as if she were entering a firefight, rather than exploring.

Falto could tell something was off. It was the angle of the floor. The ship was not level, but there was a list of a few degrees. It was enough for her to have to compensate with her stance.

If it wasn't bad enough to crawl through this wet mess of bad memories, I have to concentrate on my footing too.

The floor was torn by a rock that jutted upward. It had been a jagged knife as the ship had slid to a landing, ripping a section of the flooring right up to a wall. All around the tear and covering most of it was as yellow crusty substance. It even covered part of the rock that had inflicted the damage. At first, Falto thought it was some sort of fungus growing on the cut, but it seemed to cover some spots entirely. She was tempted to touch it but heeded Schrivener's orders.

"What do you make of that?" one of the scientists asked as another bent down to look at it closely.

The scientist leaned over it from several angles. "I can't say for certain, but it has all of the looks of a crust or eschar."

"What does that mean?" one engineer asked.

"A scab," the scientist responded as she rose to her feet.

At the far end of the room, several flashlight beams centered on a tall slit in the wall. It was taller than a human by several feet, and pinkish in color. The scientists and Rangers looked at it in wonder since it was the only distinct thing in the chamber. Falto knew it from its almost vaginal appearance. This was one of the alien doors.

The scientists silently broke out small glass-lined insulated aluminum cylinders and at the doctor's urging gathered samples. Using scalpels and small laser cutters, they carefully removed small bits of the room, storing them for later analysis. Natalia watched them, wondering what kind of reaction the alien ship might have to their efforts.

Hopefully these cuts are so minor, it won't respond.

Nodding towards the far end of the room, Dr. Schrivener moved beside Falto. "Is that what I think it is?" she asked.

"It's a door."

"Yeah," Captain Wertan replied. "It's got a whole Georgia O'Keefe vibe to it."

Falto didn't get the reference, but looked over at him. "It's a door, trust me."

"So how do we activate it?"

"You don't 'activate' anything, you simply slide on through," she asserted.

There was a hesitancy by the Rangers that almost made her chuckle. She reached out with her gloved hand and slid it into the flaps of skin-like material. There was a fast and powerful rush of air that hit her suit as she stepped through the flap, followed by Captain Wertan and his Rangers.

The next room was smaller, almost like the corridor she had been held in. It lacked the ribs of the previous room. Where the previous room had a brownish tint to it, this one seemed more pale green. The fluid that had pooled on the floor was shallower in the new chamber, but was also more viscus. Falto was thankful that the breathing unit on her suit made it so that she didn't have to smell the room.

I'm far too familiar with what this room must smell like.

The scientists entered the chamber through the door, followed by the rear guard of the Rangers, a sergeant who, judging by his immense bulk, had to be a pumper. "Biggest damn pussy I've ever been in," he joked, only getting stern glances from Schrivener, her associates, and Wertan.

"Watch that shit, Sergeant," Wertan snapped.

The Ranger realized he had crossed the line. "My apologies."

It didn't bother Falto. She had been a Marine long enough that she had heard almost every kind of biological reference when it came to men or women. It clearly embarrassed or angered a handful of the scientists, though. Their reaction was enough to get her to chuckle privately.

The laser burn they had used to enter the ship didn't reach this chamber, which furrowed into some yet-unseen room. The lights that swept around left an eerie green trail of glowing on the walls, ceiling, and floor. Luminescent material in the structure shimmered for a few seconds after lights hit them, giving the room a light emerald glow. For Falto, the light looked far too familiar.

Walking forward, she saw the Ranger's lights focus on a dark object on the floor. It was long, over two meters in length, dark gray and purple in color. As she made her way toward it, she saw tentacles coming out from it.

As she shifted her perspective, she recognized it.

It's just like Opie.

Memories of the creature and the suffering he brought upon her made her angry.

146

"Is that one of their crew?" a scientist asked.

Falto squatted next to the creature. "I've faced these before. I called them laborers. From my experience, they fill a number of different roles." The one she saw looked wrong. It took a moment to figure it out. "Something is wrong about this one."

"What is it?" Dr. Schrivener asked, bending down next to her.

"It's like half of its mass is gone," Falto replied, pointing to it. "It's like it's been cut in half." The part that was missing was merely part of the floor. Only half of its head and body were visible, the rest was flush to the spongy floor.

"Is it being absorbed into the floor?" Schrivener asked.

That made sense, though Falto couldn't understand why that was the case. "I never saw stuff like this before."

One of the Rangers next to Schrivener on the other side of the Laborer nudged a tentacle on the floor. Suddenly the remaining eye opened, looking right at Falto. The purplish tentacle jerked to life, wrapping around the leg of the Ranger behind it, pulling his leg out from under him and dropping him into the watery-goo.

The other tentacles suddenly whipped into action. One knocked over Schrivener, another shot out towards Falto. Her new legs sprang to action, sending her flying back into the soft wall, out of its reach. The Laborer couldn't move; it was now part of the ship's floor. The remaining tentacles whipped about madly as two more Rangers struggled to pull the first Ranger free.

Gunfire broke out; Falto didn't see who pulled their triggers first. The banging was loud and the flashes of gunfire tore into the Laborer. After several moments, the tentacles went limp and the grip on the one trapped Ranger released. A thin haze of smoke was in the air as Natalia got to her feet, swinging her own ACR to bear on the now immobile Laborer.

"Well," Wertan said, kicking at the creature to validate that it had been taken care of. "There's something you don't see every day." He turned to his Ranger that had the tentacle wrapped on his leg. "You good?"

Rosales shot a nervous nod back. Even from where she stood,

Falto saw how big the eyes of the attacked Ranger had become.

"You've got to watch what you do. I said no touching, and that's what I meant," Schrivener growled to everyone in the room.

Falto's eyes fell on the dead alien. *Why was the ship absorbing it? The aliens don't do anything without purpose. What else are we going to find?*

The team advanced to another doorway that intersected the hallway. It was closed and unlike the previous one, it refused to open. The scientists checked it from top to bottom, but could not find a mechanism that seemed to trigger it.

"What are we missing?" Schrivener asked Falto.

She shrugged. "All of the ones I encountered just opened."

"I can use a laser to cut it," one of the female researchers offered.

Schrivener stared at Falto as if she had the answer, but Falto shook her head. "I have no idea. This isn't something I've experienced."

Schrivener gave the single nod to the scientist that pulled out a laser cutter as another scientist moved in beside her to assist. They huddled near the door flap and turned on the laser which hummed to life. Falto instinctively stepped backwards, and Rosales, seeing her move, did the same.

There was a hiss and a spray, like a fine line of high-pressured steam shooting out of the spot that the two scientists were working. The steam showered their suits. Then without warning, the door erupted. There was a rush of liquid, under extreme pressure, that blasted out, slamming the scientists on the far side of the hall. The rush was so fast, it knocked everyone other than Captain Wertan off their feet. Falto fell forward and was pushed past him, face down in the liquid.

She fumbled to find something to hold on to, but as the pressure abated, she was able to get to her knees, then rise. In the hood she was starting to fog her faceplate, her breath was so intense. Looking back up the tunnel, she saw that she had been pushed back almost ten feet. The two scientists were floating in the now hip-deep water. Neither moved as Rosales sloshed forward to check them. Turning one over, the face mask was covered with a film of blood and a bit of pinkish gray matter.

"We have wounded," Rosales called out. "Make a tunnel!"

149

CHAPTER 14

Operation Durendal
Alien Crash Site, East Coast of Greenland

Major McKenna would have preferred to be in his Spitfire as he approached the base of the alien craft. Instead, he was dismounted, on foot, preparing for their entry to the crashed ship. The Americans had entered a few minutes earlier, from what he saw on his DBF, the digital battlefield monitor in his helmet. The Yanks had managed to find a hole in the northern part of the ship. His drones had checked the entire site and southern portion of the ship that had been designated for the British to explore; there were no such openings. That presented both a challenge and a potential opportunity.

McKenna hated the protective gear he wore, despite knowing the reasons for it. He had a scar on his thigh from the acid spray that the aliens unleashed, one shot melting its way through his Spitfire's frontal armor and burning him. *These suits are for our protection, I get that, but they don't offer much protection if the bollocks decide to start shooting.* Everyone wore standard battle armor under their environmental protection suits, but even that was not entirely reassuring.

His chief scientist from the British government's newly formed Alien Operating Group was Dr. Marc Lahoz, formerly the lead marine biologist at Oxford. The bookish man was quirky, but McKenna was fully prepared to believe that some of that was on him. The longer he had been with the Royal Marines, the more he found himself unable to fully connect with civilians. Lahoz had studied the ship images and suggested three possible egress points, entry holes that would have to be created.

As they approached the ship, they passed through some sort of barrier. It wasn't visible to the naked eye, nor was it strong, but it was noticeable. His reconnaissance images showed there was some sort of field surrounding the ship.

"What do you make of that barrier?" he asked Dr. Lahoz.

The doctor held up some sort of instrument. "Low-level magnetics detected, but beyond that, I can't tell you what it is. We tried to monitor it the other day but got nothing useful."

"Any risks with it?"

Lahoz shook his head. "The Americans passed through it during the battle and didn't report any ill side effects. My educated guess is that it is some sort of system still operating from the ship, perhaps tied to its propulsion system."

I doubt the Americans would have shared if that barrier posed a risk. Captain Wade isn't exactly open and forthcoming with information. The man clearly had issues with McKenna's government that went far beyond the force in Greenland.

His issue raised an intriguing thought with McKenna. *How much should I share with the Americans about what we find?* He liked to believe he would be open and honest with them, but it was impossible to ignore the hesitancy that he felt. *It might do them good to get a bloody nose or two along the way; knock them down a few pegs.*

McKenna moved up to the wide prow of the ship. Only twenty meters to the west was where he had his people bury his insurance policy, the powerful fuel air explosive, against the hull of the ship. He had agreed with Dr. Lahoz on this point to enter the ship because it was the furthest away from the device. The science team had no idea that it had been brought or planted there. He had been given discretion on informing them about it, but had decided not to.

The last thing I need is them arguing with me about the need for such a device. Scientists have an overinflated sense of their stature in society. They believe that simply because of their title that somehow they are infallible and the others are beneath them. There would be no debate about the weapon with his approach.

The hull of the ship looked strange. The lower levels that had impacted the ground seemed collapsed. The outer covering of the ship buckled, but not like metal, more like deflated layers of thick skin or hide. *Whatever was keeping those chambers or levels solid has collapsed.* He mentally added it to the list of strange things he saw about the vessel.

The naval engineers on the science team felt the entry point they had chosen would give them quick access to the bridge or control center of the ship. He admired their enthusiasm, but didn't share in it.

We have no idea where anything is in this ship. At least they have a reason, where the other scientists were clearly guessing.

Whisky Company would go in with the science team, while Yankee Company would maintain a secured perimeter. *The bollocks are still out there, which means we need to be vigilant.* At the first sign of trouble, he would extract the scientists. That was why he pre-positioned his Spitfire only eighty meters from the entry point.

They had tried to use ground penetrating radar against the hull, but got confusing readings at best. There were openings, presumed to be rooms in the ship, but they were not organized in a pattern that anyone recognized. That didn't surprise him. Nothing about the aliens was predictable.

When he reached the ochre and brown hull, McKenna's hand went to touch it. Even with his insulated firing gloves, he felt as if he had some sort of tactile sensation with the vessel.

You are full of secrets, and I want them.

"Bring up the L-Breach," he ordered. Two troops from Whisky brought up the laser breach device. Far more subtle than an explosive breaching charge, the laser charge was surgical. It was laser mounded on a circular rail almost two meters in diameter. The device was leaned up against where the breach was desired, propped up by two extending legs. When activated, the laser fired into the surface as it moved rapidly in circles on the rail, each pass burning deeper. Once the hole was opened, the system could be quickly deactivated and dropped, and the hole exploited. Each Marine lit up the lights on their Mk 10 advanced helmets, illuminating the area of the hull in bright blue-white light.

As they finished the quick setup, McKenna held up his assault weapon, the sleek L129A1 Sharpshooter II, painted white from their service in Norway.

"Scientists to the rear," he ordered. "Everyone else, weapons at the ready."

He made sure that they spread out so that if the other side was pressurized, they would not be in line to be hit if the cut portion flew back. He snugged the weapon tight to his shoulder, raising it.

"Ready, sir," one of the Marines at the breach point called back.

"Open her up," he commanded.

The laser raced around the track eight times in less than a minute, the small laser retracing its cutting path with each pass. As it finished, the piece of the hull blew back, knocking the L-Breach down to the ground in the process. A rush of air and fluid shot out, dousing everyone with a grayish watery ooze. The cut portion flew back so hard, it clipped one of the scientists, knocking him the ground, momentarily dazing him. The cut portion was thicker than he imagined it would be given the number of passes of the laser, just over sixteen centimeters. The seared edges oozed a sickly yellow liquid out of several spots, staining the snow.

The hole itself was dark, even as several of the Marines' lights flickered inside. Nothing immediately came out, for which he was thankful.

"Alright, Lance Corporal Thun, take your team in."

Lance Corporal Jana Dae Thun gave a nod and moved in front of the opening, crouching low, then stepping inside. The rest of the Royal Marines moved in, closing in on the breach, wondering just like McKenna, *Are we going to have to go in to assist them?*

"Clear, sir," came back Thun's voice over the comms channel.

McKenna didn't hesitate, he stepped through the breach and into the room beyond.

The chamber was easily fifteen meters long running north, but only two meters high. The walls shimmered a yellowish green as helmet lights hit them, glowing lightly in the dark. Hanging down from the top of the chamber were thin sheets that wavered as the Marines and scientists entered. They were a mustard color, around a half meter in width each, seemingly hanging in the room in a haphazard manner. As much as everyone was told not to touch anything, it was impossible to move in the room without some sort of contact with the sheets.

Using the barrel of his Sharpshooter II, he moved one sheet aside, and as he touched it, he saw what looked like a blue spark that appeared where his barrel touched it, racing upward. As McKenna saw that flicker, he noticed that other bits of the material had similar reactions as his people moved in. Leaning closer, the material that hung down looked like layers of skin. He remembered as a child looking at skin under a microscope, and the structure and thickness seemed to be very similar.

What the hell are these for? They must serve some purpose.

The floor was bouncy, resilient rather than rigid. It was also wet. Bending down slightly, he saw that they were standing in fluid, eight centimeters' worth. The floor material was uneven, listing a few degrees, and there were wrinkles in it. There was something green in it, an oily substance. Even though he wasn't moving, it looked as if the fluid was moving on its own accord.

"Sir." Thun's voice summoned him from the far end of the chamber. Moving carefully forward, he came to where his lead sub-section was poised. They stood in front of a series of flaps and folds that looked remarkably like a bit of private female anatomy. "Sir, is this one of their hatches?" Thun asked.

"Damned if I know," McKenna replied. He turned and spotted Dr. Lahoz a few meters behind him. "Dr. Lahoz, what are your thoughts?"

Lahoz moved up in front of the object, eyeing it so closely that the front of his environmental body suit helmet actually bumped into it. "This is remarkable."

"Is it an opening?" McKenna pressed.

"It may very well be."

"Looks like the biggest set of beef curtains I've ever seen," muttered one Marine.

"Hold that language," McKenna snapped, enough to make the Marine turn beet-red. McKenna turned then nodded to Thun. "Take your sub-section through."

Thun's face didn't offer a hint of apprehension, the product of training and discipline. He used his gun barrel and hand to find a gap in the fleshy folds, sliding them aside. It resisted, McKenna could see that. As he pried it, the flaps suddenly opened. There was a massive rush of air and liquid from the next space. The force of the water knocked Thun down and made McKenna reach out for the wall to avoid tumbling himself.

Thun got back up, covered in a film from the fluid, followed by several members of his team. Once the rush of water eased, they pressed forward through the hatchway, into the chamber beyond. After a few moments, he barked out, "Room secure, Major." Then, "You have to see this."

Twisting his shoulders, McKenna leaned in and through the alien hatchway. The flaps seemed to hug him which was mildly discomforting. As he came into the chamber, he saw that it was lit up, at least more than from the helmet-mounted lights they wore under their environmental hoods. The chamber looked very different from the previous one. It was almost like standing in a large accordion. The walls seemed more rigid than in the previous room, with smooth angles, but inelastic.

The lights came from the walls themselves, shimmering a dull amber, and rippled down the room from the far end where Thun stood to the doorway. The pulsating waves of light came slowly as they moved. McKenna moved forward as the rest of the science team pushed through.

Along one wall of the chamber, sitting against the wall and floor was what might have been a tall creature, with tentacles for movement. At the shoulders, if that's what they could be called, was another set of tentacles. Along the torso were a series of short stubby appendages, tentacles that hung limp at its side. The alien's head was triangular, sloping forward. It was a dark purple in color, with streaks of yellow in it. Its eyes were closed, crusted over with a gritty substance.

What struck him the most was that the creature looked as if it were being absorbed into the wall and floor. From what he could see through the fluid, two tentacles had sunk into the floor, then rose a few centimeters later, arced over, then disappeared into the floor. McKenna kept his weapon on the creature, using a quick hand gesture to keep people back.

Dr. Lahoz moved next to him. "We haven't encountered one of these yet, a new species."

"Why is it seeping into the hull and deck?" McKenna pressed.

"I have no idea," Lahoz answered.

"Is it alive?" another Marine asked.

"Unknown," Lahoz replied. He reached out and pressed a gloved finger into the creature.

It moved. One eye managed to open, breaking the dull yellowish crust off. The eye swept the room, almost as if it were in a panic, as Lahoz and everyone else backed up a step.

The creature flailed, clearly trying to move, but couldn't. *It's stuck in place, like the ship was merging with it.* The tentacles flapped about, as if they were trying to grab anything or anyone, then slapped the walls, suckering onto them and trying to pull itself up.

It didn't seem like a threat, trapped as it was, but he also had no intention of leaving it there alive. "We should kill it." The Royal Marines didn't need a second opinion. Weapons that were already trained on the creature, leveled and waited for the command to fire.

"This is a unique opportunity," Dr. Lahoz countered. "We should try to take it alive."

"It's part of the ship now," McKenna replied. "If not, and it gets loose, no one knows what kind of problems it can cause."

"We could learn a lot from it."

"You can get your samples from a dead one just as easy as a live one," McKenna coolly replied. He gave a firm nod to Thun's sub-section and each man fired. Cracks of the gunfire seemed muffled in the chamber, no doubt from its organic composition. The creature splattered against the walls and floor, oozing an oily gray substance that he assumed was blood. The creature went limp except for two of the upper body tentacles that quivered for a long few moments before flopping limp.

The ripple of light in the room stopped the moment the creature ceased to move. It was still on, but no longer moving through the room. Everyone paused and weapons swept the chamber.

"Fascinating," Dr. Lahoz stated, shattering the quiet. "It's as if the ship could sense what was done to the creature."

"I'm not exactly thrilled at that prospect, doctor," McKenna replied.

"You should be," Lahoz countered. "It's something we couldn't have imagined. If that was one of the crew, it means that the crew is somehow mentally connected to the ship itself. It is like they are a single organism. It's remarkable."

McKenna wished he could share the doctor's enthusiasm. As his eyes swept the chamber, he found himself uneasy. *This ship looks like a living organism. How is its crew going to respond to our presence? What kind of defenses does this ship have?* In that moment, he realized that he didn't want an answer.

"Alright, lads, look sharp," was the only order he could give that made any sense.

At the far end of the room were two of the doors. It didn't matter which they chose, both would need to be checked. "Thun, take your boys to the one on the right. Ashcroft, you take three men and go through the one on the left." There was no need for verbal conformation, the men simply acted on his orders.

A few seconds later, Ashcroft came back through the flaps of the doorway. "This is some sort of tunnel, going down. We went about eight meters and it is flooded. Water is gurgling up in the middle of it."

Thun came back as Ashcroft finished. "We have slope upward,

lots of twists and turns. It narrows quickly. There are these door-things everywhere."

Turning to the scientists who were finishing with their sample gathering and whatever analysis they could do, he nodded to Lahoz. "Seems like our path has been chosen for us."

"Agreed. I'd like to see that flooded area though." Lahoz went through the doorway, followed by McKenna and two troopers. The hallway was some fifteen meters long, dipping down steeply in an inky pool of water. Ashcroft was right. In the middle of the water was a bubbling. He noticed that when lights hit the walls, they didn't seem to ignite a green glow. As he focused on the walls, he noticed that they were glossy, wet, and dark gray in color, as if whatever was living about them had been drained, leaving only an ashen flesh behind.

"I'll need a sample of that fluid," Lahoz said as one of the other researchers came into the hall. The short woman bent low and started down the grade towards the water, then slipped, falling on her rear and sliding right into the pool.

She panicked and began to flail and cry out, splashing the dark fluid everywhere. McKenna took ahold of Lahoz's hand, then bent his knees, leaning towards her, like a human chain. Her white environmental clothing was covered with a dull oily substance as she started to push and crawl towards him, finally taking his hand. Together, Lahoz and McKenna pulled her trembling form out.

"I'm so sorry, doctor!" She quivered, trying to wipe the substance off. "I'm fine." Turning to McKenna, she thanked him.

"That's alright. Go on back and see if we can wipe that off of you," Lahoz replied. As she left the chamber, he turned to the major. "Everyone is a little on edge."

"That's understandable. We are standing in the middle of something that didn't come from Earth. She's entitled to be nervous."

"The layout of this ship, it's strange," Lahoz replied as another researcher carefully obtained a sample of the fluid from the pool.

"I'm surprised at all of the liquid here. Given the temperatures outside, I would have thought this stuff would be frozen."

"The temperature inside is just above freezing," Lahoz offered. "As for the amount of liquids, I would venture to guess that the entire ship was likely filled with water or whatever this stuff turns out to be. It only makes sense. It's what the aliens consider their natural environment."

"The fact that this ship is warm…does that mean it is still functional?" His brain raced with the implications of that from the defensive posture.

"To be honest, I don't know," Lahoz replied after a moment of contemplation.

McKenna appreciated his candor, but it didn't quell his nerves. *Any number of things on this ship could kill us. We are messing with biotechnology that we have almost no understanding of.* He caught himself gripping his Sharpshooter II a little tighter.

Backtracking to the other passageway, he slid through the flaps, feeling a slightly different air pressure on the other side. The environmental suit he wore over his body armor seemed to hug his body tighter, and the increased pressure was noticeable in his ears. It was a narrower passage, enough so he could touch both side walls. The angle it went up was steep, though the spongy floor surface made the climb easier. At the top, he saw the passage twist to the left, then to the right, narrowing even more.

The floor leveled out at one point, and there he found Thun with his sub-section, standing before several of the flap-like doors. Immediately he saw several small jellyfish-like creatures on the ceiling and walls. They were football-sized, opaque with hints of blue and green, and were moving slowly along the surfaces, leaving behind a slick goo in their wake. They seemed oblivious to the humans standing near them.

"We haven't touched them," Thun said. "They are almost cute."

Nothing in the ship was adorable to McKenna. Everything represented a potential risk, and he was quick to remind his men about that. "Keep your weapons at the ready. Trust nothing."

"Sir," the lance corporal returned. "These are the little ones, wait until you see the big ones." He gestured to one of the ship's hatches, opening it with the barrel of his weapon enough for McKenna to step through. As he moved through, a rush of water surged past his boots, pouring into the space where he was standing.

The chamber was more like a cavern, easily some twenty meters in height, dropping at least that far down. Where he stood was a balcony of sorts, though there was no guardrail. Filling the center of the room were oblong objects clinging to stalk-like projections from the ceiling. The balcony had a steep slope off that matched the curve of the walls down to the floor where the hanging organs (*Is that what they are?*) hung. They were misshapen, strangely distorted, almost a pinkish hue, and seemed to be glowing. The floor of the massive chamber was a transparent fluid he presumed was water, about a half-meter deep. The light from his helmet reflected off it onto the greenish-gray walls.

Off to his right, he saw what Thun had been referring to, a large jellyfish creature, a blurry crimson color. It was hovering over what looked like a scar in the wall material. *I wonder if that was where the aliens were firing their cutter weapons?* It seemed indifferent to the presence of the humans on the platform. Where it had moved, the slick trail it left behind was crusting up over the cut, apparently sealing it in its wake.

McKenna noticed he was sweating more than outside; apparently the temperature was warmer in this chamber. The back of his head ached. He'd had a headache since they had come to the ship, but now it seemed more persistent and painful.

"Remarkable," said Dr. Lahoz, staring at the hanging blobs of fleshy material.

"What are they?" McKenna asked.

"I have no idea."

"Then why call them remarkable?"

Lahoz gave him a cockeyed glance. "Major, have you ever seen anything like this before?"

"Only in my nightmares."

"These are some sort of glands or organs—larger than anything we have ever seen on this planet."

One of the scientists at his side spoke up. "Sir, do you want a sample of that tissue?"

Dr. Lahoz nodded.

The science team broke out a rope to lower the man down.

"Do you really think that's a good idea?" McKenna said, casting a glance back at the jellyfish creature methodically creeping along the wall.

"We've been cutting small samples all along," Lahoz confidently replied. "We are not taking much. It would be less than a pinprick to a creature this size."

McKenna was a tough, battle-tested Royal Marine—a bloody decorated Sovereign pilot. He also had a minor hatred of getting shots. "Sometimes pinpricks can hurt like hell," he muttered back. In the back of his mind, he wanted to have them stop and pull the scientist back up.

Is this any more risky than anything else we have done?

The scientist waded into the water coming up on the closest of the hanging organ-like growths. Using a laser cutter, he cut off a small piece of tissue and put it in a canister that he attached to his belt.

Before he could let out a sigh of relief, there was a noise from above, a wet slithering sound. Glancing up, weapon at the ready, he saw a slit open. Sliding out of it was what appeared at first to be a tentacle. It dropped down quickly, attaching to one of the organs for support as it slithered down. Then came the top or head of the creature. It was an open maw, rimmed with teeth. There were no eyes, simply a mouth, ringed with smaller tentacles.

This is some sort of massive snake or eel!

Instinctively he aimed his weapon at the head. "Get out of there!" he called to the scientist below.

Frantically the other scientists started to pull their comrade up. The head of the creature let go of the organ and plunged downward with incredible speed. The scientist screamed as the large maw opened wide, coming right at him.

McKenna fired, as did Thun and his men. The bullets hit the skin of the creature but the speed it was dropping made it impossible to see if they had done any damage. The open maw came down over the scientist, swallowing him in a single gulp. The smaller tentacles grabbed him, assisting in consuming the man. McKenna adjusted his aim, not wanting any penetrating shots to pass through and kill the scientist that they were trying to rescue.

A few stray bullets hit the organs, which initiated more of the sucking sounds from above. Two more creatures slid out, dropping down the organs into the water. Duty called on the major to try to recover the scientist below, but he realized that the more gunfire that erupted in the room, the more of the creatures they would have to contend with.

Damn it all!

"Hold your fire. Fall back," he ordered, hating every syllable uttered.

"But Dr. Krane!" Lahoz called out.

Glancing down at the first creature, its devouring of the scientist was all but complete. There were indications that at least some of the bullets had hit; the water swirled with a blackish substance he assumed was blood. It quickly became diluted and seemed to vanish. There was no sign of Dr. Krane other than a bulge in the creature's body.

"All units, we are withdrawing," he transmitted to the forces aboard the alien vessel. The other two creatures that had dropped were already starting to climb the walls heading for the balcony. McKenna waited until everyone was through the flap-like hatch, then he backed through it. His mind mentally mapped their path back. "Alright, lads, we are pulling out." The aching in the back of his head was suppressed only by the rush of adrenaline he got as they began to retreat.

We pushed too hard; we pushed our luck as well, he thought. *We pushed and the bollocks pushed back.*

CHAPTER 15

Operation Sulaco
West of the Crash Site, East Coast of Greenland

Captain Wade leaned over the portable secured communications unit in the privacy of one of the empty dome enclosures. It wasn't holographic, there wasn't enough bandwidth for such comms, and in some respects, he was thankful for it. He watched the screen and adjusted his camera as he waited to sync up.

He had wanted to go into the ship, to see the interior of the vessel for himself. *I owe that to the two dead scientists we have.* He held that urge in check with the responsibility he had to keep the team secure. He could have assigned one of the other members of Omega the responsibility for the defense, but he wanted to oversee it personally, at least during the initial penetration. *If there's some sort of reaction triggered by the ship, it will come fairly fast.* So far though, his GRDs and scouts had not reported any activity coming from the sea.

The deaths of the two scientists only steeled his resolve to get the mission done as quickly and safely as possible. *This ship is full of dangers that we cannot predict or understand. Its size alone is a massive challenge.*

A conference room flickered into focus, with at least eight people facing him. The contrast of circumstances was more than evident. They were in suits, pristine, in a wood paneled room, warm and comfortable. Even through the insulated floor panels, the cold was penetrating his boots and keeping him chilled.

They will go home tonight to their family and friends, while my people and I will to be stuck here.

He recognized Colonel Slade sitting at the table. Wade didn't know him well, but from what he had heard, the man was some sort of genius. He had gotten some time with him prior to their departure from the Penetrator and respected him.

General Lawrence "Weasel" Lee sat at the head of the conference room table, as grim and gruff as ever. As the commander of US Special Forces, Lee's presence on the call only emphasized the importance of Operation Sulaco. He didn't recognize the other individuals but was thankful that Lee was present. *He's a soldier's soldier. He's forgotten more about Special Forces ops than most men know. He's the father of Omega Force as well, so he knows what we can and cannot do.* Having him and Colonel Slade at the table gave him two rational people he could trust.

"Captain," Lee began. "We've read your last report with a great deal of interest. I regret the loss of the two scientists so soon in your exploration."

"I regret that as well, sir. We are being much more careful with our exploration protocols."

"These folks from the CIA and State Department have some concerns over your cooperation with the British."

There it is—the reason for the urgent message and this meeting.

"I'm not entirely comfortable with it myself. But then again, I don't think my British counterpart, Major McKenna, is either."

"Dale Seudemeyer, State," a young man in a pristine suit spoke up. "This arrangement you've made is unacceptable. Your so-called compromise has essentially turned over half of the vessel to the British with nothing in recompense."

"Mr. Seudemeyer," Wade countered, "I didn't ask for anything because they didn't have anything to offer. They were here first, and we both were attacked by the Fish. For all we know, they are planning a counterattack at any minute. Fighting them didn't seem to be a good move and a standoff only works in favor of the Fish, not us. I made a judgment call, one recommended by the advisor that I was provided. It's not perfect, but it's the best we can hope for." He had to admit that Falto had probably been right in her proposal to work with the British. The part that he struggled with was that it was contrary to orders he had been given.

"Who is this advisor?"

Colonel Slade responded before Wade could. "Natalia Falto."

"What qualifies her to proffer any advice about the Brits?" Seudemeyer demanded.

"Nothing that I am aware of," Slade replied calmly. "She is, however, an expert on the aliens' technology. She was held as a POW for months in one of their facilities. She's one of a handful of people that has been with the Fish in their natural habitats."

"What I'm hearing is that she knows nothing about the geopolitical implications of compromising with the British."

Slade was unshaken. "That is likely true. But she is there, with Captain Wade. If she made the suggestion, I'd trust her instincts. Clearly Captain Wade trusted her too. I understand the State Department's concerns, but you need to know that these people are in the field. They've already had a battle with the Fish and likely expect another one is coming. We aren't helping them with trying to call the shots from here." Wade's liking of Colonel Slade increased with every word he spoke.

Seudemeyer opted to ignore Slade's words, turning his ire back on Wade. "Your actions have cost us," he snapped. "I don't think you see the big picture here."

I love it when someone leads with "you're ignorant." It usually means they don't have much of an argument to begin with.

"Enlighten me," he said through gritted teeth.

"Every nation on the planet is impacted by this conflict," Seudemeyer replied, seemingly pleased that he was able to talk down to Wade. "We are in its early stages. Sooner or later we are going to get the upper hand. Much of that will be in overcoming the alien technology. The countries that do that first will determine the new world order when this conflict ends. That ship, that you so graciously allowed the British to access, represents the potential to leapfrog our efforts."

Wade didn't appreciate the discussion nor the implication that he wasn't intelligent. *This fool thinks I didn't consider all of this.* "With all due respect, I know why I am here. If you wanted someone to play diplomat, you should get your own butt on a plane and drop in. In the meantime, I am the man on the ground and I'm in command. I made a judgment call. You may not agree with it, but playing Mexican standoff with the Limeys might have left us with nothing. It's not my fault that your intel people didn't make the right call and give us a heads-up that the damn Royal Marines were here ahead of us."

That made the young woman with Asian features wince. "We didn't have time for the kind of analysis that would have tipped us off that the British were on the move."

"Who are you?" Wade demanded.

"Special Agent Markin, CIA."

"Your failure is a big reason that I had to improvise a solution, Ms. Markin."

It would have been nice to know that the damned Brits were going to be here.

General Lee cut off the discussion and brought it back to center. "None of this is getting us anywhere. I won't have people blaming my people on the ground for doing their jobs." His words made even the older Seudemeyer lean back with crimson rising on his cheeks. "Captain, do you have any indication as to how the British team is fairing in their exploration?"

"They went into the ship around the same time we did. Our people have been in there for a total of three hours, but it is a slow go of things from the messages I've been passed. Many of the chambers are filled with water under a great deal of pressure. Entering those chambers floods the ones we've been in. In many places our people are waist to chest deep in water. There's been gunfire inside the ship, both from our team and the British, at least that is what we are detecting."

"Dr. Arlo Campbell," another man at the table spoke up. "Have our people found the propulsion system or the power source for the ship?"

Wade shook his head. "We have code phrases arranged for them to transmit if they do, but so far we haven't gotten it. My intel officer has been monitoring their bodycams and real-time mapping where they've been. Despite being in there a while, their progress has been slow."

"Any signs of the crew or the more hostile aliens?" General Lee asked.

"They did find several of the Class Eleven aliens."

"Alive?" the General pressed.

"Not exactly. These were mostly dead. Apparently they were being absorbed into the ship itself."

"To what end?" Dr. Campbell asked.

"Unknown."

They're the Fish. If it is something creepy and weird, that is in their wheelhouse.

There was a few moments of silence. Wade was fairly sure they were processing the information the same as he was, struggling with the fragmentary bits and pieces and attempting to make sense of it all. General Lee spoke up.

"Anything else?"

"Dr. Schrivener sent me an update just prior to this call. It is her belief that the ship itself is a living organism. There are indications that it is not entirely dead from the crash."

"We should kill it once and for all," Seudemeyer said. "If it is alive, then the Fish are going to come and try and rescue it. If we kill it, that should remove the threat."

Ashton Slade weighed in quickly. "We have no idea how the aliens would react to such an action. The one thing we know about them is that they don't always respond in a way that we can anticipate. Look at what the Russians did in Murmansk. They lobbed a nuke at the aliens, and they unleashed their own weapon of mass destruction right back. On top of that, if you blow the ship up, our ability to learn from it is gone. Assuming Dr. Schrivener is correct, we would be left with nothing more than dead bits and pieces of alien tissue. We would never be able to piece anything back together enough for it to be of use."

"Colonel Slade is right," Doctor Campbell added quickly. "Destroying the ship will remove any context for whatever samples we gather. Yes, it's freezing there and they will be preserved, but they won't be of any in-depth scientific value."

General Lee nodded as Campbell finished. "Everyone in this room needs to understand one thing—those are my people on the ground there. We will not be taking any action that might trigger a devastating response that will kill them. Not at this stage yet. At the same time, we will not allow this *organism* to be retaken by the Fish."

Wade was pleased to hear that the general had his back.

Everyone is more than willing to play dangerous games with our lives on the line. Lee understands the risks.

"Thank you, sir."

"Don't thank me yet, Captain," the general replied. "We're going to position one of our heavy drones out of Thule. If it appears that the aliens are going to retake the vessel, you will have the ability to call in a strike and take it out. This puts the burden on you to make the call."

"It's my boots on the ground, sir, so I have no issue with controlling my own fate." Saying those words, he realized that his level of responsibility had just multiplied exponentially. It was one thing to control the mission and the military assets. It was another to have the ability to blow up the thing they had come to inspect.

The participants from around the table started to leave.

"If I may, General," Wade said, "I'd like to talk to you alone for a moment."

"If you don't mind, I'd like to sit in on this," Slade stated. It made some sense to Wade. Omega reported to Lee, but ultimately, the operation was under Colonel Slade's purview.

Lee nodded and waited until the door to the room closed. "It's just us, Captain."

"General," Wade hesitated. "These parameters for this mission that I'm working with. I've got the British here and have to deal with them. Having these civvies call the shots in terms of what I can and can't do while I am here—it presents a set of risks…risks that have already cost us two people."

"I understand. I didn't want to drag you into a political turf war, but that was unavoidable."

"I need the ability to make my own calls here. Those people, they are not present. This could get fluid very quickly."

General Lee nodded. "And that may mean breaking the parameters they are dropping on top of you."

"Yes."

Lee wetted his lips then spoke. "Here's my order to you—do what you think is best. We need the intel out of that ship. If State or the CIA raises a stink, I will back you all the way to the wall. All I ask is that you try it their way. If that fails, do what you think is best."

Wade sighed heavily. "Thank you."

"What else do you need?" Lee asked.

"From the sound if it, the team has gathered a lot of biosamples. If the Fish show up, I don't want to risk losing what they've already gathered. If we can arrange for getting these out of here each day, it would be appreciated. Also, one of our generators went belly up, making the habitats a little cold for the civilians."

"We can make that happen," Lee assured him. That was all the general had to say. His word was worth anything in writing from anyone else in the room facing him.

"We appreciate what you are doing there, Captain," Colonel Slade added. As he glanced at the two men at the table that were looking at him, it was hard to believe. Several of the people there hadn't talked at all, but were furiously making notes on their digipads, no doubt outlining his perceived incompetence.

Other than the military people on the call, the others are all here to criticize how this was executed. If this is a success, they will claim the credit for it. If it fails, it will be an albatross around my neck.

The screen went blank after that, and he sighed. Bryan found himself longing for his ASHUR cockpit. *I am a warrior. I worked hard to get into Omega Team because of that. My career has been focused with being pointed at what people want destroyed and fulfilling that mission. This level of bullshit is annoying. These Washington-types all think they're in a Tom Clancy novel, calling the shots from the Situation Room. They are in way over their heads. If I'm in my Python, I have complete control of everything I see. That is where the universe has meaning—from my saddle.*

Wade knew he had given up a lot to be in the military, and even more to be in the Omega Team. Congress had hauled General Lee up to Capitol Hill several times to grill him for the activities of the unit, and that was before the Fish showed up. Bryan found it impossible to maintain relationships or start a family being in Omega. *I couldn't ask someone to marry me knowing the kind of work I do.* The only people he could confide in were those in the unit. Given the secrecy of the operations he took part in, the things he saw and experienced simply stayed compartmentalized and stored in the dark recesses of his mind.

He had assumed that at some point he would retire and start living a "normal" life. With the Fish showing up, that was a forlorn fantasy. The word had unofficially been spread throughout all of the services that retirements were on hold. Everyone was needed for the war effort, especially seasoned fighters. He accepted that reality intellectually. Emotionally, it had been a gut punch. It wasn't that he wanted to leave right away, but losing that option was still mentally painful. He remembered General Lee's own dictum: *I have to accept the things I cannot control; destroy the things that are attempting to shatter my calm.*

Shutting off the satellite comms system, he laid his left wrist out in front of him and punched in the channel to talk to the team that was still aboard the alien vessel. "This is Crockett to Crosscut."

Captain Wertan's voice came back. "This is Crosscut."

"Sitrep."

"I was just going to contact you. We found something here,

something that we think you ought to see."

"You want to transmit it?"

"Negative," Wertan replied. "I think this is something you need to lay eyes on."

"I'm on my way." As he rose, there was a feeling in the pit of his stomach that he wasn't going to like whatever this was.

* * *

Captain Wertan met him at the egress point. The hole that had been cut by a laser had been enlarged, that much was obvious. He had left Lieutenant Davis in charge of maintaining their security perimeter and keeping his eyes out for the return of the Fish. Davis was good, a thoroughly trained killer. His squat, wide Honey Badger had been repaired from the last engagement and he took the assignment without so much as a question. That alone gave Wade a sense of comfort.

"What is it?" Wade asked as Wertan led him through the hole.

"We found some aliens…a kind we've never seen before." Wertan led him through chambers and corridors that Wade tried to take in.

I feel like a microbe moving around inside some animal.

"Dead?" he asked as they came to a large fleshy slit. Wertan parted it and Wade entered, masking his trepidation. On the other side, he paused and glanced back at the doorway.

This is just as they were detailed in Falto's reports—giant lady parts.

"No sir, not exactly alive either." They climbed and twisted through several doors and corridors. The passageways were waist deep in cold water. The soft bounce of the floor gave him the illusion of good footing as he sloshed through the film-covered fluids that were everywhere. The slight list of the ship made him almost lose his balance at times.

It's bad enough that we are doing this in this cold water, but the angle of this ship throws off my footing.

It took nearly twenty minutes of wading through the deep corridors, both up and down. In the lower ones, the water was as deep as his head, forcing him to hold his weapon above him as he sloshed through. Along the way, he passed Rangers that stood on guard, each giving him a nod as they passed. Finally, Wertan led him to a large chamber. It was nearly forty meters in length, easily five meters in height. The rest of the science team was present, along with the Rangers—all of which had their weapons trained on the objects in the center of the room.

The room was very deep in water, he saw that through the reflections of the lights that everyone carried. Rising from the floor were translucent tubes, apparently filled with a light green fluid. There were ten tubes, and as he looked closely at them, he could see bubbles rise from the floor and drift up in the fluid—like an antique lava lamp.

In each of the tubes was a creature curled up into an oblong shape. They looked slightly like Crabs, but only vaguely, and they were smaller than any Crabs Wade had ever seen. They lacked the big front claws, instead having large bony hook-like appendages. The tail section didn't look like the familiar scorpion's, instead it was a thick muscular tentacle with a flap at the end, covered with little spikes. The head was covered with urchin-like spikes sticking backwards over the raised torso.

It was the mouth…*no, maw,* that got his attention. It had a large glossy black beak, much like a giant squid. The eyes looked closed, but it was hard to tell. They were ball-like orbs of darkness that seemed outright evil. The color of the creatures was difficult to discern given the green liquid they were in. Their bodies were curved and coiled up to fit in the tubes. While none of them moved, they seemed to emit a sense of danger—that at any moment they could emerge and attack. There was something menacing about the creatures that was hard to define.

"Well, those are sufficiently creepy," he said. "I take it they are alive."

Dr. Schrivener spoke up, "There's no way for us to know for sure. We've seen some mostly dead aliens so far, laborers. Those are being absorbed into the ship. These aren't. To me, that means they might be alive."

Wade's mind was trying to process everything as he stood inside the alien spacecraft. *The ship is absorbing its dead? If these things are alive, why? They aren't the usual Crabs—these things are different. What purpose do they fulfill?* What finally kicked in was his military thinking, ingrained and imprinted in his brain for years. "I'd like to kill them, but if we start shooting, in this tight space, they might be on top of us before we emptied a single magazine. This isn't the place for gunplay."

"Agreed," Wertan replied. "We could plant some charges in here, pull back, blow them to hell before they wake up."

Memories of the importance of the ship came back to him. "We have no idea the amount of damage explosions in here might cause, and there's still a lot of ship we need to explore. Let's set up a camera to monitor them, relay the signal to CP. For now, I'd rather not blow up a part of the ship and risk us destroying something important."

"Thank you," Schrivener said. Clearly Wertan had already suggested blowing them up before Wade's arrival.

It isn't the wrong call. It's just the wrong call right now. We have been in this ship for six hours and from the reports I've gotten, we haven't found any of their critical systems yet.

"We are just about at the end of the power on these breathers," Wade told the gathered teams. "Let's pull back and get cleaned up, then plan for the next penetration."

Six hours in this place is like six hours in a house of horror at Halloween. Everyone has got to be ragged. We need to get out and rest up. There's a lot of ship we have yet to explore.

CHAPTER 16

Operation Sulaco
American Base Camp, West of the Crash Site,
East Coast of Greenland

Falto had almost been numb during the scrub down in the decontamination chamber. She had been surprised at the amount of material that had come off her suit that she had carried with her from the ship. The samples that the scientists brought back were secured in a special containment unit. Even her weapon was washed with a UV beam to supposedly kill off anything she might have brought with her from the wrecked spacecraft. The short personal shower washed away more than her sweat—it flushed away anxiety.

We already lost two people. Should I have done or said something differently? It had been a surprise, one that she didn't want to go through again.

Being away from the ship brought about a sense of relief. The team shuffled into the commons area for a meal. She ate, but by the time she finished, she struggled to remember what it was she had eaten. The only part of the meal that stood out in her mind as she sat at the table was the Tylenol she took to ease the headache she had gotten during the exploration.

It wasn't that the food tasted bad or good; her mind was elsewhere. In some ways, still back aboard the ship. The sights she had seen were different from those of her captivity, but eerily similar. They stirred memories that she had hoped had faded but were brought to the forefront of her mind, especially now as she relaxed and was away from them. She stared down at her empty disposable tray, lost in her memories.

"You okay?" a voice shattered her jumble of dark reminiscences.

Turning, she saw the Ranger that had been with her during the firefight. She glanced at his name tag, WO Rosales, then to his penetrating hazel eyes. It was one of the few times she could see his entire face, given the masks on the ECHs. She could finally associate a face with his name and voice. "I'm fine. Just detoxing from the crawl."

"I know what you mean. That was pretty nerve-wracking."

"Are you following me?"

"Don't let it go to your head. I have a natural tendency to keep close to people that might need some assistance. I was wrong in your case, I think."

"I can use all of the help I can get."

"I'm a little surprised to hear you say that, Sergeant. You're the expert—you lived with the Fish. Everyone knows your background. I just knew it had been a while since you fired a gun in anger."

She was thankful his response had nothing to do with her being a POW. "I don't think my expertise is of much use so far. This ship is different from where I was held."

"I don't know. You identified those Class Elevens, the laborers."

"That was nothing. I'd seen them before. Aside from that, I'm not really much of an advisor."

"Don't count yourself short. I know you are contributing. When the Fish showed up, you grabbed an ACR and went topside to fight them."

"That was me just doing Marine shit."

"Well, there are times when we need Marine shit," Rosales offered. "After all you've been through, you didn't have to come here at all. Word is you volunteered for this."

"I had to," she confided in a lower tone of voice. "I've been through a lot of shit. I half-assed hoped that coming would somehow give me some peace."

"How's that working for you?"

Falto winced. "Not great."

"Well, we've only spent a few hours in the ship. There's a lot of it we haven't explored yet."

Flato dipped her head, looking down at the empty food tray. "All I have managed to accomplish is to piss off Captain Wade."

"I would have thought that pissing off officers was a finely honed trait in the Marine Corps." The mention of the Corps gave her momentary focus as he continued. "While I grant you, most Marines are incredibly disciplined, they are also bull-headed, at least from my personal experience."

He's not too far off from the mark.

"We know our jobs and do them well."

To his credit, Rosales knew enough not to push Falto's Marine Corps button too many times. "So you pissed off Wade. So what? Did you do it for the right reasons?"

She returned her gaze to his face. "Yes. Squabbling with the British wasn't going to get us anywhere. If anything, it might have cost us when the Fish come back."

"You think they will?"

"I do," she confidently replied. "They don't stop. They don't give up. From all of the footage I've watched, they don't experience fear, not like we do. We bloodied them, but that just tells them to come back with overwhelming force."

Rosales nodded in agreement. "That's been my experience as well. We slugged it out with them in Seattle, down in Florida, New York, and, God help me, the Battle of Secaucus, New Jersey. If they are afraid, I've never seen them show it—at least not the Crabs, Frogs, or Bosses. I think the Foxes are less afraid than they are sneaky. They will run when you shoot at them, but I don't think it's fear. It's because they are looking for a better position to kill you from."

"They don't have any...what's the word? Empathy. That's it. They don't care what they do to humans." Falto's bitterness crept through her words. "They experimented on me—painful stuff. I lost parts of my body to them, but they never seemed to care."

"If you don't experience pain the way we do, I guess it's hard to show any mercy," Rosales theorized.

Mercy was a word that Falto couldn't apply to the aliens. She remembered the Alpha, the Boss, that seemed to relish what was happening to her. "There's more to them than a lack of emotions or pain. They seem to enjoy what they are doing. I've seen it up close and personal."

"It must have been hell."

"When you go to church, they talk about hell being fire and brimstone. It's not. I spent months in hell. It's cold, wet, and dark. You're hungry all the time. When you do eat, your stomach cramps and you shit yourself. There is torture and pain. You have to watch people you care about die, sometimes in your arms. The demons, they are real. The agony is real. The Church has a lot of learn about what hell really is."

"After all you've been through, do you still believe in God and Satan?"

Falto nodded once, slowly and firmly. "More than ever." *I've been a good Catholic most of my life. No one ever asked me if I actually believed the Church.*

"I would have thought that losing all that you did would have shaken your faith."

"Before all of this, I never was deeply religious. Oh, I went to church and all, but mostly out of obligation to my madre. Like most people, I believed in Jesus and the teachings of the Church, but I had a lot of questions. Then I got captured. There were times I wondered where God was. I questioned how He could allow the things that the aliens inflicted on me to have happened. I committed a sin, I questioned whether God existed."

"What changed?"

"I survived. God had to have had a reason to let me survive all that I went though. I don't know for sure what that reason is, but I know He has some sort of design for me. It's the only thing that makes sense."

Rosales cocked his head. "I was never the religious type. My parents were diehard Episcopalians, but not me. I did everything I could to get out of going to church. I've fought in a lot of battlespaces and never saw a hint of God anywhere there. I *did* see a lot of suffering and death, though."

"You lived."

"Thanks to my training, skills, and the firepower I carry."

"Perhaps He hasn't revealed His plan for you yet."

Rosales chuckled. "If He does exist, I hope He makes it clear soon. We work in a dangerous profession. I dance with death often and when I do, it's hard and fast."

Falto smiled at the warrant officer. "The thing about faith is simple—you just never know." She rose to her feet.

"Never know what?"

"Exactly," she said, turning and putting her tray in the recycler. She started down to the sleeping quarters for the civilians where she was housed. She came upon Dr. Schrivener, toweling off her hair from a shower.

"Getting ready to crash?" Schrivener asked.

"I need a little downtime."

"Me too. We started some tests on the samples we gathered. The AI-banked electron microscopes we brought will be going through what we collected for hours, not to mention our DNA sifters. The neutron bombardment set is already giving us some great data to go over. I have another small exploration team going back during the night to get more samples. After all of the things that I've seen today, it's going to be hard to sleep though, no matter how tired I am."

For Falto the sights and images that she had seen were not exciting. They stirred bad memories and flirted with the nightmares in the dark corners of her mind. "We barely scratched the surface in terms of exploring the ship," she said, avoiding a discussion about excitement and why she didn't share it.

"True. We've already learned a great deal more than we knew. A few more days on that ship and our knowledge about them and their technology is bound to leap forward. I had theorized that the ship was one large biological organism. A lot of that was confirmed today. This isn't a construct; this ship is a giant living creature. The aliens we did encounter, they are like microorganisms in our own bodies. Those laborers that were killed in the crash, they are like antibodies in your blood. Even the damage that we saw being repaired, it is growth, like a scab over a cut you might get."

Falto understood why Schrivener was excited. In her mind, she tempered that thrill with the realities that ship represented. *We are just like little microbes in its system. At what point will the ship think we are a threat and respond to remove us?* She was sure she didn't want to be present when that happened. "That ship is dangerous."

Schrivener cocked her head. "We are being careful."

"I know. But you saw those squid aliens. They are there for a reason. At any point they may unleash them on us. Who knows what else we are going to stumble across as we poke around. If it is just a big living thing, it might look at us like an infection and send stuff to get rid of us."

"That's possible—but so far, we haven't seen an indication of that. We are so small, we're just insignificant."

"That could change at any time," Falto cautioned.

"True. But risk is part of the mission."

"We are poking around with technology that we don't understand. My experience has shown that doing that is dangerous—deadly even."

The doctor smiled. "Sergeant, that's why we have you here." She then turned and headed down the narrow corridor.

Everyone thinks I possess some sort of locker full of knowledge that can save them. I'm afraid they are going to be disappointed.

Falto had no intention of letting anyone down, but there were always things that were beyond her control.

She made her way to the bunks that had been set up. They were five high, which the scientists complained of. *Clearly none of them served in the Marine Corps.* She claimed the top bunk, mostly because the others in the quarters didn't want to climb that high to sleep. Sleeping on the floor simply didn't appear to be an option.

The lighting was already dimmed for the night when she climbed in, sliding into her thermal bag. Pulling the bag up around her face, she curled tight. The room was neither warm nor cold, it hovered near the edge of both, so the bag felt perfect. *I would have killed for a night this comfortable when I was a prisoner.*

As she adjusted herself in the bed, her mind went back to the ship. *Tomorrow will be harder. I can already see that some of the team members are gaining confidence—and with confidence, there is a chance of overconfidence. People can get sloppy. Also we haven't found the engines or power source. There is a lot of pressure to be the ones to find those first.*

* * *

The briefing the next morning was full of renewed energy; at least that was how it felt to Natalia. The team that had gone in during the night had added to the map of the northern part of the vessel. They had found what appeared to be glands or organs in several areas of the ship, large, the size of automobiles. Their exploration had not found the elusive power source for the ship, the bridge, or anything that looked like it could be the engines.

The water situation was frustrating. Some chambers were filled to the ceiling with pressurized water and couldn't be explored without cold weather SCUBA gear, which the team didn't have. Others, those near the outer skin of the hull, were empty of water. There were no decks, no levels, so it reminded some of the Rangers of spelunking, or so they said. There was talk of getting the diving gear brought in, but it had to come from the States and would take days.

The biggest revelation was a lot of biological techno-mumbo-jumbo, as far as Falto was concerned. Dr. Schrivener indicated that the tests that the scientists had been running all night had made a "remarkable discovery." The mitochondrial DNA that they had been analyzing showed that it was generating an amazing amount of power. Falto had been spared to ask what that meant by Captain Wade.

"At the DNA level, the atomic structure of the cells seems to be able to create energy, a startling amount of it. Our cells all generate some energy, but the stuff we have seen in some of the samples from the ship is beyond anything we could imagine." Different samples came back with varying levels of this energy, or so Falto gathered, but the power was there. When asked if it was dangerous or a threat, Schrivener had been less conclusive. "We haven't seen any indications that this is dangerous. What it does mean is that this ship is still very active, though, despite the crash." For Falto, that was more than enough to make her more cautious.

The weather was clear and crisp. The sun hung low on the horizon, but was there, creating the illusion of warmth. They entered, this time taking a different path, one mapped out by the night team. It took them towards the bow of the ship and downward, where the naval engineers hypothesized the vessel's engine room could be.

WO Rosales moved up beside her as they took one narrow corridor downward, twisting and turning along the way. It was chest deep on Falto, which she hated. It made for slow going and she was thankful when they got to a raised portion that was shallower.

"You sleep last night?" he asked.

"I'm a Marine. I can sleep anywhere."

Rosales chuckled. "I'm a Ranger, I work best with sleep deprivation."

"One thing that the military teaches us that these scientists will never understand is that we can function on little sleep, and when we do drop off, we can do it in any position, any condition, in any environment," Falto added.

They reached an intersection of three of the flesh-doors. Two were marked with spray-painted symbols. One mark indicated that it had been explored already. One was marked with a W, indicating that it was likely filled with pressurized water. There was a tiny digital recorder that had been stuck on the wall, and as Falto passed it, she noticed that the texture material of the wall was starting to envelop the sticky mounting plate of the camera already. *In a few days it will simply be part of the wall.*

The Rangers led through the unmarked doorway. The passage was narrow, wide enough for one person, and required everyone to hunch down to keep their environmental suits from rubbing along the ceiling. Falto followed the Rangers, holding her ACR tight to her suit. Her boot slipped, no doubt thanks to the list angle of the ship, but she caught herself on the wall.

The passageway down got steeper, which made for slower going. Team members slipped and fell several times. After going down and, according to her compass, east, they reached a massive chamber, emerging at the bottom.

A blue spider web–like material filled the chamber. Inside the heart of the room was some sort of transparent bulbous shape, a massive gland-like projection. It was nearly thirty-five meters in diameter, looming overhead. It was suspended in place by stalks, dozens of them, acting like tree trunks holding the web sac in the air. Larger strands of web extended out from the organ and into the walls, ceiling, and floor. Falto and the Rangers were careful to avoid touching those web-like projections. Inside the mass, where multiple web strands connected, were small blobs of a spongey material, with holes. *This is very much alive.* The floor was shin deep in a clear fluid, which sloshed about like water.

As she looked up and around, she saw tiny flickers of amber light, smaller than a pinhead, flashing rapidly through the webs so fast that they were almost a blur. As more headlamps flicked upward, it became harder to see the pulses of light. Some of the lights entered the trunk-like supports that adhered to the chamber's maroon walls. There were millions—*no, billions*—of tiny threads filling the air above her. Her breath picked up tempo as she looked upward as the scientists filed into the chamber. Falto found herself caught in a mix of awe and nervousness.

For a few moments, no one spoke. Falto's headache surged back to the forefront, starting as ripples of dull pain in the back of her head and coming up over her ears, right to her temple. They had taken Tylenol before leaving the compound, but it had been overpowered by the pain she felt. Glancing over at Rosales, she saw that he too was wincing. "Are you feeling the headache too?"

He nodded and she saw that the other Rangers were also narrowing their gazes, their foreheads wrinkling in pain.

This room might be the source of the headaches we have been feeling.

Dr. Schrivener also seemed to struggle with the pain, but it didn't stop her from drinking in the details. "This is beyond remarkable."

Another scientist said, "It's like neurons firing in synapses."

"What does that mean?" a Ranger asked.

"This could be a brain of some sort. If not, some sort of nervous system control center."

"My head is killing me," another Ranger spoke up.

"I need to see if I can measure this," Schrivener said, swinging her pack around and looking for something inside. She struggled to keep the pack out of the water and failed.

"I'll get a sample," another researcher said, pulling out a laser scalpel and leaning on a stalk far enough to reach the sac that hung over them.

Falto focused on that researcher. *This is a mistake!* "No, don't do that!" she called.

The researcher ignored her, or didn't hear her. Either way, she reached up and started cutting a tiny piece of the sac with her scalpel. Another researcher splashed over to her, clearly meaning to help. A thin wisp of smoke rose from the cut as the first scientist secured it in a tiny container, then moved back to the floor, sloshing in the water.

A small softball-sized jellyfish-like creature rose from the water they stood in, sliding up a stalk to where the cut had been made. It was greenish in color and moved with remarkable speed. It adhered to where the cut had been made and stopped. The second researcher took out a camera and snapped several shots. The flashes reflected all over the chamber.

The water near the researchers that had gotten the sample seemed to churn and bubble. A gurgling noise came up. The one with the camera lowered it and looked down to see that it was all around their feet.

Falto was a good five meters away, unsure what to do next. "Move!" she called out.

This time the pair of scientists heard her. Both tried to run, but in a panic, in deep water, one stumbled. As she rose, someone else did from the churning water—another jellyfish-like creature. This was not a small one, but large, almost two meters in size and bright crimson. In a quick motion it shot across the surface and onto the back of the waterlogged researcher, its long tentacle arms wrapped around the scientist as she struggled. The second researcher, in a panic, fell.

Rosales and another Ranger moved in to try to help the scientist as the jellyfish pulled her down in the water. Tentacles wrapped around the second scientist, pulling her under. There was no rushing in the watery fluid. One tentacle lapped up at the Ranger trying to assist Rosales and hit him. "Ow!" he called out. Rosales grabbed his fellow Ranger and pulled him away.

Then came the scream from the scientist with the sample. It was agony and terror swirled together into one piercing shriek. There was no sound from the one that had simply been grabbed. Another Ranger aimed his weapon down at the alien, but held his fire, knowing his shots would only go right through the creature and hit the pair of researchers.

Falto felt a surge in her headache. She wanted to grab her head, but with the sealed hood over her helmet, that was impossible. The helmet lights seemed to only intensify her agony. She saw one of the scientists rip the hood off his environmental suit and grasp his own head.

It's not just me!

The scientists with the jellyfish stopped struggling and the water started to show churns of pink, then crimson. The jellyfish contracted for a second, and in doing so, seemed to suck the scientists into its body. The translucent material allowed everyone to see what was happening, and what Falto saw tore at her soul. There was a movement in one of them, her arms and legs twitching violently, but Falto hoped that it was involuntary—because if it wasn't, it meant that the scientist might still have a bit of life.

Most of the scientist's environmental suit was gone, it was melting away into thin blackened bits of material moving inside of the jellyfish. Her right leg was oozing blood, and the white marrow of the knee joint was easily visible. The hood she had worn was gone, and her jaw bone and teeth were exposed. Where her flesh remained, it was dissolving, half-melting, half-bubbling and fizzing away inside of the creature, turning into bloody eddies. The inside of the creature seeped with swirls of her blood. The only thankful aspect of the image was that the scientist was no longer suffering.

The second scientist started to struggle, almost as if she were dog-paddling. Like her comrade, her protective suit dissolved into tiny black bits. The motion stopped, replaced with a pinkish blood inside the jellyfish.

Falto knew they were dead.

"Sweet Jesus," cursed Rosales as he dragged the wounded Ranger up towards the door.

Schrivener stood there, stunned, almost statue-like. Her eyes were rolling back, no doubt from the headache. The doctor's knees started to buckle, and Falto caught her before she fell.

"We need to move! Everyone out, now!" she commanded.

Some moved, but others were like Schrivener, paralyzed by the agony in their brains.

Natalia dragged the doctor by her armpits up the slope and out, slipping once. When she got her to the next chamber, she went back and grabbed a Ranger, who had toppled over into the water. He was significantly heavier, given the additional gear he was wearing. Falto's flesh arm ached from the pull along with her lower back, but she was thankful that her bionics didn't give her the feedback of stress. Methodically, one foot after the other, she stomped her way up. Rosales passed her, going down to retrieve the scientist that had torn his hood off.

The throbbing of her head was far worse when in the room with the giant jellyfish and the organ, but she pushed through the agony. It took three more trips, but she managed to recover everyone other than the scientist who was being reduced to nothing more than a skeleton. All had fallen over in the pinkish water and were floating in their environmental suits. It made them easy to find and difficult to extract, but she had the advantage of having bionic limbs.

Once outside of the room, the headaches subsided. Slowly people who had passed out regained their consciousness. After retrieving the last one, she stood, wet with sweat, looming over a jumble of bodies. It was the only blessing of the deep water, it made pulling them out easier.

"Richardson has gone into some sort of shock," Rosales said, kneeling next to the Ranger that had been stung by the jellyfish. "We've got to get him back to the base."

Two more Rangers forced themselves to their feet, slung their weapons, and started to move and drag their fallen comrade out. One toppled over face-first into the water. Reaching out with her bionic arm, she locked her grip on the back of his environmental suit and pulled him out of the room where Rosales helped her get him clear. A passing glance at Rosales showed the wrinkles on his forehead filling with sweat and his left eye horribly bloodshot, almost to the point where she wondered if he could see out of it.

"What about you, did that tentacle get you?" Natalia asked.

He shook his head. "I felt a little sting but so far, so good. My head is killing me."

Falto moved next to Dr. Schrivener, whose face was drained of color. Her eyes were bloodshot as if she had been drinking heavily the night before, and there was a small droplet of blood coming out of one nostril. She lay slumped, half in and out of the water, limp. "Doc, we need to pull back—get out of here."

Schrivener nodded numbly. Falto looked over the half-conscious bodies that were stirring, still in agony. "I know everyone is hurting, but we need to get out of here—now!" The tone and temper of her voice was not hers, but she recognized it—it was the same as

Hannibal's. It was the Marine command voice.

People started to grope themselves up to a standing position. "Come on, people—move it!" she urged, and they did, one by one. Those that struggled the most, she helped. The team that had been so enthusiastic an hour earlier was shaken, battered, and exhausted. Somehow, in all of that, Natalia found a reserve of strength. She shared that energy to help the team start the long lumbering stagger out of the spacecraft.

CHAPTER 17

Operation Durendal
Crash Site, East Coast of Greenland

Major McKenna looked at the chamber and was just short of awestruck with its size. Having served aboard aircraft carriers in the past, he had seen large rooms aboard ships before. This one was different in several aspects. First, no one knew for sure what this room held, and second, this was aboard an alien spacecraft.

The room was irregular in size. He was looking in at it from what was best described as a portal, a mostly transparent organic material that allowed viewing the room beyond. The interior was illuminated by the walls, a dull yellowish green glow that his scientists claimed was some sort of bioluminescent material. The chamber was filled with a fluid; occasional bubbles drifted by the viewing portal, moving slowly...an indication of how thick the material was. Beyond the fluid were what looked like tubes, half a meter in diameter, and running in an erratic pattern from one side of the room to another. The tubes were shimmering white or so it appeared through the fluid. There were nearly fifty of them, each seemingly randomly placed in the liquid. The ends of the tubes were a series of snake-like vines running to the chamber's walls.

"Alright, doctor, what exactly am I looking at?" he asked Dr. Lahoz who hovered near him.

"Look at the radiation readings we are getting from this chamber," Lahoz said, putting a Geiger counter in front of him. The needle was pointing to the upper right and the device beeped at a high pace.

There was a moment where his nerves failed him. *Radiation!* Fear was something that Andrew had courted his entire life. It was part of his chosen career in the Royal Marines. He had always prided himself in hiding any fears he had from others. The thought of radiation, and hearing the beeps on the Geiger counter, had caught him unprepared. His face flushed as he looked down at the device, then back at Lahoz. "I can't read this. Are we in any danger here?" Just saying those words, he bought enough time to get on top of his moment of panic.

"We are relatively safe here. You'd have to be in this area for hours before you get your max dose of rems."

That's a bloody relief!

"I take it the fact that these are radioactive is important."

"It is indeed, Major. First off we are not picking up any specific radioactive isotopes in that room."

"Meaning?"

"Radiation usually needs a source, be it uranium or other refined elements. These are all organic. What is making them radioactive apparently is biologically based."

McKenna wasn't sure how to interpret that bit of information. *We know their weapons and everything else is biologically based, so I guess this isn't entirely a surprise.*

"I take it that's remarkable."

"It is. Radiation is a physical or chemical phenomenon, not biological. That is accepted science. Somehow the aliens are able to generate radiation without the physical components, but biologically. It shouldn't be possible, but it is. Further proof of that is that the radiation levels we see here are changing. So this isn't some material that has been exposed to radioactive elements; it is increasing and decreasing in a pattern."

There was a time in Andrew's life when he enjoyed science. He had fond memories of chemistry class, watching the unique interactions of chemicals. This was different though. It was a level of complexity that went over his head entirely. "Is this a risk to the team?" was all he could muster.

Lahoz shook his head. "We don't think so, not unless they increase dramatically."

"Doctor, how exactly is this information useful for us?"

The question clearly caught Lahoz off guard. "I'm not entirely sure. This seems to be a power source for the ship, or part of one. It's the first sign we have had of an energy source of any consequence."

"So this is their engine room?"

"We don't know. It is simply an energy source. Those objects could be large batteries that power the propulsion of the ship. Since we do not know how it moves, it is difficult to know if we are looking at the engines, or simply a source of stored energy."

McKenna's eyes went to the objects once more. *Nothing about the bollocks is easy. Just once I would like to be able to have the upper hand on them.* He wondered if that sentiment would ever be fulfilled. "You said there was something else you wanted me to see."

Lahoz nodded and led him on a ten-minute hike through the ship, twisting, turning, climbing, and dropping. They passed through a half-dozen of the hatch flaps, and he noticed that the water on the floor seemed deeper than it had been before.

Was it just this part of the ship, or is it rising everywhere?

They arrived at a hatch guarded by three of his Marines. They weren't relaxed, then again, no one aboard the alien ship seemed to be comfortable. It wasn't just the persistent headache, it was the creep-factor; that was what Lance Corporal Highbridge had called it during the morning briefing. Fighting the aliens was one thing; at least that was done on your home turf. Being inside of one of their ships was something else.

There was something bad behind the alien hatch, otherwise there wouldn't be his men standing there. As he stood at the hatch flap, he thought about Sergeant Falto. MI6 had sent him a data dump on her, most of which came from interviews that she had given, though a few documents were clearly smuggled out of the American's ETF control. *She was a prisoner of the aliens in a habitat not too different from this ship. They held her for months, experimenting on her. She lost her legs, an arm, and an ear to them...yet she came on this mission. That speaks a great deal about her as a fellow Marine.* McKenna respected her even more after reading her profile. *She's one of the few people here now who might have an understanding of all of this. It makes sense why she's here.*

"What do you have?" he asked Sergeant Fitzhugh.

"Sir, it's Lobsters, and something else, something new."

The mention of the scorpion-like Lobsters stiffened McKenna. "Let's have a look."

Fitzhugh opened the hatch flap and McKenna slid in. He saw a circular chamber, dark maroon in color. The levels of liquids in the room were almost knee deep as he sloshed in. Lining the walls were what looked like transparent panels, three meters tall and two wide. Behind each one was an alien Lobster, curled up, its small legs wrapped tightly around the body and tail. None seemed to be moving, but that wasn't something McKenna wanted to test.

There were others present too. There was one that was a hulking obsidian creature, similar to a crab in terms of propulsion, but sans the wide spindly legs. They were replaced with thick wide tentacles. At least a dozen or so of some new creatures were present. Shaped much like the Lobsters, they were smaller in size. Their tails were like an octopus tentacle. Their faces were ringed with spikes of some sort. In the center of their face was a black pincer, much like that of a squid, but larger. The front legs did not have the lobster claws, but nasty spiked hooks. They too appeared dormant.

There were easily thirty aliens in their semi-transparent cocoons, all seemingly stored, silent but seemingly waiting for something, some signal or some reason to come to life. Even though he was joined by his Marines in the chamber, he felt dangerously outnumbered. He didn't want to let those under his command see the fear he felt knotting at his stomach. *Three of my men guarding the door is a joke—this is a big enough force to pose a threat to all of our forces.*

He backed out of the hatch slowly as he reined in his composure. Once on the other side, he turned to Dr. Lahoz. "They seem to be hibernating or in stasis."

"That was our assessment as well."

"Why?"

"I'm not sure I understand, Major."

"We are crawling around their ship. That seems to be a good enough reason for them to activate or respond—but they aren't. Why?"

"I wish I had answers for you, but I don't. We found a smaller chamber with about a dozen or so more of the new ones, the squid creatures, along with two of some form of Skenks with tentacle legs."

"It doesn't make sense."

"Maybe the ship doesn't perceive us as a big enough threat."

Memories of what happened to Dr. Krane, who had been devoured by the alien snake-creature the day before, surged to the forefront. "When we've interacted with the ship before, the ship responded."

"Perhaps who or what is controlling the ship doesn't feel that the time is right. We have been using less invasive means to gather samples since yesterday."

"How much of the ship have we explored?"

"Per your agreement with the Americans, we split the ship pretty much in half. Of our portion, we have explored around twenty-seven percent or so. Some portions of the vessel we cannot get access to at all without cutting holes in the passageways or the rooms—which neither of us wants to do after yesterday."

McKenna's mind tried to process the information. Twenty-seven percent in two days.

We still don't know if and when the aliens might make another play for the ship.

"I take it that it's possible that the Americans have found similar caches of aliens in their part of the ship."

"We have no way of knowing."

"How about an educated guess, then?"

Dr. Lahoz nodded. "We don't know what they have found or not, but if we found these, they may have found the same, or even more."

Damn. For a millisecond, his mind raced to the hidden fuel air explosive planted up against the hull of the alien craft. *If they start to surge out, I have the means of dealing with them, but it could kill a lot of Americans in the process. That would play out horribly. I'm under orders to not let the Yanks know about the bomb, but I'm also not to create a bigger diplomatic incident than what we currently have on hand. The Foreign Office will have my testicles on a platter if I leak the info to Captain Wade and his people.*

That didn't leave him with a lot of options for the situation. "We only know what we know," he muttered, mostly to himself.

Lahoz replied to the comment. "That would be most accurate, sir."

"I think we should share with the Americans. Not our technical data, but on the threats we've encountered and aspects of the ship, like that radiative chamber, that we have discovered. They may very well have found things that would complete parts of this puzzle."

"Do you think they would be willing to share?"

His initial reaction was that he doubted it. Captain Wade didn't seem to enjoy the level of scant cooperation they already had. The thought of exchanging more information was not likely to go over well. At the same time he felt that not sharing information that might lead to the deaths of American researchers...something he could have prevented...would be too agonizing to contemplate. *I am in a situation I cannot hope to win. It has been that way the moment the Americans arrived.*

"We need to consider carefully what to share with them. I need you to come back with me and get prepared. In the meantime, I need to meet with my American counterpart."

"This may be the best course of action, Major."

"I agree. That doesn't mean that the Americans will."

His communicator in his helmet earpad chirped. "Major," came Lieutenant Phil Walling's crisp voice.

"Go ahead, Lieutenant."

"We just had an attempt to penetrate our battlespace."

The bollocks! Bloody hell, we knew they would show up sooner or later.

"How many?"

"Sir, it's not the bollocks. It is a small aircraft."

Instant relief washed McKenna's body. "Aircraft? American?"

"Negative, sir. It is commercial. It was requesting permission to land in our BS, but I informed them that wouldn't be allowed. They diverted to the south of us and landed there."

Who the hell is it? If it's not the Americans, is it another government attempting to make a grab for the ship? How could a commercial aircraft land on the ground here? He had far more questions than he had answers, and it wasn't a situation that he enjoyed.

"Lieutenant, what kind of aircraft are we talking about here? Did they give you any identification of where they are from?"

"Yes sir. It is a small propeller-driven airplane, five-seater from what our drones could identify. The occupants claim they are members of the press and that they have permission from the government of Greenland to be here."

Well, that's more than we have.

"The press? Whose press? Is it the BBC or Sky News?"

"Sir, it isn't one of ours. It's the Americans. A journalist and her people. They claim that they are here to cover the recovery efforts on the ship."

The American press. He wanted to moan out loud with that news. *That's all we don't need.* He preferred them to news that the aliens were attacking, but not by much.

"Tell them to bugger off."

"I tried that, sir, but they declined my suggestion."

McKenna said nothing as he thought through his options. *This isn't my problem at all to deal with, it is Captain Wade's. This may be a good lever for me to use to facilitate a meeting.* He had to admit, there was a certain amount of inner glee at the thought of Wade being forced to deal with the reporters. *Why should I have all of the fun?*

"I'm on my way back to the base. Hold the reporters there until I arrive. I'll escort them over the American base," he sent.

"Doctor," he said to Lahoz. "You will need to accompany me. It's time we share with our American colleagues, whether they want to return the courtesy or not."

CHAPTER 18

British Base Camp
South of the Crash Site, East Coast of Greenland

Veronica Diamond was flanked by Fizz and their security person, Verret. Verret's first name was Justin but he never went by that. A retired Marine pumper, Verret was a mass of muscle and aggression. When the British had suggested that he surrender his weapons, he merely scoffed at them and the matter was dropped. *Even they don't want to mess with him.* He was worth every penny that the network had paid his employer, Ravensheart PMC, for his time. His fiery red hair and beard only added to his intimidation factor. *Add on the numerous firearms he carries, and he's downright frightening.*

Verret was there because Fizz and her bosses had insisted they have heavily armed protection. Fizz had complained about almost every aspect of the trip. He was too cold, his feet were numb, the plane ride was making him sick, etc. Veronica responded with each whine that he made, and a few times she saw him smile. *He's used to Dana's style, so the more I mimic her, the easier this transition is going to be for him.*

Securing the gear for their trip had been challenging all on its own. The network picked up most of the responsibility for it, getting food, cold weather tents, parkas, sleeping bags, solar charging stations, and other gear. It all had weighed almost as much as the passengers on the airplane they had come in on.

Getting to Greenland in the middle of a war had been a nightmare of logistics, threats, payoffs, and outright lies…all of which she found herself willing to do. The tiny government of Greenland had been more than willing to let them fly up to the crash site and film it, mostly because it would give them the first glimpse of what had landed there. They were furious at the Americans for violating their sovereignty, and highly irritated at the British for the same.

Both governments have assured them they will be compensated, but they do not know what is actually on their soil. We are their best chance to get an unbiased view of the crash site.

Fox had paid handsomely for a bush pilot that would take them from the Danmarkshavn landing strip to the wreckage site. Veronica couldn't pronounce his name correctly, despite several attempts. He had a heavy accent, quasi-Danish, which made him hard to understand. Before they took off, he had valiantly tried to convince her that the flight was dangerous…that he would be landing, dropping them off, and leaving. He wanted nothing to do with crashed spacecraft or the imminent threat of the Fish coming to take it back. She quelled his concerns with a fist full of dollars.

Finding the British there had not been a surprise; her contacts in Greenland's government had told her they would be there. As their plane approached the site, Fizz managed to get some aerial footage before the Brits ordered them to land south of their base. She had pressed her face almost on the ice-cold glass cockpit, looking out as he had filmed. The ship was huge, larger than she could imagine. They saw figures on the ground, and at first she assumed they were troops, but only when Fizz pointed them out as ASHURs did she realize just how large the vessel was.

No wonder everyone wants a piece of this. There has got to be a lot of stuff in there, a ton of alientech. I'm shocked the French or the Spanish haven't made a play to secure the site.

The sight of the British ASHURs approaching to escort them had been intimidating. They had also refused to answer any questions she'd asked. "Talk about excessive. All that firepower for us. Do you think they're overcompensating for something?" she quipped to Fizz.

"They were abused as children," Fizz replied as he struggled with his gear. "I thought this place would be easier than LA. I was baking in the Valley during the start of the invasion. Now I'm so cold I can't feel my nuts."

"I assure you," Veronica replied. "They haven't fallen off. Did they, Verret?"

The security person who trudged at her side cast her a look of mild annoyance. "I'm not responsible for his nuts. Check my contract. No nuts clause." It was one of his longest contributions to a conversation since they'd left.

Maybe he's finally warming up to us.

"Excuse me," she called over at one of the British ASHURs. "Where are we going?"

"The major wants to meet you," came a voice over a small speaker on the rig.

"Major who?" she pressed.

"That's for the major to share, ma'am." The armored suit's footpads crunched the snow under them as it stood on their flank.

I wonder, are they here to protect us, or are they the threat?

"You almost get the idea they don't want us here," Fizz stated.

The purring of their airplane behind them made all three of them turn. The pilot taxied on the massive almost cartoonishly large balloon tires of the plane, whipping it around and taking off with a roar.

We are stuck here now. A part of Veronica liked that thought; it meant that they couldn't simply be expelled. *That doesn't mean we are going to get any access. That footage that Fizz shot during the landing might be all we get if they zip-tie us and lock us away.*

The war had melted away all the rules when it came to journalism and the military. The Pentagon had, for decades, been courting reporters, embedding them with the troops. This war was different. The official word was that the services didn't have the resources to embed reporters anymore. For reporters like Veronica, it created a sense that this was a war that could be lost still—that every service person was needed for fighting, not helping reporters get stories. She had heard rumors of some units smashing journalist equipment, even assaulting them.

I don't think they'll do anything like that to us, but I need to be appropriately delicate or we will have come a long way for nothing.

The British camp was several portable modules and a series of tents, whipping in the frigid wind. Veronica noted that these were the 45 Commandos of the Royal Marines; she had picked this up from their distinctive up-thrust dagger logo painted on the white-and-gray ASHURs. She leaned over to Verret. "The Royal Marines…what do you know of them?"

He cast her a glance as if she didn't exist. "Pussies compared to our Corps."

"You know, it's not all about who has the biggest swinging dick. What do you know about them?"

Verret cocked his head. "They are front-loaded with Sovereigns. They are elite, even by our standards. Between them and the SAS, it's debatable as to who is better at special operations."

"What's a Sovereign?" Fizz asked.

Verret pointed his gun at the rig next to them. "That's what they call 'em. You know the Brits, they think they invented the English language."

Veronica was pleased with his response. She could finally get her hired gun to engage in something more than menacing glares and grunts. Veronica prided herself on being able to connect with people at a level that got them to open up. It was one of the gifts she had as a reporter.

They were led to a portable unit, similar in size to a cargo container. This one was bristling with antenna and two small satellite dishes. The Sovereign pilot gestured to the door. "That way, if you would."

"Thanks for flying British Air," Fizz muttered as Verret opened the door for her to enter. She noticed that the retired Marine only held the door for her. He let Fizz fend for himself.

Inside was a small antechamber where coats were hung and boots were drying. They stripped down too, embracing the light warmth. Verret re-slung his weapons after taking off his parka. "You can probably leave those here," she suggested. The hulking man frowned, then stacked his assault weapon, his two pistols, and his kit filled with magazines against one wall.

One door opened and a lance corporal ushered them inside. An officer, wearing a dull green jumpsuit, stepped forward, his arms behind him at parade rest. He was short, but even with the clothing, she could tell that he was all muscles. His brown hair was short and combed back neatly. "I'm Major Andrew McKenna." She caught just a hint of a Scottish accent. *Southern Scotland, not the Highlands.*

"I'm Veronica Diamond," she replied. "This is my production man, Theodore Hart," she said, gesturing to Fizz. "And this mountain of flesh is our security, Verret."

"Yes," McKenna said, his eyes quickly scanning the trio. "I must admit, we had not anticipated your arrival."

"I must admit, I hadn't expected to find British troops here," she countered. Before he could respond, she brought up another subject. "Would it be alright if my cameraman recorded this conversation?"

McKenna chuckled. "Hell, no."

"Well, we are here with permission of the government of Greenland. Which I think is more than you have."

"My government might feel differently about what constitutes permission. Nuuk is a long ways from here and frankly, I don't care what the government of Greenland thinks. That is for our Foreign Affairs people to address. I am here, dealing with the singular most important crash site since the *Titanic* was discovered."

Veronica thrived on the conflict, the battle of words. *I learn a lot about people from what they say and how they say it.* "I take it your government has no issues with us recording the crash site."

"I have been given no direction on how to deal with the media. I doubt anyone anticipated that someone would be foolhardy enough to make the journey here, given the risks."

"Risks?" Fizz asked. "What risks?"

"We have already been attacked by the aliens once. Which is

why I have so little time to deal with the likes of you three."

Veronica's attention focused on what the major had said. The Fish had struck once already. *We are in the right place at the right time. If we play our cards correctly, we get to film an alien spacecraft for the first time and we are going to get a battle on top of it!* "We have no intention of being underfoot. If you can help us get established, we would like to get some footage of the ship, perhaps follow one of your teams into the craft."

Her words forged a grin on McKenna's face. "I don't think so. I'm under no obligation to assist foreign press while we are conducting military and scientific operations, nor will I be responsible for you."

"I brought our own protection," she countered, glancing over at Verret.

McKenna looked over at him with a casual disregard. "So I see. I doubt that one person is going to be enough to protect you once the shooting starts."

"You may not be familiar with my portfolio, but I have had some experience covering the war from the front lines."

"This is nothing like that," he assured her. "Regardless, you are not my problem to contend with." Usually she found a British accent to be a little sexy. Given the flippant tone that Major McKenna was taking, she was starting to find it irritating instead.

"You can't deny us our right to cover this story. A crashed alien ship—no one has ever seen that before. This is huge."

"Quite. I believe I am slightly more aware of what the implications are than you, Ms. Diamond, if that is, indeed, your real name. Your zeal for plying your trade doesn't change my options or decision."

"You can't just block us from doing our job. We have rights."

"I'm sure you think you do. I'm heading over to the American base of operations. It is my intention to escort you there. You will be the problem of the American commander."

"And who might that be?"

"One Captain Bryan Wade of Omega Force."

The mention of Omega Force told her how serious the situation was. For the Army to have pulled them from wherever they were fighting and send them here, they are playing for keeps. "I can live with that."

"It isn't like you have a choice, ma'am," McKenna replied. "Reginald, here, will take you to get some coffee and something to eat. We will leave in a half an hour." He glanced over at a private and stood before them, then gestured down the hall. The conversation was over, Veronica could sense it.

Fine. I'm sure this Captain Wade will be a little more open to our presence.

Regardless of McKenna's standoffishness, a cup of coffee and some food were sincerely welcomed.

* * *

Veronica liked to believe she was physically fit. She paid for a trainer five days a week and worked out even when she was on an assignment. At the start of the war, she had done her bit as a war correspondent in her attempt to claw her way back up the broadcasting corporate ladder. That had been grueling as well, lugging equipment and wearing plate carriers and helmets. She had thought herself in good physical condition. But the march to the British camp, then the long slog through deep snow to the American base, left her sweaty and exhausted.

They had been accompanied by Major McKenna and a young man who was clearly not military, based on his lack of uniform or muscular build. She had approached him in a friendly manner during the traipse, asking his name, but McKenna had cut him off. "Don't tell her anything." It was rude but reinforced McKenna's opinion of the press.

The American camp was different. Portable dome structures, tunnels, and some cargo-carrier modules were connected. Whipping violently over the camp, whipping in the icy wind, was a small American flag. They were met with some white-clad Army Rangers who escorted them to one of the modules.

Fizz was wet with sweat as he pulled off his cold weather gear. "For the record, I hate Greenland."

"Fizz, we need to play nice," she said, reaching up to adjust his flannel shirt. Leaning in, she whispered, "You still wearing the, you-know…"

He nodded, his grin barely visible through his ice encrusted beard. "Old habits die hard," he assured her. The two of them had taken the time to equip him with a micro video recorder which replaced one button on his shirt. It fed to a tiny device in his pocket that allowed him to control turning it off and on. He could record hours of material without anyone being aware.

A trio of people entered the chamber with them, led by Captain Wade, or so his jumpsuit tag indicated. His shoulder bore the tabs for Ranger, Special Forces, Special Missions Unit, and the ASHUR wings with two rig patches. On his other shoulder he wore the Omega Force patch. *It's like an extra layer of sewn-on body armor on one sleeve.* His face was dour, his jaw so chiseled, that it looked like it was stone.

The other two individuals that came in were female. In Veronica's trained eyes, both were in need of supporting makeup. One was tall, light-skinned, with straight black hair that desperately needed a stylist. The other female was in a Marine jumpsuit, lighter in color than her Army counterpart. She was Latino, with skin that Veronica envied. Her black hair was worn short and as soon as she stopped walking, she crossed her arms almost defiantly.

Her face is familiar. Where have I seen her before?

"I got your message, Major," Wade said. "Who are these people?"

"Dr. Lahoz is from my staff, per my message. These individuals," he gestured to Veronica, "are members of the free press. Being Americans, I'm turning them over to you."

Veronica didn't give him a chance to think or talk. She stepped forward and jutted her hand out in front of her. "Veronica Diamond, Fox News. This is Verret and Fizz. Verret is my security, Fizz is my producer." Fizz smiled and gave Wade a welcoming nod, all of which the captain seemed to ignore. Sniffling, her nostrils had thawed enough for her to catch a whiff of the room and could slightly detect body odor. It instantly reminded her of her last venture in the AIZ on the west coast.

Glancing at Veronica's hand, he disregarded it and turned to his British counterpart. "You didn't mention them."

"They showed up unannounced," McKenna stated. "We don't have the personnel to deal with them. Since they are from your country, I assumed you would take possession of them." If McKenna was trying to hide his smirk, he failed.

Wade's face got furious red and his rigid jaw seemed to find an even more firm setting. He locked his gray eyes onto Veronica's. "We do not have the accommodations or facilities to deal with you. I don't know how you got here, but you'll have to leave—immediately."

"Impossible," she replied, still maintaining a grin that had cost her tens of thousands of dollars to sculpt. "Our airplane departed. We are stuck here."

Veronica got a heavy sigh in response. "This operation is classified."

"I understand. If you know who I am, you know I'm one of the network's top reporters. This story is huge. We haven't seen any footage of the Fish's ships and you have one right here. Covering this will give the people back home hope. We've lost so much of our coastline and cities, yet the image of that crashed ship should give them a belief that we can win this war."

"I don't think you appreciate just how dangerous this situation is," Wade replied. "Your leaving might be the thing that saves your lives."

"We've already taken a hell of a risk to get here," she countered. "My people and I knew the risks when we set out for here."

"I don't think you do," Wade replied, glancing for a moment over to McKenna. "We've already lost someone just poking around that ship, not to mention our casualties from the Fish attacking us.

This is more than a scientific expedition. People are dying."

"We can take care of ourselves," she assured him—hoping and praying that Fizz didn't counter what she had just said. "We can't leave. Our ride is long gone. We won't be in the way."

The tall black-haired woman spoke up. "Having extra cameras recording can't hurt. If anything, they may spot something that we miss." McKenna gave her a squinting angry sideways glance.

"Sir," the female Marine spoke up. "We don't have the ability to lock them up or guard them. You can't just have them start marching back to wherever they came from—it's freaking winter in Greenland. They made it this far. You may as well let them do their job."

"I didn't ask you, Sergeant," Wade said.

"I know."

I like her!

"I have zero instructions on what to do if the press showed up, which pretty much means your being here is at my discretion."

"Understood."

"You will transmit nothing until it gets approved by the military PAs and the State Department. The last thing we need is an army of the media descending on this place. It's bad enough that you are here."

"Agreed. While we are here, I will put nothing out on the air or the net," Veronica replied, knowing full well that she would find a way around Wade's edicts.

I phrased my response deliberately. What he doesn't know won't hurt him. Besides, once the story is out, it's not like they can recall it. He doesn't know that Fizz is recording this right now.

"If you don't mind, Ms. Diamond, I have need to do some coordination with the major."

"Why not let them stay?" the Marine asked, increasing how much Veronica liked her even more. "Besides, we don't have anywhere to put them yet."

Wade glared at the Marine, then turned to Veronica. "Your bodyguard isn't needed, he can stay outside. As for the two of you, just stay out of the way and be quiet," he growled.

"Of course, Captain. I'm the model of discretion." She shot a fast glimpse at Fizz who only smiled.

CHAPTER 19

American Base Camp
West of the Crash Site, East Coast of Greenland

Major McKenna had enjoyed dumping Veronica Diamond and her people in his lap; that much Wade could see in his face. He did what he could to keep his composure at first, though the intervention on the part of Staff Sergeant Falto once more grated him.

I will never again get saddled on an op with someone who doesn't report to me.

In reality, he saw the arrival of Diamond and her team as a mental speed bump. Omega didn't undertake operations where reporters were present. He had dealt with them earlier in his career and found most of them to be friendly targets. Nice people, naïve about the risks they put themselves in. Since the war with the Fish had started, a lot of good reporters were either dead, wounded, or out of the business.

Wade knew he couldn't send them away even if it tempted him to. *They got themselves a one-way ticket in here. Their only way out is with us. I have to admire Diamond for her craftiness.* When Falto suggested they stay, there was no reason to not have them there. *Someone back in the States will have to figure out what to make public and what to keep secret. I'm not going to burn brain cells trying to juggle what they get away with.*

Captain Wade knew he was violating orders by allowing the meeting. *The CIA and State Department will want to hang me for all of this.* His mind went back to General Lee telling him that he would "back him all the way to the wall." Wade knew he was putting a lot of faith in the general, but he also knew that it was a safe bet. *I need to do what my gut tells me is right, not what the bozos in Washington think is best.*

His attitude towards the Marine staff sergeant had changed when he heard from Wertan how she had pulled several of the Rangers and scientists out of danger, most likely saving their lives. He hadn't talked to her about the incident yet. *She's proving more useful than I had expected.*

"Alright, Major," he said, leading them to the commons area, which his people had cleared minutes earlier. The only person who remained there was Captain Wertan. Tommy was a kindred spirit; both men had completed Ranger training and his people had been aboard the ship providing security. "This is Captain Wertan of the Rangers," he said, gesturing to Tommy who nodded. "You told me we should have our scientists share some information—that lives might be at risk."

"That's right," the British officer replied. "I realize that we have no reason to trust each other, and from what you have conveyed before, your government doesn't want cooperation. My team has suffered a loss during our exploration—and we have found enemy aliens that are not dead yet."

There was genuine remorse on McKenna's face. Gone was his haughtiness mixed with arrogance he always felt from the man. It was something that Wade felt as well. *We lost a person too. If they have indeed found a potential threat, knowing it will save lives.* He knew that meant him sharing what his people had discovered, the Squids, as the Rangers had dubbed them, as well as the Crabs they had discovered in some sort of hibernation or dormancy. It was the right call to make. *God only knows what they've come across.*

Once the door to the room was closed, they made introductions. They took seats around the commons table, with Doctors Lahoz and Schrivener sitting across from each other. Falto settled in at one end of the table alone, opposite Veronica Diamond and her producer.

"My government has advised against sharing of data, but they also put the ultimate decision in my hands. In other words, it's my neck in the noose," Wade stated grimly. "I also have no desire to lose any more lives when that might be avoided."

"Thank you, Captain," McKenna replied. "I feel the same way. We're both military men. Good intelligence can save lives. Let us strive to save a few."

Wade knew he had to start the effort, if only to show good faith. "We have encountered a few aliens that we have never seen before." He nodded to Dr. Schrivener, who pulled up a video on her slim laptop.

Schrivener took the reins on the conversation. "These are the ones we found. So far, we have found one chamber of these, with nearly thirty of them. From what we can tell, they are still alive, apparently unaware of our presence."

Dr. Lahoz spoke up. "We found many of those, along with Lobsters." He opened his laptop and it took a full minute to pull up the video feed. Wade leaned in at the images in the video, as did Wertan. "We also discovered a large crab-like creature, black as all night. We saw some other creatures similar to Skenks, but with multiple legs."

"Is a Lobster a Crab?" Wertan asked.

"Apologies," Lahoz said, pointing to the image. "Yes. We tend to use our nomenclature. Skenks are your Foxes, I believe."

"On these new aliens, can we agree to call them Squids going forward?" Wade asked.

There were nods around the table.

My first diplomatic victory...hardly worth celebrating.

"There is another alien we encountered," Schrivener said. "We came across a large chamber, which we think contained a brain or large synaptic relay of some sort. When we interfered with it... well..." She loaded the video for the British to see. The large jellyfish attack played out in horrific detail. Wade watched his counterparts across the table wince at the crisp images.

When the footage stopped, the captain spoke again. "We lost one person and another is still being treated for some sort of toxic shock he got in the attack." Richardson was conscious, but in a great deal of pain from the stinger attack by the giant jellyfish-like creature.

A grim sense washed over the room after everyone had viewed the images. Wade had reviewed the footage himself a dozen times, looking for every detail he could get from it—everything from the speed of the alien to the way it enveloped its victim. He had to mentally detach himself from the wails of agony and the gore.

This is an enemy and the more I understand it, the better.

"We lost one of our scientists as well, but not to that kind of creature," Lahoz replied, loading his own video. "This was Dr. Krane," was all he could say as the video started. The five-meter-long eel dropped down with its open maw surrounded by fast-moving tentacles. The speed with which the appendages helped seize and pull the scientist into it was chilling to watch. Wade found himself thankful when the video ended. *These damn Fish keep coming up with new ways to kill us.*

The videos had sucked the air out of the room. No one knew what to say. It was Dr. Lahoz that shattered the quiet. "Our people have been experiencing headaches after being on the crash site. Have you had similar experiences?"

Those words seemed to shake Schrivener out of her stunned state and back into the room. "We have. When we were in that brain chamber—for lack of better words, many of our people were incapacitated by it. I had several monitors out and we tracked what is causing it."

This was news even to Wade, who leaned in on his elbows over the small table. "What is it?"

"It's a form of brain wave. It has characteristics of beta waves from humans, but these are amplified and so active, they are generating a field in the electromagnetic spectrum that seems to conflict with our own brain waves."

"Are they dangerous?" McKenna asked.

"Our people were injured, some temporarily rendered unconscious, but there is no indication of long-term effects," Schrivener said.

Wertan weighed in, "Doc, mine still hurts like the worst hangover I've ever had…and I've had a few in my day."

Lahoz ignored the Ranger captain, staying focused on Schrivener. "I take it there's no way to block it."

"We just figured out what it was. My recommendation is that we avoid that chamber at all costs. Our interactions in there are what triggered the giant Scyphozoa attack and the surge in these waves." Her clinical definition of the jellyfish didn't soften the impact of the video they saw.

Major McKenna spoke next. "So how do we address the aliens that are in stasis?"

Wade reacted first to that question. "I toyed with planting explosives on each one of them as a fail-safe if they start to wake up, but there's no guarantee that the blasts would kill them. As we have all seen, the Fish are pretty resilient. We all wanted to shoot them, but that was a recipe for a greater reaction that could get out of hand fast. Also, I doubt that either of our parties have explored all of our parts of the ship yet. We do not know how many other aliens are tucked away that we haven't found yet. We have explored a remarkably small portion of the ship."

Schrivener joined in again, "We found several Laborers—Class Elevens. They were being *consumed* by the ship, like the ship was absorbing them."

McKenna nodded. "Are these the ones that are covered with tentacles? If it is, we found a few of those as well, in the same state you did."

Wade continued. "Those aliens were not quite dead, but were becoming part of the ship. We didn't see signs of that with the Squids or the Crabs that we found. They are not melting into the ship. For some reason, the ship is keeping them alive."

"Perhaps to respond to force if we use it," McKenna said.

"My thoughts exactly," Wade responded. "So far, we have been an annoyance. When we've triggered the ship into reacting, it did so, violently. Right now, it probably doesn't see us as much of a threat. The moment that situation changes, they could start releasing those aliens against us."

The British major replied, "That is a situation I think it would be best for all of us to try to avoid."

Captain Wertan spoke. "We may not be the ones in control of that situation. Remember, the Fish have already attacked us once. There's no reason for us to assume they won't be back."

"Our team reviewed the data from that skirmish. What struck us as odd was that the bollocks were firing on their own ship." Dr. Lahoz added.

"We have found nothing that points to this actually being a ship," Dr. Schrivener stated. "Our attempts to find a bridge or propulsion system have proven fruitless."

Lahoz shifted in his seat. "It is our team's general assessment that this is less of a ship as much as it is a giant living organism. Shooting it down did not kill it. That is evidenced by what we have all encountered. The ship is very much alive."

Wade spoke up. "I am not a marine biologist, but I tend to agree. We have found organs. We've been wading through what appear to be giant blood vessels. No bridge though, definitely no engine room."

Dr. Lahoz looked over at McKenna, who gave him a single nod. "We found a chamber that was giving off radiation." He fumbled with the keyboard for almost a minute before he pulled up the images.

Wade looked at the large tube-like devices pulsating with light and power. "We haven't picked up any radioactivity in our exploration. Was it at a dangerous level?"

"No," Lahoz replied. "What was strange is we didn't find any material that would have generated radiation."

"There has to be some," Schrivener replied.

"There wasn't. These tubular projections have varying levels of radioactivity but there is no source for it. We believe that somehow the aliens have learned how to generate radiation organically."

"That's impossible." Schrivener shook her head. "It requires a physical or chemical reaction."

It was Falto that shattered the discussion thread with a chuckle. "Nothing is impossible—not when it comes to the Fish. The sooner that we come to accept that, the sooner we can move forward."

She's right, Wade thought. *The war thus far has been us applying tactics and weapons from the last war to the aliens, with spotty results at best. We have a war playbook, but the damned Fish are refusing to play by our rules.*

"Sergeant Falto's right," he said. "From the sound of it, neither of our parties has found any sign of the key systems that we would think of as a ship."

"Having been over in that ship, I can tell you that you need to shake your *Star Wars* and *Star Trek* mentality. Looking for engine rooms and control surfaces is a waste. When I was being held by the Fish, the control systems they had for us were so simplistic. I doubt we would know what a bridge looked like if we were standing on it. There probably isn't an alien piloting the ship, not in the traditional sense. The ship is probably flying itself," Falto added.

While her words were off the cuff, they hit home for everyone in the room. Wade glanced over at Diamond and her producer, and saw the talk had mesmerized them.

They must be salivating over all of this. I bet this is the news story of the year. We've been living this ever since we dropped here, but to them, this is all new and exciting.

Dr. Lahoz dropped another minor bombshell. "The water levels are rising on the ship. We've seen evidence that some of the holes torn in the landing are healing over. The water levels in the lower portion of the ship have increased so much that we have been forced to concentrate our efforts on the higher sections that are forward, where the ship seems to have ruptured on impact."

Wade could tell that was news even to Major McKenna, who turned to stare at the doctor. Lahoz didn't seem too shaken by the stares he was getting. "I measured and marked the depth in several of the corridors and rooms as we explored them. They have rising in some chambers by anywhere from six to twenty centimeters."

"They can't be drawing water from the ground where they

crashed. If they were, the ship would sink with the loss of ice under it, and we haven't detected any appreciable movement," Dr. Schrivener stated. "Besides, snow melt is at a rate of six inches of snow for every inch of water."

Captain Wade shifted. "So where are they getting it from—and why?"

"It's got to be from the sea," Wertan replied. There was no rebuttal to the conclusion.

"That can't be good news for us," Falto added.

"It's got to be somehow drawing in sea water," McKenna stated.

For Wade, it was something that was going to need to be investigated. *That's all we didn't need, another mystery.* "Obviously we will need to check that out."

"Agreed," McKenna said.

Wade shifted in his seat, then said, "Something that has been nagging at me since we were attacked. Why did the Fish fire on their own ship? If it is indeed alive, why shoot at it?"

McKenna fielded that inquiry. "I do not know, Captain. You're right; it doesn't make any sense."

"Another mystery to throw on the pile," Falto said.

Damn, I'm getting tired of her being right.

* * *

The scientists shared information for an hour, even making copies of their videos. They had agreed to connect their battlespace surveillance of the surrounding ground. No doubt the State Department would grill him for the exchange, but he had already accepted that. As they broke up and the scientists of both nations departed, Wade arranged for Diamond and her people a place to crash in the shelter, as opposed to pitching a tent outside. As people filtered out of the room, the last two left in the room with Wade were Falto and McKenna.

The British commander moved in close to him. "When we first

met, we both dug our heels in. You've changed, Captain. What brought that about?"

Wade looked at him, not at a British officer, but his comrade-in-arms. The patches and uniforms were different, but they had the same enemy. "I have the State Department and the CIA demanding I not so much as talk to you. My commanding officer told me to do what was right. Well, I've lost people, four so far. I've got troops that have been wounded and injured. I wouldn't be able to sleep at night if you lost people in that ship and it could have been prevented by something we knew."

McKenna grinned. "You are not alone. MI6 and the Foreign Office aren't exactly fans of you and your government. Like you, the only blood that I want on my hands is alien."

"This *isn't* an alliance. It's cooperation. Even at that, I'm keeping it to a minimum," Wade said.

"It is common sense."

"Something that diplomats and spies would never understand."

"Quite."

"Hopefully we can glean more from this vessel before the bloody bollocks decide to return."

"Good luck, Major."

"Godspeed, Captain."

With that, McKenna turned and left, leaving him alone with Falto, who was grinning.

"I thought you two might hug and kiss there for a moment," the Marine staff sergeant said.

"That conversation doesn't leave this room, understood?"

"Yes, sir."

"I've been in uncharted territory since I got this mission. I'm more comfortable at destroying a target and moving on. All of this *help* I've gotten from State and the CIA is not the kind of thing I ever wanted to be involved with. I certainly didn't ask for a Marine Corps NCO for me to babysit."

The last word got to Falto. She opened her mouth to rebuttal, but Wade cut her off.

"But I've discovered that, in one instance, you have been a blessing in disguise."

"I—" she began, unsure what to say.

That alone was satisfying.

"Sergeant Falto, I want to thank you."

"Thank me? For what?"

"I heard what you did when that monster jellyfish attacked. A lot of Rangers and the science team dropped. Captain Wertan claimed that you saved them."

Falto blushed. "I just did what I could."

"Why weren't you affected the way they were?"

"I asked Doc Schrivener the same thing. She thinks where I was held was probably a lot like this ship. If that's true, they subjected me to these brain waves for a long time. She thinks because I lived with that damned headache for months, I was more resistant."

"That was a blessing then."

Falto let a thin smile creep on her face. "I guess it was. I've been wondering why I was here. Maybe it was for that—to help those people."

"I'm not much on divine intervention," Wade confessed. "I was never the church-going type."

"I went, my mother insisted. Like so many people, I went through the motions. I sang the songs, read the Psalms, and prayed. Then I became a prisoner."

"You find religion down at the bottom of the ocean?"

"No, sir. I did pray a few times, but I came to realization that all that I could count on was myself and the people that were with me. I didn't blame God for being there, and I didn't expect Him to get me out either." There was a deep resolve in her voice as her memories were clearly coming back.

Looking at her, it was hard not to admire her spirit. *She defied everything the Fish threw at her and overcame the odds. When the battle started, she didn't run from the fight, she joined in the battle.*

"You have far more experience than I do with the Almighty," Wade conceded. "Being an officer, I don't like the thought of an unseen deity guiding my destiny. At the same time, your being here can't just be a fluke. You were in the right place at the right time. For that, you have my thanks."

"Maybe we are both more religious than either of us is willing to admit."

Wade smiled. "Sergeant, you might make true believers out of all of us before this is over."

CYCLE IV

DIA Extension Office, aka the Auxiliary Site (the Aux)
Crystal City, Arlington, Virginia, the United States

Slade had stopped by the DIA facilities in Crystal City to get a few briefings before his return to the Penetrator. He hadn't enjoyed being summoned to Washington, DC, for something that could have been handled with a video call. The fact that the summoning had been at the behest of the Director Wilson of the CIA had made it even more unpleasant.

I have no idea what I did to piss him off, but he's like a dog with a bone when it comes to work my people are doing.

He liked being back in the Aux. It reminded him of more simple times before the invasion. It was getting harder to remember what life was like before the Fish had shown up. A part of Ashe longed to be nothing more than an analyst. *Back in those days, it was monitoring the Russians and the Chinese. Now I have to look into space and the bottom of oceans for data.*

The temporary office that he was using was sparse. In one corner were storage boxes filled with printout reports. The desk had seen some action too, with scuffs and dings that betrayed its abuse. *There was a time when I was down working in the dark, doing analysis, that I longed to have an office. Now I can have any one I want, and I find myself longing for that dingy analyst desk.*

A knock came at the door, and a corporal stood there. "Colonel, you have a visitor."

That struck him as odd. Very few people knew he was going to be in the office. "Who is it?"

"A general, sir."

With a nod, the corporal went off and returned with General Lee. Ashe rose and saluted and the general returned the gesture. "Sir, I hadn't expected the honor."

"It's no honor, Colonel," Lee said, making sure the door closed behind him. He took a seat across from Slade, who also sat down. "I came with words of warning."

"Warning?"

"You have a handful of powerful people gunning for you, Colonel. I thought you might like a glimpse of the battlespace before the festivities commence."

"Go on."

"No doubt you know that Director Wilson wants control of the Extraterrestrial Task Force that you are heading up."

"I suspected as much. I'm not sure why he wants it so badly. It's a daunting job."

"From what I heard, you were the only person who spotted the threat before it came ashore. You were responsible for some of our key victories so far, like Republic."

"All I did was make good educated guesses. There were many people under me that made those victories possible—especially the forces that were in the field."

"That's the other thing," Lee said, crossing his left leg over his right at the ankle. "You are humble and honest."

"Thank you, sir."

"Those weren't intended as compliments," Lee warned him. "Those are weaknesses."

The general's words caught Slade off guard. "Sir—I—"

Lee waved his hand. "Let me finish. Those are weaknesses for a person having to deal with Washington power brokers. Art Wilson is a hard-ass who lives for the power. You shun the authority that you've been granted. You see your work as a means to end the war. People like Wilson see it as a means of exerting power and control. Men like him have ambitions. Men like you want to do the job because it's the right thing to do."

Ashe felt his face get warm.

He's right; I have no ambition other than winning the war.

"General, I have tried to work with the CIA. I have been stonewalled, and in the case of Greenland, outright misled."

"That's why I'm here. That prick Wilson put my men at risk with this little stunt. I have confidence in my officer-in-command, but he misled both of us, keeping us in the dark about the British. Either the CIA was incompetent or he blindsided us. Either way, he doesn't deserve the chair he's sitting in."

"That isn't for me to say, sir."

"Well, you need to change that attitude, Colonel. Wilson will leverage his connections with the president to oust you. He's already aligned a certain powerful senator to work against you."

"Carson?" Just stating his name brought back unpleasant memories of the confrontations that the two had exchanged since the start of the war. It made perfect sense for Wilson to ally with Carson; both wanted to control his task force.

"That's him," Lee assured him. "He's gotten a few others to join his little cabal. It's only a matter of time before they make their play. And if they do, you'll be booted from command of the task force."

"If they knew how hard the work was, they wouldn't want the job."

General Lee tilted his head towards him. "They don't care about the work. Like I said, this is about power. You have it, and they want it. It's like a new toy or a shiny object. They want to play with it, boast to their friends that they control it. For men like Wilson and Carson, it will give them a toehold in defense contracts, and for politicians, that's a chance to line their pockets."

"What do you recommend I do, sir?"

Lee uncrossed his legs and rose to his feet, as did Slade. "Colonel, you got this job because you are smart. If you want to keep it, you need to be more than intelligent, you need to be wise. You have people that are gunning for you. You're an obstacle. Their goals are not yours. Watch your back and cover your ass."

"Yes sir."

"They are going to make this political and personal. Wilson already reached out to me to see how I felt about you. That's what prompted me to drop by. You and I are fighting a war. These jackoffs are playing power politics. It's time you up your game. They are choosing the field of battle. You're a warrior deep down. I heard about you during the Battle for Washington, DC, and read your records from the Russo-Bratva War. Well, this battlespace is political. I think you are important to us in winning the war. If you believe that, you will need to figure out how to fight in their arena and win."

Slade appreciated the warning. It confirmed what he suspected, though the scope of the conspiracy against him was more formidable than he had guessed. "Thank you, General."

"I'll do what I can," Lee assured him. "Just do me a favor and make sure our people get out of Greenland in one piece."

"I can't guarantee what the Fish will do, but I will do my best, sir."

As General Lee departed, Slade realized that his life was getting far more complicated.

Pituffik Space Base, 821st Space Base Group
Thule, Greenland

Lieutenant Georgia Johnstone liked the new kill marker stenciled on the sleek carbonweave skin of her X-62. It was a pretty good approximation of the ship that she had shot down. It was much larger than the Sputnik-like icons already painted there that represented the Russian satellites she had taken down.

Until she had downed the alien spacecraft, being at Pituffik had been like being sent to Siberia. It was cold, isolated, the facilities were decades old, built for a war that never happened. *I put this place on the map. Most people did not know that we even had a base in Greenland.*

There had been a ceremony the day before where the base CO

had congratulated her for being the first ace in the war. The Fish had not been engaged in an air war up to this point, so the Air Force had only ground kills to their credit. Even though most of her kills had come during the last war, she was the first American aviator to achieve the status of ace since the start of the war. It had been a real shot in the arm for the Space Force. As her CO had said, "For the first time, Space Force has shown the rest of the armed forces our true value." It was an indirect shot at the Air Force, one that Johnstone secretly was proud of.

The Air Force pilots and joyboys always get the glory. Not this time. Space Force scored this one, big time.

As she admired the artwork, she glanced over at the new drones that were in the hanger. One tech saw her looking at them and weighed in. "Pretty slick, eh? Those are the new Vultures."

"Why would we be getting bomber-drones here?" she asked. Thule had a long and less-than-illustrious military history. During the Cold War, it was one of the most northern airbases that the US used. After the fall of the Soviet Union, it got routinely stripped of equipment and importance. That changed with the Russo-Bratva War, but by then it had stopped being a strategic air command base and become one for America's fledgling Space Force. When new equipment arrived, it drew a lot of attention.

"It's all hush-hush with the brass," the tech replied, wiping grease off on his coveralls. "The word I got from the joyboys that came with the stuff is that they are going to be positioned to blow up that ship you brought down."

Johnstone wasn't sure how to react to it. First, word of her victory was known at the base, but to her knowledge, hadn't gone any farther. Everyone knew there was some sort of recovery force at the crash site. She had followed the ship all the way to the ground after shooting it, if for no other reason than to record the ship. The military, at least for the time being, was keeping a lid on the downing.

But this…this was something else. *This isn't about getting images or providing CAP—those Vultures are for destroying shit on the ground, plain and simple.*

"I thought we were short of ground support munitions."

The tech grinned. "Funny how that works. They made this a priority and voila! They scrounged up some bombs. Seems like a waste to me. I mean, you already shot the damn thing down, right?"

Why destroy something of such value? No one had ever even seen one of the alien ships until she shot it down. Now they seemed to be shuffling resources to destroy it.

"This is fucked up."

"Welcome to the Space Force," the tech replied, then walked off to start his next task.

CHAPTER 20

Operation Sulaco
Crash Site, East Coast of Greenland

The Americans had split their science teams. The majority were still exploring the ship, but Natalia had opted to go with the smaller team that was looking for how the ship was obtaining water. The helicopter that had come in to take out their samples had brought equipment used by utilities to detect underground pipes. No one knew if it would work in this application, but the equipment was easy to obtain and use. The gear looked almost like a jackhammer, though was far lighter.

Standing next to the wall-like hull of the ship was intimidating. She preferred being topside, where she had been during the attack. There was a sense of being hemmed in along the base of the ship, walking along the jumble of broken pieces of ice. The hull was a barrier that couldn't be crossed. It had plowed up ice and snow in front of it as if done by a giant plow blade. Not far out was the ocean and more rock-like ice formations, though much more widely dispersed. From where she stood, it was impossible to know where the actual shore was, but according to the scientists she was with, it was some seventy-five meters out.

Before the war she had never traveled. Certainly she hadn't planned on living on the ocean floor for months, nor had she ever expected to be in Greenland. She almost fell at one point, saved from the inevitable bruises by Warrant Officer Rosales who grabbed onto her parka sleeve and swung her for a moment until she regained her footing.

"You gotta watch your footing out here," he reminded her.

"I don't have a lot of experience with ice. It was never an issue in Los Angeles."

Rosales chuckled. "You don't have to tell me. I'm from Waco. Of course, I did a stint with the 10th Mountain at one point, so I got some hands-on with this shit."

As they slowly moved, the scientists used the equipment to try to find some sign of moving water under them. It was a slow go given the uneven terrain. Falto welcomed it. Inside the ship, there was a feeling of claustrophobic terror. The alien craft surrounded everyone, but for her it was worse. She was surrounded by not only the ship but her memories of captivity.

At least out here, I'm not having that constant sense of worry or fear that something is about to go wrong.

Natalia knew that wasn't entirely true. The ship had an alien crew. Under the frozen ice of the North Atlantic, the Fish were present. The sense of safety that she embraced was a lie, like the lies everyone tells themselves to get through their days. It wasn't delusion, just a normal human coping mechanism.

Strangely enough, since the first battle with the Fish in Greenland, her PTSD seemed to have diminished. While the bunk cots were far from comfortable, she had managed to get more sleep than when she had been back at the Penetrator. Some of that came from mental and physical exhaustion, the rest came with her confronting echoes of her past aboard the ship. *I'm sure my shrink will have a field day going over all of this with me.*

As they walked, her eyes kept drifting more to the sea. *They are out there. We still don't know why they attacked the ship.* She knew the prevalent thinking was that the Fish wanted to deny the humans access to their ship. To her, that never felt right. *If they wanted to stop us from getting to their ship, they would have simply concentrated on killing us.* She was sure that her instincts on this were correct. She had never witnessed any noble or honorable self-sacrifice by the aliens. *They wouldn't destroy the ship and leave us here. They were firing on the ship for some other reason, something we don't understand yet.*

"Falto," Rosales said, nudging her coat. "Didn't you hear me?"

"No. Sorry. Lost in my thoughts."

"I asked why you came out here rather than go into the ship?"

"I've had my fill of being in their ships or habitats. At least for the time being."

"I hear you. Those environmental suits made me sweat like all hell. Worse, they limit my field of vision."

Falto climbed up on one thick piece of broken ice and used the perch to look out further over the seas.

"You looking for the baddies?" Rosales asked.

She didn't stop her surveillance with her answer. "They will be back."

"Is that the voice of experience speaking?"

She jumped down, crunching in the snow on her landing. "No. I only fought one engagement with them. When I was recovering, Colonel Slade arranged for me to get access to combat footage of them. He thought it might enhance my analysis. I studied them for weeks, watching them, reviewing after-action reports and BDAs. I wanted to know them as well as I knew my fellow Marines."

"We've done at lot of that in the third," Rosales replied. "We were always looking for vulnerable spots, places that might give us an advantage."

"You see anything useful?"

He nodded as they trudged forward. "A little. The Crabs are softer on the underside. You get a stackable grenade under them and it can do some serious damage. Foxes are not super tough, but fast. They rely on those big damn arms to get around. You take one of them out of commission and they don't move well—makes them easier to hit."

"What about the big ones—the Bosses?"

"Persistence. You need to keep up a steady fire on them. That skin of theirs absorbs kinetic energy well enough, but you can fatigue it locally during a firefight. You can get it to where your regular small arms fire can do some serious damage."

Falto nodded. "They are formidable."

"I've seen footage of them removing a damaged limb, and it is downright freaky to watch. I mean, imagine one of us removing an arm or a leg like that."

She glanced down at her own bionic limbs. "It's not that hard," she said. "I'm more hardware than flesh in some areas. If I had to, I could remove a leg or an arm."

"That's different. You're talking bionics. Their limbs are flesh. To be able to do that, to build them genetically so that it's even possible, it's evil."

"I try not to think of them in terms of good or bad. They just are. When you try to think of the aliens in the same way you think of men and women, nothing adds up."

They cut their conversation off when one of the science team called out, "Hey, I think I've got something." Falto moved in his direction as he held the yellow device that had its tip buried in the snow.

"What is it?" another scientist asked.

"Water movement," he said, turning towards the ship and continuing to move the tip-head of the device along the ice. "I've never used this stuff before, but according to the instructions we got with it, I'm detecting some water movement here." He continued to trace an invisible line along the ice right up to the pile in front of the ship. "It's right here," he said, nodding downward.

Another scientist broke out some florescent pink paint and made a dotted line on the snow and ice where the tip had been dragged, marking the line. "You want to track it all the way to the water's edge?"

The scientist with the device looked nervous at that suggestion. "I'm not sure that is necessary."

Falto understood. She was a Marine, Rosales was a Ranger—they had signed up for the service to face the enemy. The scientists did not. *They have seen some of the same things we have aboard the ship and that makes even a strong man afraid.*

Another of the science team, a young African American woman, pulled her glove back to reveal a wrist comp. "Doctor Schrivener, we think we've found some sort of line or connection between the ship and the water." Falto couldn't hear the response, but the scientist nodded. "Roger that." She then turned to the others. "We are to hold here."

Falto looked around and found a tall block of ice leaning at a steep angle. She moved next to it and rested her butt on it. Waiting was something that she was used to. It took almost an hour for Captain Wade and Dr. Schrivener, along with an ASHUR rig, to join them.

Schrivener asked to see the readings and the scientist complied, tracing the pink dotted line on the ground with the device. Falto moved over near Captain Wade as he watched. "If he's using the device correctly, he's found moving water down there."

Wade contemplated that, saying nothing as he considered his next steps. "Alright, let's melt a hole and see what we have down there."

His words sparked an immediate reaction from Falto. "Is that a good idea? I mean, what if this ship decides to react to that?"

Wade almost smiled at her words. "I've already pulled out people from the ship. And I told the British what we found. They are on their way here now. Further," he glanced upward along the tall hull of the ship. At the top she could see Rangers and at least another ASHUR suit right at the edge. "Omega and the Rangers are set up in case this ship starts spitting out soldiers for us to deal with."

From his smirk under his goggles, she could tell that he enjoyed beating her to the punch. "Apologies. That's exactly what I would have recommended."

"See, Sergeant? We are getting to know each other."

A few minutes later, Dr. Lahoz and Major McKenna arrived, coming up from the south where their camp was. The scientist that detected the readers briefed everyone. Dr. Lahoz seemed excited. "We need to see what the ship is doing under all of this."

"Suggestions?" McKenna asked.

One scientist produced a flamethrower out of a large pack he had been carrying. It wasn't a military-grade flame unit, but a hose attached to a small propane tank. Falto had seen them before, usually when Buffalo had been socked in with snow and the Weather Channel covered the storm. People used them to clear driveways and sidewalks of ice and snow. He went to work assembling it as the other scientists conferred. There was some tension. She could hear it in the tone of their voices. She leaned in enough to hear what was being discussed. Everyone was worried if or how the ship might react. Looking above her at the looming long wall of alien construct, it was a nervousness that she fully understood. Even though she didn't see any signs of an alien, she pulled her ACR a little tighter to her body.

The scientist with the flamethrower began slowly, picking the lowest spot on the dotted line. He used it to cut out a large hole, almost two meters in diameter, with a series of consecutive passes. The moisture rising from his work hit the cold air and turned into tiny snowflakes, landing downwind of the hole.

It was slow and meticulous work. *This is what separates scientists from Marines. If we had been given this task, we would have used explosives to blow this wide open.* She appreciated the care with which the scientists were working. *We have no idea what is down there.*

Someone showed up with an additional tank of propane, and it was needed a few minutes later. Water pooled in the hole, trying to freeze as the flamethrower continued to cut deeper. There was a pause at one point to recheck the readings with the probe, then they continued to melt their way down to whatever the source was.

At about two meters down, something dark appeared under the water and ice at the bottom. The scientist, to his credit, moved slowly, melting around the dark object that seemed to bisect the bottom of the hole. Bit by bit, it became visible to everyone hovering at the edge. It was gray, almost like a tentacle, only much larger and thicker than Falto had imagined. It ran from the alien ship out towards the sea and was almost like a thick pipe. As the surrounding ice melted, she could see that it was moving, almost pulsating…

drawing water from the sea towards the ship.

One scientist entered the hole with a cup and bailed out the water that remained. As he finished, they got their first clear view of the appendage. Falto glanced at the ship, then back down to it.

I wonder if it can sense us. Now that we've uncovered it, what do we do? Other questions percolated in her brain. *Did it grow this thing? How did it get through the ice pack? If it can grow this, what else can the ship grow?*

That was the subject of the conversation that followed. The scientists were satisfied that they had found this…appendage…or whatever it was. Major McKenna and Captain Wade were in favor of destroying it. "Nothing good can come from this ship getting water. If it is, indeed, a living organism and aquatic, then cutting it off from the sea makes sense," McKenna pressed.

The concern that Wade raised was what the reaction from the ship might be. The scientists called for more study and research, perhaps exposing the entire appendage. Captain Wade wasn't in favor of it. "Uncovering this thing doesn't give us anything new in terms of information. Water levels are rising, it's drawing water with this thing. I say we blast it."

He then surprised her by turning to her. "What do you think, Falto?"

For a few moments, she said nothing, stunned as all eyes fell to her. She rallied her thoughts and charged them into the discussion. "We have no idea what this ship can do if it somehow recovers. At the same time, we cut this thing, it may react by unleashing those aliens we saw aboard. We can't win this war by playing it safe and sitting back and doing nothing. I didn't come all this way to see this thing heal up and take off. I say we get our people off of this thing, cut it, and let's see what happens. We should be prepared for a reaction, whatever form that might take."

The scientists were not happy with her words. "We should study this more?" Dr. Lahoz argued.

McKenna shut him down. "What more can you learn from it— how much water it can suck in? Staff Sergeant Falto is right. She has more experience than any of us with the aliens. We need to cut this thing off. The sooner the better."

That surprised Natalia. *He knows who I am. He's studied up on me.* Of course, it made sense. *He probably has files on all of us.* Still, it felt strange to have support from the Royal Marine commander. She gave him a nod of approval which he returned.

Captain Wade agreed and started to signal his people to get out of and off the ship. McKenna walked up to him and Falto caught their conversation. "I've got explosives with me. If you don't mind, the Royal Marines would like the honor."

"Frankly, I think we can handle it," Wade replied.

"I don't want to squabble over it, but it's really no trouble. We would consider it an honor."

"My people can handle it," Wade said.

Falto intervened, more out of frustration with the egos she saw being displayed. "Does it really matter who in the hell blows it? Give me the charges, I'll do it."

Clearly she upset Wade more than McKenna, she could read it on his face. He glared at her, then at McKenna, eventually waving his hand at the hole in a gesture to the Royal Marine.

He can be pissed off if he wants.

The charges the Royal Marines used were small, can-shaped black blocks. One Marine had a handheld trigger mechanism and unspooled wire between him and the charges as he moved to a safe distance. They were set in the hole and the team evacuated the entire prow of the ship, with the British heading south and the Americans heading north. It was a lot of explosives but she understood the thinking. If there were other hidden tentacles in the ice nearby, the concussion would damage them as well.

Falto still wasn't far from the bulk of the ship, but followed Rosales behind a big slab of ice for cover. While she couldn't see up on top of the ship, she had little doubt that they were falling back towards the camp. The lone Omega ASHUR that had accompanied them even took cover behind some ice.

After a quick check to make sure his people were safe, Captain

Wade called out, "Clear!"

There was a crack-boom of the explosives going off. Even from where Falto was huddled down, she could see bits of ice flying skyward over the ship and a faint hint of gray smoke curling in the wind. For a few moments, there was silence. In the back of her mind, she wondered if the ship could feel what had just happened. So many of the aliens seemed to be resistant, if not immune, to pain. *Maybe that tentacle-tube-thing was so small, it was like us losing a hair.*

A dozen yards further down, the ice burst upward and a spray of liquid shot up, much of it turning to snow when it hit the frigid air. One of the scientists ran up to the hole and peered in. "We got another one over here that is burst."

Then it came, a deep moaning sound. It reminded her of when her stomach would growl when she was hungry. It was a low gurgle followed with a deep bass tone lasting for two full seconds.

Aw shit! It did feel it.

Raising her ACR and aiming it at the ship, she realized the folly of her gesture. Shooting at it with small arms fire was a waste of ammo. Still, holding her weapon with her finger poised above the trigger gave her a sense of control.

The sound died off.

"Any signs of activity?" Wade signaled in his wrist communicator. While she couldn't hear the details of the responses, she didn't see him shift into action.

"Alright, people," Wade said coolly. "So far, so good. We're going to check the rest of the front of the ship, just in case this thing has more of those things in the water." Slowly, the scientists and the protectors started back around the corner of the ship to continue their search.

"All we got was a moan," Rosales said as he and Falto started walking. "I got more out of my last date." When he realized what he'd said, he blushed. "Sorry. My barracks-brain kicked in."

"I'm a Marine," she assured him. "I've heard worse, from worse."

"That wasn't much of a reaction from the Fishies."

Falto shook her head. "I'm thankful, but cautious. Just because we haven't seen a reaction doesn't mean that one isn't in play."

CHAPTER 21

Operation Durendal
British Base Camp, South of the Crash Site,
East Coast of Greenland

Lieutenant-Colonel Frye's image came up on the secured satellite comms device in McKenna's tent. It surprised him to see the image on the screen. *I wish we were in a place with better reception. At least we could have used the holoprojectors rather than these antiquated flat-screens.* He leaned in as the wind rippled the exterior of his tent, causing some unwanted ambient noise.

That was one thing about the Americans, they had more posh settings than his people. *They have hard shell portable domes and interconnected buildings. We have cold weather tents.* He wondered what it was like to have the kind of defense spending that the United States enjoyed. *They aren't flaunting it, but I have to admit I'm a bit jealous.*

"I hadn't expected the pleasure, sir," McKenna said.

"Good to see you, Andy," he said. "I trust things are going well."

"That would depend on your definition of 'well,' sir. We found the ship was siphoning water from the ocean and we, shall I say, severed its ability to do that."

"Any reaction from our aquatic friends?"

"Per my last report, the ship is definitely alive, sir. It reacted audibly."

"Audibly?"

"It moaned, sir. At least, that is the best way to describe it. Quite

234

loud, actually. We are considering ourselves lucky that it didn't release its cargo on us."

"Yes. I can only imagine your relief at that. Is there anything you need from us?" His voice faded over the hiss of static from the dicey atmospherics. McKenna adjusted the fine tuning, hoping to clear some of it. *It wasn't this bad in Norway. I wonder how much of that is because of that damned alien ship?*

"We have received the airdrop of fuel for the LCAC-Hs. One will depart soon to deliver the samples we have gathered so far. We have enough fuel now so that if we are forced to vacate our position, we can." During his first few days in Greenland, McKenna had been concerned that if they had to flee, they would have to go by land along the coast—a cold and dangerous prospect at this time of year.

"Well then, this is not just a status call. Your initial reports reached MI6 and the Foreign Office."

His pause made McKenna stiffen slightly. "I see."

"Quite," Frye replied. "Needless to say both of them are less than supportive of your decision to share information with the Americans."

"We didn't share any technical data, sir. Only the risks that we were facing. I felt it was necessary at the time."

"Well," the lieutenant-colonel sighed, "they feel you exceeded your remit. I have been asked to inform you that you have gone beyond your authority."

"Sir, I haven't compromised what our scientists have found."

"I know. I told them the same. I told them that you were on the ground there in Greenland and that the last thing you needed was us telling you that your decisions were in error or questioning what you were doing."

"Thank you."

"They were, shall I say, displeased. No doubt when you are back from all of this, they will demand an inquiry. They will attempt to exert their authority. They will attempt to make you the scapegoat for everything that they perceive goes wrong up there."

McKenna didn't like the sound of that—politicians ganging up on him. *This could ruin my career. They will drag me through the mud just to demonstrate their power.*

"I stand by my decisions."

"As you should," Frye affirmed. "I told them that if you tried to make this an issue, you wouldn't be alone in any testimony that you might have to give. I would be there at your side, along with all the upper command of the Royal Marines. I like to think that talked them down from doing anything rash, but you can never tell with these political types."

Hearing those words was heartening for McKenna. "You saw my report on the American media that showed up?"

Frye's face wrinkled. "Yes. Damned fools if you ask me. As you are painfully aware, at any point, things could take a turn for the worse there. Only a madman would go up there to film for the news. Interestingly enough, the Foreign Office suggested that they allow the BBC to come up there…to capture the British perspective of matters."

It was Andy's turn to wince. "Please tell me you talked them out of it."

His senior officer chuckled. "That was a target that I took great pleasure in shooting down myself. I told them you were a Royal Marine commando and didn't have time to babysit reporters."

Thank God.

"That is most appreciated, sir."

"Have you seen any sign of the bollocks responding at all to your actions to sever them from the water source?"

"Not yet, sir. Of course, we do not know if this was significant to them or not. I have taken the precaution of interfacing our battlespace with that of the Americans, just so both sides have a full view of the surrounding ground. I've also poised several of our drones out on the ice for an early warning system."

"There is a chance that they might never respond. If that is the case, you may be there for some time."

Glancing around his tent, he caught the faint aroma of sweaty socks. "If that is the case, sir, we will need facilities that are more spacious and permanent."

"You are breaking up a bit. Please repeat."

McKenna tried again to adjust the signal.

"Sir, if that is the case, we will need facilities that are more spacious and permanent here."

"Understood. I have a team of engineers working on that right now."

McKenna didn't think that would be needed, though he dared not say it out loud. *The aliens have come once and are bound to come again. When they do, we may face them and whatever is aboard that ship.*

"We are still early into this operation. It will be some time before we need any semi-permanent structures."

"I understand. It doesn't hurt to be ready. Are you sure there is nothing else we can provide you?"

He wanted to say "more troops," but he knew the folly of such a request with the bollocks making inroads into London proper and several other coastal cities. One thing he'd learned as a Royal Marine was that it was always best to learn to work with what you had.

"I would prefer some thermal diving gear and the usual. Toilet paper and some uniform changes for the people here."

"I will see what I am able to get to you. Andy, you're doing a good job in a difficult situation. I will help with any problems that might arise when this operation is over. One thing I cannot allow flexibility with is allowing that vessel to return to enemy control. If that is going to happen, it must be destroyed. Fail to do that, and you will face wrath from within the Navy and from the outside."

"I placed the device, sir. I will do what is necessary."

"If that means the deaths of some of the Americans, so be it. Understood?"

"Completely." As he said that word, there was a moment of cringe that grappled with him. He had thought about the dangers to the Americans if he set off the bomb several times before. The lieutenant-colonel's comment drove that point home. *I hope it doesn't come to that.* While had no fondness for the Americans, he disliked the thought of killing them.

"Very well then. Carry on and please keep me posted," Frye replied.

The image went off, plunging the interior of the tent into darkness. McKenna slid into his sleeping bag and zipped it tight up near his head. Outside another gust of wind ruffled the tent fabric.

Someday I hope they send us someplace warm. Between here and Norway, I doubt I will ever feel my toes again.

* * *

The next morning he had been awakened early with a report of a pair of Skenks out on the shore ice. One had been shot by the sentry, a long-range shot. The other had scampered back out over the ice. *The Skenks are scouts. If they are showing themselves, our time is limited.*

McKenna joined the science team in their exploration. The team had been moving with a sense of urgency. They understood that the aliens might return at any time. As such they had opted to scramble through the parts of the ship that were more exposed, where the hull had ruptured and much of the water had been drained out. Everyone on the team was tired. Wading through icy waters for hours at time burned calories and patience. His Marines were getting frustrated with the scientists who seemed rushed in their work.

He and the Americans had discovered several other tentacles extending from the ship into the water and had destroyed them. The ship had not responded as it had the first time. Wade put a team on patrol along the shore, constantly looking for more.

That's fine by me. Let them do that while we try and plunder this ship.

As they entered the ship through their breech, he noticed that something was different. It was hard to put his finger on it, but something felt different. The headache that was common with the exploratory teams was there, despite the aspirin they took.

No, something looks different.

"What has changed?" he finally asked.

"I notice it too," Dr. Lahoz said. "Wait, look at the luminesce of the walls," he said. "They have been more of a yellow color, but now they are greenish."

"The chamber seems smaller than the last time we were here."

Lahoz looked around. "I think you're right."

"I'd ask what that means," McKenna started. "But I'm willing to bet no one knows."

"It is a reaction. The only thing that has changed is that we cut the ship off from its water source," another scientist said. "It's entirely possible that change is connected to that, but we don't have enough data to validate that hypothesis."

As they moved through the ship, other changes became apparent. "Where's the alien that was on the floor?" Lahoz said. The octopus-like tentacled creature that had been semi-absorbing into the deck of the ship was gone. There was no sign that it had ever been there.

"Tell me, did it just soak it up, or did something come and clean it?" McKenna asked, his hand drifting down to his sidearm in his holster that he wore on the outside of his environmental suit.

Lahoz bent over and stared intently at the liquid on the deck. "It was here yesterday. The ship must have absorbed the rest of it."

"That was a lot of organic mass in a short period of time," one researcher stated. The comment did not alleviate the nervousness that gripped at McKenna one bit.

As they crept through the winding tunnel systems, he noted he was on a pathway that he had not been on before. His wrist communicator throbbed and he activated it. "This is McKenna."

"Sir, there's been an incident," came a tense voice he identified as Lieutenant Kendall. "We've already called the medics."

"What is it?"

"It's Lance Corporal Beale. Something attacked him and now he's stuck."

The response only generated more questions than answers. "Send your coordinates. I'm on my way." The map layout for the explored sections of the ship uplinked to his helmet's DBF, Digital Battlefield Monitor, giving him the exact details of where they were. It took three minutes to reach them, mostly because of one wrong turn that only added to his frustration.

What McKenna saw was startling. Beale's environmental hood had been taken off. He was being propped up in an awkward sideways reclining stance on the floor, with one hand, sans his glove, sunk in the watery goo and into the floor.

Beale's face looked horribly sunburned, his eyelids cracked and bleeding and the tissue around his eyes seared to the point that it looked as if his eyeballs might fall out. They were dilated, more than he would have thought possible, and the whites of his eyes were crimson with blood. Beale's mouth was open and he sobbed as Kendall tried to help him.

"For God's sake, man," McKenna started, "what happened?"

"I'm sorry, sir," Beale cried. "It's my fault."

Kendall filled in the details as crisply as he could. "He took off his glove to reach in his hood and wipe something from his eye. Something attacked him, hit him with one of those damned blinder rays the aliens use. The lad fell down and tried to push off with his hand." Kendall nodded down to his hand and McKenna's eyes followed.

Beale's hand was sunk up to the wrist in the ship's floor. "Can't he pull it out?"

Beale cried out in agony and Kendall continued. "It's not just that he's stuck. The ship is absorbing his hand. We have tried to pull him out and we can't." There was a hint of desperation in Kendall's voice that was hard for Andrew to ignore.

The medic rushed into the room and immediately wrapped the face and eyes of the injured man. The blinder rays were nasty weapons, using a flash of intense radiation to fry eyes. Kendall continued in a lower tone of voice. "We need to get him out of here to treat him."

"Can you cut around his hand?"

"Sir," Kendall said. "We tried that."

"It makes me feel like my hand's on fire," Beale said.

Looking over at Lahoz, McKenna clearly wanted an explanation or at least some guidance. "It's possible that the material of the ship is integrating with his hand."

"What in the bloody hell does that mean?"

"We've seen it with the dead aliens being absorbed. Their tissue becomes one with the ship."

Damn it all to hell!

"We were going to try and cut him free, but when we start cutting into the ship, it *responds*."

"Sir," Beale said as he clenched his teeth in pain. "I don't want a snake thing to swallow me or a jellyfish to eat me." His words were enough to have everyone look up and around the narrow chamber where he lay.

McKenna leaned in and looked at the wrist that was simply now anchored to the floor. As he did, Beale wailed again, loudly. "What is it?" the medic asked.

"I'm not sure about my hand. I can't feel it. My entire arm feels like it's on fire."

The medic reached out and cut his environmental suit and uniform sleeve off. The arm was bright red, swollen. Ugly greenish streaks, like new ugly blood vessels, rose from where the wrist was stuck up through his forearm. Several of the normal blood vessels had burst and dark purple bruises were present. The major stared at them, unsure of what to make of it. He glanced at the Marine medic, who only silently shook his head.

"What can we do?" McKenna asked the medic.

"I—I—this isn't anything I've ever seen before, sir," he stammered. Once more, Beale cried out in pain.

"We have to do something."

The medic nodded. "I can use the laser scalpel to," he gulped, "cut off his arm at the elbow."

"His elbow?"

"Those greenish streaks stop there. It's the only way to be sure, sir."

"You can't do that, sir," Beale panted between ripples of pain. "I'll never pilot a Sovereign again if you do."

McKenna looked at him with deep pity. People hit with the blinder ray only stood a chance if they had their visors down—and it was clear that Beale didn't. *Despite all of this pain, he's worried about piloting his Lancaster.* He was angry that Beale had broken protocol by removing his glove and hood. At the same time he was proud of him. "Don't you worry about that, Beale. It's more important that we get you out of here." Turning to the small gathering of his Marines. "You lads that don't have your visors down, activate them now."

The medic rallied himself and took action, wrapping Beale's arm in an auto-tourniquet. Using a preloaded hypodermic, he gave him two shots, presumably of painkillers. If it was designed to ease his pain, it was hard to tell. Beale was close to hyperventilating.

"Best to move fast," McKenna said.

The medic pulled out the laser scalpel and activated it. It took a moment to cut through the elbow, and as he did, Beale howled in agony. Smoke rolled from the cut as he finally got all the way through. The injured lance corporal collapsed, caught by two more Marines who were present and ready. Even with the environmental suit on, the major imagined he could smell the cutting of the flesh.

"Move him out," the medic said. "We need to get him back to the camp."

McKenna reached out and grabbed Kendall by the shoulder. "Something is loose on this ship and dangerous. I want everyone informed about this creature with the blinder. Everyone needs to be on alert. In the meantime, get back to the base and pull Beale's chest and helmet cameras." He wanted to withdraw everyone.

"Already on it, sir," Kendall said, rising to his full height and following the others.

McKenna took a few moments and looked around the chamber. Beales's severed arm wobbled slightly as the ship devoured his flesh a millimeter at a time.

This ship is getting nastier towards us. I should let the Yanks know what happened.

CHAPTER 22

Operation Sulaco
Crash Site, East Coast of Greenland

Veronica Diamond was stunned at the size of the ship. From the air, it looked huge. As she followed the Rangers towards the ship, she got a different sense of the scale of the craft. As they walked, she looked back to make sure that Fizz was filming. It was unnecessary, Fizz was always filming. She activated the microphone inside her environmental suit.

"One cannot fully appreciate the immense size of this vessel until you walk up to it. It stands easily four or five stories in height. The front of the ship is wider than the rear, which makes it look non-aerodynamic. Since we do not know how this shop moves through space, we don't know how efficient this design is."

In her mind, she was already thinking about how to edit this imagery with what Fizz had captured from the air. *So far, we have the scoop—but that could disappear any time, either because of the competition or the Fish.*

Deactivating the microphone, she turned to Fizz who gave her a thumbs-up. Captain Wade had not been in favor of them coming aboard the alien ship at first, but Diamond knew she was like sandpaper and she slowly, methodically wore him down. She laced her requests with reminders that her cameras were far above the military spec gear the Rangers were using, that the images would show Omega Force in a positive light as opposed to their usual brutality. It took a lot of convincing, but Veronica was unrelenting.

I'm pretty sure he's letting us aboard simply to shut me up. I can one hundred percent live with that.

As they approached the ship, she felt the slight tug of the field that surrounded the vessel. Her people had been warned about it, informed that it was some sort of brain wave. They gave her Tylenol to deal with the headache that was to come. Within a few minutes of crossing the barrier she felt it, near the back bottom of her head, far below where her extensions were woven in. It was a physical reminder that this ship was extraterrestrial and as such inherently dangerous.

"How you doing, Fizz?" she asked as they got near the opening where the Rangers were already entering.

"I feel like the morning after tequila. A lot of tequila."

"I would have guessed you more of a vodka-hangover kind of guy."

"I prefer my potatoes fried."

Leaning forward, she called out to Verret two paces ahead of her. "How are you, Verret?"

"Frosty and underpaid," he replied.

I guess that's a positive thing.

"Fizz. I want you to get a shot of me entering the ship. Wait until Verret goes in first."

I don't want people to know that I've hired my own security. It's better for ratings if they think I am brave and risking my life to get the story.

"That's the plan, pretty lady," he replied.

She waited at the entrance until Verret was completely through the slit. Glancing back at Fizz, she cautiously slid in. It wasn't that she was afraid, but she wanted people to get a sense of fear from her, an emotion that she was overcoming.

I want them to feel like they are going on this exploration with me.

She was momentarily in awe of what she saw. *I've watched too many movies and shows about spaceships. I was expecting corridors and lights.* This, this is something else. There was a wetness to it, and a feeling that it was very much tissue rather than some sort of construct.

Fizz entered. "Whoa," he muttered as he adjusted the tiny bright camera light and swept the chamber.

Veronica activated her mic again. "This is not at all what you might expect. If you're like me, you were expecting something *Star Wars*-ish. This is something that was genetically grown or engineered to be like this. I can tell you, there is almost a feeling of dread when you enter it." As she spoke, two of the Rangers turned around. She made a mental note to have Fizz make sure that their rolling eyes didn't make it into the final edit of the piece.

Some members of the military liked the media. She understood it; it was a chance for friends and family at home to see them, perhaps bump up their social media ratings. Others viewed the press like annoying and painful blisters on the bottoms of their feet. There wasn't much they could do about them, but they were more of a nagging feeling than a threat.

What they feel isn't what's important. All that really counts is how the viewers feel when they see the final piece.

As they snaked their way through the ship, she couldn't escape the mix of claustrophobia and awe. Fizz was on his game, sweeping everything he could with his camera, zooming in on the things that were more colorful or downright strange.

Each room was a visual treasure trove of footage. In one long hallway, the water on the floor sloshed as the doors at either end opened and closed. Veronica once more went into narration mode. "As you can see, the ship seems to be alive all around us. There are subtle movements from time to time…a reminder of how bizarre the alien technology is."

As they sloshed into the next chamber, she spotted the female Marine that she had liked so much. Veronica moved up beside her. "You look remarkably familiar."

The Marine said nothing in response. She simply lowered the visor on her helmet to obscure her view.

It didn't deter Veronica. "What is your name again?"

"Falto. Natalia Falto."

Diamond's mind raced. "Of course! You were one of the POWs that the Trident team rescued out on the west coast."

Falto said nothing in response, just continued to scan the chamber as if looking for a threat.

"I'd love to get some time with you. Your perspective about this ship given your experiences is priceless."

"I'm not here for you," she replied flatly. "I'm here to advise them." She nodded to the nearby Rangers.

"Your point of view would really enhance this story."

"Go fish."

Even Veronica admired the double meaning of her response.

There was commotion, quick and immediate, up ahead in the long chamber they were in. Water was splashing madly as Rangers started to swing their weapons into play. Veronica froze in place though from behind her, she saw Fizz's light dance off the walls, leaving glowing spots in its wake. "Get it!" someone called. There was a brilliant flash of white light that illuminated the entire chamber for a moment, then came the gunfire, short bursts and single shots. Verret moved back, placing his body between her and whatever was causing the disturbance.

The disturbance looked to be more than one, at least from what she could see by leaning around the mass of her bodyguard. There was scurrying, quick and jagged, along the walls in two places. Shots followed the blurs she saw moving. One was hit—its erratic course was terminated by a *bang*. It slid down the wall into the water on the floor. The other, apparently sensing the danger, did something she had never seen a Fish do, it fled. It dove for the vaginal doorway... *I'm going to need a way to describe those doors that doesn't use that word*...then disappeared.

Whatever it was, it was down, surrounded by Rangers with their weapons aimed. Falto stood there, unmoved, her ACR poking downward at whatever was in the water at their feet. The Rangers had all been in motion, but she had remained impassive, wrapped in an eerie calm. The Rangers' voices were tense, loud and crisp.

"What the fuck is that?" came one voice.

Another rang out, "Is anyone hurt?"

"Get some guns on that door and get a line to Crockett."

"My vision is messed up," one called.

A fellow Ranger leaned in, looking at his face. "Raise your visor," he said, and looked at the man's eyes intently. "Flasher hit. Good thing you had your visor down."

"I feel like my face is sunburned." His lips were cracked and the upper one was bleeding.

"Yeah, it looks almost as bad as it probably feels. Let's get you back to the base," the Ranger said. Another one of them started leading him out. As he passed, Veronica moved forward to fill the void to get a better look at what had caused the commotion. It was a spider-like creature, with a body roughly the size of a football. Its ten legs were long and spindly, covered with tiny little spikes, as was its body. The two forward claws were short. One leg twitched slightly as a Ranger moved it up out of the water with the barrel of his weapon, pushing it up along the wall. Its coloring was a strange blur of pastels, pink to green. She saw where it had been shot through the body—the hole oozing a black oily substance that swirled down the sloped wall down to the water where it was diluted. She eyed the holes in the wall of the chamber where the missed rounds had struck. The walls were bleeding, an ugly pinkish fluid that trickled down.

"Fizz," Veronica muttered. "Please tell me you are getting this."

"I am. What the hell is it?"

One of the scientists squatted down and looked at the dead alien creature. "It looks like a mutation or variation of the deep sea Lithodid crab, only with more spider traits. This one has two additional pairs of legs, and they have an additional set of joints on its legs. Very strange." She pointed to the body of the crab where a strange series of bumps appeared. "I take it that is the flasher."

The mention of a flasher had meaning for both Veronica and Fizz.

That is how Dana Blaze had died.

Without warning, one Ranger called out and grappled with

something on his arm. Another swatted at something on his hood. Diamond felt the tension in the chamber ratchet up several notches and she found herself crouching, looking upward.

What had hit the two Rangers was something that looked a lot like a jellyfish. They were the size of a basketball and the Rangers struggled to pull them off, flinging them to the water that was knee deep in the chamber. As she watched upward, a slit seemed to open, and another came out, slithering down the wall to one of the bullet holes. It stopped there, bluish in color, giving off a light azure glow as the lights hit it.

One that hit the hood of one Ranger somehow got a slippery tentacle through the hood, slapping onto the face of the soldier, who wailed in pain. Another Ranger pulled the big jellyfish off, tossing it to the wall where it slid down into the water. Veronica saw that where the creature had landed on the hood, there was a hole, as if the protective gear had simply melted. His comrades helped the wounded man up. From what she could see of his face, there were welts on his bright crimson skin where he had been stung. His cheek was distorted, swollen already.

"What are those things?" Diamond asked nervously.

A Ranger whose name tag read "Rosales" responded to her question. "These are the little ones. We had a big one devour one of our people. They can eat right through your protective gear. If a big one gets you, it will dissolve your flesh right down to the bones." There was no hint of exaggeration in his voice. It sounded like a sincere warning.

"What's their purpose?" Victoria asked.

"Evidently they're here to fuck with us," Rosales replied. It was clear that he was still burning adrenaline as he spoke.

"So this has happened before?" Diamond asked.

"The jellyfish, yes," Falto replied. "Not the spider crab thing. He's new."

The scientist produced a plastic cylinder from her pack. "We need to take this back."

"You go right ahead," one Ranger said, moving again to cover the door.

The scientist used a set of tongs to pick up the dead spider creature and slide it into the clear cylinder, then closed the top. A tiny green light appeared which seemed to confirm that it was sealed. It was only then that Veronica noticed that her heart was pounding in her ears.

We just got attacked and didn't even know it.

Veronica's eyes locked on Natalia Falto. During all of the commotion, she hadn't moved. There hadn't been so much as a flinch. *Is she really that calm, or does she just lock up?* The fact that she had not panicked when so many others had made the sergeant very interesting. *I need to get her to talk to me.*

One Ranger was adjusting his comms link on his wrist, clearly carrying on a conversation. Fizz continued to film as he did. When he stopped, he turned to the group. "Alright, folks, we are leaving."

"We just got here a few minutes ago," Veronica protested.

"It seems these things are loose in other places in the ship. Crockett says the British just told him that one of these spiders badly wounded a Royal Marine. We need to retrograde and secure this chamber. To do that, we need the civvies out of here."

"But we've only been filming for few minutes."

"Protocol, ma'am," the Ranger said, motioning for her to turn around.

"I have my own security person. Can we stay and get a little more filming done?"

Verret turned on her with an expression of harnessed rage. "You can't pay me enough to stay inside this ship without them."

Everyone has a price—but perhaps now isn't the time to try to find it.

"Fine." Even Veronica knew there was a line she shouldn't cross. That didn't stop her from trying, just not now.

"I gotta say, boss lady," Fizz weighed in. "I'm siding with the Rangers on this one."

"You afraid, Fizz?" she asked, cocking him a smile.

"Just a lot."

Me too. The difference was that Veronica was more than willing to confront her fears. That was what going up against Dana Blaze had taught her. It had been an emotional, and somewhat physically painful, lesson. "Alright, let's hightail it out of here." She did what she could to make it sound like her decision, despite knowing full well that the Rangers were more than willing to drag her and her team out—even Verret.

They marched back to American base while the Rangers did their sweep of the ship. Diamond hated the winter in the US. She'd finally found something worse, winter in Greenland. *Why couldn't this thing have crashed in the Bahamas?* No matter how many layers of clothing she wore, the cold seemed to find a way through. The hood covering her face broke the biting wind, but she could almost feel the pores on her face drying up. *This is going to take days of spa treatments to correct when this is over.*

When they got back, she was forced to queue up with the others for decontamination. It reminded her of the girl's locker room after a volleyball tournament in college, only more assembly line. While she hated the procedure, she also preferred it to being exposed to some microscopic alien organism.

Once inside, she pulled Fizz aside. "You got everything, didn't you?"

"Of course I did," he whispered back as she leaned in close. "Scared the shit out of me, but I got it. The company satellite is going to be overhead in the next six hours. I can shoot up everything we have in raw form when it does. Of course, that will be a violation of our agreement with Captain Wade."

"I told him I would not put anything out on the air. I never said that we wouldn't transmit it up to the satellite for storage. He can't be pissed at us for having an off-site backup."

"Something tells me he isn't going to see it the same way you do."

As she huddled with Fizz, she saw Falto start to walk past her. Veronica reached out and gently grabbed the sergeant by the arm. It was solid as a rock.

That's right, she's had bionic replacements.

Falto pivoted in place and looked at her fiercely. "Let me go," Falto spoke in a low tone.

Diamond did. Something told her that Falto wasn't the kind of person to give two warnings. Fizz was behind her, and she prayed that he was discreetly capturing their conversation on film. "Sergeant, I'd like to sit down with you and talk about your experiences, both as a prisoner and here at the crash site."

"No thank you."

"Sergeant, please. You have a perspective on this ship that is different from anyone else's. You lived with the Fish for a long time."

"I've done all of the interviews that the PAs asked of me. I've already told my story many times."

"There's always more to the story."

"Not this time," Falto countered. "I'm just a Marine here to advise."

"When that spider-thing attacked, you didn't flinch or duck. I watched you. The Rangers responded, but they were frightened, I could hear it in their voices. You just stood there, taking it all in. You have to be a pretty cool customer to not get rattled with those things jumping all over the place."

"I'm sure it looked that way to you."

"So you were frightened?"

"No. I just don't shake easily. I had my life threatened every minute for months. I lost friends, limbs, and every shred of my decency and humanity. The Fish take from you, that's their nature. You want to know what I was thinking in that moment?"

"Yes."

"I wasn't afraid, but I also didn't react. I was numb. Some might call that courage under fire. I don't think I was brave—I was waiting for the right moment to deal with the threat, if I had to."

"The big brave Rangers were panicked. What I saw was a female Marine who didn't flinch."

"Maybe I should have. Did you ever consider that?" Before

Veronica could answer, Falto turned and walked away.

"Tell me, Fizz, did you get that?"

"Video, yes. Audio is going to be weak. I'll have to run it through the AI buffer to enhance it…but yeah, I got it."

"She's fascinating."

"She's hurt," Fizz countered. "Hurt in ways that we can't possibly understand. You would be wise to let her be. She's done her part for her country and then some."

"If that's the case, why is she here?"

Fizz leaned in slightly. "We all have our personal demons. Hers are worse than any of ours. Maybe she's trying to purge them, or face them down. I can't tell for sure. I do know this—you aren't going to want to be there when that happens."

"You're wrong, Fizz. That's exactly where I want us to be."

CHAPTER 23

Operation Sulaco
Crash Site, East Coast of Greenland

Captain Bryan Wade stared at the vast chamber and could feel his stomach knot up. He stood with Captain Wertan, the other Rangers, and three scientists. The last time he had been in the chamber had been days before. There had been large green organic tubes in the room filled with a new breed of aliens. They had been dormant, or at least that was the assumption.

Now the room was unfamiliar. Four of the tubes were empty, their green viscus fluid puddled on the floor, mingling with the water that was pooled there. The occupants of the tubes, the squid-like aliens, were nowhere to be seen. The others were still in their tubes, curled up tightly, but there was no way to know for how long.

"When did it happen?"

"During the night," one scientist said.

"Please tell me you have it recorded."

The scientist nodded, handing him a digipad. With his gloved hand, he tapped the play button and watched intently. For a full minute, nothing happened; all of the alien-filled tubes were simply in place. Then the tube on the far end opened at the bottom. The thick green liquid splashed out on the floor, splattering everywhere. The creature inside the tube didn't drop out, it slid down slowly, unrolling from its organic cocoon, unfolding its limbs.

It wasn't as large as the typical Crab, if there was such a thing, but was still large enough to look menacing. Its skin was grayish on top, almost white on the bottom. Its body had an almost sea urchin-like appearance, crossed with slender but deadly spikes along the head. Like the Crab, it had a long body, and a raised upper torso. It was there that the similarities ended.

As it moved and extended the six thick, carapace-covered walking legs, he saw that it was about two and a half meters long, not including the tail. It didn't have a stinger like the Crab; instead, it was more like an armored tentacle. There was a large, slender flap with squid-like suckers at the end. Near the base of the tail was a separate, smaller tentacle. They moved like snakes as the creature stretched.

The front appendages were more like arms coming out of the torso. The Crabs had claws, but this creature had hooks, thick and menacing. As it stepped away from the tube it had been in towards the camera, he saw the maw in action. It consisted of two large sleek black beaks, opening the closing around the teeth. The pair looked like they could crush a man's head without flinching. Their glossy blackness and size made the mouth menacing.

Behind the creature, one by one, three more tubes disgorged their contents. The creatures moved slowly, but in Wade's mind, he knew that was probably a result of their dormancy. *Once they fully awaken, they probably can move as fast as a Crab.* It was a sobering thought, having faced their larger counterparts in battle. *We have no idea what weapons these things may have or how they will perform in battle.*

The creatures milled about for a few minutes, then moved to one of the walls. There was no door present. They simply pushed, and the wall opened up to accommodate them. Wade found himself unconsciously stepping away from the wall where he had been standing, giving it a glance as the footage ended. *They can move freely through the ship, while we are limited. Not a good situation at all.* His training kicked in. The threat just soared. *Those things are wandering around the ship and can pop out from anywhere. I need to get my people out of here.*

"Crockett," came a voice in the earpiece in his ECH. "Priority message from Major McKenna."

He closed his eyes for a moment. "Put him through."

"Captain. We've had an incident in the ship. One of my men was hit by a small crab-like creature that had a blinder ray. He fell and his hand sunk into the floor and, well, it hooked onto him—wouldn't let him go. The bloody ship was absorbing him. We had to cut his hand off to get him out."

"How is he?"

"Not good. The radioactive burst fried his eyes. He didn't have his visor down and caught it square on. The footage we got from his helmet camera is a mess, but I am going to send it to you. Needless to say, I have pulled my people out of the ship."

"If you need anything to treat him, just let me know," he said. It was more of an instinctive response. For a moment, he suppressed the thought that McKenna was British. This was soldiers helping fellow soldiers.

"I appreciate that."

"So you've seen what they look like when they aren't hibernating?"

"I will send you the footage of what we have."

"Most appreciated," McKenna replied.

"I have some additional news on our front. We just found out that four of the squid aliens were… released, during the night. They moved right to the wall of the chamber and passed through it."

"We had some sightings out over the ocean ice—a pair of Skenks." McKenna's words came as a warning.

"The Foxes, yes, we tracked them as well. I think it is safe to say that the enemy is planning something if they are sending scouts out." He had not relayed the information to the Brits because the Rangers had seen them shoot and kill one of the Foxes.

"I have contemplated pulling my science team out, but we have barely scratched the surface on this ship."

I will keep those people in there as long as I have to. There's too much at stake with this vessel.

"We will likely be doing the same."

"It can't be a coincidence that we've had two of these, dare I say, escalations."

"I concur. I'd ask the scientists, but this tech is far beyond what they know," Wade said, thinking, *We have been poking around in the dark with this ship. So far, we've been lucky, with just a few injuries. I believe we may need to rethink what we are doing with these recons we've been running.*

"I'm starting to feel the same way," McKenna confided.

Wade knew he had air assets that could blow up the ship if need be. *Is now the time to employ them? If we can't explore the ship, should it be destroyed?* Telling McKenna was something he was not prepared to do. *What he doesn't know won't hurt him.* In that moment, he realized that call was his to make, but doing it now would require justification—and at the time he simply did not have it. "We're going to pull out and reassess. I will let you know where we land on this issue."

"Copy that."

Before he could lower his arm with the wrist communicator, it beeped again. "This is Crockett."

"Lieutenant Edison," the voice came back. "Sir, we have had an encounter with some sort of spider-crab creature. We have one wounded and have send the civilians back until we can secure our egress paths and make sure these are isolated incidents."

We cannot catch a fucking break.

"How badly was our person wounded?" Wade asked.

"Flasher burst, sir. He had his visor down. Radiation burns. He's throwing up but able to walk."

"Alright, we've had some grim news here, too. Follow the protocol. I want to talk to the science team and get our proverbial shit together."

"Yes sir."

Up until now, the ship's reactions have been rare. *This is an escalation...but of what?* He transmitted the orders to everyone and started the careful egress from the vessel.

* * *

It had taken time to get everyone back, send and receive files from the British team, and set up the science and military leaders for a strategy session about going forward. He had taken a few minutes to check on Sergeant Kritten who had been hit with a flasher. The radiation burns were severe, but should heal. The actual damage was the long-term risk of cancer from the burst. No one discussed that with the wounded man; such conversations were not necessary. His time on Earth was limited.

Another Ranger had been stung by one of the jellyfish creatures. Wade had checked on him and saw his face was swollen and distorted. The medics claimed that the toxin was going to make his life a living hell, but they were hopeful he would recover. Two wounded, one most likely terminal.

Damn it, we were only in the ship for an hour.

The pertinent personnel looked over all the material that the British had sent, as well as what had been gathered by body and helmet cameras. It was a meticulous review, with many requests to zoom in and review parts of the footage. McKenna was growing impatient but reminded himself that the scientists were viewing the data very differently than the military personnel.

They are immersed in the discovery, whereas my mind is focused on the mission.

Once it was completed, he looked around the commons area, making sure he looked at every face there. "We need to discuss our approach for going forward," he stated, shutting down the laptop they were using.

"We really need to learn more about these Squidwards," Dr. Schrivener said. "We are seeing more new species than we have encountered in the last six months."

"Squidwards?" asked Captain Wertan.

"It's from a really old cartoon," Diamond's cameraman said from where he stood, behind Falto and Veronica.

Wade held his hands up. "We are not naming these things after cartoons. They are Squids for now. In terms of learning more, I'm not sure that is practical. Those things could be anywhere. They could pop out behind us at any time too."

"So you're proposing we stop exploration of the ship?" Schrivener said.

"Absolutely not. Exploration of that ship is our primary objective. But we need to establish new rules of engagement that allow our Rangers to effectively protect the research personnel while we fulfill that mission."

Wertan nodded in agreement; it was his Rangers who were at the most risk.

"Why not ask for more troops?" Schrivener pressed. "Every time we go in that ship, we are taking our lives in our hands."

"It doesn't work that way," Wertan said.

"If it will help, I can talk to the Pentagon or someone on the task force," Schrivener offered.

"It's a matter of practicality," Wertan replied. "Throwing troops at this isn't going to help. Most of the chambers in that ship are small. Packing them with troops is problematic and dangerous, both for us and your people."

"We have just scratched the surface of what is potentially there," Schrivener replied, her voices raising in pitch. "We all knew the risks when we came here. We need to press on."

Wade shifted his stance and crossed his arms. "We've got wounded and dead from this expedition already. So have the British. The risk factor in this operation is going up more with these new species roaming around the ship, able to spring out at us from any direction. This isn't a matter of us just encountering them. They have attacked us. That ship is reacting to our presence, and there's no reason for us to believe that they will not continue to escalate." He was well aware of the body count the team had suffered so far. Four dead from the exploration of the ship alone, along with two wounded.

That doesn't even address the personnel we lost in the battle.

"You don't know that," Schrivener snapped. "No one knows that."

She's right, but she is blinded by her scientific perspective. Her people are at risk, but she sees Tommy's Rangers are bearing the brunt of that.

"Before you make that call, doctor, I think you should know that we spotted enemy Foxes out on the ice."

"Meaning?"

"Chances are the enemy is preparing to attack. They use the Foxes as scouts," Wade said, thinking, *She should know this, but she doesn't think like we do. We evaluate and respond to threats. Her people just want to explore.*

"Then let us get back out there and do our job." Schrivener demanded, leaning forward was she spoke.

Wade leaned right back at her, unintimidated by her stance. "I am going to do just that. But you and your people need to understand something. When the shooting starts, you will not have any Ranger protection in the ship. I will be pulling those forces out to deal with the enemy. When that happens, you and your people will be on your own."

"We came here knowing the risks."

There's no way she could have. None of us knew what this was going to be like. "Also, you have to know, I am under orders to ensure that this ship does not fall into enemy hands."

"I would think so."

She doesn't understand that I have two bombs to destroy the ship. Wade didn't want to bluntly tell her. The scientists would argue against that. For a moment, he said nothing. It was Sergeant Falto that interjected.

"I think the captain is dancing around the real issue here, doctor. When he says he can't let the ship fall into enemy hands, that means he will destroy it."

Schrivener's face fell with those words. Wade was actually glad that Falto had said the words. "You wouldn't?" she asked of him.

"I will follow my orders to the letter. That means if you get the signal from me, you need to hightail your asses out of that ship. Do you understand?"

"This is outrageous. I want to contact Colonel Slade. He never —"

"He knows my orders," Wade snapped. "He approved them himself."

Schrivener's face fell but, collecting herself, she said, "This is the greatest find of the war and you would risk squandering it out of fear."

"Doctor, if you are actually ever responsible for people's lives, you might feel differently. We cannot risk the enemy regaining control of this ship. It is that simple. I will follow those orders. So, if I tell you it is time to get out of there, you and your people had best run. I've already lost a number of people on this operation; I would hate to lose you too."

"Then we need to suit back up and get out there."

"Agreed."

The doctor departed along with the scientists, leaving only the military personnel and Veronica Diamond and her two people remaining. Falto moved up next to Wade as the scientists moved out. Diamond seemed to loiter just within hearing range.

"This is the right thing to do," Falto told him.

"I know."

"Why didn't you tell them you'd destroy the ship earlier?"

Wade dipped his head slightly in response. "I was hoping that it wouldn't come to that."

"It still might not," Falto offered.

"Not unless my luck changes."

Before she could respond, his earbud chirped to life. "This is battlespace command, we have movement on the outer perimeter markers to the east. Enemy forces are starting to emerge from the ice. Multiple contacts."

I'd hoped we'd have more time. Damn it.

Wade turned to everyone in the room, tying in his wrist communicator as he spoke. "This is Crockett. Enemy forces are incoming. Omega, sound Boots and Saddles and saddle up. Tommy," he looked over at Wertan, "deploy per Plan Charlie. Comms, send out the code word Stormbringer to our support in Thule. Everyone else, arm yourselves."

He switched channels on his wristcomp. "Dr. Schrivener, the enemy just showed up. You need to get in there and grab whatever you can. I'm pulling your Ranger protection."

"Damn!"

"Get in gear. Keep on this channel if I have to give you the word to pull out. The code word will be Wildstar."

"Wildstar, got it."

Wade started to gather his kit. They bustled past the trio from the media who were the only ones looking slightly dumbstruck by the change of events. Veronica Diamond stepped towards Wade as he moved to depart. "Where do we go?"

"I doubt you'd stay there if I told you," Wade said. "You wanted a story. Well, this is going to be one. Let's hope you live to send it."

CHAPTER 24

Operation Durendal
British Base Camp, South of the Crash Site,
East Coast of Greenland

Major McKenna stood in the portable command shelter and looked at the images being relayed by their Bulldog drones. At least a half-dozen Stegosaurs burst out of the ice floe, throwing big chunks of greenish ice skyward. Emerging next were several Golems, their ebony skin flickering with colors in some places, yellow and orange. Lobsters—too many to count—followed, their pinkish color, tinted crimson on the top, seeming to defy camouflage concepts. Thanks to the connection to the American battlespace feed, he saw even more enemy signals flicker on the holographic display.

This isn't a feint or a probe; this is an all-out assault.

"Communications—contact HQ and let them know we are under attack. Sound general quarters—all pilots to their Sovereigns, all Marines to their designed posts." He grabbed his pilot's helmet and pulled it on, as well as his tactical gloves and body armor. *Damn bollocks showing up like this.* Thoughts of exploring the ship further, given the new threats, evaporated as he once more prepared to face the enemy.

McKenna threw on his coat and headed to the maintenance shelter. The wind was blowing and a light snow fell. As he made his way down the well-worn path, he noticed the orange and purple sky looming over him. The sun attempted to flank a dark cloud formation, but was failing.

How can a place so beautiful be so deadly?

His eyes fell on the alien ship and there he found his answer.

They have a way of ruining everything they touch.

Moving into the large tent, he saw the row of Sovereign pods. "You're ready to roll, sir," his tech said, gesturing to the pod on the end. Rounding the corner, he shed his coat, tossing it on a tool chest, and his body tensed under the stunning cold as he climbed up into his cockpit. His fingers flew over the buttons and controls, powering up the Spitfire around him. His virtual displays shimmered on, showing green lights across the board.

His focus shifted to the tactical display. The signals showed the alien forces as they emerged about a half a kilometer out from the ship. There were three distinct groups, one heading for his base, one moving north, apparently to flank the crash site to come down on the Americans. The third force bore straight at the alien ship.

It puzzled the major for a moment. *Why go after the ship? They can hit us and the Americans and recover the ship once we are wiped out. If we are no longer in the picture, they can do whatever they want with the ship at their leisure.* He assumed that Captain Wade was seeing the same data as he was, and he hoped he was just as confused. *Why should I be the only one with a headache over this?*

Switching to the command channel, he adjusted his microphone as he stepped out of the pod, crunching in the snow. "This is Vindictive to Meteor and Bluecap, we need to establish our first line of defense at Phase Line Corgi. Bring our drones back to that point —before the aliens take them out." He adjusted the angle of his Spitfire and began a steady run, his legs pumping to keep the war machine moving. Leaning forward, he could feel each footfall as if it were his own feet crushing the snow and ice under him.

To his left, the alien craft loomed, rising like a monolith against the midday sky. "Bluecap, put a few of your boys on the left, just in case that ship decides to unleash some of its cargo on us."

Lieutenant McCranie's voice rang back, "With pleasure, sir."

"Sir," came Meteor—Lieutenant Walling joining in. "I have

established our heavy mortar team at point Zulu."

"Good work. Have them prepare to fire once the aliens begin to close on us. Don't have them wait for the orders."

His Marines were a mix of Sovereigns and ground troops—with an emphasis on the Sovereigns. He saw a section of ground forces rushing forward, not flinching at the line of aliens that were becoming visible in the distance. As their adaptive camouflage came on, they would become a momentary blur until they synced with his system. The *thunk* of outgoing mortar fire was followed by explosions tearing into the alien's ranks. Echoes of the blasts bounced around him as he moved into the firing line, commingled with the unison grunting of the Toads.

The line of aliens rushing toward his camp was daunting, the largest force that his people had faced since the start of the war. There were several dozen of the light blue Toads, though these seemed tougher, thicker, better armored than those he had faced before in Norway. The Lobsters scampered right at his line, oblivious to the explosions of mortar rounds that fell amongst them. There were several Golems leading the charge. At the rear of the line were a few Stegosaurs.

As they approached his maximum range, McKenna brought his Gatling laser to bear, firing off a power shell. His gaze tightened as he aimed his reticle on the lead Golem heading for his line. The moment the reticle flashed emerald green, he fired. The whirring barrels spun on the extended arm as small white flashes flickered, the only real indication that the weapon was firing. Tiny puffs of white smoke streaked across the body of the Golem, proof that his shots were finding their mark.

If the attack was bothering the hulking alien, it didn't show it. An N-LAW rocket fired from another Sovereign exploded on its left forearm, rocking the limb back hard and fast. As the limb came forward, it squirted several streams of liquid that instantly turned into snow as it ran.

A mortar round savaged one Lobster, blowing two of its lower mobility legs off spinning into the air. Firing another power shell, he continued to blaze away with invisible bursts of laser fire.

The Golem raised its undamaged arm and fired something—most likely a large bony spike projectile. He couldn't see it in-flight, but the air rippled along the path as it streaked out, slamming into a Typhoon that was off to McKenna's right. He didn't see the impact damage but knew it had to be savage; it overloaded his cloaking technology and left the Sovereign plainly visible. McKenna had seen such weapons punch through the transparent aluminum of a Sovereign and kill the pilot in his seat. The Typhoon reeled to one side under the impact, but somehow managed to keep upright.

Another N-LAWS rocket hit the rushing Golem in the leg, this time twisting him around hard and sending it falling on its side into the snow. It skidded for several long meters, churning up ice and rocks. McKenna didn't have time to grin as an alien cutter beam stabbed into the upper legs of his Spitfire. Bits of armor crunched while others flailed off. His damage indicator showed one spot on the right leg flicker to amber.

The firer was one of the Lobsters that closed on the British line. Gunfire from the heavy automatic weapons riddled the creature but it seemed immune to the pain it should be feeling. Some shots cracked the carapace on its long upper body, others made ripples as the thick hide absorbed them. A rail gun round cut off the end of the tail completely, sending a spray of oily bloods shooting skyward. Still the Lobster advanced. One by one the adaptive camouflage systems overloaded and the Royal Marines became visible.

McKenna shifted his position, advancing and turning to get a better angle on the side of the approaching alien. Lining up his target reticle, he fired one of his own N-LAWS rockets. On a twisting smoke trail, the warhead tore downrange, hitting where one of the enormous claws attached to the upraised body. The explosion wrapped the creature in a moment of flames and he saw the claw fly over the creature.

The Lobster sprang forward, landing on one of the Sovereigns in the line. Its remaining claw clamped onto Cobbler's Hurricane, grasping its arm in its pincers and twisting it hard. The metal groaned; even McKenna could hear it in his cockpit. A hydraulic line broke and hot green fluid—the blood of a Sovereign—squirted upward and splattered the alien in the process. The creature twisted hard, using its entire body, and ripped the arm off of the Hurricane entirely, throwing it at a nearby Spitfire.

Lance Corporal McComb's Gladiator rushed at the Lobster, its heavy automatic weapon blazing. It jumped up at the upraised torso of the creature, colliding with it hard. The Lobster twisted off of Cobbler, as McComb landed several hard punches at the eyes and head of the alien. One blow found a hole, punching deep into the head tissue. The entire creature seemed to throb under the hit, then went limp.

A cheer went up, one that McKenna joined in with. "Good work there, Otter," he said as McComb backed up to where Cobbler was struggling to his feet. The rejoicing was short-lived as the first wave of the Toad warriors sprang towards the line. One's head exploded, heat-fried from a large laser hit. Many others were riddled with small arms fire. Even when their limbs were torn off, the Toads didn't stop.

He discharged another power round and strafed the line of advancing Toads with his Gatling laser. He saw the shots sear black marks on the blue Toads, cutting a swath across their midsections. Two fell; the rest seemed to reel from the hits for a moment, then continued to rush forward. Another exploded from a shot fired from further down the line. Two more were turned to a bloody pulp as shots ripped them apart.

Still a few reached the line of the British forces, springing forward, and unleashing their smaller cutting beams on the Sovereigns. One diverted and headed straight at his Spitfire, grunting loudly as it sprang into the air.

It crashed into his Spitfire hard, staggering him back a little from the impact. His own camouflage system went offline instantly from the blow. Acting less on instinct than on his targeting system, he unleashed his torso-mounted chain gun. The weapon purred as he cut a line of shells under the Toad. He cut it in half at the waist as the creature's big claws grappled with him. In an instant, he looked the alien in the face, right in front of his cockpit canopy. Its eyes glared at him and it spat. A glob of greenish-brown goo, toxic on human flesh, splattered his lower canopy. Then the body went limp, flopping to the ground in front of him.

A Bulldog-class drone bounded at a pair of Toads, its mini-rockets blasting them both. The Bulldog was front heavy like its namesake, and was one of the few ground drone models that the British employed. While the drone skirted the still smoking remains of the two Toads it had blasted, another alien fired its cutting beam at the drone, hitting it square in the torso, toppling it over on its side.

McKenna's eyes went to the tactical display. The aliens were pressing his line hard. The temptation was to hold their positions, let the aliens bleed themselves. That was an emotional response. His brain crunched the numbers and processed the damage indicators from his forces. Three Lobsters were moving along the right flank. "This is Vindictive," he barked in his mic. "Meteor, you are being flanked. Oblique the line and retrograde with us. All other forces on Zulu, we are falling back to Phase Line Lambda."

As he backtracked his steps, he saw one of the lumbering Stegosaurs start to charge at the line. A Marine rail gun round hit it squarely on one of its huge armored plates, cracking it but failing to penetrate. McKenna brought his targeting sight for his N-LAWS into play, dancing it on the head of the charging creature, and sending two of his missiles streaking at his foe.

Both hit; orange flames and rolling black smoke briefly obscured his view as he struggled to see the results of the impacts. More shots tore into the creature as it lumbered forward like a charging elephant. He saw blackened marks on the body where his missiles had hit. A slick black streak oozed from one of the small craters his N-LAWS had caused, but otherwise it seemed undaunted.

From the creature's enlarged head, air rippled in concentric waves as it unleashed a large sonic blast on the British line. The ripples were unavoidable, though McKenna did lean in towards them as they came. The sound filled his cockpit and ears—a deep roaring, almost like thunder. A painful throbbing filled his temples. One of the smaller Mosquito-class Sovereigns fell over, awash with the sound waves.

Lieutenant McCranie's Hurricane II fired another rail gun round at the creature. The plume of superheated air roared from the barrel, and while he couldn't see the round mid-flight, he saw it strike where the creature's neck joined its body. Gore sprayed the snow, turning the churned white ground a sickly gray-black as the Stegosaur staggered. Then it spun fast, its fully-extended tail slamming McCraine's Hurricane II with a side blow that sent the Sovereign skidding along the ground, crunching armor in its wake.

The downed Mosquito rose and unleashed its flamethrower at nearly point-blank range, dousing the creature in flammable material that roared as it seared the thickly armored flesh. The beast reeled back around to face its foes, just in time for two more N-LAWS rockets from other Sovereigns to blast it, one in the leg, the other near the already injured neck.

The creature opened its snapping turtle–maw and roared—not its sonic weapon, but an angry cry of animalistic pain. Then its feet simply gave way and it thudded to the ground.

"Come on, lads," McKenna called out to his men. "We need to keep falling back."

As he spoke, a spray of small explosions rattled his Spitfire. Three burst on his cockpit canopy, making him wince. Some of the so-called spike or needle weapons that the aliens used had explosive tips and he had been caught in a burst of them. His armor was still holding, though his damage display showed more amber warning lights than before.

There was a blur off to his left, something dark, almost like a shadow. As he turned to face the threat, he saw it, a Golem, its dark black skin broken by a lightning bolt pattern that glowed bright blue. It was some ten meters away and swinging something over its head. As he brought his mini-chain gun to bear on the creature, peppering its thick skin with a steady burst of fire, it swung down one arm towards him.

It was holding a whip-like device, which lashed out at his Spitfire, wrapping around his left arm and torso. McKenna jerked back hard to break free, but then sparks flew down the whip, crackling over his Sovereign, azure flickers of energy that danced along the armor. His secondary systems and readout screens went off, including his tactical display.

That bugger has shorted me out!

A faint whiff of ozone wafted through the cockpit.

There had been reports of this weapon, but this was his first actual encounter with one in battle. His training and knowledge of the Spitfire took over. Bending at the waist, he leaned over and popped the circuit breaker panel, then reset the ones that had been tripped. As he did so the Golem closed with him, balled a fist, and landed a punch to his cockpit canopy that cracked the transparent aluminum around the large fist-shaped dent.

The Spitfire came back to life, and he sidestepped to avoid another devastating blow. Firing off two power rounds, his Gatling laser whirred and he kept feeding it energy. Dozens of little white spots marked the burning he was doing to the flesh of the creature. Raising his arm slightly, he wasn't using his targeting system to track his fire, simply eyeballing the damage he was inflicting as his guide. He brought it up the neck of the Golem and at the narrow crimson-lit slit eyes.

The Golem threw up an arm to deflect the laser and staggered back. That allowed McKenna to fire another N-LAWS into its upper chest. The two were so close that hot bits of the exploding rocket pinged and dinged off of his Spitfire's armor as the Golem was squarely hit. It raised its whip that was now free from his Sovereign and looked to be swinging it for another strike when another explosion tore into the alien.

This time the blast was larger, more devastating than before. It knocked McKenna off his balance and sent his Spitfire falling backwards on the snow behind him. The impact was hard, throwing him against the restraining strap in his seat digging the harness into his flesh. His ears were ringing as he struggled to get his bearings for a moment. Sweat stung to the corners of his eyes as he looked skyward, then he attempted to sit up.

Something grabbed his Spitfire, he could feel a strong pull on his left arm. Leaning forward to get a view, he saw McCranie's Hurricane II grappling with him, helping hoist him upright. Standing from a fallen position was tricky with any Sovereign, but it was greatly aided by his junior officer.

"You alright, sir?"

He glanced over and saw that the Golem he had been fighting with was down, splayed out on the white snow, smoke rolling from where a recoilless round had hit it. "Thank you, Lieutenant. Let's get back to Phase Line Lambda before we are overrun entirely," he managed with a ragged breath that came from fighting his Spitfire to get upright.

Glancing down at the tactical display, he saw that the Americans had problems of their own. His mind went to the trigger for the fuel air explosive. *The Yanks are too close. If I set that off, they will be caught in the blast.* Should he trigger it now, risking killing some of them to deny the aliens the ship?

No, not yet. This battle is still young.

CHAPTER 25

Operation Sulaco
American Base Camp, West of the Crash Site,
East Coast of Greenland

Falto put on her gear without even thinking about it. That was what training did, it made the mundane instinctive. The STG-W gear she strapped on felt familiar, if not strangely comfortable. She counted her magazines and grenades, making sure that her grenades were secure. The armor went on over her cold weather clothing. When she was done, she donned a thermal winter poncho, white with light gray streaks. It was Ranger gear, but she liked it, less for the warmth than for the freedom of movement it gave her. *I wonder if the Corps has these?*

She cleared her ACR and made sure it had a fresh magazine in it. Her assault weapon was more than a gun; it was the difference between life and death. The Marine Corps drilled that into her and she adopted it as one of her mantras. With a weapon, she felt she had a degree of control in her destiny. Without it, she was just a target.

Warrant Officer Rosales moved in beside her. "How much are you carrying?"

"Eight mags, four stackables."

"Good, that will do. You're with me."

"I don't need a babysitter," she replied, eyeing him suspiciously for the first time since they had met. *He is with me everywhere I go; this can't be an accident.* "You don't have to babysit me. I can handle myself."

"I'm well aware of that. Captain Wade asked me to shadow you."

There it was, in the open.

"Why would he do that?"

"I can't say," Rosales responded. "But I've been told to keep you in my sights and watch out for you."

Falto gazed at him, searching for the right words to say. *He can't be worried about me getting hurt, not at this point. No, this is something else.*

"Doesn't he trust me?"

"As I said, Staff Sergeant, he didn't tell me."

Falto's mind filled with a rage. *This is because I was a POW. He isn't sure if the aliens got to me in some way, if I'm going to sabotage him in some way.* It was a gut punch. Natalia knew she had not done anything that might make him think that she was some sort of traitor, but he still put a Ranger on her tail. She knew she was not some mole that the Fish had turned against her people. By the same token, she wondered what else they may have done to her while in captivity. Unconsciously she reached up to where she still had a bandaged area of scales where her DNA had been altered. *Is it possible that they have put something in me that the doctors all missed, something that can control me? No. Hell no! I've done nothing but my duty since I was rescued.* Her mind wondered if this was what others thought of her. *Do they see me as some sort of traitor, lurking around, waiting for me to stab them in the back?*

She didn't want to go there, to that dark place in the recesses of her mind. Falto liked to believe that she didn't care what people thought of her. That was part of her she liked about herself, her tough exterior. Most of that was true. But there was still a part of her that cared what others might think, and that tore at her, fueling an inner inferno of rage that she somehow kept in check. "If he doesn't trust me, he shouldn't have brought me along," she said as her jaw slowly locked.

"Look, Falto, I'm just a Warrant. It's a purgatory rank, trapped between NCOs and officers. The senior officers don't exactly confide their inner thoughts to me. I do what I'm told to do, and I do it very well. The standing order I have with you is that I shadow you, nothing more, nothing less."

She wanted to rant more, but Rosales was not the person to do it to. *I haven't done a damn thing that would cause them to be suspicious of me.*

"Fine, shadow-away. When this is over, I will have words with Captain Wade."

"You've earned that, if my opinion matters."

"It does. To me at least," she replied. Rosales was doing his job, which was something she understood. "Where should we go?"

"I'd recommend following the Rangers," he said.

"Big shock. You *are* a Ranger."

That brought a flash of a smile to his face. "RLTW. We are deploying to the north of the crash site onto the top of the ship again, like during the last attack. Omega is primarily covering our southeastern flank."

Memories of being on top of the alien ship came back to her. *Things are different now. We know that there are aliens in that ship that might pop out when we least expect it.*

"I say let's head north," she decided. "With that ship starting to wake up, I'd rather not be on top of it."

"They aren't putting much on the ship. Just enough to dump grazing fire down on the Fish as they approach," Rosales replied.

"Hard to argue with that logic."

Rosales pulled on his own cloak, pulling the hood up over his ECH. "You tied in with the battlespace?"

Falto reached up and adjusted her helmet, lowering her visor. "I've got eyes and ears. Let's roll." Starting down the passageway, she came to the door. Waiting there, just off to the side, was the media trio, trying to get their gear on. The cameraman, the one called Fizz, looked like he was more excited than frightened. Their bodyguard was helping both of them tighten straps on their body armor. Veronica Diamond somehow managed to look like she had just been in makeup for a movie, despite living in isolated

Greenland. Her STG gear had a stitched patch on the front that read, "Media—Don't Shoot," where everyone else either had their call sign or their last name. *As if the aliens can read English. Then again, she's in the press. Maybe that isn't meant for the Fish to read.* Fizz's simply read Fizz, which she decided really wasn't his actual name. *He should have gone with, "I'm with her."* It was enough to make Falto suppress a grin.

"Where are you heading?" Fizz asked as he tightened the strap on his helmet.

"Following the Rangers, if that's possible," Falto replied.

"Mind if we follow you?" Diamond asked.

"I'd rather you didn't," Falto replied. A cluster of people in battle tended to draw unwanted attention. "There are plenty of other people here you should be tailing. Why not tag along after Omega Force?"

"I'd rather follow someone like you, Sergeant."

Falto wanted to protest. She had gained a dislike of the media while the public affairs people had paraded her around after her recovery. *I heard it from them all the time—I was giving hope to families that had missing loved ones. Well, I'm not doing that here. I'm here to advise and fight.* As much as she wanted to argue with Diamond, she didn't have the time. The rising crescendo of fire in the distance reached her ears telling her that the battle was unfolding. Deep down, the young woman in her wanted to move away from the bangs, cracks, and booms that were starting. The Marine staff sergeant in her yearned to see and be in the fight.

"You go where you want," she finally conceded, moving through the doorway, "Just don't get in my way."

* * *

As she walked in the worn footsteps of the Rangers that went before her, stretching her gait to land where the holes punched in the snow, Falto felt the cold wind chill the thin sheen of sweat on her skin. *I never thought I'd miss wearing the environmental suits.* The cold air penetrated her ECH visor and filter, stinging at her nostrils. Looking to the north of the ship, she saw gray-black smoke rising in the bitter breeze, and saw flashes that could only come from combat. Several times there was a bright flash, followed a moment later with a thundering boom—each one with a smaller gap between the two as she got closer.

Falto moved fast, but numbly—not from the cold. The battle drew her in. It was a strange seduction. There was no fear of it; if anything, there was a desire to engage in it. It was as if deep down she knew that validation in combat might somehow purge her of the other dark thoughts and memories. They were there, secreting themselves in the nooks and crannies of her brain.

She saw one of Omega's Honey Badgers flicker out of ACS concealment, shimmering into full view. It raised its right arm and slung the Remington M2-S rail gun upward at a charging Crab. The gun flashed a burst of orange and red superheated plasma as the round sped into the approaching alien, striking its side and legs. Flesh flew from the hit, as did a grayish spray of blood. Two of the legs simply went limp, slowing its charge but not its intent to plow into the Honey Badger.

The pilot backstepped his ASHUR a little as a power shell banged off, the spent casing pinging like a cowbell as it hit the ice. There was a flicker, a momentary flash, from the left arm laser. As Falto continued to close, she couldn't see the laser beam itself—but where it hit in the lower torso of the Crab charred black instantly, leaving thin contrails of white smoke from the hole.

It leveled one of its claws and a deadly cutter beam stabbed at the Honey Badger, sending bits of armor plating flying. The pilot broke off, juking left hard as another Omega rig, a Bronco, tore into the Crab with its chain gun and a single, perfectly aimed LAWS rocket. An explosion engulfed the creature in a flash of flames and shrapnel, and the chain gun riddled the already breeched carapace. The Crab dropped face-first into the snow, sliding to a stop some ten meters from the Bronco.

Swarming over it were smaller creatures. They had humped backs that reminded her of armadillos, but these were decisively not from Earth. Scampering on four legs, these were deep green and flowed over the dead Crab like a wave breaking on shore. Their size was roughly that of a bowling ball and packed remarkable speed. The ASHURs dumped small arms fire at them, blasting a few apart, but they kept coming.

Dillos—that's what they are. She had seen footage of them in the intel reports.

A dozen or so swarmed the Bronco, scaling it, biting and clawing at the armor. Their effects looked minor at best, but from the way the Bronco pilot was twisting, attempting to shake them off, it was clear to Falto that they were inflicting some sort of harm. The ASHUR staggered back, attempting to fling them off as the creatures tore at the rig, clawing at hydraulic hoses.

The Rangers nearby sprang into action to save the Bronco, opening up with their XM7 assault weapons. For all of their deadly biting and cutting power, they were not able to shrug off bullets. Most exploded...an emerald liquid burst that rained down on the Bronco, giving it a new paint scheme.

The gunfire from a new source attracted them like moths to a flame. Leaping off the Bronco, they were joined with a wave of their kin, surging forward towards the Rangers...*towards me.* For a moment, she was lost in the scene; she saw them rushing toward her, some being flung back or exploding from controlled shots by the Rangers. The gunfire banged all around her but in those few moments, Falto did nothing. It was as if a calm had washed over her, an eerie resolve. She wasn't afraid; it was something else, a feeling she couldn't quite define—nor did she have time to.

Movement returned, as if a rubber band had been stretched to its maximum then released. The Marine in her raised her ACR and aimed. She couldn't feel the trigger as she squeezed it, she didn't have to. The kick of the rifle into her shoulder was all the tactical feedback she needed. She wounded two of the small scrambling crab-like creatures, snapping off legs in the process. Then her shots became more controlled, tighter groupings. Several of the Dillos she aimed at exploded in a mist of emerald green.

Almost in lockstep with the Rangers, she paced backwards as she fired, reloading like a machine as her muscle memory took over. She knew the drill; keep the enemy at a distance. The Rangers on the flanks of the swarming Dillos took up positions to form a kill box with the Dillos in the middle.

If that realization frightened the aliens, they didn't show it. They fanned out from the center, heading right at their attackers—rather than attempt to punch through the kill box in a single point of friction. One of the anchors on the right flank kept up a brisk fire with a M245 light machine gun, devouring the wave of Dillos in bursts of deadly fire. Falto actually admired the Rangers, despite being an Army unit. They were an effective killing machine, which was something even the most jaded Marine respected.

On the opposing flank, the Dillos managed to reach the Rangers. One toppled forward as he reloaded, and the Dillos scaled his body, biting and clawing at his STG gear. His winter cloak was shredded as they went about their vicious work. As he fell, the small aliens climbed all over him, flinging ripped bits of uniform, his blood squirting on the snow and air.

The other Ranger that was taken out lost his footing on the ice as he attempted to put some distance between himself at the aliens. He fell on his back and the Dillos pounced. Unlike his fallen brother, he wailed in agony as blood flew up from where he had dropped. The Dillos biting his neck and ripping at his mask were slick with his gore, giving them an ugly blood covering.

Two of the creatures made a rush directly for Falto, making the battle suddenly very personal.

Rosales and the other Rangers saw that their comrades were permanently down. They fired at the Dillos that were clustered and feasting on the downed men, actually making them easier to kill. Falto kept up her fire and, in a matter of seconds, the Dillos were eliminated as a threat. "Check that fire," one Ranger called out, clearly worried that stray shots might hit the men. Falto understood what she was looking at. These were not wounded personnel, that much showed on her visor display—they were dead. The snow and ice were intermixed with a sickening blend of bright crimson and light green.

Out of the corner of her eyes, she glimpsed Veronica Diamond and her team. They were behind her, cameras as poised as her ACR, unflinching. Her security person was firing, but not with the same intensity as Natalia and the others.

He's conserving ammo to protect Diamond.

A Crab, brilliant pink to an almost orange color on the upraised torso, rushed the Bronco ASHUR rig. The Omega piloting it fired off power shells so fast, she wondered how he was managing the power so quickly. Its left torso mounted L-2.5 laser barrel didn't reveal its beam, but Falto could see that the end of the barrel was glowing red. Its M-2 rail gun was an entirely different matter. When the projectiles were fired out of the barrel, the air in the barrel was super-heated to a plume of hot plasma that flared out for a half a meter or more. The rounds cut the air so fast you couldn't see them, but could see the ripples of the air as they sped towards target.

The Omega pilot moved the Bronco in ways that Falto could never imagine. After the loud bang of each power shell went off, a weapon fired, and the approaching Crab either rocked back, or developed a new blackened circle from the laser. The rail gun rounds punched into the flesh of the Crab's big body, but somehow the alien kept closing the gap between them. Falto took aim with her ACR, but knew at the distance that hitting the fast-moving target would result in the waste of ammo…and in a firefight, ammo meant survival.

Finally one of the Bronco's rail gun rounds hit dead center on the Crab's upraised body part. It penetrated, then went out the back of the Crab, spraying out internal organs. The impact was so violent that the short stubby arms and large pinchers seemed to fold inward on the hole. The Crab went rigid, then slumped over, limp and unmoving except for one claw, that twitched and flexed as if it had a mind of its own.

A part of her wanted to cheer, but couldn't form the sounds in her throat. It was the calm, that strange, almost detached feeling again. Since Guam it had been there, almost as if it were some sort of protection mechanism that she had looking over her. It kept her emotions in check and gave her focus.

Her eyes darted to her ammo count in her visor and told her she still had half a magazine, which was oddly reassuring. Out of the right corner of her eye, along the prow of the ship, she saw motion. Falto's head whipped around and saw a Crab claw pulling up a fellow creature, followed by several others doing the same.

"We are being flanked," called out Warrant Officer Rosales as her mouth opened to alert the others. "They are coming up over the front of the ship. Multiple Crab contacts." The Rangers responded to the new threats with firepower—pouring it into the Crabs that threatened their position. She joined in, raising her ACR and carefully firing four rounds in a steady procession.

Captain Wertan's voice followed. "Second platoon, take positions on the right flank and cover us. Rangers, we are going to pull back seventy-five meters to Point Morgan." On Falto's helmet display, the image flickered into existence. The new position was closer to the American base camp, which, in her heart, she knew was the last line of defense. More Crabs moved in from the north, supported by dozens of alien Frogs.

"Down!" came the crisp order from Rosales, followed by a violent shove. She lost her footing, almost toppling over, then something hit Falto and exploded. She felt her sheer thickening armor stiffen and the pressure of the blast shove her body armor into her breasts and chest. Bits of something scored her helmet's visor, and she staggered backwards, then fell over. Falto never saw which alien shot her and as she winced in pain, she didn't care.

Her entire chest throbbed, as if she had been hit with a log. Glancing down at her breast, she was instantly relieved that the armor had held. Her body armor plate had a blackened pock mark with a splatter of black star-like splinters that fanned outward from the center. Her mind quickly processed that it had been one of the aliens' needler spikes. The Fish had been employing new ones that, rather than simply penetrate, they exploded. It hurt, right through to her back, but that hurting served to remind her she was still alive.

A hand reached down for her and she looked up, seeing Rosales. His own chest plate had an almost identical impact scar like hers but was far more cracked. *He's lucky it was a small needle, not one of those ASHUR-killing ones.* His face mask was cracked, badly. *He took one of the shots that was meant for me.*

"You in one piece?" he asked.

She grabbed his hand and welcomed the assist to standing. "I think so." A part of her was still bitter about him and his role of shadowing her, but that was melting away rather quickly.

He may have saved my life. Time to shed that betrayal stuff.

"Then let's haul ass," he replied.

Falto nodded, her jaw setting. "Agreed." She made a mental note to thank him later for the warning and shove.

CHAPTER 26

Operation Sulaco
The Crash Site, East Coast of Greenland

Veronica had been standing behind Falto when she and the Ranger with her had been hit. She had been amazed at the reflexes of the Ranger. The Crab that shot them was coming from the north, skirting around the wrecked spacecraft. It had taken careful aim. It had hit the Ranger in the chest, just as it had Falto, with some sort of explosive. Bits of the shrapnel had hit Veronica as well, causing a moment of panic as she checked to make sure she was okay. When she turned back, Falto was down and the Ranger was kneeling over her, his own body armor pockmarked with a black scar.

"Fizz," she managed to say. "Did you…"

"You don't have to ask. I got it, boss-lady," he replied, his face anchored to the camera which was focused on Falto.

This is golden…a Medal of Honor recipient in battle, getting hit, getting back up. This is the kind of image that is like the Marines raising the flag on Iwo Jima!

Her eyes swept the battle, not evaluating the enemy for weaknesses but looking for filming opportunities. Seeing the Crabs climbing over the front of the ship, she pointed off in their direction.

Everyone has seen a Crab, but we don't have a lot of footage of them climbing—not like this.

"Fizz, over there!" she called out.

Fizz didn't jerk, he pivoted and kept his camera level as he moved.

282

She actually admired him. *I've had a lot of production crews. Most are good when things are calm. It takes a true professional to be this calm when things are chaotic.*

"I gotcha covered," he replied.

The hulking Verret moved next to her. "Rangers are pulling back and so are we," he said. It wasn't a request, it was a statement of fact. Veronica saw the Rangers, weapons blazing and cracking, making their moves of violence and force. Looking up at Verret, she could only see his jaw below the visor of his helmet, but in her mind she could see the fury in his eyes.

Time to trust the professional on the payroll.

"Fizz, we're moving," she ordered. They shifted position, moving back through the crash site toward the American base camp. The concussion of an explosion made her body quake momentarily, as a trio of Frogs were engulfed in a grenade blast off in the distance. Bits of their bodies, arms and legs included, whipped around, landing on the churned up snow. A part of her hoped that Fizz had captured that image. Deep down, she knew he had.

As they moved, she came up alongside Sergeant Falto. "Are you alright, Sergeant?" she asked as the two of them moved.

"I won't be alright until this fight is over," Falto replied, turning, aiming, and squeezing off three shots. Even outdoors, the crack of the ACR so close to her made Veronica's ears ache. She looked at what Falto had been shooting at, but couldn't tell which target she was going after.

Veronica's eyes fell on the Crabs that had come over the bow of the ship and were starting to move towards them. Their legs were a blur of action, their claws pointed and fired weapons—cutters and spikers. She continued to move back, keeping close to Falto. The sergeant was a survivor, and there was a sense of security being near someone like that.

One of the Crabs rushed forward, leading the others. It stabbed a claw forward and sprayed an ugly goo across three of the Rangers. Screams were the immediate result, at least from where Veronica stood.

Acid—it's got to be that bioacid stuff!

One Ranger dropped to his knees, fumbling quickly with his STG, stripping it off. Another threw off his helmet, its visor had been almost totally eaten through by the time he got it clear. The last Ranger collapsed, falling face-first as his two surviving comrades scrambled to get clear. Smoke rose from the fallen man and the damaged bits of armor and helmet that had been discarded. She caught a glimpse of the soldier who had tossed his helmet. His face was pockmarked with holes from the acid, one eating through a cheek to the point where she could see his teeth and jaw. The remaining skin was crimson. Despite the pain, he didn't look panicked. He paused, firing five rounds at the offending Crab, then running to the rear. She caught a hint of the acid smell on the breeze, an almost sweet aroma, but one that made her tongue taste as if she'd licked a battery.

Even at this distance, that stuff might be deadly.

Verret fired, emptied a magazine, and smoothly replaced it with a new one. An explosion went off from a stacked grenade that had been tossed under the acid-spraying Crab which was closing its distance quickly. Despite the risk, Veronica kept close to her hired gun, mostly out of fear. The blast blew upward and outward, tearing through the Crab and throwing bits of its flesh in every direction. One small piece hit Veronica in the right thigh. Looking down, she saw the unidentifiable bit of organic material and the ugly blackish wet marks that had been left on her thigh armor plate.

For a moment, she fixated on the bit of Crab lying at her feet. It was a reminder of how dangerous this fight was, and that frightened her for the first time.

She had been told early in her career that you could get too close to a story, and when you did, it could consume you. *That is what happened to Dana Blaze. She became part of the story and the story ate her. Now I have dragged Fizz back into this. I lied to myself and him, telling him it would be good for him. In reality, it's only good for me.* It was all about ratings and bylines and awards. Diamond craved the spotlight so much, she was willing to risk the lives of others to bask in it.

In those long few moments, as she stood mutely looking at the small chunk of pinkish flesh that had hit her, she knew that she had been wrong. As she raised her head, she saw Verret, just slightly off to her left, his weapon up and firing single controlled shots. *This is what my profession does, it kills people for ratings. It isn't about news; it's entertainment. If I—no, we—die here now, the network will run the last bit of footage recovered. They will create music and a logo for it. They will package our deaths for the public and sell pillows and vitamins in the process.*

A resolve grew in her. It started not in the pit of her stomach, but in her soul. "Alright, we need to fall back! Let's get out of the way and let these Rangers do their job."

Verret nodded and Fizz continued to sweep the line with his camera, his free eye darting over to her. "You sure, boss-lady? This is where the party is."

"This isn't a party, Fizz. These guys may be overrun. If they are, what hope do we have? Time for us to drift back and pray that doesn't happen." As she spoke, she felt a surge of new energy, a vitality that was hard for her to define. Doing the right thing was so rare that when it happened, she wanted to embrace it. Unfortunately, there wasn't time.

She ran. Unlike before, there was no turning around, no looking back for a great camera angle. She, Fizz, and Verret raced away from Natalia Falto, who had dropped to one knee and was firing away steadily at the approaching aliens. Her feet were a blur as she ran faster than she had in years. They sprinted for nearly a hundred meters before she stopped, putting her hands on her knees, and struggling to get her breath. The cold air stung at her throat and made her lungs ache, but Veronica didn't care.

Wheeling about as she panted heavily, she saw that the Rangers were making their way towards them, slowly, with a degree of precision she could never fully comprehend. The Ranger's Bronco fired its rail gun and the plasma plume filled the air between the ASHUR and one of the Crabs. There was an immediate violent tug of the alien at the head, as the hypersonic slug impacted and penetrated the bony skull. The Crab fell over, only to have another Crab climb right over its newly fallen comrade, firing a cutter beam at the Bronco. Bits of armor flew off behind and to the side of the Bronco, but it didn't waver. Leveling its laser, she heard the bang of a power shell and saw a white flicker and a black scar along one of the Crab's large claws. There was a cracking noise, and the claw seemed to pop, fracturing with the burst of laser fire. It dipped down, limp.

Fizz was still gasping for air, but continued to film. Verret reloaded and knelt in front of her, his weapon adding to the bangs and cracks of gunfire. As the Bronco closed with the Crab, the alien's tail whipped around and the stinger slammed into the Bronco hard, nearly breaking the charge of the ASHUR. Somehow, the Bronco pilot recovered, though for a moment Veronica wondered just how badly the stinger had damaged the rig.

The Ranger ASHUR jumped forward and swung one of its big arms at the alien, thudding into the side of its torso. As it swung, another power shell went off and in the moment of impact, the rail gun fired. Superheated energy cut into the flesh followed instantly with the projectile. The side of the Crab exploded, with the flames of the plume burning through. The upper torso was blown through and the head twisted in agony as oily smoke rolled from the hole. Amid the smoke, the Crab collapsed and the Bronco pilot planted one of its footpads on it, as if to pin it to the ground.

"Don't even ask, Veronica," Fizz said off to his side, still breathing heavily. "I got that kill on vid."

A sound occurred, one she had heard before, a guttural, deep bass groaning rising out of the ship, only eighty meters away. This time it was long, and it almost sounded like there were horn noises or tubas that were part if it. It was so deep, it made her entire body shake, and so loud she covered her ears with her gloves. *Now what?* Her left ear popped painfully from the reverberation.

When the noise ended, her eyes fell on the ship. From the rear of the vessel, she saw two black holes open up, seemingly right on the hull. Out of them came Crabs, and the Squids as well. They surged out, dozens of them. Some Crabs headed right for the Rangers, but the majority seemed to be heading south and east, towards where Omega Force and the British were engaged.

The Squid creatures were smaller than the Crabs, but faster. Their thick bony legs stabbed into the ice and snow with a blur. They were moving quickly as their tails flicked about, almost like a playful cat, though there was nothing playful about them. The big hooked front claws extended out, sunk into the ice, and seemed to pull them along with lightning speed.

She made sure she was on a clear open channel and called out, "There are aliens coming out of the ship!"

"Get off this damn channel!" snapped someone. "We see them."

A few moments earlier she thought they had staved off the Fish's assault. Now things had changed. The ship was very much alive and the odds had dramatically changed.

If the Rangers and Omega boys are wiped out, what chance do we have? In that instant she wondered if anyone was going to emerge from this fight alive.

"Verret," she barked. "Get me a gun, now!"

CHAPTER 27

Operation Sulaco
The Crash Site, East Coast of Greenland

Captain Wade angled his Python alongside others of Omega Force. He moved in an arc that extended across the rear hull of the crashed ship, all of the way to the edge where the vessel dropped to where the British were engaging. From the expanded view of the battlespace in his cockpit, he saw that the Royal Marines were anchored off the end of Omega's line. They were spread in an arc in the other direction from his, extending down to the shoreline. Glancing over, he saw the muzzle flashes of their outgoing fire. Explosions pounded the seemingly endless swarm of aliens.

Wade's own force was blazing away at the Fish as they surged toward his positions. The front of the crashed ship slowed their advance in the middle. Wertan's people held the northern flank, where the aliens were already on top of the Rangers. Extending his right arm, he could almost aim by iron sights down the twin chain gun barrels—but he relied on his targeting system. As one Boss strode to the front of the lines, it unleashed a deadly spray of gas that swirled outwards towards Omega's ASHURs. Bringing his targeting reticle onto the Boss, Wade got a green lock light and unleashed the chain guns.

They purred, spewing a deadly spittle of armor-piercing bullets downrange, thunking into the massive body of the Boss. The strange etched pattern on the creature's black body flared from yellow to bright orange as the shots made ripples on its armored hide. Several finally found their way through. Their penetrations were marked with sprays out of an oily black fluid that initially spewed like a fire hose, then stopped. It made the Boss turn to face him, its slit-like red eye seeming to stare at him out of the line of ASHURs.

The Boss moved forward, clearly sluggish from the damage it had taken, shoving aside the Frogs that clogged its path. As it reached a stretch of open space, it broke into a run. Brimstone swung the big arm of his Croc at the Boss as it passed, hitting its shoulder, but barely slowed its run. Suddenly it was through the Omega Force line, gaining speed as it headed right at Wade.

He drew his breath slowly in through the mouth, discharged another power shell, and brought his reticle on the charging ebony creature. Wade didn't wait for the reticle to confirm his targeting, he fired. The M-D-01X Directed Energy Weapon hummed in a high pitch as the invisible focused microwaves hit the Boss in the head and upper body, super-heating the contents.

The Boss skidded to a stop, putting its big clawed hands up on both sides of his head. Wade didn't hesitate and fired another power round, channeling the energy into the same weapon. This time he narrowed the aim, zooming in on the center of its head, and fired again. The high-pitched whine told him that the shot had discharged, but he looked to the target for some sort of confirmation.

For a moment, he thought he saw steam rising off the black shark-like hide of the head as the Boss reeled from the hit, staggering backwards against the invisible source of agony that was hammering it. The alien seemed to shiver, which grew quickly into a tremor. It dropped to its knees with a dull crunching thud, only eight meters from him as he fired another power shell off, preparing for the kill shot.

He didn't need it.

The Boss's head exploded. The thick hide peeled off with a geyser of flesh and liquid, exposing the creature's bony skull. The liquid turned to ugly gray-black snow around the humanoid alien. The skull was knobby, dark tan, and looked horrific on its own. As the Boss fell forward with a *thunk* that shook his Python, he saw that the top and back of the skull had blown out, no doubt from the super-heating of the microwaves.

A voice rang out on an open channel…something about aliens coming out of the ship. He thought it was Veronica Diamond; there were very few females in his force and the tone was like that of a broadcaster. The battlespace officer cut her off, but now Wade turned to see what the threat was.

They moved in a wavelike fashion. The leaders were the new aliens, the Squid. Their gait was fast, with bursts of speed from their extended hooked arms jerking them forward. Their tails, complete with suction cups on the flapping ends, flickered in near unison as they moved. Behind them came a slew of Crabs.

For a moment, he hesitated. *Do I inform the British about this?* They had access to his battlespace feeds, so he assumed they saw it, but there was no way to know for sure. He wanted to tell them, but still felt they deserved to find out for themselves. *I owe them nothing.* A part of him wanted to see them hurt.

The complex mathematics of battle overrode his emotions. In the end, the debate was settled quickly.

We are going to need their help to crush these bastards.

He shelved his patriotism and focused on winning the fight. While the decision was easy to reach, he didn't like it. From the moment he had arrived in Greenland, he had been forced to contend with their unwanted presence. At least now they were going to have to pay a price for the ship that they had wrongfully laid claim to—a price in blood and borne in battle.

"Battlespace Command—inform the British that we are about to be hit on the flank here by aliens from the ship."

"Yes, sir. Sending now."

"Omega, we have a threat on the left flank. Saint, have your platoon pull back and see if we can channel them in front of us. Do not allow any of them to get in behind us. Pudknocker, you and your platoon have that responsibility." His officers confirmed his orders quickly. As he spoke, he started to hear a clicking sound over the explosions and gunfire. Glancing at the Squids, he saw it was the pincers at their maws, snapping together like bird beaks as they moved. It was as menacing as the grunting that the Frogs did when they advanced, made worse in his mind because he had not seen them in action.

Omega Force redeployed with a precision that only an elite unit could execute. Two Crabs rushed into the ranks of the ASHURs. One got close enough to Warrant Officer Peter Pearson's Rattlesnake that it clamped an enormous claw around the rig's waist. As Wade brought his twin chain guns into play on it, the creature tightened its grip, the rig looking like a doll in its grasp, and thrashed it from side to side. Pearson leveled his plasma carbine and fired. The searing hot crimson plasma splashing about wildly, some of it hitting the Crab, the rest sending up plumes of steam as it splattered the snow.

Wade's shots were hitting the Crab, but not forcing it to shake its grip. Then a fast-moving GRD, a Landshark, moved under the alien's hulking body. The box near the head popped open and it unleashed two missiles at point-blank range, right under the Crab's belly. Guts and gray ooze rained down on it, drenching the drone as it darted away.

The Crab dropped Pearson's crumpled and battered Rattlesnake hard onto a chunk of ice, adding to the mangled armor. "Dribble," Wade called out on the discreet channel. "You good?"

Pearson's rig moved slowly, as if it, not the pilot, was in agony. It struggled for a moment before he was able to get his footing and stood up. A slick of bright emerald hydraulic fluid ran from the right armpit down the side of the rig, staining the snow and ice. Its armor where the claw had thrashed him about was torn, bent, and wrinkled to where it was hard to see the original pattern.

"I'm leaking and creaking," Dribble replied, breathing heavily. "But I can still stand and shoot."

Normally he would have ordered Pearson back to the repair bays, but the odds were not in their favor and there wasn't time for even spot repairs. So he just said, "Do what you can—"

"—with what I've got," Pearson finished. "I'm on it. I'm going to need two minutes to reroute the hydraulic line and the damaged power feed."

Wade didn't reply. There wasn't time. A cutter beam struck Wade's Python in the right arm. Bits of his armor flailed off and a red warning light flared for one of his chain guns. Instinctively, he sidestepped, hoping to throw off another shot, as his eyes looked for the Fish that had dared fire on him. He didn't see which of the sea of aliens had fired, so he held the arm out in front of the cockpit canopy for a visual inspection.

The damage indicator hadn't been wrong. The cutter had chewed through the upper receiver as if the metal were made of soft plastic. There was no way that the gun could fire again. Reaching out to his weapons controls, he disabled it rather than risk a jam or another problem if it were engaged.

He wanted to curse, but knew it would not help anything. *At least I have one functional CG.* Another glance at his battlespace feed showed a sea of confusion that his mind sorted through. Aliens coming out of the ship were attacking both the human troops and the Fish coming from the shoreline. The Fish that came from the ocean attacked the ship, the occupants of the ship, and the humans.

The new Squid creatures broke from whatever their formation was and closed on the Crabs that had come from the sea. It was as if the two species were natural enemies. A part of Wade was thankful. *If they are firing at the ship, they aren't firing at us.* Still, their behavior puzzled him. He hoped if his people survived the battle, they might be able to get to the bottom of what was driving the Fish's actions.

The lead Squid was fired upon by Chan's tricked-out Mamba. The big .50 caliber assault weapon hit the creature's thick armored legs, fracturing the chitin armor there, badly mauling one of the legs to the point where it was turned into a pinkish pulp that dragged behind the creature. It jerked in response, turning to face the new threat.

It moved with lightning fast response as Wade fired off a power shell and targeted it. Chan was good. He lowered his stance to sprint away. The problem was that the Squid was faster. It lunged out at him with a speed Wade thought impossible, its big front hooks extended. A splash of black liquid, almost the consistency of paint, covered Chan's rig. Then the squid planted one of the big hooks into the Mamba's shoulder, piercing the armor there. The other overlapped the other shoulder, grabbing the back of the ASHUR, holding it captive.

Wade fired his directed energy weapon. The microwaves either missed or had little effect as the creature pulled the Mamba towards it, moving Chan between Wade and the predator. He sidestepped his Python to get a good line of fire, but as he did, he was shocked at what he saw.

The Squid's upper body tentacles wrapped around the rig and the hooks retracted, pulling the rig towards the now-open maw. The tail whipped around the Mamba, attaching itself with the suction cups on the back of the ASHUR as Chan struggled. The paint-like liquid obscured Chan's view. He heard the automatic weapon firing, but Wade knew that he didn't have a good shot. It was panic-fire.

The massive beaks opened wide and came down on the Mamba, then closed. The beaks clamped down on the cockpit canopy and as they closed, the ASHUR's cockpit frame crumbled and crunched. Metal groaned in protest. Chan screamed as the canopy broke, folded, and collapsed inward on him. The beaks continued and there was a *poof* as the hydraulic system fractured, squirting the green fluid skyward. The rig was bleeding to death.

Wade didn't need to check his battlespace feed to know that Chan was gone. With icy precision, he brought his targeting reticles to bear and fired off a power shell. Locking on the Squid, he saw the creature slither and loosen its tentacles, breaking its grip on the now dead ASHUR. It turned and seemed to stare at Wade, then moved towards him.

The moment his reticles lit up, he fired. One rocket, his energy weapon, and his remaining chain gun. The Squid twitched, no doubt from the microwave heater doing its job. The chain gun rounds stitched along the tail, with bursts of thick black-to-crimson blood squirting outward. The creature recoiled, but not enough to avoid the LAW rocket slamming into its raised upper body. It exploded, viciously and violently, its hooks still planted on the fallen Mamba as it slumped over dead. Bits of its ugly internal organs hung over the dead ASHUR and pilot.

Usually he felt some momentary surge of joy over a kill, but not this time. It had come with too high a price. Sandor Chan had been an exemplary soldier. He had known him from when they had gone through Ranger training together in Georgia. Now he was dead—not fighting to defend his home, but in damned cold Greenland. This isn't where American soldiers should be fighting and dying.

The Crabs continued to wade into the Omega line of battle, while the Squids seemed to divert to the east, towards the front of the crashed ship. Wade moved forward a dozen meters and leveled his targeting reticles on another approaching Crab. A power shell banged off to his left, the spent casing *cling*ing against a rock. The energy surged into his capacitors and he waited patiently for a lock. The Crab shook off an attack by Sergeant Bill "Brimstone" Smith's Croc, lashing at the ASHUR with a claw and unleashing a spray of acid on the rig. Brimstone reeled about, losing his footing on the ice and falling into the snow. Steam rose from the acid. The snow may have actually helped his situation—it was difficult to tell with the Croc lying face-down and struggling to get rolled over.

Wade's target tone hummed in his ears as he unleashed a pair of missiles first. The metallic snapping sound and *whoosh* of the weapons as they cleared their racks was strangely satisfying. The missiles seemed to twist midair and slammed into the Crab's upright portion of its body. Flames and a pair of rolling black and gray smoke plumes billowed out into the breeze as the alien rocked back from the explosions.

Wasting no time, he unleashed his directed energy weapon. The DEW hummed loudly as it discharged, and he watched as the Crab jumped back, giving Brimstone time to get on his feet. More gray steam rose from the blasted holes the LAWs rockets had left. The legs on one side of the alien collapsed, tipping it downward.

The Crab's tail whipped out at Brimstone's quasi-melted rig as he staggered to bring his Croc back into the fight. Its stinger pierced the left leg of the ASHUR in the thigh, punching through the blast plates, the STL layers, and stabbing deep into the internal components. Despite the dangerous range, Smith opened up with his left arm's grenade launcher, sending three of the explosives into and under the Crab. Wade knew at that range the Croc was taking damage too, but it was the kind of cold decision-making that kept SMU pilots alive.

The explosions did their job as the Crab collapsed, its stinger and tail still stuck in the Croc's thigh. Smith's ASHUR grabbed it and extracted the stinger.

"Talk to me, Brimstone," Wade transmitted to him.

"I must be a magnet for these damn stingers, Captain. This is the third damn time I've been hit by them. I'm operational, but I can't say for how long." There was a weariness in Smith's voice that told of his struggle to get the ASHUR upright in the middle of the firefight. Looking at the damaged rig, Wade saw that the acid spray had melted much of the canopy, leaving only part of the support struts. Streams of smoke rose from the armor that looked like butter left in a microwave. Parts of the internal rig structure were visible.

Damn, it's a miracle he's standing.

"Retrograde back by me," Wade ordered. *At least if he is back here, I can provide him assistance as needed.* The tactical display told him that four ASHURs were down, two with pilots whose biochips were reading them as dead. Every one of his rigs was damaged, some bad, and the battle was still early.

For a moment he thought about the scientists that were still inside of the alien craft. *Do I order them out now?* With the combat raging all around, they would be soft targets for the enemy…easy prey. *No. It's better to have them do their job and stay out of the line of fire.*

The Crabs that had emerged from the ship charged toward the 45 Commando rigs. In the distance, he heard the discharge of several of the large sonic weapons aimed at the ship. These were louder than those used by the regular troops, and were mounted on the giant Turtles, which must have climbed out of the sea while he'd been focusing on the closer battle. Wade watched as the air rippled skyward from the front of the ship where that attack was taking place. His mind went to his air support, somewhere above the clouds. On the tactical display he could see it, a Vulture. With a simple order, he could order the bombs dropped. They had been slated to destroy the ship, a last-ditch means to ensure the prize didn't fall into the enemy's hands. There was a temptation to employ the drone bomber. Blowing up that ship might just end all of this; it might save lives. At the same time, it would be handing the aliens a victory in that the Americans would not have access to their ship. That was the last thing he wanted to do.

No, now isn't the time. But that time might be coming...

CHAPTER 28

Operation Durendal
The Crash Site, East Coast of Greenland

Major McKenna and 45 Commando found themselves wedged in by two forces. One had been the initial alien assault from the sea. The other had emerged from the rear of the crashed ship. The Americans, for better or worse, had blunted their drive through their forces, but the result had channeled the enemy right into his Royal Marines. He didn't have time to wonder how deliberate that gesture was, though he had his suspicions that it was a conscious effort on the part of Captain Wade.

Most of the Crabs were plowing into 45 Commando with a vigor that he both envied and hated. Only a few of the Squids seemed interested in his force—they were skirting the firefight, heading to the north end of the ship. The rest were quickly lunging towards the aliens attacking the crash site. Their awkward pulling movements with their large front hooks and skittering armored legs were disturbing to watch. *I'm glad we are not facing them. If they want to tear into their fellow bollocks, more power to them.*

The fact that Captain Wade had his people warn him was not something he could ignore. Wade's apparent disdain for his Royal Marines almost was on par with McKenna's thoughts about the Americans. The warning had given him a few precious seconds to issue orders to redeploy his forces. Though the visual that he was soaking in of the staggering number of aliens was not leaving him with a positive perspective.

Since the start of the war, 45 Commando had been fighting the aliens. The odds always felt against them; the invaders consistently brought that advantage to every firefight. This felt markedly different; far more menacing.

Even if we were fully coordinated with the Americans, there's a good chance of us being overrun.

McKenna leveled off his Spitfire's stance and aimed his Gatling laser, firing off two power shells and routing the surge of energy to that weapon. He targeted the Squid that was rushing Sergeant Major Shoemaker's Hurricane II. One of the big hooks came down fast, hitting the Sovereign near the cockpit, digging deep, securing a deadly grip. The creature seemed to envelop the Hurricane II. Something sprayed from it, a black liquid that covered the target, no doubt blinding the man in the cockpit. The squid's smaller tentacles wrapped around the war machine, pulling it in tight. The tail whipped around, snake-like, grabbing and holding the legs.

Shoemaker fired his hulking assault weapon, but his aim was wild and he only seemed to pepper the creature's thick legs. McKenna had been holding his shot out of fear of hitting Shoemaker in the process. That changed when he saw the creature's mouth open —its massive black beaks click, then open. The mouth moved forward, clamping on to the Sovereign's right shoulder, then contract. The beaks crunched through the armor slowly, as if the Hurricane was in a vice being crushed.

He couldn't afford to play it safe. McKenna brought his reticle onto the head of the Squid and fired his Gatling laser. The barrels purred and hummed as the weapon unleashed an invisible burning-hot assault on the creature.

Smoke rose from blackened marks on the slithering creature's face and it immediately stopped crushing the Hurricane II. Its head snapped back to look around, its tail releasing the legs of the Sovereign. McKenna didn't hesitate. He fired another power shell and kept up the stream of fire. Soon there were at least twenty scorched holes seared into the beast's head.

The creature acted swiftly. It ducked down, putting the Hurricane between itself and McKenna, breaking his line of sight. He juked his Spitfire to the right and ran to change the angle, but the Squid kept it up sliding around and changing its position. "Cobbler," McKenna called to Shoemaker on the discreet channel. "I need you to drop flat."

A wet cough filled his ears and a gurgle, followed with Shoemaker's voice. "With pleasure, sir."

Damn—he's wounded.

The Hurricane didn't drop, it collapsed, exposing the Squid.

Got you!

His lasers whirred as he fired another power shell, concentrating fire on the already pock-marked face. It only took a moment before the Squid fell limp.

"Cobbler, how bad is it?"

All that came back was a strained breath and more gurgling.

"Medic, attend Sergeant Shoemaker," McKenna called out. Normally, the Royal Marines deployed with a Commando Forward Surgical Group (CFSG). That hadn't been the case with this deployment. He had three skilled medics, almost as good as doctors, but that was it. If they couldn't stabilize the fallen pilot quickly, he would be dead before he could be treated by a surgeon.

"On our way, Major," came a medic's response.

A thundering sound, followed with a blast from a large sonic weapon, shattered McKenna's attention. The deep tones came in waves, slamming into his Spitfire with a savage fury. For a moment, it felt as if his head were going to explode inside of his pilot's helmet. The vibrations were so intense. The air in front of him rippled, blurring what he could see. His transparent aluminum cockpit canopy dented inward in one spot.

He had been hit with sonic weapons before, but this was much larger. As it stopped, the ringing in his ears still detected the thunder-like noise. Squinting slightly, he saw two of the bollocks' Stegosaurs running right toward his line of Sovereigns off to his right. They were charging, sounding like stampeding elephants.

"Range Rover, Whippoorwill, Galahad, move!" McKenna called

out as he shifted towards the charging creatures.

As he spoke, the lead Stegosaur slammed head-on into Colour-Sergeant John Bear Ross's Tempest. The creature flicked its greenish head at the moment of impact, hooking the Sovereign on a bony spike on the front and flinging it in the air. The Tempest rolled over broken ice and jagged stone, leaving bits of armor in its wake. His battlespace feed told him that Ross was still alive but with weak life signs.

McKenna let loose with two of his N-LAWs rockets, aiming for the heavily armored flank of the creature. One rocket missed, exploding under the tail as the creature tore through the British line. The other slammed dead on target, right in the thick plate-like covering. Its explosion was a flash of yellow and crimson, and while the impact smoked as the beast continued to run, he could see that it had not penetrated enough to slow the massive beast.

The major mentally plotted the path of the pair of the aliens as they rushed forward. *They are heading for our camp!* McKenna broke into a run to keep up with the Stegosaurs and transmitted to the scientists at the base.

"Evacuate the base! All personnel, make for the LCACs—now!"

He aimed and fired two more N-LAW rockets at the rear of the creature he had already hit. The missiles twisted in the air, their contrails caught in the arctic wind and fading into nothingness as they flew. The explosions hit the rear and tail of the beast, wrapping it in flames and smoke—but barely slowing it down.

"Range Rover, Whippoorwill, Galahad, with me," he commanded.

"On them, sir," came Lieutenant Kendall's voice as his Liberator unleashed a rail gun round into the other Stegosaur. It hit, enough to make the creature turn to look behind it, but it didn't stop it. As McKenna sprinted, he fired off two more power shells and brought his Gatling laser to bear. The hum of the capacitors discharging and the whirling of the barrels confirmed the weapon was firing. It was hard to see if any of the shots on the massive creature were effective. Meanwhile, the creature was putting distance between them, and seemed to close in on the command trailer.

Ensign McComb's Gladiator opened up with his recoilless warhead on the lead Stegosaur. The round was a blur in flight. All McKenna could see was the rippling of the air as the round slammed into the second beast and exploded. Big pieces of flesh, green and crimson, sprayed out near its rear leg. The Stegosaur skidded to a stop, turning to face the Sovereigns that had dared fire on it. It reminded McKenna of a bull turning to face the matador.

"Good shooting, Whippoorwill," he said. "You have his attention."

"Not exactly my plan," McComb replied.

"You pissed him off," Galahad said, firing his Tempest's rail gun again. The hypersonic slug tore a gouge down the creature's side, but failed to penetrate. Smoke rolled from the wound, the flesh superheated from the fast-moving slug.

The Stegosaur lowered its head, charging at Whippoorwill's Gladiator.

McComb was a cool operator. He fired off another power round and took his time to aim as the creature bore down on him. The shot went off, the flaming plume marking the trajectory of the round that slammed into the creature above its head. A blur rippled the air as the round went in. A splash of gore marked the penetration, but the monster didn't stop. Its thick feet tore through the snow and ice. McComb waited for the last moment, then dove his Gladiator off to the side.

The alien seemed to anticipate the move. Its snapping-turtle-like mouth opened and clamped onto the rail gun as it passed the Gladiator. It started dragging the Sovereign with it, then under the massive feet as the gun tore loose. For a few moments, McKenna lost sight of Whippoorwill. When he found the Sovereign, it looked as if it were an old automobile that had gone through the scrap metal compactor.

There was no time to mount a recovery. The lead Stegosaur tore into the camp, crushing tents and temporary units that the British had brought with them. It aimed at the long white command center trailer, opened its wide mouth, and clamped down on the structure, ripping the metal as if it were wrapping paper. Its big tail whipped around, tearing apart tents and sending supply boxes skidding in its wake.

McKenna's battlespace display went off line, as did his communications system. His jaw set as he closed on the Stegosaur, bringing a pair of N-LAWs rockets online. He aimed at the already damaged side of the creature, zooming in on the previous damage as the beast climbed up on the crippled command post. Its enormous feet sunk and sparks flew from the equipment inside that was being destroyed.

Triggering the missiles one at a time, he sent them in on a tight pattern. The first explosion was followed with a pause as the second warhead passed through the burning hole created by the first rocket, punching deep. The second explosion was muffled, and for a moment, it looked as if the entire Stegosaur was an inflating balloon. As it deflated, gray smoke rolled out of the hole and the creature collapsed. Some internal organ, dark purple and covered with a spiderweb of crimson veins, slid out of the hole and onto the trampled snow. It was a visual distraction that he had to shake himself from seeing. The loss of the command post was something he could no longer disregard.

Getting battlespace command back up was going to take a miracle and without it, the forces of 45 Commando would be forced to work with limited comms and coordination. He stared at the ruined trailer under the fallen alien and a wave of desperation came over him.

Time to earn my bloody damn pay!

Pivoting with precision in place, he saw that the other Stegosaur was immobile, but it had come at a high price. His troops were trained to not be dependent on battlespace command, but losing it was something that would have to be compensated for. He switched to one of the auxiliary comms channels and found that conversations were already buzzing on that channel as his people fell back on their training. For a moment, he was proud he had trained them for this very situation.

"This is Vindictive. Can the chatter, lads," he ordered, and the voices dropped off. "As you probably have guessed, we are now blind to the big picture, but this fight will be fought on the small screen. We need to fall back to a line anchored on the bow of the ship and swinging back in an arc to the LCACs. They hit the command post; we need medics in there. Move and move with purpose, gents—this fight is far from over."

"Sir," came the voice of Lieutenant Walling. "You do realize that the enemy is between us and the ship at the moment."

"I do indeed, Meteor. That is something we will need to change. Understood?"

"Yes, sir!" Walling replied vigorously. A litany of confirmations came on the channel as his people redeployed.

McKenna moved as well. He was down to two N-LAWs rockets, and made a note to swing by the tech pods for a fast rearming. That would take three minutes; three minutes that he wasn't sure that he had. *I'm no good without power shells and rockets.* Fortunately he was running at sixty-eight percent power—not great, but not bad. He broke into a trot to the pods.

As the techs did a hot-reload on his Spitfire, his mind went to his last straw—the thermobaric bomb planted near the bow of the ship. With the battlespace down, he could arm it, but he would have to be at fairly close range. The enemy was between him and the ship. While he didn't think that this was the time to detonate, that time might be looming closer.

Should I warn the Americans? They would have noticed that the British battlespace went off-line. *No. Not yet. I'm not even sure we will need it.* While he felt that time was still on his side, the hourglass of battle was emptying fast.

CHAPTER 29

Operation Sulaco
The Crash Site, East Coast of Greenland

As she reloaded her ACR, Falto watched in amazement as two of the Squid creatures attacked a pair of Crabs that had climbed up over the bow of the ship. The Crabs had bulk and were menacing, but the Squids had speed on their side. Rather than distance themselves from their adversaries, they both moved to close quarters combat range. Their sucker-covered tails whipped at the Crabs. They latched on to the Crabs' backs, their front hook-like appendages extended, grappling with their foes, and pulling them together.

Their tentacles slithered around the Crab's quickly, and their beak-like pincers opened wide. One Crab jabbed its claw into the maw of a Squid. The Squid's pincers snapped onto the claw. For a moment, nothing happened, then the big claw audibly and visually cracked, with parts of it pulled into the mouth. The Crab used its free claw to pinch off two of the tentacles. Black liquid sprayed out from the maw of the Squid onto the Crab. For a moment, the Crab fell back a few steps. That didn't stop the Squid from using its beaks to latch onto the body and squeeze until the points of the beaks met. The alien Crab thrashed for a moment to try to throw off its foe, then it simply fell dead.

The other Crab fared far worse. Its head was pulled in and the Squid's pinchers closed on it. The chitin armor plates cracked and popped as the Squid pinched off the Crab's head. Oily goo shot up from the stump where the head had been as the Crab fell limp onto the hull of the ship.

Both Squids slithered away and headed to the front of the ship, where they scampered down, no doubt looking for more prey.

"Did you see that?" Falto asked as she made sure her weapon was ready.

Rosales moved next to her. "Weird shit."

"I'm just glad they are killing each other, rather than us," she said, raising her weapon at a group of Frogs that were charging at their position. Natalia fired three shots, two into the same Frog, sending it toppling down. To her dismay, it rose back up.

The grunting of the Frogs grew louder as they closed with them. These weren't like the cannon fodder Frogs that troops usually faced. These were the tough ones, the Uber Frogs. Some service personnel referred to them as Uruk-hai Frogs, but Falto didn't get the reference. What she knew was that they had a form of organic body armor, and their deadly spray-spit went farther than their weaker cousins. Their upper bodies and backs were a dull light blue that faded on their chests to a light blue-gray color. And when they came at her and Rosales, their rumbling croaks reverberated all around her.

Falto lowered her ACR and pulled out two stackable grenades, attaching them to each other. Rosales continued to fire in controlled bursts, reloading with a speed she envied. He glanced down at what she was preparing and gave her a slight nod of approval.

"Chuck it right in front of them," he muttered between shots.

Falto didn't reply. She moved. Attaching the grenades, she pulled the safety tab, then pressed the blast button. She arched her back as she had been trained to do years before, extended her arm, and threw, putting her entire body into the lob.

The grenade spun in the air, landing right at the feet of the closest Frogs. Falto brought her ACR up before the explosion came. The boom was devastating. Shrapnel, small hot bits of fast-moving death, ripped into the alien flesh. Legs flew in the air, along with at least two of the Frogs, spinning end over end. The explosion had devastated their haphazard formation. Two of the creatures were badly wounded, but kept closing, both hopping on a remaining leg, dragging a useless one behind them. Smoke rolled from the explosion, but Falto filtered it out.

There were six of the creatures still upright, though Rosales reduced that number by two with head shots. Her ACR rejoined the fight, with shots that downed two aliens. She started to step back as the Frogs got within striking range. Then they spat.

The streams they sprayed were toxins deadly to humans. Where the slower unarmored Frogs fired a blob of goo, the Uber Frogs spat a long-range stream. Falto dove for the ground in a roll, hoping to avoid the hit. As she came up, she fired again, this time four fast shots, downing another Frog. All that was left were the two that were dragging their pulverized legs. Out of the corner of her eye, she saw Rosales throw a grenade, then stagger back as if he were wounded. The explosion devoured the two remaining Frogs, turning them into a mist that froze in the air almost snow-like on the wind.

He was struggling with his helmet, trying to rip it off and failing. His fingers flew to his belt and pulled a wipe-rag out, commonly used to clear a helmet. Rosales dragged it across his face mask, his fingers trembling. He tried to use the rag to remove some of the Frog goo from his upper chest, then dropped the rag.

Something is wrong. He's been hit by the Frogs!

The stocky Ranger stopped moving for several seconds, his head dipped down. He let out a moan, and fell forward. Her eyes surveyed the area and she didn't see any sign of an immediate threat. The Rangers were engaging several Crabs off to her left, but none were closing with them. Falto darted over to Rosales who lay on his side. As she rolled him over, she could see that the Frog's toxic spray had hit him in the face and chest. The crack in his helmet may have been enough for some of the spittle to get through. His body was convulsing hard, and for a few moments, she tried to hold him steady but it was a losing struggle.

Moving fast, she carefully unhooked his ECH and tossed it aside. He was unconscious, his skin crimson. There was a frothy substance near his lips, she wasn't sure if it came from him or from the Frog's deadly spray. *I've got to be careful. If I get this stuff on me, it can have the same effect.* His tremors stopped and his body went limp as she searched for where she had stashed an EpiPen. They weren't perfect, but rumors were they could help arrest some of the reaction to the poison Rosales had been sprayed with. Every soldier carried one or two. Falto couldn't remember where she had stuffed hers, and she fumbled with her arctic pants pockets and her belt. Finally, after what seemed an eternity, reaching, she felt the EpiPen in one of her rear pouches. Falto nervously fumbled with it, trying to remember the simple training, finally pulling off the cap and letting it fly into the snow. Jabbing it in his neck, she found herself praying that she had been fast enough.

Her eyes kept checking for threats, then returning to Rosales. There was no mist rising from his mouth or nostrils. From what she could see, some of the spray had gotten to his neck and chin, no doubt aided by the crack in his visor. His blasted chest armor was wet with the dark green spit. *CPR—I need to give him CPR!*

She struggled with his STG straps, careful to not touch the spit herself. Once she got it off, she started with compressions, knowing she couldn't breathe on his face since it had been compromised. "Corpsman! I need a corpsman over here now!" she called on the tactical channel.

A Ranger medic moved up alongside of her, pulling her off. "It's Frog spit," she cautioned. The medic gave Rosales another shot. "Is he going to be okay?" she asked. The medic didn't respond. Instead he slung straps onto the body, stood up, and started back to the base, dragging Rosales behind him.

She knew the truth. He was dead. *The only reason he was here was to watch over me.* A wave of emotion swelled within her, uncontrollable sadness, almost consuming her. Falto fought it back as she had so many times before as a POW. Death was no stranger to her. Natalia barely knew Rosales, but he had been there for her since she had arrived in Greenland.

I've seen a lot of people die that I was close to. Why is it his death is affecting me the same way?

Tears streaked down her cheeks as she sniffled and regained her composure.

Through the distant smoke of battle, she saw a dark looming figure emerge. It was an Alpha, what everyone else called a Boss. It lacked a discernable neck, only a slope of ebony flesh that crowned an almost turret head. Unlike the other aliens she encountered, the Boss lacked eyes; it had only a slit that glowed crimson. Its obsidian skin looked wet, almost glossy. Across the chest, shoulders, and lower torso there was a jagged pattern that shimmered light green, almost like erratic bolts of lightning on its skin.

For a long few moments, she didn't move. It was as if her body could no longer respond to her mind. The Boss rushed to two Rangers, swinging its massive webbed claws, batting them aside as if they didn't matter. Grenades went off at its feet, the shrapnel causing ripples on its black hide, but none seeming to penetrate. The creature moved with an eerie grace, swaying as it strode forward, oblivious to the firepower being dumped into it.

Natalia stood there, mesmerized by the sight. The Boss raised its arm towards one Ranger and a cutting beam stabbed out. The high-pressured water beam almost completely severed the soldier's arm. It threw him back with the flailing stump that barely held on flipping wildly beyond him. Memories came to her as if a mental dam had burst. She remembered the Boss that had killed Rickenburg on Guam. He had taken her prisoner, hauled her down to his abyss, and had tormented her. She knew it wasn't the same one, but the sight of it seemed to hold her in its grasp and she could not move.

A rocket, fired from the Ranger's Cobra ASHUR, hit the creature's upper shoulder, wreathing it in flames and smoke. It staggered from the hit and for a few moments, tiny jets of water sprayed out under high pressure from where shrapnel had penetrated its hide. They stopped, and the Boss stabbed its arm towards the ASHUR, hitting the Cobra square on with the blast from its cutter. The Cobra lurched under the blast, tottering over with a crunch.

The Boss seemed to look at her, then closed the gap towards her.

Falto wanted to move, but was paralyzed. It wasn't fear that held her frozen in place; it was something else almost as sinister. All she could do was watch the creature close with her.

"Falto, move your sorry ass!" The voice in her head was that of Sergeant Rickenburg from Guam. Like a ghost from the dead, he still was with her, still was helping her be the Marine she strove to be.

The memory shattered her strange calm. She darted off to the left, where more of the Rangers seemed concentrated, raising her ACR and taking two snapshots at the creature.

Her sudden movement drew the Boss towards her like a shark moving on a slow swimmer. It broke into a run, its footfalls sinking deep in the snow and ice as it came. More shots came from the Rangers, but nothing seemed to stop the alien from closing the gap.

Falto slipped as she ran, falling, the staccato of gunfire around her. Pushing up, she got to her knees, when the shadow of the creature fell upon her.

With one big arm, it swept her up, wrapping its elbow joint around her thighs and squeezing tightly. Her bionics gave her the feedback, but her ears could hear the strain of her carbon reinforced legs flexing under the grip. Twisting as it lifted her up, she managed to turn enough to face the alien.

The eye slit was right in front of her, glowing crimson. She felt another tug as it tried to hold her tighter. If she had human legs, they would have broken already, and the pain would have taken her. Her bionics had sensation limits, which gave her a few fleeting moments of hope. Natalia glared at the eye slit and the malice she had felt for the Alpha that had taken her prisoner surged forward.

She had fantasized about killing her captor many times. SEALs in Trident rigs had done that for her. It was in that moment she realized that the desire to kill that particular Boss had never faded. It had been lurking in the back of her mind ever since. The desire for that vengeance was ever present, a nagging mental itch she could never quite scratch.

Until now.

Curling her fingers into a bladed fist with her bionic hand, she looked into the glowing eye slit and felt a smile rise to her face. Like a pile driver, she thrust her artificial fist forward, right into the eye slit. Her metal fingers didn't register the extreme pain she would have normally as her fist dug deep into the alien's head.

A fast blast of fluid, greasy black, sprayed out like an open fire hydrant from the hole she had made. The grip on her legs disappeared and she fell, wet from the alien's blood or whatever it was. As her back hit the snow, she saw the creature looming over her unmoving for a few moments. Through her arctic cold weather gear, it was hard to evaluate the damage she might have taken. Looking at her bionic hand, she saw that the artificial flesh-covering on her fingers was gone. Two of the fingers were bent in a way that no human hand could. Most of it was peeled back, either from the punch or the rush of fluid coming out of the alien. But the hand, what was left of it, worked. She slowly got to her feet and was surprised that she could stand.

As she moved to pick up her ACR with her good flesh-and-bone hand, she felt different. It was as if she had been carrying a sixty-pound ruck and suddenly had dropped it. An intoxicating feeling of elation, relief, and joy washed over her, an uncontrollable sense of justice and a feeling of retribution. It was as if she had been working toward an insurmountable goal and had suddenly achieved it—though in this case she was unaware that the goal had even existed.

"Falto," came the voice of Captain Wertan. "Are you alright?"

For the first time in a long time, she could truly say, "Yes."

"Then shag that Marine ass of yours back with us," he ordered.

As she looked, she realized the Rangers had fallen back again, closer to the American base camp. She started to run to join them, her speed hampered by a pronounced limp in her left leg. As she moved, she made a mental note that they were just past the rear of the crashed ship. From the dark holes further back, more Crabs and Squids were still emerging, though at a slower pace than before.

We had no idea there were that many of those things tucked away in there. We were lucky we didn't wake them up.

An explosion went off behind her. She glanced at the battlespace display and noticed that the feed from the British was black. Reaching up, she banged the side of her helmet, just to make sure it wasn't the result of damage, but the image didn't return.

Something has happened to the Brits.

When she reached a pair of Rangers, she pivoted in place, checking her ACR status in her HUD. It took some effort to steady her weapon, but she clenched the exposed bionic hand tight on the forward grip and focused her control. Looking back where she had run from, a group of advancing aliens were closing on the fallen Boss that she had killed. With a renewed vigor, she raised her weapon and fired away, hitting Frogs in the distance with a zeal that was hard to deny.

"That was one hell of a thing you did," the Ranger at her side said as he reloaded. "I have never seen anything like it."

"Thanks," she replied, firing another two-round burst. Praise from a Ranger meant a lot to her suddenly, even if he was just in the Army. "What's going on with the British?"

"No word to us yet," he replied, firing another shot. "I'm sure Captain Wade is on top of it. I saw what you did for Rosales."

Falto tried not to think of him laying unbreathing in the snow. She wasn't sure how to respond. She thought he was dead; he looked it the last she had seen of him.

Who knows, maybe the medics got to him fast enough.

"He's good people," was all she could say, taking careful aim and exploding the head of one of the Frogs.

"Something had better change quick," the Ranger at her side said. "I don't like the math we are facing here."

Falto understood the math, the equations of battles. The numbers of the enemy, the firepower, the numbers of bullets—they all fed a mythical math formula that determined victory or defeat. She had always been told, "Don't fight the math." It was something she deeply understood in that moment, standing in the wake of a crashed alien ship in isolated Greenland.

We can't get reinforced here. The odds are against us, but maybe that will allow us to fudge the math a little. The aliens have

*no souls. We do. They just fight where we fight to save what is ours.
Let's hope that's enough to alter the equation…*

CHAPTER 30

Operation Sulaco
The Crash Site, East Coast of Greenland

It mesmerized Veronica Diamond—the sight of Staff Sergeant Falto knifing her fist right into the eye of the Boss, killing the creature. The liquid that sprayed out turned into a fine snow and was caught in the wind, billowing away. It tempted her to ask if Fizz had gotten the shot, but from what she could see, he had. There was something inspiring about seeing a female warrior, a battle hardened Marine, taking down the worst that the Fish could throw at them.

"Alright, people," came the voice of Captain Wertan. "We need to haul ass and form a new line up at the base perimeter."

As she surveyed the aliens that were approaching—Crabs, Frogs, Dillos—it was frightening. *Can we actually destroy all of them?* A number of the Rangers were already either dead or wounded, and Omega Force had its own problems. It had been a while since she had to question whether or not she was about to die. Now that she was staring at that reality, Veronica gathered her wits and opted for action.

"Come on, Fizz," she said. "You heard the captain."

"Right," he said, lowering his camera as Verret moved in between the two of them, pausing long enough to fire off a pair of shots at the approaching enemy. The hulking bodyguard was breathing so hard, she could see his chest rise and fall under all of his body armor.

"We need to move right now!" he commanded.

Veronica started to move, as did Fizz. After twenty yards of running, she felt something cut the air near her head. Then came something hitting the back of her left shin. It first felt like a bee sting, hot and small. She made it a few more yards and noticed that her left leg below the knee was numb, as if it were asleep…nothing more than a hot tingle. Her run became a limp and the paralysis seemed to grow.

Oh shit—I've really been hit!

Pausing, she looked down at her white thermal pants at the back of her leg and saw a small smear of blood. "Verret—I've been shot." Fear chewed at her thoughts. *Can I even walk?* Testing the leg, it felt as if it were going to collapse under her.

Verret kneeled next to her and checked the wound. She felt a tug as his beefy gloved fingers poked near the bloody smear. Pulling his hand back, she saw a blood-smeared projectile. It was like a sliver of bone, dripping with blood—her blood. It was almost five inches long. Veronica was stunned at the sight.

It didn't feel that bad when I was hit.

Verret rose next to her. "Can you move?"

"I—I don't think so." Her voice was tense, and she realized she was starting to breathe heavier, flirting with hyperventilation.

Her hired muscle slung his weapon over his shoulder and picked her up. "It's probably not that bad," he offered.

Veronica wrapped one of her arms around his thick neck.

Probably?

How he ran carrying her was something that she couldn't understand. It was as if she weighed nothing. *Whatever I'm paying him, I need to double it if we get out of here.* The numbness reached her hips and seemed to slow or stop there. Verret was moving so fast that he actually was able to catch up with Fizz, who had stumbled on the snow once and was struggling to put some distance between the aliens and himself.

"Is she going to be okay?" Fizz asked as he moved alongside Veronica and Verret.

"She'll be—" Verret's body tensed, her upper body could feel it.

There was a gurgling sound from his throat. Looking up, she saw a similar projectile that had hit her, somewhat longer and thicker, sticking out the front of his lower neck. Blood squirted on her as Verret dropped to his knees. His face never looked down at her. It was as if his visor were looking at the camp, almost as if he were lost in thought.

His grip released and she fell in the snow. Then Verret fell across her legs.

Veronica screamed, a short high-pitched screech unlike any she had ever let loose in her life. *He's dead! I can't stand. I'm going to be dead.* Her hands tried to wipe off his blood from her coat but only smeared it, making it worse. She was trying to keep panic at bay, but it was swirling all about her.

Her head snapped around towards the aliens and things went from horrible to fatal. Three Dillos were springing towards her. Their sharp fangs glistened as they bounded from side-to-side, closing rapidly where she lay. She knew what they could do. They would rip her apart, shred her, and there was little that she could do.

She had a sidearm, and she fumbled to pull it out. While she had trained to shoot, the odds of her hitting the aliens were somewhere between slim and none. For a moment, she held the M-18 and contemplated sticking the weapon in her mouth and pulling the trigger. *It would be better to kill myself than be shredded alive.* As they got closer, she gripped the gun tighter.

Suddenly there was a sound next to her, the unmistakable bark of a Remington ACR firing in full automatic. Turning, she saw Fizz. He had grabbed Verret's ACR and was spraying the raging Dillos. She was instantly relieved. Turning to the aliens, she saw he had already shot one and then Fizz hit another one, exploding the alien into an ugly mist.

The remaining Dillo sprang towards her and she brought her own pistol into action. Aiming, she pulled the trigger and nothing happened. *Fuck!* She had forgotten to chamber a round. She fumbled with the slide, trying desperately—uncoordinated—to chamber the round while ignoring the leaping Dillo in her peripheral vision.

It sprang at Veronica. Then a blur hit it just inches from it landing on her. It was Fizz, he had used the stock of the ACR as a bat, swinging and hitting the creature, sending it flying a good thirty feet away. It rose, shook its ugly head, and started moving towards her, much slower than before, as if dazed by Fizz's hit.

Veronica took the extra second to control her hands, rack the slide, and take a breath to aim at the little Dillo scrambling back at her for the kill. The pistol kicked her arm and elbow joint hard as she unleashed three shots faster than she thought possible. The creature was hit on the second shot, flying backwards from the kinetic impact. Fizz had swung the ACR back to a firing position and unleashed the last rounds of his magazine into it, turning it into a pinkish mush.

She could see that Fizz was trembling and realized that she was as well. He pulled several magazines from Verret's gear, reloaded the ACR, and slung it over his shoulder. Bending down, he grabbed the shoulder epaulettes of her jacket and started to drag her out from under the bodyguard. Veronica could hear his strain, but Fizz continued to pull her as he walked backwards. He was panting, but didn't complain.

A sense of relief washed over her as they reached the line of Rangers moments later. "She's injured," Fizz wheezed. Someone called for a medic as the Rangers poured on their gunfire.

"Thank you, Fizz," she said.

"I lost one partner. I'm not about to lose another. Besides, I wasn't done breaking you in yet," he said, bending over slightly at the waist, still fighting to get his breath. "You going to be okay?"

Her butt was numb, but the loss of sensation stopped at her waist. "I think I'll make it. Will you?"

Fizz nodded. "I need to get in better shape." Pausing for a moment, he gathered his breath and stood back up. "Before you ask, I had on my bodycam."

Veronica grinned. "I honestly hadn't thought about it."

"That's a first."

"Getting shot changes your priorities."

The medic came and checked her wound, giving her a shot of something right through her coat sleeve. Veronica didn't ask what it was, but assumed it was working as warmth passed through her body. She carefully holstered her pistol and the realization came to her that she had actually shot an alien.

I'm no longer covering the story, I'm in the story.

The Rangers continued to fire grenades and their weapons and the intensity only increased. They were close to the base, only fifty meters behind them. A part of Veronica wanted to go to there, as if it would provide security. As she watched a Crab that had been pursuing them seem to shake off the shots hitting it, she realized that the base was just a target and didn't offer any safety at all.

There is no safe place here.

CHAPTER 31

Southwest of the Crash Site

A spray of explosive projectiles detonated across the thighs of Captain Wade's Python, throwing bits of armor into the snow. *How the hell did they hit me at this range?* He didn't want an answer to his internal question; it was more a cry of raw frustration. His damage indicators didn't show any critical damage, but it was only a matter of time before a lucky shot tore up something he needed, or hit him personally. Glancing around the displays in his cockpit, he still felt oddly safe. He remembered his father's words from his youth, talking about a tough SOB that lived in the neighborhood. "He's got hard bark on him." That was how he felt in the Python.

The battle had not been going as planned. Captain Wertan and the Rangers had fallen back to the perimeter of the base. There was nowhere else for them to go beyond that except into the frigid snowy wilderness of Greenland. As he angled his ASHUR towards the end of the British line, he could see that their base had been already hit. Several of the temporary structures were shredded and battered, which had explained why he and his people had lost the British battlespace feed. As he surveyed the line, he could tell that 45 Commando was suffering a great deal. Several of the ASH—no, Sovereigns—lay as dead hulks on the battlefield. One had a battery fire that had turned the potent war machine into a funeral pyre. In the distance, he could hear the roar of sonic weapons, big ones. Their ripples in the air led him to the source: two Turtles. They weren't firing on the British or his own Omega Force; they were blasting away at the ship. Their shots were so strong, they moved like plow blades.

Why are they so determined to destroy their own ship? If they turned those things on us, they could wipe us out and have it to themselves.

With the British battlespace down, he knew he would have to move in close to Major McKenna to try and see if there were any opportunities he might be able to exploit. Cooperation wasn't what he sought. Wade was a professional.

I want an edge, and if that comes from the British, I'll take it.

He spotted McKenna's distinctive Spitfire. It was painted in the grays, white, and black streaked pattern of the 45 Commando. He had a red domed upper armor plate that helped make it stand out. Wade angled his Python towards the major as McKenna fired his Gatling laser at one of the many targets that were downrange. As Wade came alongside of him, he saw the target, a Crab, with two blown off legs, which was still lumbering towards the 45 Commando forces.

Instinct took precedent over politics. Wade brought his targeting reticles on the Crab and banged off a power shell as he drifted his aim dead center on the Crab. His capacitors hummed as they discharged the concentrated microwave energy. The Crab twitched violently with the hit, though there was no physical indication of how much damage he had done.

A rocket, no doubt a British N-LAW, streaked out of the Spitfire next to him, slamming into the creature's body with a thunderous boom. Bits of flesh flew in the air as the smoke rolled past the Crab. It staggered, almost drunkenly, then fell over. The upright portion of the torso flopped down on the ice and snow.

Wade hit the scan button on the comms system, searching for whatever fallback comms channel the British were using. It was a safe assumption that with their battlespace down, they had some other means to communicate. He narrowed it to three channels, and toggled in the first one. Immediately he was greeted with British accents. The most dominant was someone acting as a forward observer, sending coordinates for mortar fire.

"Major McKenna, this is Captain Wade," he said, canting to face the cockpit of the Spitfire next to him.

"I saw you there," came back McKenna's voice as he aimed and fired his Gatling laser.

"What is your status?"

"We lost our BS. The command post is now trash and the people are casualties. We still don't know how many of my researchers are injured. My force is being forced back. And you?"

"Omega is on your left, but we are being pushed back from the north and from on top of the ship."

"I would kill for a few moments of bloody air support," McKenna said, firing off another power shell.

Wade paused. He had air support. It was supposed to be used to destroy the ship if matters called for it. Now he contemplated using it in a different way. "I've got some air support." The words came out and he almost wished he hadn't spoken them.

"We could use some help."

"I am supposed to use it as a last ditch, to destroy the ship."

"Doing that might stop them, but it might not."

Wade was forced to agree. "I've got two bombs, that's it."

For a few moments, McKenna said nothing. Then came a sigh. "Meet me on 15016.0."

Wade adjusted the comms frequencies. "I'm here."

"My government felt the same as yours. I brought a bomb with me. Thermobaric. It's planted up against the hull of that ship."

"You planted a bomb under the ship while we were in it?"

"Sorry. It was a necessary precaution. We felt the ship couldn't be allowed to fall back into their hands."

A part of Wade understood completely. Another part of him was furious. "How big is it?"

"Big enough. It is set for a ground burst. I have the arming system in my Sovereign."

His military mind went into action, processing options and choices open to him. *I can use my bombs to break up the enemy attack on our troops, and we still have the means to destroy the ship.* To do that required a level of cooperation that he was struggling with. *What choice do I really have? Wertan has fallen back. We can't win the ground battle, and if we do, we still have aliens attempting to destroy that ship all on their own.*

He hated the decision he was planting his boots on. It required him to trust the Brits. While they had not knowingly acted against his people, they had planted a huge explosive up against the ship…a vessel he had people exploring. Still, he wondered if McKenna was acting honorably. There was some evidence of that. *He asked to go on a private frequency for this talk, which means that his own people might not be aware of the bomb. Is he showing me trust, or is this part of some ruse?*

"The problem is, I don't entirely trust you," Wade said coolly.

"The feeling is mutual, I assure you."

"I really hate this," he confessed.

McKenna unleashed another N-LAW rocket downrange at the seemingly endless supply of the enemy. "Whatever we are going to do, we need to do it fast. My lads are good, but we can't hold forever."

He wanted to let the British die. It would be just retribution for them abandoning America in the last war. A dark realization grasped him tight in its clutches. *I can't let my personal feelings lead to the death of my people.* For Wade, it became a matter of cold calculation. If he let the Brits get overrun, the Fish would be able to concentrate on him…and those numbers didn't look good. "Fuck it then. I will use my bombs to break up the alien attacks as best we can. After that, we will, should the situation merit, use your bomb to deny the Fish access to the ship."

"Agreed. I am most appreciative of your support."

"Don't rub it in. I feel bad enough already."

"You are not alone in that. Stand by on this channel."

Wade tied in his own battlespace feed. "Whiplash. What is your situation?"

Captain Wertan's voice was ragged and frayed around the edges. "I'm running out of places to fall back to. The Fish are massing just west of the ship. I'm not entirely sure I can hold them when they make their run at us, but we will do our best."

"I have access to an air strike. One bomb at your disposal. Send me your coordinates of where you want it and pull your people back. The iron rain is coming."

"Thank you, Bryan!" A few moments later, the coordinates came up in the chat display.

McKenna's voice came on as well. "Relaying you our target information now." The coordinates were the old NATO system, but he understood them. "I'm ordering my scientists out of the ship now, just in case."

"Coordinates received," he said, as he saw an Omega Force ASHUR be torn apart by a Crab. It was Lieutenant John Jacob Lessman's Panther. The Crab used both of its claws to grasp and crush the rig, tossing it violently side to side. He fired a power shell and aimed at the Crab, knowing it was at far range, unleashing his directed energy weapon at the creature's long body. The Crab twitched, tossing Gold Rush's Panther rolling in a snowbank. A trio of LAW rockets slammed into it, finally taking it down.

Too many balls are in the air. I've got the Rangers, Omega, the bombs, and my own scientists to be concerned with.

Wade tied in the frequency for his air support. "This is Crockett 219 to Bumpercar."

"This is Bumpercar. Go," came back a voice so young, it made him cringe.

"I have two drops. Coordinates coming to you now." He dragged both sets of coordinates into the comms relay window and sent them. "Set for low altitude bursts."

"Crockett, these coordinates are not the target ship."

"That's correct. You are providing ground support."

"Crockett, my orders are to bomb the ship when ordered."

"Bumpercar, I'm changing your orders. Drop those bombs immediately at the coordinates provided."

There was a pause, which Wade despised. "Crockett, I'm not sure I'm authorized to change the drop coordinates."

"*I'm* authorizing you, Bumpercar. Drop the bombs, now! If you don't, you will be responsible for the death of American and British forces here on the ground."

"Sir, I understand. It's just that the duty officer is not available. I'm not—"

Wade cut him off. "Damn it, boy, drop those bombs as ordered. If you don't, I will bring a wrath on you that you will not survive!"

"Stand by," a clearly shaken Bumpercar replied.

A few moments passed. "We are cleared for drop. Get your forces from the blast zone now. Awaiting final release code."

He breathed a sigh of relief.

"Thank you," McKenna said.

He had forgotten to mute the conversation for the major. A part of him was glad; it demonstrated his sincerity. "I'm sorry you had to hear that."

There was another pause, and he saw the British forces fall back, coming at both his and McKenna's positions. His own battlespace display showed that Wertan was doing the same.

"Omega, we have incoming at the front. Retrograde one hundred meters and re-form at—" he drew a new phase line on the display, "Phase Line Sierra."

Omega's still operational ASHURs started back. Lessman's Panther was not among them, though he saw the pilot running, his green pilot's suit standing out against the stark white of snow.

Wade switched channels. "Wildstar," he transmitted to the science team. "Repeat, Wildstar."

Dr. Schrivener's voice came back. "We need a few minutes."

"Now, doctor—that or you may be killed." There was no response, so he assumed the doctor understood the gravity of the situation.

The clock was running and he knew it. He wanted to send the code but waited to give everyone as much time as possible.

"Still on station," came back Bumpercar's voice.

"Just another few moments," Wade said, eyeing the battlespace feed. Then he saw it, the scientists scrambling away from the ship. They were little more than white dots, but they were moving away.

He believed they were at a safe distance but time was running out. The Fish were interpreting the falling back as retreat, and were advancing.

God help me.

"Drop authorization zero, zero, one, drop."

"Ordinance released," came back Bumpercar's voice.

The bomb hit to the north first. The concussion wave tore through the air a few moments after the flash of the explosion. Greenland throbbed under his ASHUR. Then came the boom, riding the wave from the detonation and mildly buffeting his Python.

Let's hope that took the wind out of them.

A few seconds later, off to his right, the second bomb went off. There was no distant reaction time—this time the flash and the reverberation hit him almost instantly as a large cluster of the Fish simply vanished. Bits of rock and ice rained down on his rig, freezing to it hard. The explosive burst forced him to compensate his balance to remain upright. Glancing over at McKenna's Spitfire, he saw the major was leaning into the blast. The sleek streamlined style of the Sovereign seemed almost built for this kind of battlefield event.

His focus was on the American bombing site. A black cloud rolled skyward, curling in on itself before eroding in the icy winds. The crater that the bomb made was an ugly scar on the surface, one that lacked the stark whiteness of the snow that covered everything else. It was shallow, black and gray from the up-churned rocks. Smoke rose, twisting in the wind. Surrounding the wide blast zone were pieces of Greenland, vast slabs of ice, and thousands of bits of indistinguishable alien flesh. The only thing that he saw that he could identify was a large piece of a Crab's tail, complete with a stinger, lying atop a massive piece of ice.

"Nice work, Bumpercar," he transmitted, cutting off the feed to his air support. There would be no more help from that direction.

I will probably have my ass chewed for having them bomb the Fish rather than the ship. I'd rather be alive for a butt-reaming than dead for following obsolete orders. Besides, General Lee will have my back. He always has before.

As the smoke cleared from the blast radius, Wade got his first view of the changes to the battlefield. The explosion had blunted their charge. The ground was cratered from the explosion, littered with rocks, chunks of ice, and bits of aliens. The explosion had rocked the alien ship hard, sending huge ripples across the surface, knocking over all of the aliens on top of it, throwing some back out towards the sea. There were several spots where the thick outer skin of the ship ruptured, spilling out as liquid. *I hope that the science team is still with us.*

The British explosion had seemed to stun the aliens that remained standing. The blast radius extended almost to the side of the ship, whose upper portion had been damaged by the concussive force. Water oozed out of several fresh gashes, splattering down the side of the ship and freezing. The crater was a swirling hellscape of white smoke, blasted bits of Greenland, and littered with dead alien parts.

The Fish on the far side of the blast radius stood, clearly stunned by the turn of events, looking at the British force, as if waiting for an order to rush out and risk the fate that their brethren had. Wade hoped that whoever was commanding the aliens would pull back, fearing more death from the clouds.

They have no way of knowing that I have shot my wad with this attack.

Omega Force made it to their new positions, turning to face the stalled enemy.

Come on, you bastards...fall back.

Even their attacks on the ship with sonic weapons seemed to have stopped with the bombing.

We haven't been able to throw up much air support after the first few weeks of the war. This is something they must not have been prepared for.

One of the Bosses stepped forward, towards the blast zone, walking defiantly for a few steps. Then he broke into a full sprint, rushing right towards the British line. The rest of the Fish surged forward, charging again.

Fuck me!

The ASHURs and Sovereigns opened up at long range. Wade knew what his people were feeling, a toxic combination of exhaustion, frustration, and a dash of despair. His battlespace feed showed that the Fish were charging forward towards the Rangers as well.

I had hoped we'd broken their spirt, sent the fear of God into them. Apparently not.

He aligned his targeting reticle on another Boss that was sprinting towards where he and McKenna stood.

"Shite," signed McKenna. "I thought we'd broken those twats up."

The charging Boss was getting closer, almost as if he were focused on the pair of them.

Do they understand our command and control?

Wade fired a LAW rocket at the rushing creature. The warhead went off on the creature's swinging hand. The alien paused for a moment, still in the blast zone from the bomb. Two of the Boss's fingers were blown off in the blast and were spraying oily liquid. The alien reached over with its other huge clawed hand and seemed to twist it, removing the mangled stump off at the wrist, stemming the flow. It glared at Wade and McKenna, its crimson eye locking on them. Its body tattoo shimmered bright azure, like living lightning, all across its hulking body.

It resumed its rush. Power shells went off, both from Wade and McKenna. He aimed his DEW and the major's Gatling laser spun, flickering occasional bursts of white, barely visible to the naked eye through the all the debris in the air.

A British drone got close and opened fire on the charging Boss. The alien angled off towards the drone, jumping and landing in front of the GRD. Before the drone could put any distance in, the Boss grabbed it by its rear legs, and carried it along with it.

Wade was sure he was hitting the Boss, but the fire didn't seem to deter it from rushing forward. The charging brute extended its handless left arm and a long stream from the cutter weapon tore into McKenna's Spitfire. One piece of his armor was thrown off, crashing into Wade's Python as the Spitfire turned to deflect some of the damage. Turning back, McKenna sent an N-LAW rocket at the creature, followed a moment later by a missile from Wade. Both weapons hit, the ripples on the thick hide of the creature were visible as the Boss seemed to shake off the assaults.

Wade started to sidestep away from McKenna, who was moving as well, increasing the distance between them. The Boss sprang with the captured GRD still in its clutch, aiming right for the Spitfire. Wade fired off another power shell as he spun to try to assist McKenna.

The Boss's lunge was an organic torpedo of energy and death, slamming right into the Spitfire's torso. McKenna fell backwards, with the Boss right on top of him. The alien used the GRD like a club until it was so shredded, it flew apart as bits of debris. Then the creature threw blow after blow into the already damaged Spitfire, its thick obsidian arms a blur of speed, savaging the Sovereign under it. Metal few off, as Wade closed once more on the fight, leveling the directed energy weapon before him.

The Boss jammed its sharp claws right into the Sovereign's cockpit, compromising the transparent aluminum projection. McKenna's voice came in Wade's earbuds as he moved, a deep moan as he struggled. Swinging one of his Spitfire's arms like a club, he collided with the head of the Boss with a dull thud. That only forced the alien to grab that arm and twist it. Metal screamed and hydraulic fluid squirted as the arm was torn off and thrown aside.

Wade jammed his weapon up against the head of the Boss and fired. The capacitors hummed their tune of hot death as the weapon fired. Instantly, the Boss stiffened, almost like an animal that had been given a high voltage shock. It then ceased to be a hulking mass of muscle…it had turned into dead weight, collapsing down on McKenna's crippled Sovereign.

Wade set down his DEW and used his rig's hand to grab the

shoulder of the Boss, peeling him off McKenna's Spitfire. It was far from easy and he almost lost grip, barely catching himself as he strained his own muscles to move the Boss off.

The Spitfire was a crumbled mass of worthless metal. Its once sleek prow was flattened, mangled. There were holes in the lower canopy where the sharp claws of the alien had penetrated. "Major, are you alright?"

He got a cough back, which was a good sign. "I'm alive."

"You need help standing?"

The Spitfire didn't move. "My computer system is badly damaged as is my battery under me. All that weight it must have come down on a rock…my power levels are nearing zero."

That diagnosis hit Wade hard. He had lost a rig before. Pilots had a bond with their equipment and the loss of a rig was hard to shake. "Are you okay, though?"

"I think so," McKenna said, coughing again. "I may need some help with egress. The latches and hinges are twisted and almost in my lap."

Wade knelt his Python next to the Spitfire and struggled to find the hatch edges, the Sovereign had been so badly mauled. When it did, it was a new battle to get the fingers of his ASHUR under the lip of the canopy to pry it off. Precision with the fingers was something that every Omega pilot took extra training in, and it paid off. With a tug, then a hefty jerk, he managed to open it.

McKenna lay before him. Fresh blood stained his jumpsuit. His pilot's helmet was dented on one side. The British officer winced as he struggled to sit up, fighting to pull his cold weather parka out of the storage next to his saddle. Wade brought his Python to a standing position and swept the area to make sure no other aliens were closing on them.

"Looks like we are going to have to go with Plan B," Wade said as McKenna sat up in front of him, his face streaked with blood on one side, his skin pale.

"About that," McKenna said between heavy breaths. "My master arm and the bomb triggering system were crushed in the attack."

Wade could feel his face sag with the news.
Damn it!

CHAPTER 32

Southwest of the Crash Site

Major McKenna bore an expression awash in desperation as he looked up at the Python ASHUR looming before him. Blood soaked his flight suit and he found several ugly cuts. Pulling out his auto-suture, he applied it to one set of cuts on his lower torso, hoping to seal the wounds. His head ached as he moved, and a wetness oozed down the neck of his turtleneck sweater he wore under as cold weather gear. Reaching up, he found something dangling below the damage done to his helmet. A slight tug pulled off the tip of his ear. As he tried to move, everything ached, especially his lower chest.

I've got bruised or broken ribs from the feel of it.

It wasn't the first time in his life he had suffered that pain. Using a small sprayer of skin-seal, he sprayed his damaged ear, hoping to stem the bleeding there.

Wade had surprised him, using half of his air capability to blow up the aliens that were pressing his troops. The American had always seemed to be fighting some inner anger when he met with him. Now he had come to McKenna and had rendered critical aid.

The lads...how are my boys? With no battlespace or display, he felt blind. As he started to push and pull himself from the remains of the cockpit, he tried to eyeball what was left of his troops. Seeing Sovereigns still moving, still shooting, it gave him a momentary sense of pride. As he rose to his full height, he used a pain numbing agent on his ribs, which gave him instant relief. He knew he'd pay the price for using it later, but for now, it allowed mobility.

Looking at Wade's Python, he wondered if he had been wrong

about the Americans. In that instant, he realized it didn't matter. The battle was still on, and in the distance, more bollocks were coming around from the sea-side of the ship, shifting towards the long British line.

We could still be overrun. I have a bomb, but no way to detonate it.

It was a bitter pill to swallow and only seemed to fuel his worries. Worse, his Sovereign lay under his feet, mere scrap metal now. For the first time in a long while, he felt exposed on a battlefield. Without a Sovereign, he was just an infantryman, one that was feeling the sting of cold penetrating his uniform.

The bombs had not killed all of the aliens by any stretch. The Squids that came from the ship seemed to be getting reinforcements from the vessel still. The ocean-borne aliens were getting additional forces as well. The aliens were still fighting each other all around the ship. The Stegosaurs were still blasting away at the ship from the seaside. There were plenty of the enemy close enough to the ship where they could be caught in the bomb blast—if it could be set off.

His mind bore in on that subject. It was possible to set off the bomb without the signal. He could hand code it in. It would only take a few seconds of work. There was a significant issue. There was no timer. If he manually coded in the triggering sequence, it would detonate instantly. Death would be blissfully instant, but there was no escaping it.

So I can die here, with the aliens overrunning what is left of 45 Commando, or I can set the bomb off and save them.

The choice became easy.

McKenna didn't want to die, but it was inescapable at this point. His men came first, then the science team. *What matters is getting our samples home.* His father would understand, even if the rest of the family didn't. *I have to do this. It is my mission.*

Glancing at where the bomb was concealed along the hull of the spacecraft, he felt an emotional weight press down on him. McKenna knew that he would have to run some two hundred meters over blasted ground...ground that was now crawling with aliens. *I must try, at least.*

Raising his wrist communicator, he looked at the US Python towering over him. "I can manually detonate the explosive. There's no timer, though. Once I key in the last digit, it will go off."

Wade's voice came back to the earbuds he wore. "Where is it?"

McKenna pointed to the ship. "Right there, against the hull."

"Was it damaged in the blast?"

McKenna squinted in that direction. "It should have been clear."

"You'll never cross that ground alive."

"I will. I'm a Commando."

I must do this. No one else can. With all of the attention being drawn by the Sovereigns, there's a chance they might ignore one human.

There was not an immediate response from Captain Wade. McKenna turned and started mentally plotting where he would sprint to avoid the aliens as much as he could. It was disheartening, there were so many ways to die between him and the bomb. Still, it was the only way.

If I do this, I save both of our forces.

That mental acknowledgement gave him the strength to try.

He reached into the mangled cockpit, pain shooting through his back, and pulled out his white L129A1 Sharpshooter II. He checked to see if it was cleared, chambered a round, and stuffed three additional magazines in his coat pocket. His legs were already getting numb from the cold, but he was counting on the sprinting to keep them from giving out before he reached the bomb.

✳ ✳ ✳

Wade looked down at the Royal Marine Commando checking his weapon. *He can't make it out there without armor. The Fish will swarm him before he gets halfway.*

I can get him there. He knew what that meant.

"Hold up, Major."

"Why?"

Wade drew a long breath of air. *Things would have been easier if his rig hadn't been destroyed.* Easy wasn't part of this conflict, though; that was something he had come to accept long before arriving in Greenland. *Now there are new species, the Squids and the others we found in the ship. They are coming at us, unrelenting. We don't even know what it is they want other than us to be dead.*

Looking down at McKenna, Wade came to the understanding that the two of them were more alike than different. He hated that thought.

He is going to sacrifice himself. It's damned noble. He's the only one with the know-how to set off that bomb. If he gets himself killed, we are really screwed.

His eyes raced through his displays. Power levels were low, and Wade could tell that he only had a few rounds of ammo left.

My ability to be effective in this fight is fading fast. This is something I can do that makes a difference. I can still win this battle.

"Major, I'll go with you."

***

"Damn it all! I can do this," McKenna declared.

"Oh shut the fuck up," Wade replied, barely reining in his disgust. "This day has been bad enough as it is. Look, you can't get across that open ground without an ASHUR and I'm the one that is here. There are handholds on the rear of the rig used for maintenance. You should be able to hold on to them. I will get us to the bomb; you set it off."

McKenna nodded grimly. *The last thing I want is to die with a bloody Yank.* Refusing his help would endanger the mission, and that was what mattered. There was no guarantee that the two men would survive the rush through no-man's-land to begin with. But the odds were far greater with Wade than without him.

He moved to the back of the Python and climbed up on the small handholds, wrapping one arm at the elbow around the upper rungs near the battery. Every joint on his body seemed to protest. Despite the drugs he had pumped into himself, he knew his body was battered—badly. The rig's battery next to him radiated a small amount of warmth, which was the only welcoming feeling.

"I'm up," he transmitted.

"Hold on tight, this is about to get bumpy."

The Python lunged forward, accelerating up to as close to a full sprint as he could manage on the uneven ground. McKenna's arm ached and the cold numbed his legs, a welcome relief as it helped suppress the pain he felt. He heard the metallic click and whoosh of a LAW missile firing, much louder than it sounded from within the cockpit. Off to one side, the Python's chain gun purred, spent casings flying past McKenna as the Sover—no, ASHUR—rushed forward. It was strangely reassuring, that the Python was firing.

The rig sidestepped, throwing him hard, swinging around on the back of the rig, only held in place for a moment by his locked arm. It ached and throbbed, but McKenna ignored the pain as he regained his footholds.

What does it matter? When I set that bomb off, any pain I have will be gone.

Something collided with the Python, he felt the all-too-familiar jerk of a kinetic impact with the ASHUR. A piece of armor plating flew over the shoulder, narrowing, missing the top of his helmet. Another LAW missile fired, and he found himself wishing he had a forward view of the battlefield. All he saw was that they were rushing past charging Crabs and Dillos that were surging across the frozen ground right at 45 Commando.

There were two more jerks from impacts that tossed McKenna about. One hit made his already cracked and battered helmet collide with the ASHUR, making his vision darken for a moment. He pushed through a moment of nausea and maintained consciousness, refusing to release his grip, despite the cold starting to make his fingertips feel as if they had needles sticking into them. *We have got to be pretty close now. It can't be too much further.*

The Python skidded for a moment, turning around in place. He saw the hull of the spacecraft looming above him like an orange and brown wall. At the foot of the alien craft was the bomb. Only a small part of the long gray device was exposed, the rest covered in snow.

"Is that it?" Wade asked.

McKenna relaxed his aching elbow and dropped to the ground. His feet were freezing and his knees protested the landing, but he managed to keep upright. "It is."

"How long do you need?" Wade said, his chain gun purring once more with a long burst of fire.

McKenna moved next to the thermobaric device and using the side of his hand, chiseled out the access plate. It wouldn't open, and for a moment he was afraid it was somehow jammed.

That's all I bloody need!

His numb fingers fumbled with his tactical knife as he locked battle with the access plate. Twisting the tip of the blade, he managed to pry it free.

A bang of another power shell went off and the expended casing fell next to the bomb as Wade blazed away at some unseen target. McKenna's focus was the bomb.

"All I have to do is key in the code and hit enter."

"Let's get our people back then," Wade replied, firing off another power shell. The discharge of the directed energy weapon was a high-pitched, almost static-sounding hum as it fired again.

Reaching to his wrist communicator, the major tied in on the channel his people were using. "This is Vindictive to all commands. Fall back from the ship immediately. We are setting off an explosive that will destroy the ship and, we hope, most of the bollocks that are here. You have a minute to detonation. Lieutenant Walling, you have command—take care of our men and the scientists. The rest of you fall back and take cover immediately. Vindictive out."

He didn't want to hear responses from his men. Andrew was committed to what was about to come.

* * *

Sweat burned in the corners of his eyes. The physical exertion to run his ASHUR while carrying an extra few hundred pounds of Royal Marine Commando had pushed him hard. Getting his breath, Wade toggled his communicator on. "This is Crockett. All US forces fall back and take whatever cover you can. I'm assisting the British commander in setting off a thermobaric device that will hopefully destroy the ship. You haven't much time, so haul ass. Brace for an air rush and fireball. Captain Wertan, you are now in command of this task force." He switched off his communications system. There was nothing else left to say.

This wasn't how he had envisioned his death—certainly not fighting to protect a Brit. He had always assumed it would be a random death, like so many he had witnessed during his career. At no point did he think he would know how he would die, or when.

His Python was out of ammo. It was nothing more than a big target at this point. A Crab was moving towards him and all he could do was throw punches or kicks at it. If the major did his job, it wouldn't come to that, though. Glaring at the Crab, Wade smiled.

You have no idea you're about to die, and I have a front-row seat to it.

It was a grim satisfaction, and one he savored.

"I've gotten word out. I told them they had a minute."

"Same here."

McKenna's voice sounded winded, and from the blood he saw on the major, he understood why. "I hope you aren't expecting any sort of thanks for this."

"I'm not. My opinion of your nation remains the same. You're all still assholes."

"I think you Yanks are nothing but the lowest form of wankers."

"This isn't how I wanted to go out," Wade said.

"Nor I," McKenna said, glancing off to the aliens between their position and where that last of his Royal Marines were fighting and falling back. "The clock has been running. I suppose I should get on with this." He leaned in over the panel to cut the faint glare.

Wade looked out and saw two Crabs that seemed to have noticed them. Both of the creatures turned away from the British and started to scurry towards them. Seeing them made him smile. *That's right... get in a little closer. We have a surprise for you.*

"It looks like they've noticed us."

McKenna chuckled at his words. "Time's just about up."

"See you in hell then," Wade replied with resolve.

"I will beat you there," McKenna assured him.

"Asshole."

* * *

McKenna checked his chronometer quickly and saw that more than a minute had come to pass. He tuned out anything that Wade might be saying. *Let him have the last word. Time to muck up these bollocks once and for all.* He thought about his family, then his mind went to his men. *Lay a wreath for me at Graspan, lads.*

His fingers were trembling, not from fear but the invisible needles of the stinging cold, as he pulled off his glove and started the key sequence, 1-6-3-0-9. The enter button pulsated white. He carefully placed his finger on it, closed his eyes, and pushed. For a millisecond, he felt something hit him as the casing of the explosive went off, then sweet oblivion washed over him.

CHAPTER 33

Operation Sulaco
The Crash Site, East Coast of Greenland

Natalia Falto heard the order to get to cover from Captain Wade and dove behind a thick slab of ice that had been churned up by the crash of the spacecraft. She knew better than to question such an order. Curling up, she braced for something, something big.

There was a crack-boom in the distance that shook the ground, thundering over the sounds of the sonic weapons that the Turtles had been pummeling the ship with. She had witnessed thermobaric weapons in grenade form and had been shown a vid of a bigger one during training. Her mind tried to process what they did and how they worked. Glancing at the ice, she remembered the intense heat such bombs made. *Should I dive and try to find better cover?* Those thoughts evaporated when she saw a flash and the orange shadows that were cast from it creeping around the ice block where she lay.

A few moments later, the fuel aerosol that the initial blast released ignited with a tremendous roar. Her chest strained, struggling to get in air as her diaphragm felt the concussion. Both of her ears painfully popped. For a moment, the air rushed away from the epicenter of the explosion. Then it reversed and rushed towards the blast as the massive fireball sucked up all the oxygen around it. Falto curled up into the tightest ball she could and clamped her eyes shut hard as the flash shone right through her lids. Bits of snow, ice, and stone slapped into her body as they flew inward toward the massive ball of flames. She could feel the heat around her and the upper crust of snow misted in the rushing air.

As the rush of air stopped, Falto slowly raised her head and looked up over her makeshift cover. The fireball was rising over the battlespace, ugly, black and orange, like a miniature sun. The spacecraft was mostly gone, though bits of structure and wreckage were falling off to the side of the crash site and the parts of it that still stood to the north were ablaze. Bits and pieces of charred flesh were everywhere in the blast radius, all of it burning. The ground snow and ice had melted, leaving pools and troughs of water steaming. She knew that in a few minutes the entire blast area would be a giant pond of ice, but for the moment it was a bizarre combination of wet and burning.

She spied a charred stump that had been a Boss, listing slightly, most of its arms gone. A Crab claw near the edge of the blast zone popped and cracked open, letting out a hissing sound. Through the haze of smoke, she didn't see any signs of the Fish. At least not any live ones. The explosion had gone out to the sea, no doubt melting the shore's ice floes.

Will they be back?

Her eyes went to the HUD in her ECH and she looked for a signal from Captain Wade's Python. It was offline. His implanted chip was no longer pinging. She knew what that meant, and she bit her lower lip for a moment. *Wade killed himself in getting that bomb detonated.* She appreciated his sacrifice. More importantly, she understood it. *He did what it took to take care of his people and completed his mission.* Memories of Sergeant Rickenburg flared once more in her mind. Completing missions was something she understood deeply.

Regardless of how Wade had clashed with her, she admired him for what he had done. *How many of these kinds of victories must we die for to win?*

A Ranger moved up next to her. "Are you alright, Sergeant?" he asked. Looking around to her sides, she saw the troops were standing, she was the only one still keeping low.

Rising to her feet, she nodded her response. The air was warm, radiating from the epicenter of the blast, but it was losing its grip to the icy winds of the arctic. She was transfixed like those troops near her, surveying the carnage where the ship and their enemy had been only a few minutes earlier.

"Listen up, people," came the voice of Captain Wertan. "They may come back. I want ASHURs to rotate back to the pods for rearming and battery swaps. Let's get our wounded back to the base. I want a tight perimeter with eyes on that shoreline."

His words shook the strange hypnotic calm everyone was caught in. With orders, soldiers move, and so do Marines. She knew her bionics had been damaged but had no idea how bad.

I should get back there just to see how bad "bad" is.

She slowly began to limp her way back.

After walking for a few minutes, she saw Veronica Diamond, her leg stained with blood, being dragged by her production person. Gone was her bodyguard. Falto didn't need to ask. *If he's not there, he's dead or injured.* She moved up to Diamond and her production person stopped. It was clear that he was winded.

"How bad are you hit?" Falto asked the reporter.

"Not sure, my legs and hips are numb."

Falto bent down and checked the wound. It was ugly, but then again all wounds were. It looked as if it wasn't still bleeding, which was a good sign. "You're probably lucky. The cold weather slowed your blood flow." She rose and looked over at Fizz. "Do you need some help?"

He nodded, his beard a tangled and frozen mass, refreezing the further they got from the blast zone. "My fingers are numb and, I'm not sure, but I think my balls have frozen off."

It was enough to make Natalia grin. She bent down and grabbed the shoulder straps of Diamond's coat. "Let me take her for a few minutes." She started to walk, using her exposed bionic hand to help with the pulling.

"What kind of bomb was that?" Fizz asked as he lumbered alongside her.

"Not sure. It could be the mother of all bombs, the father, or the distant cousin. Thermobaric device, that is for sure."

"Was it British?" he asked.

"I think so. Captain Wade went in with them and helped them set it off."

"Is he dead?" Veronica asked.

"I think so," she said in a low tone.

"Will the Fish come back?" Veronica pressed, a hint of nervousness in her words.

It was a good question, one she did not have the answer to. "I don't know. But if they do, we need to be ready."

Will we ever be ready? We keep killing them, they keep coming. We find new ones and they are just as deadly as their predecessors. I can only hope that we gathered something here that helps us win the war.

* * *

Veronica was finally getting the feeling back in her legs and hips. The medics at the base camp had treated her along with the other wounded and injured. Her talks with them on their cots gave her a good sense of what had transpired during the fight. While it was a jumble of memories and the usual rumor mill, what she had gathered had confirmed what Sergeant Falto had told her. Captain Wade had gone to help the British. He had been the one that had called in the air strike and had gone in with Major McKenna to set off a bomb that the British had brought with them. It was a good story, and she was confident that with the right packaging, she could make Wade a household name.

America's newest hero in the war against the aliens. That is the bundle people will want back home.

Fizz sauntered in, his head dipped down. Some of his beard was missing in little patches, no doubt from freezing and breaking off. He moved alongside her cot and kneeled down. "How're you feeling?"

"I can feel my ass again. I can move my legs, but they are still a little numb."

"You're luckier than most," Fizz confided to her, keeping his voice low so that the other wounded didn't hear his words.

"Thank you." She quickly wiped away the tears that were forming in the corners of her eyes. *A lesser man...partner...would have abandoned me.*

"For what?"

"Dragging me out of there. If you hadn't, I would be toast—literally."

Fizz shrugged. "You're welcome. For what it's worth, I did it more for me than for you. When I lost Dana, I lost a little bit of who I was. So much of my life was about Dana, I was just a shadow. When she died, I guess a part of me went with her."

"That had to be rough."

"I tried to hide. I told myself I had to...you know...to keep away from Drake. In reality, I was hiding from myself. I didn't know how to operate in a world without Dana Blaze."

"Are you mad I came and brought you back into this shit-show?"

He clearly was pondering her question carefully. "No. This is who I am. I don't want the limelight, I just love the work. I didn't know how much I missed it. I'm actually glad that you came along when you did. If you hadn't yanked me back, who knows how long I would have been moping around that house alone."

Veronica understood, and Fizz's words made her smile. "Welcome back, Fizz."

He cracked a smile. "You should know, they are sending in the choppers to get us out of here."

"What about the Fish?"

"Apparently they don't like big-ass fireballs of death and doom. So far, they are gone. There's no ship left to be destroyed, or recovered, or whatever they were planning to do with it."

"Good," she sighed. "I've had my fill of them for a few days, at least."

"The British are loading up to go as well. Major McKenna and

Captain Wade set off that bomb together. I don't think that will patch up the bad feelings between the countries, but what do I know? They are very appreciative for the support, or so I'm told. I was able to get some long-range shots of them loading their hovercraft up for the trip back to England."

Fizz is still working. I am damn lucky to have him as my producer.

"Squirt our stuff to the satellite when you get a chance."

"Next pass is in two hours, but I've got it all set up. The helicopters are not coming in to haul us out for another four. Hopefully, that will give you some time to rest up and heal."

She nodded once, feeling the weariness tug at her. "We both could use some rest."

Fizz chuckled in response. "My work is just starting. We have dozens of hours of footage that have to be edited and cleaned up, especially the audio."

"You can take a few hours to rest up, Fizz."

"This is a big story. Dana would never forgive me for not getting it ready to rock."

Veronica lowered her head back on the pillow. "You don't owe her anything, Fizz. You never did. She didn't make you who you are. You were always the best damn camera guy and producer out there. You made her. The sooner you come to grips with that, the sooner you will get some rest." Her eyes fell on Fizz to watch his expression.

He sighed, long and hard. "You know, I needed to hear that. Thanks."

"The honor is all mine." With that, she closed her eyes and succumbed to the tug of sleep that had been struggling with her consciousness.

EPILOGUE

Extra Terrestrial Task Force (ETF) HQ,
DIA Intelligence Annex, the Penetrator
Los Alamos, New Mexico, the United States

Dr. Bailey Fleming had been waiting for this moment for a long time. She was finally alone with the samples brought back from Greenland. She had been on Dr. Schrivener's team on Operation Sulaco but had never been able to finagle being alone with the alien samples. This opportunity had presented itself solely because she volunteered to catalog the samples. It was the kind of dull administrative work that most scientists were willing to pass down to their grad students.

Fleming knew she was being videoed by the security monitors. She also knew that no one was likely going to be studying them. After all, who wanted to watch a lonely doctor catalog organic samples? Her plan factored in the laziness of human beings.

The storage room was cold, mostly to preserve the tissue and bits of the ship that had been recovered. Starting her work, to anyone watching, it was dull. She logged the sample, its dimensions, and the audio field note files that had been already transcribed and put in the local cloud.

As she moved, she went to some of the more unusual samples and opened their outer shell. Using a small disposable needle, she was able to go through the access port and extract small bits of tissue. After resealing the sample, she transferred the cells to her covert transport container—an antiperspirant container. The false container had rows of little holes on the top which normally would

344

have released the antiperspirant when a small knob was twisted in the bottom. In this case, each hole was a specially designed receptacle that would store the samples she was stealing.

To anyone checking, it would appear that she had brought along the plastic tube simply for hygiene purposes. If the knob was rolled, it would even eject a small amount of gel. She admired the construction of the device both in terms of its covert nature and its appearance.

Then again, she expected nothing less from JayTech.

Bailey's family consisted of her father, who was a cancer patient. A secretive contact from JayTech had reached out to her when he had been diagnosed. They offered new medicines and a promise to reverse his stage-four status with drugs JayTech had developed. All she had to do was get her intelligence and samples from the ETF.

There had been no hesitation to take up the offer. True to their word, her father was experiencing what doctors called "a miraculous recovery." She had kept up her end of the bargain for months, sneaking data and classified reports out. When the chance had come to take part in the mission in Greenland, she was encouraged by her JayTech handler to sign up. A part of her wondered if they had something to do with her getting her name on the shortlist to go to on Sulaco.

I wonder how many people in the ETF are on the payroll with JayTech?

Deep down, she knew she didn't want to know the answer.

The work took three days to finish, three days of not being bothered or interrupted. Bailey didn't feel like she was a traitor. There was no sabotage in what she was doing. After all, what she was doing was taking a few innocent cells. The ETF had plenty of material to work with. Giving Jay Drake and his people the samples wasn't an act against the United States. It was only the action of a daughter working to save her father's life.

What harm am I really doing?

***

Falto walked into Colonel Slade's office and his clerk closed the door behind her. Slade sat at the desk, reviewing something holographically projected over the desk. He held up a finger and she went to parade rest as he finished his work.

For the last few days, she had been in the hospital getting repaired, at least that was what she called it. Her left prosthetic leg had been damaged so badly by the crush of the Boss that the physicians had opted to scrap it, replacing it with a new one. Her bionic hand had suffered numerous failures and three fingers had been completely replaced. The flayed off synthetic skin on her arm was replaced, but the skin tone had not been set yet, so it was almost a pale white. She had an appointment in two days to match her skin color, and was looking forward to it. The sight of the pale hand was strangely disturbing.

During the downtime, she had been giving interviews with the ETF team members about things she saw and encountered. She had caught the news and was surprised to see the footage of her in Greenland. During the evac, she had lost track of Veronica and Fizz. Seeing the story on every network confirmed they had gotten out relatively intact. While she hated the new press coverage, from what she saw, most of it was positive—if not overly so.

I'm not the heroic Marine that Diamond said I am. I just did what I needed to do.

During the flight back, she had spoken with Dr. Schrivener. Their last few moments in the ship had netted a strange sample that the doctor had showed her. They initially looked like dime-sized white balls, hundreds of them floating in a dull green goo. Upon closer inspection, she saw that each one was a Crab, tiny, suspended in a translucent white egg material. "We didn't have time to get as many of these little buggers as I would have liked," Schrivener told her. "That ship was carrying an army all on its own." Falto liked the thought that the destruction of the ship had prevented mankind from having to fight more alien forces at least.

Slade rose to his feet, then gestured to a chair. "Have a seat, Sergeant."

Falto slid into the chair and the colonel continued. "I have been going over the reports on Operation Sulaco. I have to say, your performance was outstanding."

"I did what any Marine would do."

Slade grinned, cocking his head slightly. "A little more, I think. Bad news about Captain Wade dying like that."

"He and Major McKenna likely saved both our op and the British's."

"For what it's worth, he mentioned you in his daily reports. He said you were irritating, that you countermanded his desires. That you were, in his words, frustrating."

That bothered her a little, but Falto knew that the words were well earned. "He isn't wrong."

"He also said you were invaluable to the mission. Despite your getting under his skin, he was going to put you in for a commendation."

A pang of guilt and loss swelled in her. For all of his bravado, Wade appreciated her. That meant more than any vid that Veronica Diamond and Fizz produced.

"It's a shame we lost the ship," she said. "I feel like we could have gotten more."

"We did just fine. The science team is going to be going over the samples they recovered for months. In the meantime, we learned a hell of a lot."

"Did we?" she asked, not entirely sure.

Slade nodded. "Damn right we did. The fact that the Fish were firing on the ship, and at each other—that is big. We have been approaching the aliens as if they were monolithic, that they were all in lockstep. We've seen genetic differences in different coastal regions, but we just wrote that off. The fact that they were firing on each other, that they wanted that ship destroyed, that means there are *factions*. They went after themselves. That means there are potential divisions, perhaps even splinters between groups."

"And that helps?"

"It might. We are still early in this fight, so every nugget of intel we get is important."

"Well, I guess that's something."

"It is. The team's efforts also learned that their ships are not piloted by aliens, they *are* alien organisms all on their own. Somehow, they have figured out how to creature a nuclear reaction biologically. You were crawling around inside of an alien creature. Dr. Schrivener has floated the hypothesis that when you were held, chances are you were being held on a ship that had been somehow organically altered to be a colony of some sort. Finding all of the hibernating aliens and the eggs she recovered is significant."

"You make is sound like it is huge, but these are just fragments."

"I'm an old-school intelligence analyst, Sergeant. My past life was all about piecing together seemingly disconnected bits of information to form a picture. You gave us a few more pieces to a massive jigsaw puzzle. I call that a victory."

Natalia could not counter his words. *He's looking at the big picture. I rarely get the chance to do that. The Corps pays me to stack bodies. Maybe we were a success. It just doesn't feel that way, not yet.* In that moment, she came to truly appreciate Colonel Slade on a new level.

"You've given me something new to think about."

"Sergeant, tell me, are you doing okay?"

"Sir?"

"I know you were wrestling some demons. I struggled with some of the same ones after the last war. Did this mission help, or make matters worse?"

Falto drew a long breath. "I'm fine, sir. Better than I have been in a long time. I slept in a bed for a few nights straight, though the doctors had a lot to do with that. I don't think I'll ever be able to get rid of my demons. But I have them cornered with a gun to their heads. That might be the best that I can hope for. Whatever my problems are, after Greenland, I don't think I can solve them here giving lectures or writing reports."

"You want to be in the fight, don't you?"

"Don't you?"

His grin broadened. "You know, with bionics, the Marine Corps is likely to assign you to some rear area job. With a Medal of Honor, you might get roped into recruitment."

"A good friend of mine found himself in the same situation. He managed to work his way back to a combat assignment." She mentally pictured Reid Porter.

"That may be. What if I told you there might be another way?"

"What is that?"

Slade reached to his desk and jabbed a control. "Send him in, please."

The door behind her opened, and she turned to see an Army master sergeant enter the office. His short cropped hair was gray. He wore the wings of an ASHUR pilot and enough salad on his chest to fill a hundred trips to a bar with stories of past glories. He had an aroma, that of cigar smoke. As he moved up next to her, he looked down at her, then at Slade.

"I take it she's the one you were telling me about?" His voice had a gravelly tone to it, a hint of more toughness.

Slade rose to his feet. "Staff Sergeant Natalia Falto, this is Master Sergeant Adam Cain."

She extended her hand, and he shook it hard enough to feel the callouses on his hands grind against her own. "I've heard a lot about you," Cain said, retrieving his hand and crossing his muscular arms. "You're an expert on the Fish. Allegedly you are some sort of hot-ass crayon-eating jarhead too."

The crayon comment was easily deflected, as was the reference to being a jarhead. "I've heard of you too, Grandpa. They say you saved the Pentagon. That had to endear you like all hell with every NCO in the Army," she snapped back. Their eyes locked onto each other for a tense moment.

"Grandpa?"

For a moment, she thought she had gone too far, and for Falto, that was fine.

"Jarhead?" she countered proudly.

Cain laughed heartedly. "Oh, I like her already," he said, glancing over at the colonel who gave a grinning nod in response.

"I told you, she's a handful."

Falto wanted to deflect what the colonel had just said, but didn't. "That actually seems pretty fair."

Slade sliced the mocking faux tension like a master swordsman. "We've had Sergeant Cain working with the engineers on some new ASHURs. I've tasked him with assembling a new force, something of a prototype team. I thought you might be a good fit for it."

"I'm not ASHUR qualified," Falto said. "The Marine Corps standards say that pilots with prosthetics can't pilot rigs."

It was Cain that replied. "Fuck the regs. Let's just say I have something of a special dispensation when it comes to who is on my team and what role they can fulfill. The Army and Marine Corps don't call the shots with my force. In fact, they won't let me recruit from their ranks. That's why I get to call my own shots as to who is in and who isn't."

"The sergeant is right," Slade said. "The ETF operates outside of the normal military chain of command. We break the rules from time to time. We aren't going to win this war with the operations manual in-hand."

"So, you're saying I can get back into combat? That I might even qualify as an ASHUR pilot?"

Cain weighed in quickly. "You'll get a chance. That's all I can promise. If you want to get another stab at killing Fish, I can possibly make that happen, whereas the Marine Corps is likely to give you some office duty. What you do with this opportunity is up to you."

She looked back at Slade, then at Cain. "I'll take the shot."

"Good," Sergeant Cain said. "Then let me tell you about the Fox Hunters…"

CIA Headquarters
Langley, Virginia, the United States

CIA Director Art Wilson glared at the news broadcast of Veronica Diamond, his face red with fury.

This was supposed to be a goddamned top secret operation. So what the hell is the news media doing there? This is one more thing that Slade needs to be held accountable for.

While the public was elated over the operation in Greenland, Wilson was not. In his mind they lost the ship they had been sent to explore. Worse yet, it had created a diplomatic clash with the British.

This is all Slade's fault. He has mismanaged the ETF from the start. His cowboy attitude has cost us the best chance we ever had for learning how to master the alientech. Wilson was so angry, he pounded his fist hard into the desktop.

I won't let him get away with this. When I'm done with him, they will shuffle him back to the basement where he started. The Extraterrestrial Task Force needs a firm hand guiding it, someone that can navigate the political waters and lead us to victory.

He took the glass on his desk and emptied it of his nightly drink of brandy. It no longer burned in the back of his throat as he set the glass back down on the coaster. *The country...no, the world, needs someone leading our effort against the Fish that can see the strategic landscape and align all of the resources of the nation to winning the war. That isn't Ashton Slade. When I am done with him, he will plead to hand the reins over to me.*

If not, well, accidents happen during wartime.

About the Author

Blaine Pardoe is a *New York Times* bestselling and award-winning author. He has been an author and designer in the gaming industry since 1985. He has written countless sourcebooks for games including the *Star Trek RPG*, *Space 1889*, the *Robotech RPG*, *BattleTech/MechWarrior*, *Twilight 2000*, *Renegade Legion*, and *Leviathans*. He has authored numerous science fiction novels in the BattleTech/MechWarrior universe. His political thriller, *Blue Dawn*, was an Amazon bestseller in its category. Outside of the gaming industry, he is an accomplished historian and bestselling author in the military history, business management, and true crime genres. He has twice won awards from the Military Writers Society of America and was awarded the Harriet Quimby Award from the Michigan Aviation Hall of Fame for his contributions to aviation history. He has been a guest speaker at the US National Archives, the Smithsonian, and at the US Naval Academy.

About the Creator

Brent Evans is a long-time illustrator and an award-winning art director, as an artist and noted game line developer. He has been freelancing since 1987 and worked in many genres including political cartoons, comics, and children's books. In 2005, he was hired by gaming visionary Jordan Weisman to work on several games, and immediately distinguished himself as one of the core illustrators for the *BattleTech* franchise. His creative design and project management style inspired his elevation to Senior Art Director in 2009 for many legendary gaming franchises including *BattleTech*, *Shadowrun*, D&D's *Dragonfire*, the *Valiant RPG*, among others. From 2017-2019, he took on the additional role as line developer leading the overhaul of the *BattleTech* product line, catapulting the brand into the industry-leading global success that it enjoys today. Of Brent, it is said that his "superpower" is the ability to recruit and develop creative talent.

Additionally, Brent is a graduate of and serves as a board member for the Game Design & Development program for the University of Washington.